KEEPER
AT THE
SHRINE

KEEPER *AT THE* SHRINE

DOMINI HIGHSMITH

WARNER BOOKS

A *Warner* Book

First published in Great Britain
by Little, Brown in 1994

This edition published by Warner in 1995

Copyright © Domini Highsmith 1994

The moral right of the author has been asserted.

A CIP catalogue for this book
is available from the British Library.

ISBN 0 7515 0692 3

Printed in England by Clays Ltd, St Ives plc

Warner Books
A Division of
Little, Brown and Company (UK)
Brettenham House
Lancaster Place
London WC2E 7EN

Acknowledgements

The author would like to thank the following for their help and encouragement, and for the loan of important books from private collections:

The Reverend Peter Forster of Beverley Minster.
David Thornton, Head Verger of Beverley Minster.
Pamela Martin, Head of the Reference Section,
    Beverley Library.
Librarian Jenny Stanley and staff at Beverley Library.
Barry Roper of The Beverley Bookshop.
Alan and Beryl Parrot.
Amy Dawes.
Peter and Edith Webster.
Pauline Brown.
And special thanks to Father X of St John's.

AUTHOR'S NOTE

Keeper at the Shrine is the result of many years' meticulous research into the medieval history of Beverley, East Yorkshire, and its magnificent Minster Church.

The map of Beverley, bearing its original name, 'Beaver Lake', is the author's reconstruction from archive material giving descriptions of ancient watercourses, woodland, marsh and building.

The author lives on the site of St Peter's Enclosure, in the shadow of Beverley Minster.

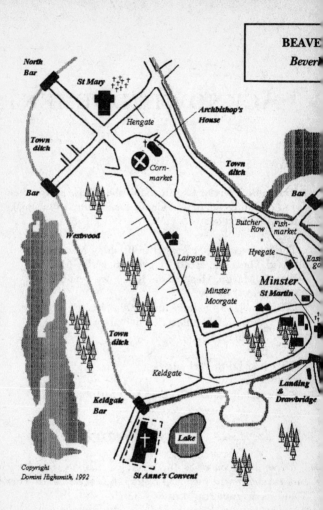

North
Bar

St Mary

Hengate

Archbishop's
House

Town
ditch

Town
ditch

Bar

Corn-
market

Bar

Butcher
Row

Fish-
market

Westwood

Lairgate

Hyegate

East
ga

Minster
St Martin

Minster
Moorgate

Town
ditch

Keldgate

Landing
&
Drawbridge

Keldgate
Bar

Lake

Copyright
Domini Highsmith, 1992

St Anne's Convent

BEAVE
Bever

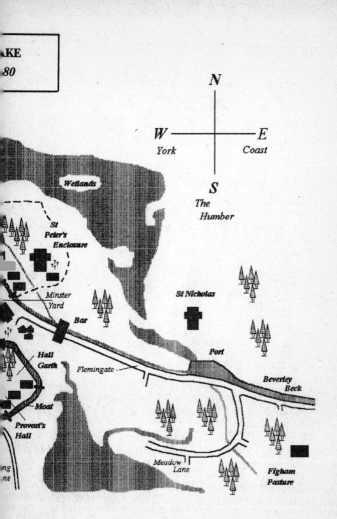

N

W ——————— E
York   Coast

S

The
Humber

Wetlands

St
Peter's
Enclosure

Minster
Yard

St Nicholas

Bar

Hall
Garth   Flemingate

Port

Moat

Beverley
Beck

Provost's
Hall

Meadow
Lane

Figham
Pasture

This book is dedicated to the unknown priest whose tomb now rests in the North Transept of Beverley Minster.

CHAPTER ONE

The horror came to Beverley on a bitter winter's night in eleven hundred and eighty. It came without warning, a raging tempest set against a bright, star-jewelled sky, and those who survived its passing swore that it moved with the deadly intent of a hunter running its prey to earth.

England was then at peace, though no less troubled in its soul than in more turbulent times. The rich, as always, were over-burdened by great wealth, the poor by even greater poverty. The Lawgiver, Henry Plantagenet was king, and had been so for twenty-six long years. He ruled a vast province whose two chief capitals were separated by two hundred miles of road and a hundred miles of sea: a daunting empire, but he governed wisely. He might have proved an even better monarch, had he not been cursed with bickering barons, a scheming queen and a brood of rebellious sons. All this and a powerful pope in Rome who would make himself the overlord and puppeteer of royal princes. Uneasy times. When was it ever otherwise?

The horror came while kings and bishops and all good Christian souls were in their beds, when only the ungodly and the priests were at their mutual nocturnal devotions. It struck the little town of Beverley in the see of York, and it left five hundred dead and as many maimed or seriously injured.

1

More than half the occupants of the town were rendered homeless at a stroke. Many were simply lost, wiped from the face of the earth as if by magic, vanished without a trace. It was the time of greatest human sin, those hazardous early morning hours dividing night from morning. That day had been the shortest of the year, St Lucy's feast day. It was followed by the longest night of a biting cold December, and in that barren, pre-dawn darkness Hell itself was running loose.

The storm came from the east, from a sea whipped into frenzied waves that hacked and scythed at the vulnerable coastline. From there it gathered its energies and flung itself inland, leaving a trail of havoc in its wake.

A single rider galloped ahead of those fierce elements, hooded and stooped and bearing a precious burden. His mount was a destrier, a massive beast muscled for the plough and bold enough to bear an armoured rider into battle. Its hooves pounded the ground, flinging up turf with every desperate stride. Its breath was damp, laboured and hot, and blew pale gusts of frost into the air. The rider stooped low in the saddle, hunched protectively over the bundle clutched in the crook of his arm. At his back the night sky boiled and seethed in the gathering storm. Ahead the darkness lay like a heavy blanket over treacherous marshy ground scarred here and there by steep-sided dikes and crooked, half-hidden ditches.

'*Onward, my friend! Onward!*'

His heels jabbed at the muscular flanks they straddled. The big horse snorted once and tossed its head. Silver-toned moonlight touched its flying mane and shone in the whites of its eyes as it threw itself against the darkness, reaching for the last reserves of strength within itself. Man and beast outran the elements, flying inland with a snarling force like Hell's own furies racing at their heels.

On higher ground a lonely man, a simple parish priest whose life was hard, trudged homeward hunched against the biting wind. He was weary to the bone, for he had sat out the tedious deathbed hours of a stubborn old man who lacked the grace to heed his Master's call with a willing heart. Caleb the Salter would not go meekly into the Great Unknown. He was too large, too brutish a man for that. He scorned the solemn rites of the Holy Catholic Church and mocked the careworn priest brought there to offer absolution. He shook his gnarled fist in the face of death, clinging to life with unrepentant indignation. But in the end the Good Lord had His way and Caleb the Salter, still voicing his blasphemous objections, went kicking and screaming into that other place.

'And unconfessed,' the young priest spoke into the wind. 'You died without confession, without repentance, daring to curse the Lord and all His servants.'

The knowledge of his personal failure sat like a gnawing cancer in his heart. Another soul had slipped from his grasp unsaved. God would not judge him well by this night's work.

'You've earned your place in darkest Hell, Caleb,' he told the darkness. 'And by default I have helped you into it.'

Muttering still, the priest stumbled on the uneven ground and fell to his knees with a small cry of discomfort. The sky at the horizon was bright with stars, so that the humped shape of his village with its modest wooden church crouched darkly against it. He was nearly home, where he could sit and brood at his own quiet hearth, watching the logs burn bright and red and slowly dim like the fire in Caleb's eyes.

'May the Redeemer look upon thee in pardon and mercy.'

He spoke the words aloud and in the English, rather than the Latin tongue. The prayer was voiced less for the dead man's benefit than for his own. One reluctant soul was all he had been required to claim in God's good name, one lost soul hanging in the shadow of eternal damnation, and he had failed. In the face of Caleb's overwhelming unbelief his own small faith had proved inadequate. He had been tested and found lacking, and in his failure a worthier man was damned.

He saw the rider then, hunched over a wildly galloping horse so that the two were like a single beast of mythical

3

design. Rubbing the tears and the tiredness from his eyes he stared again at horse and rider bearing down upon him. In that strange light it seemed to him that the flapping hair of mane and tail licked out at the air like hungry tongues of flame. The burnished harness glinted and jangled. Massive hooves tore at the earth with every stride. Muscle and sinew strained, and the great beast plunged through the night, bearing the dark-clad rider onward at a killing pace.

Still on his knees, the priest looked beyond the horse to the distant coastline. He saw the sea rise up above the cliffs, its waves, steel-tipped with moonlight, writhing and twisting in the howling wind. He saw the sky become a cauldron and the storm gush from its heart like black pus from an open wound. It poured across the land, dragging the sea after it, screeching and roaring like a thing possessed. Ahead of it the big horse flew as if pursued by a deadly pack, a brave and noble beast, but surely doomed.

The priest lumbered to his feet and shaped the sign of the cross in the air before him. What vision of Hell was this? He had seen the heavens open, and what the sky spewed out was hideous and ungodly. He could not move. His feet were rooted in the ground while the wind caught the edges of his heavy cloak and flogged him where he stood. He faced death and he knew it. Escape lay neither to the left nor to the right, and no mere man could hope to outrun this awesome spectacle. He felt the rush of wind against his face, heard the pounding hooves and labouring breath, smelled the sweet sharpness of the beast's sweat as it passed close to him. Then he turned back to face its dark pursuer, the broiling tempest.

'Dear God,' was all he said before it struck him down.

CHAPTER TWO

Fleeing before the tempest, the hooded horseman urged his mount to a faster pace, pushing the already labouring beast to the limits of its endurance. Across the flat diked fields the destrier raced, crashing through gate and fence alike as if those sturdy barriers were the flimsiest of impediments to be scattered in its passing. Hooves pounding, it traversed marsh and tangled woodland at the same rash pace, crossed the dark waters of the river Hull, where heavily laden boats and barges already squirmed and pitched in the path of the coming storm.

At last a coppery glow appeared in the distance, marking the lights from the diverse lamps, candles, torches and campfires of the prosperous little town of Beverley. The town's many watercourses, its stagnant moats and dirty ditches, its litter-filled streams, brooks and open sewers, ran through the streets and skirted every field, all glowing molten with reflected light.

'*Forgive me, Beverley,*' the rider cried, knowing how many would not survive this night, and that those who did would never forget his passing. '*Forgive me Beverley, and pity me, as I surely pity you.*'

The big hooves clattered over the hump-backed bridge spanning the older beck whose waters ran outside the boundaries of the town. Here crude vessels and makeshift dwellings hugged the water's edge where people scraped a living as they could. Beyond it the land was wet and treacherous, for this was winter, when much of Beverley was impassable except by boat. The horse reared up, turned upon its massive hooves, whinnied once and lunged to the right on an altered course.

'St Mary's, then,' the rider cried. '*Make haste, Cephas. The storm is at our heels.*'

The great destrier galloped on through the darkness, trusting to drier ground as it sought a less hazardous point at which to cross the formidable boundary ditch. As it reached the steep slope that banked the ditch near Walkergate it faltered and its body jerked sideways, struck by a crippling bolt of pain. It snorted and tossed its head, showing the whites of its eyes and baring its teeth. The great beast's balance was undermined, and though it battled bravely to keep upright its efforts came to nothing. Whinnying, it lurched, half-reared and crashed to the ground with a thud, then slithered helplessly down the slope towards the icy water.

The hooded rider leapt clear as his mount went down. Unhurt, he scrambled after it, descending the muddy incline with his darkly wrapped bundle closely held against his body. At last he crouched to rest his free hand on the hot, damp neck of the animal that had paid such a price for bringing him this far.

'*Rest easy, old friend. For you the race is over now. Rest easy.*'

Across the ditch to the south of the town stood Beverley's ancient guardian, the Minster Church of St John, where rested the golden shrine of Bishop John, the town's own saint. It rose up to meet the coming storm, its single tower pale and imposing, its tolling bells deep-toned and mournful in the depths of night. The horseman touched the bundle in the safe crook of his arm, then stroked the horse's cheek once more in sorrow and gratitude.

'*Farewell Cephas, my faithful friend.*'

The dark head lifted briefly and fell back, the eyes rolled, white-edged and wet with grief, and even as its master bade farewell, the brave heart, pushed too far beyond its measure, quivered a final spasm and was still. The first flash of lightning lit the sky with a cannon-blast of accompanying thunder, and by its light the hooded figure crossed the ditch and melted into the shadows of the town.

Nearby, a woman and a man were agape at these events. They saw the destrier stumble and the rider turn his steps towards the town, and they saw their fortunes altered in the gift of meat and costly leathers and brasses left in the mud beside their hovel. Their small son's body lay in a shroud of rags inside the house, unburied for want of the church's burial-fee, born into the world and gone from it without receiving either the first or the final sacrament. The man saw a handsome profit suddenly dropped to him like manna from above, but for his wife, still choking upon a mother's grief, the means to raise the precious burial-fee for her child was placed within her reach.

The beast was still warm when a dozen furtive hands stripped off the magnificent leathers and the jewelled and burnished metals. It merely shuddered, an involuntary reflex, when the ice-cold point of the first butcher's blade pierced through its hide.

The horseman hurried onward and did not turn to see the hands that fell like a swarm of hungry flies upon the carcass of his beloved destrier. He lifted his head to the sound of the Minster bells, his features lost in the shadow of his hood, and he heard the rush of wind that was the enemy running swiftly in pursuit.

'*Let it begin,*' he whispered, and suddenly the pack of snarling wolves that was the storm fell upon the sleeping town in an orgy of destruction. It tore down buildings large and small, uprooted trees, flattened walls and fences, lifted fully laden carts of timber and grain and tossed them effortlessly through the air. By now the lashing rain had become torrential. As cold as ice and sabre-sharp, it was driven before a lethal wind that flattened or mangled everything in its path. Thunder shook the town to its very foundations. Flashes of harsh white lightning set the ravaged skyline in ghostly silhouette.

Those who survived the terror swore that the great Minster Church of St John took a monstrous battering by elements determined to part it from its foundations and scatter its ancient stones to the four winds. It stood like a solid fortress under siege while violent squalls were flung at every door and window. There were many who feared the wrath of God had come to punish those sins not brought before the priest for absolution. As many more believed it to be the Devil's own doing, for Satan too is a jealous God, impatient of his enemies.

Within minutes the streets and alleyways of Beverley were awash with filthy flood-water. The town ditch, running a swollen, crooked course toward the lower level of the beck, burst its banks at every turn to dump its stinking contents where it could. A crowded tenement building collapsed in Eastgate, its poor foundations undermined and its timber walls enfeebled by the storm. The common sewer at its rear rushed wreckage and bodies alike downstream, its foul waters hampered to one side by a huddle of squalid homes, to the other by the stout wall of one of the church enclosures. These grounds marked the eastern edge of the settled area. They were held by the little prebend of St Peter, divided from the Mother Church by Eastgate and the sewer, but as much a portion of St John as was the glorious Minster Church itself. Beyond its brick and stone defences, shivering men bore witness to the brutality of the storm.

'May the Saints in their mercy preserve us.'

'And the Lord in His mercy deliver us from all Evil.'

Two priests, an elderly man of nervous temperament and his much younger companion, sought sanctuary in the narrow gap between the store-house and the infirmary wall. It was a paltry place barely wider than a grown man's shoulders, a draughty tunnel strewn with debris and sheltered by the sloping overhang of the infirmary roof. For those neither troubled by its shadows nor daunted by its uneven ground, it provided alternative access to the high boundary wall and the narrow, little-used gateway into Eastgate. Though barely adequate, on this night it offered some respite from the storm, a place where a man might draw in his breath without the harsh wind snatching back the air before it fed his lungs.

Father Willard held the prebend of St Catherine and was a canon of the Minster Church. Now in his sixty-third year, he found that neither good health nor stoutness of heart had followed him into old age. Too rich a table and too fine a cellar had slowly increased his bodyweight to barely manageable proportions. Too easy a living and too few demands upon his courage had left him ill-equipped for the harsh realities of the outside world. Now he crouched in the darkness in terror of the storm, his shaven head protected by his hood and his thick lips muttering a garbled, barely coherent prayer.

'Holy Mother, we beg your protection in adversity ... forgive us our sins ... while we, the unworthy ... for our deliverance ...'

Father Willard's silent, grim-faced companion called upon no higher power for his personal safekeeping. Young Father Simeon was a chantry priest of St John's, serving the altar of St Peter and the little church dependent on it. He was a gifted translator and copyist, a scribe and a keen historian, with a talent for assessing the hidden qualities of other men, of weighing and measuring almost at a glance. And because his judgment was often unnervingly accurate this, among his many and varied talents, was least appreciated by his fellow priests.

The younger son of a family of quality, he bore an outward flaw, a rigid ankle that guaranteed him a lower status in the estimation of his peers. Such imperfections, men believed, were moulded by the hand of God for His own purposes. Like Cain, this young priest bore the Lord's mark so that men would know him, and even those who had learned to trust his goodness still viewed that disabled foot with apprehension. Simeon de Beverley was also a contemplative man

9

whose calm exterior concealed a thousand undertows. None knew his secrets, yet many were dismayed to find their own unveiled before his steady gaze.

Now Simeon's searching, deep blue eyes were narrowed to slits, his hands drawn back into the warmer folds of his fur-lined winter cloak. He was drenched with rain and chilled to the bone, having braved the deluge to help his terrified companion to the shelter. Then he had struggled back to set two lanterns on the wooden bridge that crossed the drain between the lesser buildings and the tiny, modest chapel of St Peter. In one short hour that exposed section of the drain, bearing the double burden of a deluge from above and increased seepage from the marshy ground below, had overflowed to rush like a frantic torrent through the grounds. His main concern was for his companions still at Matins in the chapel. In the dark an inattentive priest, scurrying for shelter ankle-deep in rain, might miss his footing and plunge into its unsavoury flow. The lanterns, of sturdy iron and horn, were hung on weighted hooks at either end of the bridge. They danced and jerked before the wind, struggled a while and spluttered into extinction. When the scribe set out to replace them he was driven back by the fury of the storm. Defeated, he limped for cover with the elements pounding viciously at his back, his lungs sucked empty by the wind and his unyielding foot dragging stiffly in his wake. And there he remained, imprisoned in the space between the eaves, looking out on chaos.

'As God is my judge,' he murmured calmly, moving his head slowly from side to side as if to deny his words even as he spoke them. 'As God Himself is my judge, this is no earthly tempest.'

Between him and the chapel lay the cloister field, and next to it an open garden once neatly planted and tended. Here too was the upper section of the graveyard, the whole criss-crossed with narrow footpaths and flanked by wooden, stoop-backed buildings never intended to withstand such a battering. That whole area had now been stripped of its shrubs and hedges. Seats and fences were blown away, wooden crosses stripped from the graveyard, window-shutters torn from their hinges, roofs snatched away or demolished by the onslaught.

Father Simeon shuddered, feeling the penetrating chill of something more than ordinary cold. It drew him back into the deeper shadows of his shelter. He was a man of instinct as well as intellect. While reason argued that here was a natural storm and nothing more, some deeper part of him could sense an aim, an evil purpose at its core.

Most of that small community of priests were still at prayer, keeping the long night vigil of Matins and Lauds, building a solid wall of prayer between mankind and his constant predator, the Evil One. Sheltered beyond the raging gale, their mellow voices rose in soaring expressions of praise or sank in supplication to their Maker. They either knelt in prayer or lay prostrate before the little altar with its single sanctuary lamp. They believed themselves protected by the Grace of the Almighty from the awesome power unleashed beyond the chapel walls.

Squinting out between the darkness and the ice-blue lightning flares, Father Simeon felt the fingers of fear begin to pluck at the very fibre of his being. His lips moved automatically as he recited in lilting repetition the familiar lines of the *Jesus Prayer.*

'Lord Jesus Christ, Son of God, have mercy upon me.'

For seven long centuries untold numbers of priests and monks had built their spiritual lives upon the chanting of the *Jesus Prayer.* Done correctly, the combination of chanted words and steady breathing produced a state of quiet euphoria from which a man might more easily make communion with his God. For Simeon it had become a personal mantra, an aid to deeper contemplation and a key to almost instant inner quiet.

'... have mercy upon me. Lord Jesus Christ, Son of God, have mercy...'

He saw a shadow taller than a man unfasten itself from the black hold of the orchard gate. It seemed to move without effort against the storm now raging like a fury within the

11

enclosure. Walking erect and with a shapeless bundle clutched against its chest, the hooded figure met the vortex of it head-on and kept to a steady, diagonal course across the open ground. Father Simeon raised his hand and called out in alarm: '*Have a care, Brother! Beware the watercourse!*'

His warning was plucked away by the wind the instant the words were past his lips. He wiped rainwater from his eyes and stared again, this time with disbelief. The drain was wide. Even at its narrowest part it matched the combined height of two grown men, and yet the figure had moved from one side to the other without disturbing the balanced length of its stride. Simeon did not trust his eyes. Even sheltered as he was in that dark space, he could feel the storm tugging at his robes and stinging the exposed areas of his skin. How then was that figure passing through the worst of it as if uncaring of its turbulence? The lame priest licked a sudden dryness from his lips and felt his scalp prickle and grow tight across his skull. His right hand moved to shape the sign of the cross.

'Lord Jesus Christ . . .'

'*Simeon!*'

He started in sudden alarm at the sound of his own name, not knowing if some disembodied voice had yelled into his ear, or if the storm itself had called to him. Father Willard huddled at his feet, his terrified face protected by his hands and his voice reduced to a guttural sobbing. He too had heard the voice and he too feared it.

'*Simeon!*'

Now the figure in the midst of the storm was standing quite still, the heavy cloth of its habit barely disturbed by the pounding rain or the wind that howled and screeched all around. In the darkness it had no face, only an area of shadow framed by a weighty hood. Even so, for an instant it was as if their eyes met and their gazes locked, and in that look was forged a curious bond. They stood thus, watching each other, until the figure lifted an arm to point a finger in the direction of the chapel. As it turned its head Simeon felt himself released from the magnetism of its unseen stare. He

12

looked across the courtyard as a meagre light briefly illuminated the chapel's tiny porch. Some sixth sense made him want to scream a warning, but his mouth shaped only a soundless, meaningless cry. He stood like a man transfixed, stunned by the certainty of what was about to happen.

Three priests in coloured hoods over their choral white emerged from the chapel, their bodies bent and stooped against the elements. The instant the door slammed behind them they were at the mercy of the wind: now pulled, now pushed, now cast aside like helpless toys before the greater force. One man was flung backwards across the chapel steps. His head struck the stone and he lay motionless, his face upturned, his mouth wide open to the deluge. Another fierce gust lifted one of his companions off his feet and hurled him against the chancel's outer wall. There his body dangled like a rag in the wind, impaled by the neck upon an iron lantern-hook.

'Oh God, help them,' Simeon muttered, knowing they all were doomed.

The third priest battled to maintain his balance before being borne wildly off in the opposite direction, his every movement snatched from his control. His arms were extended ahead of him as he was carried towards a row of stout supports bearing the heavy eaves of the dormitory roof. He clutched for a solid anchor, a place of safety, but the first oak post loomed out of the blinding rain to halt him in mid-flight with sickening impact. He hung there for a moment in a weird embrace, astonished by his pain, then slithered unprotesting to the ground. Another howl of wind and his body began to tumble and roll at a rapid pace across the muddy grass. It met the drain's edge some way below the bridge, slithered over the edge and vanished.

Father Simeon tried to move but found himself held fast. There was nothing to be done for his ill-fated fellow priests. What hope had he of reaching them, hampered as he was by a stiff-jointed foot and a halting, uncertain gait? What hope while more than an acre of ground lay between himself and them, with deadly pitfalls at every stride and something inhuman loosed between the two?

'My God,' Simeon muttered between dry lips. 'What is it? What in the name of Heaven is happening here?'

'We are going to die,' Father Willard whimpered in terror. 'You saw him too. The Angel of Death is here. We are all of us doomed ... we are all going to die. Oh Jesus Christ, have mercy ... have mercy ...'

'That hooded figure is no angel of death,' Simeon declared with firm conviction. 'He is not the cause of this. The reason, perhaps, but not the cause. Pray for our souls, and calm yourself, my friend. We are in God's hands.'

Father Willard shook his head in terror. 'Not God's hands, Simeon. You saw it ... the Angel of Death ... we both saw it.'

'*Simeon!*'

The figure held him with its hidden gaze and raised its arm again to the little chapel of St Peter. It was showing him, demanding that he bear witness. Father Simeon turned his head and looked toward the bell tower dividing the roofs of the chancel and the nave. In a sudden lull that followed the thunder he heard the fitful tolling of the bell, the rush of water in the nearby drain, the pounding of the rain, the distant cries of men and women terrorised by the elements. And above it all, briefly sweet, the deep, incongruous sound of pious brothers still at their night's devotions.

A flash of lightning lit the sky as it struck the summit of the tower a shattering blow. The bell jerked once and clanged, a dull and tuneless sound, and after a heartbeat's hesitation was dragged down in a hail of collapsing masonry.

'Oh Dear God in Heaven,' Simeon whispered, making the sign of the cross as he stared at a gaping hole made in the chapel roof directly above the altar where the priests were gathered.

'Dead ... all dead,' Father Willard moaned. 'We have seen the Angel of Death, the Grim Reaper himself. We are all doomed.'

The two priests shared their narrow shelter, one standing erect, the other crouched in terror. Out in the open the sinister figure stood watching them from the hollow darkness of its hood. Then it gathered its bundle more closely to its body, turned once more into the heart of the storm and moved away. When it reached the wall that marked the lower boundary of the enclosure, it joined the deeper shadows there and vanished where there was no opening.

'*The Angel! The Angel of Death!*'

With a piercing scream the terrified Father Willard clawed his way out of the narrow shelter and, before Simeon could make a move to hold him back, surrendered himself to the madness of the storm. It took him with an unholy glee and pitched him about like so much windblown litter. While Simeon looked on in horror the fat old priest was dragged through pools of choking mud, bounced along rows of paving stones, tossed against walls with bone-shattering force. When at last his ordeal ended, his broken and bloodied body lay jammed, spread-eagled against the bridge that spanned the swollen drain.

Shocked to the core, Father Simeon gaped out through a curtain of wind and rain. His friend was pinned to the timbers with his neck twisted at an angle and his arms outstretched like a crucified Christ. Even as Simeon looked on, the little bridge was riven free of its mountings and cast with its human cargo into the drain. He saw it rush downstream and vanish underground, and he knew that when it reached the Beverley Beck it would continue on to the River Hull, a mile away, and from there to the Humber and the open sea.

Father Simeon made the sign of the cross and his mouth shaped the words of the final sacrament, but in the face of that sinister storm his prayer for the souls of the dead and the dying seemed but a hollow gesture.

CHAPTER THREE

'*Simeon!*'

He started at the sound. The voice had a peculiar quality, a certain resonance that might have originated inside or outside his own head. Instinct told him that the hooded figure was now standing at his back, watching him. Something in the atmosphere was altered now, as if that other's presence filled the sheltered place at the expense of everything that had been there before. For a moment the storm seemed very far away. Its angry sounds were muted, its claws withdrawn. He could see it raging less than two strides from where he stood, only now he was insulated from the force of it, held in a pocket of silence in which even the air he breathed was somehow changed.

'*Simeon.*'

He turned without haste and pushed the heavy hood back from his head, determined to meet his adversary head-on. His strong-boned features, too handsome and too arrogant, some thought, for a man of holy orders, now betrayed nothing of the fear that hampered his tongue. Questions tumbled in a clamour inside his head, finding no voice.

'Who are you?' His mind screamed out the words. 'Why are you here? What do you want with me?'

The figure stood at the far end of the shelter, its face

concealed in the dark folds of its hood. With its left hand it cradled its bundle to its chest, with its right it indicated the great Minster at its back and beckoned slowly to the priest. It had come for *him*, and it expected him to follow where it led.

Simeon shook his head and managed to say aloud, but softly, without defiance: 'No! I will not come to you as Daniel meekly stepped into the lions' den.'

The figure, in deep black silhouette, beckoned more urgently. Once again the lame priest stood his ground.

'Do your worst, whatever you are,' he told it bravely. 'I will move neither hand nor foot to assist you in my own destruction.'

'Come, Simeon, my brother. Come!'

The delicate hairs at the nape of his neck leaped to attention, risen like the hackles of a nervous animal. That thing had called him *brother* and now it turned and moved away, expecting him to follow after it. Simeon seemed to be suspended above that endless chasm dividing one heartbeat from the next. He recalled the terrible sense of wonder that had humbled him to the point of tears during the ceremony of his ordination. The sacred words borne upon nerve-tingling music, the intoxicating aroma of incense, the blinding colours of glass and gold and silver made feverish in the light from a thousand candles: all this and more had swelled his soul to bursting. Trapped within the majesty of it all he had been compelled to participate in the shaping of his own destiny, and now he could feel the experience repeated. He started forward, drawn by a force too compelling to resist, moving with an unfamiliar ease and grace. For the first time in half a lifetime, his ill-matched feet moved with equal co-ordination under him, one after the other in smooth, unfaltering strides.

When he reached the far end of the shelter the acrid smell of urine met his nostrils from the shadowed area where a long succession of priests, himself among them, had ducked between the buildings to lift their habits and relieve themselves. After that was open ground as far as the high wall of red brick, patched here and there with borrowed stone,

17

enclosing the grounds of St Peter's church. A tall, narrow gate of worked iron opened on to the timber bridge spanning the common sewer. Across the bridge was Eastgate, and beyond it the grassy slope, now a sea of glistening mud, that skirted the Minster churchyard.

Out there the storm was at its most ferocious. Rain beat a frantic tattoo on the single oak beam of the bridge, making its surface treacherous to negotiate. The wind continued to howl and tear at everything in its path. Through it all Father Simeon moved with an ease that was bizarre, his tread unfaltering and his path unhindered. He saw the muddy shapes of men and women huddled against the church walls like so many effigies moulded in glistening clay. The body of a small child hurried by, borne on the current of flood-water rushing along Eastgate toward the greater beck. It struck the churchyard wall and became trapped in an angle there with its little arms outstretched, pausing with its face up-turned as if to beg the blessing of St John before the current rushed it on its way.

'May God have mercy on your soul,' Simeon muttered after it, shaping a tiny cross in the air with his fingers.

He followed obediently after the hooded figure, passing untouched through the mayhem all around him. He could feel no rain on his uncovered head, no harsh wind in his face, no slippery wetness beneath his sandalled feet. At the Minster yard he hesitated, shocked by the sheer numbers of people crowded there. Every inch of space inside the walls had been claimed by frantic victims of the storm. Pilgrims and townspeople, sailors, students, travelling monks and priests, all clamoured for a place of safety in the shadow of St John. Many were injured, as many more were dead or so close to death that they had slipped beyond the natural fear of it.

'*Simeon!*' The figure turned ahead of him and beckoned. '*Not here. Not yet. St Martin's first, and then the holy shrine.*'

This time he did not hesitate but followed quickly where the figure led. Ahead of them, on the south-west side of the Minster, stood the small parish church of St Martin, hemmed

18

in on every side by the schools and residences of the collegiate church. Much of its roof was damaged, its windows cracked, its modest tower crushed and scattered in the muddy yard. Nearby the prestigious grammar school, after standing firm against the seasons' worst for almost a hundred years, was reduced to rubble in the south-west corner of the Minster Yard. Above the howling of the storm he caught the cries of men and women and only with some effort turned his head away.

St Martin's was packed from wall to wall with frightened people who had fled there in droves in search of refuge. They huddled together in dark stone corners and crouched, trembling and sobbing, in every shadow. Terrified priests in their colourful copes and surplices were huddled together in the choir aisles, their voices hushed to furtive whispers before the elemental roaring at the doors and windows. Others clung to the altars, trembling and afraid. They were closer to God in spirit, having purchased a safer place in the hereafter with the purer currency of their devotions, and yet they too were cowards when confronted by their own mortality. The prospect of death had levelled all distinctions, proving the cleric brother to the serf.

'God's mercy on you,' Simeon muttered, knowing that fear made brutes of honourable men. He closed his eyes and his ears to their helplessness. God would forgive them. Neither common man nor priest should dare do less.

One priest was jammed against the chancel wall by a crush of stinking, muddied people sheltering from the storm. In the darkness a young girl groped for the wooden crucifix at his breast and clung to it for comfort.

'Spare me,' she wept. 'For God's sake, Father, spare me.'

The priest restrained her clawing hands and struggled to escape the frenzy of her hysteria. Finding no space in which to move, he stiffened his arms to hold her off, and by a flash of lightning saw her clearly. She was young and pretty, a child just blossoming into womanhood, a helpless little thing in muddy rags. She squirmed in his grip and cried out as a cannon-clap of thunder echoed through the church. The

19

priest drew breath with a gasp as every nerve in his body leapt in response. He wanted her. If he was to die in this tempest then let it be as a man, with heated blood and throbbing loins and a yielding female body under him.

In the blackness after the lightning he yanked the frightened girl towards him and pinned her small body to the ground beneath his own. In a moment his heavy woollen habit was hoisted to his waist and he was ramming his distended organ into her. His fingers raked her skin and he growled like an animal as he pounded his pent-up lust into her small body. Her shrieks were to no avail, just one child's cries among a thousand others.

At the end of it the priest roared in satisfaction and collapsed, elated, with the child still pinned beneath him. Just for a moment he felt himself to be more than any ordinary man, for in the face of death he had never felt more potent, more alive. But the moment of his victory was brief. When his ebbing energies slowed in their outward rush and began their natural homeward flow, cold reason cooled the fires in his head. Revulsion almost choked him.

'Get thee behind me, Satan!' he spat. 'Vile creature! Get thee gone from me!'

His voice was a vicious snarl. He could have killed her then, for the evil, filthy thing she had made him do. More than that, he could have damned all womankind to eternal Hell for the way they played so easily upon the weaknesses of manly flesh. He rushed away, stepping on dead and injured alike in his scramble to find a cleaner and a safer hiding-place.

A Matins light still burned on the nearby altar of St Mary. It jumped and spluttered as the storm's breath found it, then settled to a flickering, uneasy glow. In the uncertain light within, Father Simeon followed the hooded figure toward the sturdy Norman font that stood between the high altar and the nave. The wooden cover of the font, kept locked to protect its blessed contents from thieves and desecrators, now stood wide open. Its metal locks were hanging loose and its little pool of holy water glistened a dark quicksilver in the half-light. The figure beckoned and once again Simeon found himself unquestioningly obedient to the sign. He stepped forward as lightning flashed at the church's windows, and by its light he saw that the bundle the figure carried was a living child wrapped in a thick fur cover.

'A child? You bring a child?'

He stepped forward to look more closely. It was indeed a child. The twisted birth-string on its belly showed that it was newly-born, a boy, perhaps no more than a few hours old. It was a tiny thing, naked and carelessly unswaddled in that draughty place. The sudden flash of light beyond the windows touched a blue sheen to its eyes and lit its hair in a fragile halo around its tiny head. And for an instant that same light fell upon the features of the hooded figure. Simeon glanced up and with a jolt he saw, or imagined that he saw, a face he recognised.

'Lord God in Heaven . . . how can it be . . .?'

The words were torn from his lips, but even as he stammered his consternation the hooded figure raised its hand to warn and to silence. Then the water in the font was gently stirred and the child brought closer in preparation for the sacrament of baptism.

'*I adjure you, unclean spirits, be gone . . .*'

As the first solemn words of the ritual were spoken, the storm beyond the walls bellowed like an enraged beast pricked into fresh fury. It was as if the hooded figure roared defiance in the baptism words, and the elements running loose beyond the walls took up the challenge with increased savagery.

The figure touched each tiny ear in turn with its dampened thumb and spoke the command, '*Ephpheta! Be thou open!*'

A thunder-clap exploded overhead. Glass shattered and men and women screamed in terror.

He dampened the veiled blue eyes, each one in turn, and commanded: '*Ephpheta! Be thou open!*'

Thunder exploded and lightning flashed. A section of the

21

roof collapsed. A column shifted, unseating its massive load of ornate stonework.

'*Do you renounce Satan, the Evil One?*'

Simeon's response on behalf of the child was instinctive.

'I do renounce him.'

'*And all his works?*'

'I do renounce them.'

Simeon's heart was pounding in his chest. He felt himself caught between two awesome powers, one the merciless elements unleashed outside, the other a single hooded figure standing in that sacred place beside the holy font. In these, the bleakest hours of St Lucy's feast, when the night was supposedly deeper and more prolonged than any other night of the year, this newly-born child was to be baptised before God, no matter if Hell itself rose up in protest.

'*Do you believe in God the Father Almighty . . . ?*'

'I do believe.'

'*. . . Are you willing to be baptised?*'

'I am!'

Simeon shouted the words, speaking from the heart on behalf of a child unable to speak for itself, adding his own strong voice to that of the figure standing on the other side of the font. From its bed of soft fur in the crook of its guardian's arm, the child looked on impassively, disturbed neither by the deafening cry of the wind nor by the startling crash and flash of thunder and lightning.

'*. . . shall all bear witness to this blessed sacrament.*'

Now several cowering monks and priests were stirred to lend their voices to the holy rite, all of them finding strength and comfort in the familiar words. As their voices rose in unison the clamour of the storm increased to a tumultuous pitch. And above it all that single voice intoned the words of baptism with a penetrating clarity, the unwavering force of it competing with the cacophony of sound beyond the church walls.

'*. . . and receive the Holy Spirit.*'

A section of the roof above the nave was ripped away and several wailing voices were silenced when it fell. A pillar cracked and shifted on its base, shattering the great stone arches overhead. The stone slabs of the floor began to splinter and rise up, breached by the enormous pressure of water rushing underground in flooded streams and over-burdened culverts. As the ground beneath their feet began to gape, people clawed at anything within their reach and so dragged others with them to their deaths.

'*Name your child.*'

Simeon hesitated. 'What?'

'*Custodian, name your child.*'

'Custodian? I?' Simeon flinched as the elements seemed to shriek a protest.

'*Make haste, my brother. Name your child.*'

Simeon glanced up at the modest window arching above the high altar of St Martin. He glimpsed the face of St Peter in the glass and remembered his own church dedicated to that same saint, the vicar of Christ, the apostle who held in his keeping the keys of Heaven.

'Peter,' he cried. 'His name shall be Peter.'

'*So be it.*'

He felt the solid ground beneath his feet move sideways with a sickening lurch, saw the carved feet of the ancient font begin to shift from their solid pedestal.

'*Peter!*' the voice declared as if in triumph. '*In nomine Patris, et Filii, et Spiritus Sancti . . . in the name of the Father, of the Son, and of the Holy Ghost.*'

Sacred water glistened on the infant's head, three times marking the sign of the cross, and with a bellow of '*Amen*' the holy rite of baptism was ended.

A stone struck Simeon's head, drawing a spurt of blood and causing him to cry out in alarm: 'The roof! Beware the roof!'

Instinctively, he raised one arm to shield his head from falling debris and with the other tried to protect the child. For a moment the hooded figure stood still as stone, the infant in its arms concealed by the priest's muscular forearm, its face safely cupped in his strong right hand. Then the figure spoke again in gentler tones.

23

'*Come Simeon, we must hurry.*'

It turned and Simeon staggered after it. 'Where? Where are you taking us?'

It answered in a word: '*Sanctuary.*'

'The Minster?'

'*The shrine itself.*'

'Will we be safe there?' He leaped back with a cry as a fall of masonry crashed to the floor between them. The figure turned but briefly, and in its attitude he sensed recrimination for his doubts. He glanced at the rubble and back at the hooded face. Although he could not see the eyes it seemed to him that their gazes locked exactly as they had locked in St Peter's Yard, and that same understanding, calm and unworded, passed between them.

Simeon had never claimed to be a man of true vocation; God knew there were few of those in holy orders. His faith was simple, often uncertain, constantly questioning. It took little on trust alone, but it was adequate for his needs and had served him well enough for all his life. He called upon it now to strengthen him, and in the darkness of that other's face he fancied he could see himself revealed. In that momentary exchange both his doubts and his convictions were laid bare.

'Lead on then,' he said at last, trusting the other's extraordinary strength more than he feared his own human weaknesses.

'*Stay close to me, Simeon.*'

'I will,' he declared. Then the stone floor lurched again beneath his feet, throwing him forward so that he followed the figure from the church at a rapid, unsteady pace.

CHAPTER FOUR

Between St Martin's and the west wall of the Minster was a stretch of open ground broken only by the churchyard walls and a few defiant trees not yet uprooted by the wind. In this place the quick and the dead were now lying side by side, the status of each made level with the other. Simple graves once set below the ground now rose up and opened into pools of mud churned by a thousand pairs of fleeing feet. Here men and women fought each other for half an inch of space, for a grip on some dislodged gravestone, for the smallest degree of shelter from the storm. Those unable to keep their feet were trampled underfoot. It was a place of carnage, where neither priest nor pauper knew which would be spared and which would perish, and neither one nor the other received the last sacrament.

Simeon lifted his hood over his head, the better to blind himself to the worst of the horror through which he had to pass. There was a wetness on his face that was not from the driving rain, for it stung his eyes and burned his cheeks and left a taste of salt behind where it touched his lips and tongue.

'*Come Simeon, my brother.*'

The figure had reached the smallest of the Minster's doors, that set in the very centre of the long wall on its western end. It paused there, waiting for Simeon to approach, and moments later led him through into the chaotic interior. Now Simeon found himself in the greater transept, dwarfed by the ornate, sweeping stonework of the central vaulting. For an instant he felt the cathedral-like splendour of the Minster reach out to brush his senses in a delicate caress. Its walls of honey-coloured stone, its soaring arches and painted plaster-work, decorated marble columns, elaborate masonry and shimmering stained glass windows seemed to sing their own sweet anthem to the glorification of God. As he made the sign of the cross the moment of splendour fled, leaving behind a daunting ugliness. His ears were assaulted by a bedlam of sound, his nostrils filled with the smell of filth and fear, his eyes distressed by the pitiful sights around him. It seemed that half of humanity had crushed itself into the confines of the Minster, and half of these would not survive the night.

'My God, can there be so many?' Simeon whispered.

The place was filled with townspeople who had fled their stricken homes in search of sanctuary, and by strangers who had flocked to Beverley from every corner of the country. These were the pilgrims, the hopefuls in their thousands who drifted from shrine to shrine in search of cures for twisted limbs, blind eyes, incurable diseases. And there were those who preferred the hardship of pilgrimage to the endless, hopeless grind of certain poverty at home. All these and more had been drawn or driven here, and Simeon knew that they had come to die.

Voices cried out from all directions: 'A blessing, Father. A blessing.'

And he replied as often as he could: 'God's blessing be upon you.'

He saw a woman pinned against a pillar. No mark was on her but her back was broken. She stared back at him with eyes that shone like glass, and even as he watched, some wretched thief was prising off her shoes.

The voices were all around him now. 'Help me Father.'

'Bless me in God's name.'

'Save me. Save me.'

'God be with you,' Simeon said. 'God be with you. And with you also. God's blessing upon you. Trust in the Lord. Go in peace.'

He was caught, ensnared in the horror seething all around him. His movements were halted by a solid press of people, his robes grasped and plucked by wailing men and women clutching at anything that might provide a lifeline in their hour of need.

'*Simeon!*'

He looked up, their torment and his own showing in the brightness of his eyes. 'There are too many,' he groaned. 'There are too many.'

The figure stretched out a hand. '*Come, Simeon.*'

'I cannot move. These wretches hold me fast. My feet ... my hands ... my robes ...'

'*Come, Simeon.*'

The voice, although much softer now, was no less penetrating than before. It seemed to bear him up, though he knew his feet remained firmly on the ground. He found himself moving freely and without hindrance, passing through the press of crouching, grasping people, protected from their disquieting demands. The figure nodded a sign of encouragement and turned away while Simeon, lifting his hood that it might blinker him, fixed his gaze on the broad, dark back and propelled himself after it.

They crossed the north transept to the choir aisle, then passed the double stairway to the Chapter House where beggars, merchants and landowners alike cringed on the steps or clung in terror to the slender, blue-black columns of Purbeck marble. Here too, as in the choir and at the altar, were gathered all the dignitaries of the Minster, the superior clergy in their copes of richly coloured silk, the lesser of their number all in white. The storm had caught them as they were gathered for their night's devotions, and now it held them, penned like sheep and useless in their terror. They turned their eyes to Heaven or closed them fast in urgent prayer.

The lesser clerics, those clerks of the seven orders from

27

ostiary to deacon, the tutors and their students, the scribes and cross-bearers, all cowered in any space that would accommodate them. Each man had been disinherited of his courage and his pride, and many stripped bare of whatever measure of faith they had once professed.

Simeon and his tall, hooded companion were following now in the footsteps of those countless pilgrims who had shuffled along the north choir aisle to the narrow turret staircase leading to the reredos and the martyr's holy shrine. Here the faithful knelt or prostrated themselves to offer their prayers and beg St John's indulgence: a miraculous cure, an inheritance, a purse of gold, a battle won or lost. A thousand miracles from the trivial to the profound were petitioned here daily, and on the Saint's three feast days of each year the numbers were impossible to calculate. The deaf and dumb flocked to the shrine of their patron saint as moths to a candle-flame, and by his mercy many of them were cured. After their short out-pourings at the shrine the pilgrims were ushered out by a second staircase and moved along the south choir aisle to the arched, round-headed doors in the greater transept. Each left a whispered burden with the Saint and paid for the privilege in coin or kind that would help to swell the Minster's coffers. And some, God willing, struck an honest bargain.

At the shrine Father Simeon dropped to his knees and murmured a simple prayer for the souls of all men and women who repented of their sins. The shrine was set to rest on the reredos itself and was a work of art of exceptional beauty. It was of precious metal richly jewelled, overlaid in panels of gold and ivory, encrusted with amethysts, emeralds, rubies and glorious golden-green chrysoprases. Beside it lay the beautiful, gem-encrusted dagger of King Athalstan, Beverley's first overlord, placed there by his own hand 250 years ago. By the altar light the shrine had an eerie glow, a living lustre capable of stealing a man's breath away and filling him with a crushing knowledge of his own inadequacies.

He felt the figure close at hand. '*Pray for the child,*' it told

28

him. '*Pray for the keeper of the shrine, the future saviour of St John of Beverley.*'

Simeon did as he was bidden, and as he prayed the storm outside reared up and flung itself in screaming fury against the soaring arches of the east window. While it raged Simeon prayed against it, crying out from memory the words of the fifty-fifth psalm.

'Fearfulness is upon me ... horror hath overwhelmed me.'

His voice took on a firmness that belied the awful pounding of his heart. Only his voice had any strength, for the rest of him was in a state of dread.

'... hasten my escape from the whirlwind and the tempest ...'

As if to mock his words a fiery pain shot through his crippled foot, so sudden and so agonising that his senses reeled. He could not move. His entire weight was resting on the joint, crushing the bones together, and yet he was powerless to shift the load. Instead he sweated out the torture, gasping the words, thrusting the power of his mind against the storm.

'... for I have seen violence and strife in the city ...'

The high clerestory windows, set clear above the roof and aisles, the better to light the centre of the church, snapped inward one by one. Having no crosspiece to divide the light and act as brace, they stood but briefly before the gale and then were blown to nothing.

'... from the eye of the hurricane ...'

While the storm raged Father Simeon prayed with all his strength against it, praying as if the holy words themselves would hold it back.

Behind the high altar in the retrochoir was a little-used turret staircase winding upwards. It was cut from the ancient stones of the Minster wall, and provided a chimney-width of refuge for two priests with little but their tonsured crowns in common. Father Cyrus de Figham was a muscular man in his early thirties, splendidly garbed in scarlet and white, with a claret-coloured hood, fur-lined for warmth, and several fine jewels set into his girdle. His brow was heavy, a muddy reddish brown in colour and permanently furrowed. His eyes were grey as slate and, like their owner, rapidly adaptable to the tone and colour of their surroundings. In this dark place they were as black as pitch, glinting and flickering with reflected torchlight. His was a striking face of many moods, one moment grim and coldly dangerous, the next lit up with a boyish softness that could be disarming. Mercurial was how Cyrus might best be described, in looks and nature a man of many subtleties. He was also discontented and resentful of the restrictions of his office. He desired more wealth, higher status, greater authority over his fellows, but he lacked the wherewithal to secure his advancement. A choral priest, his ambitions patterned him for grander rank.

Cyrus's companion was a canon who held the coveted prebend of St Martin which, having the highest value, was the most sought-after of the seven prebends. Father Bernard was short and slightly built and twenty years Cyrus's senior. A well-loved, amiable man, his temperament was such that he could be moved to tears or rage or laughter with equal ease. He was that rare thing, a charitable man, who presumed no ill, no underlying mischief in his neighbour. He wore the bright blue and red robes of his everyday office under the ritual surplice, and over them all an outdoor hood of brilliant green with a golden clasp at the shoulder. While the storm outside raged on, the narrow stairwell echoed with the words and music of his prayers.

'... for He redeemeth my soul with His love and leadeth me into His own safekeeping ...'

Crouched on the higher stairs close to a candle with a fitful flame, Father Cyrus brooded in silence upon the devotions of his Canon. He glowered down at the pink dome of that shaven head and despised the older man as much for his quiet faith as for his integrity. The man was old, yet he chose to hold on to St Martin's rather than take his ease and set a younger, more able priest such as Cyrus de Figham in his place. Not a single coin from the coffers in his control had ever been put to his own use, not a drop of wine nor a crumb of bread misappropriated for his personal indulgence. Cyrus de Figham might have harvested rich pickings from the wealthy prebend of St Martin. It was the parish church and very prosperous, a source of rich donations and plump offerings. But instead the wealthy parish church had this *good man* at its helm, and by his guidance sailed a worthy but unprofitable course.

'They shaved the crown of a pious man and revealed a saint,' he spat, and with distaste he touched his elegant fingers to his own smooth tonsure. 'And such saints make public failures of us all.'

The idea came swiftly and without any conscious premeditation. If Bernard were lost, if he fell victim to this terrible storm, St Martin's might come again within Cyrus's grasp. As is the nature of it, ill-deed ran but a breath behind ill-thought. On the stair was a damaged treadstone that came loose with little effort, and in his strong, determined hands it sat like an aspiration Heaven-sent.

Father Bernard was unaware that death was standing at his shoulder. One moment he was knelt in prayer, eyes closed and hands clasped tight in his devotions, the next he was sprawled face-downward in the dirt, his skull smashed open and his brains laid bare.

Cyrus de Figham let the air from his lungs in a satisfied sigh, then released his grip on the weapon that had crushed that pious skull with a single blow. It came to rest beside the dead man's head, where the eyes were closed, as if he merely slept.

Cyrus stepped over the body and threw the candle down, then stooped and left the staircase by its little crooked door. Near the high altar he found an empty niche where once the figure of St Mark had stood. He pressed himself into it, hugging the deeper shadows gathered there. All around him the church was a chaos of cringing bodies and voices that were coarse and shrill with fear. The narrow niche offered safety from falling stones and privacy from the common rabble trapped like screaming rats in the darkened Minster, and it

31

touched upon his vanity to be sheltered thus, where once a saintly effigy had been displayed. Lifting his hood over his head he dropped into a crouch, prepared to wait out the storm in that quiet cavity. He heard a familiar voice rise clear and strong above the din, and he wondered at the identity of the tall, black-hooded man who stood with Simeon.

At the nearby shrine of St John, the lame priest's voice rang out above the roaring of the storm beyond the Minster walls and the screaming of the people trapped inside. Now the hooded figure joined him, matching its words with his.

'. . . *and filled with the braying of the enemy* . . .'

The storm snarled like a mad dog at the window.

'. . . *and the terrors of death are upon me* . . .'

The wind howled in reply. Simeon dared to open his eyes. He looked beyond and above the shrine in time to see the great east window bulge and swell and with a mighty crash burst open. The impossible was happening. The entire eastern wall of the Minster, framing as it did a masterpiece of delicate tracery and sculpted coloured glass, was in its death-throes.

'*No more!*' the figure bellowed just as the wall was ruptured. '*The deed is done, the child baptised, the blessing given.*' He flung back the fur covering to reveal the child. '*Behold The Rock, the guardian of the shrine. Behold, ye Forces, Peter of Beverley!*'

The child was lifted up like an offering to the heavens just as the great east window exploded inward, hurling a shower of jagged stones and razor-sharp arrows of glass into the Minster. For an instant Simeon froze. He gaped at the hooded figure with the naked babe held high above its head, and at the deadly torrent of shattered glass and masonry that seemed to hang above them all as if suspended by some force defiant of gravity. With a cry he threw himself forward, reaching for the child with both hands. He felt a shard of glass slice into his neck, another sink into the flesh of his exposed forearm. A chunk of masonry struck his naked crown and as his big hands closed around the child he crashed to his knees with a gasp of pain and shock. Slumped against the golden shrine he instinctively arched his back to shape a barrier against the killing onslaught from above. Crouched thus, with his infant godson pinned against him, he heard the shattered window fall to earth and then a great rush of wind roar through the church and out by the transept doors.

It was over in an instant. The unholy commotion was silenced at a stroke, leaving behind it clouds of swirling, blinding masonry dust. Beyond the Minster's huge, north-facing doors the screaming whirlwind plunged into silence with a suddenness that was uncanny. Just as abruptly the lashing rain dropped to a feeble drizzle, the thunder moaned like a dying beast and skulked away, dragging the lightning after it. In the heart-stopping stillness that followed, every voice in that crowded place was hushed, every breath stilled. After the chaos, the sudden calm rang through the vaulted Minster like a noisy peal of bells.

Close to the shrine a weary voice declared in the Latin tongue: '*Actum Est,*' and repeated in English: 'It is done.'

And Simeon answered, just as wearily: 'Amen.'

Simeon reached out to retrieve the fur covering, shook the debris from it and carefully wrapped it around the child. Slowly he dragged himself to his feet, his gaze fixed on the tiny, untroubled face. For a while it held him with that veiled yet all-knowing stare of the newly-born. Then it sighed and closed its eyes, turned its small face against his arm and slept.

'*I entrust this precious infant to your care, Simeon of Beverley.*'

'Me? But why? Why me? I am not worthy of this.' Simeon stared at the darker shadows within the heavy folds of the other's hood. 'How can I be worthy of such an obligation?'

The child stirred in his arms and he bent his head to soothe it with a few whispered words. When he looked up again the figure, like the storm it had provoked, had vanished.

'*Actum Est,*' he repeated, staring at the fragments of glass twinkling with colour and lying like added gems upon the shrine of St John. '*Actum Est.* It is all over.'

He spoke the words without conviction, for in his heart the truth was already planted. The awful events of that night portended not an end but a beginning.

CHAPTER FIVE

Simeon was in a state of near-collapse. Shocked and bleeding, he stumbled the few rubble-strewn steps from the shrine of St John to the devastated area beneath the chancel arches. Here the great columns carried a thousand wounds and the vaulting that swept so elegantly to the roof was scarred and shrouded now by a swirling cloud of dust. Barely conscious of his actions, he slumped with his back against the chancel wall, then slowly slid down into a crouch among the stones. His head fell forward and his eyes were closed, but he did not pray. Instead he sat with his knees drawn up and the child cradled against his belly. He felt wasted and empty, a hollow man from whom all sense and feeling had been scourged. He did not know what wounds he had sustained. He did not even know that he was weeping.

All around him men and women picked their way over the rubble, many of them bloody and bewildered. Those without injury rummaged in the dirt for anything that could be sold or traded, for life continues even in the midst of death, and life, as any Christian must accept, is hard.

A woman sat beside her stricken father, watching dull-eyed while the dead man's clothes were stolen from his body. Another woman recognised the cheek and beard of her husband, that part of him still visible while the rest lay crushed beneath a fall of rock. The body of their child lay by his side. He had tried to flee when the great east window imploded, and in his panic rushed to meet his death head-on while she, left unprotected, had been spared. Now she began to rock to and fro beside her man and child, wailing in grief and oblivious to the fact that her movements caused a shift of stone and dust, enough to stop up the meagre flow of air that had been keeping a buried priest alive.

To all these things Father Simeon was insensible until at last he felt a hand rest gently on his shoulder and a voice he knew spoke softly in his ear.

'The child, Brother Simeon. I must see the child.'

Simeon looked up, his face dusty and streaked, his blue eyes awash with tears. He recognised Gilbert, a priest of higher orders in a rich blue robe and hood, a man with a lawyer's mind and a claim to distant kinship with His Holiness the Archbishop of York. This man had been to Rome and Jerusalem, had spent four years as a papal clerk and double that time as a priest at the great cathedral at Canterbury. All this, yet he seemed humbled now as he crouched beside his brother in the rubble. Simeon watched his face and saw the look of wonder written there.

'Gilbert . . .?'

'Please, let me see the little one.'

'You know this child?'

Father Gilbert shook his head. 'I have no idea from where he came or why he is here, but I was present at St Martin's when he was given the holy sacrament of baptism.'

Simeon blinked his eyes in surprise. 'You were there? You saw it?'

'I saw,' the priest whispered, and bright tears welled in his eyes as he bent towards the tiny form in its nest of fur. His fingers made the sign of the cross close to the infant's head and his lips moved in a brief prayer before he said: 'Myself and many others. We were sheltering in St Martin's when you arrived, and it seems our lives were saved when we dared to risk the tempest and follow you here. The church has been

35

demolished. The font and the altar are buried now beneath a mountain of rubble.'

Thick dust caused Simeon's eyes to stream and his voice to sound so hoarse he scarcely recognised it as his own.

'The parish church? St Martin's? Brought to rubble?'

'We barely escaped alive,' the priest told him.

Simeon searched the man's face, his thoughts in turmoil. 'But you were there? You saw and heard? You will bear witness to the holy baptism?'

The priest sighed deeply as the naked child was gathered back into the warm folds of fur. 'I saw it all,' he nodded, suddenly aware of his own small part in what he sensed were events of profound significance. 'I heard the words and felt the presence of that ... Oh yes, I will indeed bear witness.'

'And I,' another said, standing behind.

'I too.' This voice came from his left and it was tight with pain. 'I too will speak of what took place.'

Another man, also a priest, held Simeon's forearm with an iron grip and signed the cross over the child. His hand was trembling but his voice was steady.

'It was a miracle,' he said, so firmly that no man would have dared to contradict him. 'We were called as witnesses and so our lives were saved while others perished, and our hurts are trivial while so many more are maimed and mutilated. Whatever else took place this night, we few have seen a miracle in the making.'

A row of tonsured crowns showed pale in the dim light as each man stooped in his turn to whisper a prayer and make the holy sign above the child. As others joined them Simeon struggled to his feet, the better to protect his tiny charge from harm. It was then, as the dust was beginning to disperse, that he saw the figure of his Canon, whom he dearly loved. A wordless sigh of relief that should have been a prayer escaped his lips.

'God's blessing,' was all the wording he could manage.

Father Cuthbert was a portly, stiff-jointed man now permanently stooped, as if the long years spent with his head bowed in prayer had knit the bones together for convenience. And yet despite his own affliction this man had, for ten long years, regularly massaged the hardened bones of Simeon's ankle, hoping to coax the bones to yield and the muscles to slacken. He made hot footbaths and ointments out of rosemary, that trusted old cure for bad bones and paralysis, but all his loving administrations came to nothing. It took a decade's proof before he set aside his oils and poultices and, facing at last his failure, sadly declared: 'My son, God does not wish your foot to mend.'

That kindly, devout old man held the prebend of St Peter's, a modest holding, but a precious one, and he was the only father Simeon knew. He was standing now by that Saint's little altar, where dust and storm had put the candle out, dressed in the choir habit, white surplice under a soft fur amys fastened at the throat with a brooch. A touch of purple and crimson showed here and there, a border of fine embroidery, a beaded panel. His robes were the property of his church, the worldly icons of his priestly standing. A man of Cuthbert's modest tastes, owning no fancy apparel and scornful of extravagance, was nonetheless required by Mother Church to display the accoutrements of his office.

The old man crouched with difficulty until he was able to touch the ground between his feet. He seemed perplexed, distracted by some mark or stain or fragment he had noticed on the ground. After a while he allowed two priests to help him to his feet and, leaning heavily on their arms for support, clambered over rubble and glass to reach the High Altar. He peered long and hard into the dust-streaked face of Simeon, his priest and scribe, and there was sadness and a look almost of reverence in his eyes. His stiffened, blue-veined hands, long grown unsteady with age, were shaking more than usual when he reached for the child. He took a fold of fur between his finger and thumb and gently drew it back until the tiny face was visible.

'You named him Peter,' he said, as if surprised.

'It was appropriate,' Simeon answered quietly.

'I too was at the font.'

Tight-lipped, Simeon muttered: 'You too? I'm glad of it.'

'And I believe I can bear witness to a miracle.'

'It was a nightmare,' Simeon groaned, 'and we, thank God, lived through it.'

Once again Father Cuthbert looked deeply into the blue eyes of the young priest, and he wondered if the man could be fully aware of the true weight of the burden that was now his to carry for a lifetime.

'I believe you came to St Martin's from our own chapel of St Peter?' he asked.

Simeon merely nodded in reply.

'Brought through the very centre of the tempest?'

Again the young priest inclined his head.

'And from St Martin's, to the Minster, across the quagmire of the burial grounds while the storm was so great not an oak nor an elm is left standing?'

'I did,' Simeon whispered.

Now Father Cuthbert nodded also, as if to confirm what Simeon himself recalled. 'I saw. I marked your progress from a window niche. You came the whole distance without harm while men and women, horses, carts and mill sails were taken up and tossed about like sticks. You came through the worst of the storm and yet ...' He peered more intently into Simeon's face, searching for understanding of his own. '... and yet your feet are dry, Simeon, your sandals clean, your robes unstained by rain and mud.'

Simeon glanced down and saw that his feet and sandals were indeed dry and clean. He shrugged his shoulders mildly.

'I was summoned and I came,' he said, as if that fact alone sufficed to explain the phenomenon.

Father Cuthbert leaned closer and lowered his voice to a confidential whisper. 'I saw it hold the child aloft just as the window shattered inward as if all Hell had hurled itself against the altar wall. It left you on your knees beside the shrine and then ... and then ... as God is my judge I *saw* it, Simeon. One moment it appeared beside me at St Peter's altar; the next it vanished in the winking of an eye. It was as if the ground had opened and a man was swallowed into it, except that he ... that *it* was not ...' He moved his old shoulders, a twitch resembling a shrug, and looked to Simeon for an answer. Their faces, then, were very close together. '... *what was it?*'

Simeon shrugged. 'A man, perhaps? A Saint? A Spectre?'

'But you saw it close. You looked into its face.'

'I did,' Simeon nodded, licking his lips, discomforted. 'And for a moment, just for the space between one racing heartbeat and the next, I thought ... I thought ...'. He closed his eyes and shook his head, dismissing the memory.

'What?' Father Cuthbert prompted. 'What did you see?'

'Nothing that common sense will not explain. It might have been a play of light on shade deceiving weary eyes, and yet ...' He shook his head again and said more firmly: 'No Father, the features were hidden. I could not see beyond the shadows of the cowl.'

Just then the frantic voice of an injured priest cried out from the curtain of dust concealing the damaged choir, and both men were made painfully aware of their surroundings. The deathly hush that had followed the storm was over now, and sounds of anguish rushed in to fill the void. Dark figures were beginning to move about the church. They picked a cautious path among the shapes still huddled together like sheep packed into a slaughterer's pen. Candles were brought and lit by those priests who had fled in terror at the storm's screaming height. Torches were fired and set in metal brackets where they spluttered and smoked in the dust-filled atmosphere. By these uncertain points of light the full extent of the damage could be seen, and in the gloom it was a sorry sight.

The Minster Church of St John still stood its hallowed ground, a battered fortress that would not be defeated despite a grievous wounding. Its windows and doors, pinnacles and buttresses had suffered enormous damage. The whole of its eastern end was laid wide open to the elements. Parts of the roof and the chapter house were down, some pillars cracked, some statues of the Saints cast down amongst the stones, some vaulting wrecked or seriously undermined.

The small tower in the centre of the crossing, being of sturdy Saxon design, modest in height and set on solid rock, had suffered several fractures in the stone but other than that appeared to be intact. In time this deception would prove costly indeed, for the ancient foundations had shifted in the storm. The stream that crossed the transepts underground had altered course so that the tower's lower parts now wallowed in its flow, the load-stones prey to its swift, abrasive current.

Simeon groaned aloud. 'My God, the damage here . . .'

'A terrible night,' Father Cuthbert nodded sadly. 'We faced the Forces of Evil and survived. Whatever else, we must give thanks for that.'

Simeon stared about him. 'The choir,' he said, squinting through the dust, 'the arches are fallen, the vaulting collapsed . . . oh God, the stalls are crushed beneath the bigger stones and there are priests still in there. We must help them. We must . . .' He started forward, reeled and closed his eyes against a sudden wave of nausea.

Father Cuthbert used both hands to steady him. 'It will be done,' he promised. 'Do not push your strengths beyond their given limits, Simeon. Leave it to others to do what must be done. You have the infant safe. Your part in this has already been fulfilled.'

Simeon nodded and leaned his head against the chancel wall. The stone was cool and he was very tired. He was weary now to the very deepest reaches of himself. He felt as if he had passed through Hell and out the other side.

Many of those who minutes ago had cringed in abject terror now found the wit to go in search of loved ones who were lost. Some began to sob and wail their personal miseries, others to call out the names of their missing, still others to lick their own wounds or to mourn their dead. A host of unfamiliar tongues, Italian, Greek and German, Dutch and French and many more, were added to the din as bewildered foreign pilgrims found themselves a part of this local tragedy. They had come to see the graves of Brithun and Winwald, two early abbots of the monastery that had stood upon that marshy ground for centuries before the Minster took its place. They had come to worship at the blessed shrine of St John of Beverley, and to kiss the casket holding the sacred prayer-beads and bones of St John the Evangelist. They had tramped great distances to earn some small remission of their torments in the after-life and many, instead, were hastened to their deaths. Those who remained protested in heart and voice against the injustice of the bargain.

Above these sounds the voices of the choral priests, at first few in number and hesitant, were gradually swelled to a song of worship. The sacred time of Matins was not yet over, and those still imprisoned by the damaged stalls and arches of the choir, some trapped beside a dead or maimed companion, returned their hearts and voices to their God.

There was fresh blood on Father Cuthbert's hands, alerting him to the fact that Simeon was injured. He held back two priests who would have gone with others to offer comfort to the injured and to bless the dead.

'Go with our brother Simeon to the infirmary,' Cuthbert instructed them in his quiet voice. 'He is to be given special care. This man and his godson must be given priority. A wet-nurse will be needed, and a crib. And guard them well. They must not be left alone, without protection. No harm must come to them.' He paused in his instructions, reached out to touch the arm of a passing priest and turned his head on its stiffened neck in order to peer into his dusty, blood-stained face. 'My son, your help is also needed here. Take brother Mark and go with these men to the infirmary. They will instruct you further on the way.'

When a concerned deacon attempted to take Simeon by the elbow, the younger man shrank back against the wall as if the touch were painful. Shrugging the helping hand aside, he hugged the sleeping child to his breast and shivered. He was now aware that his head was throbbing painfully. His arms and back were stiff and he suspected he had been injured in several places by flying glass. He blinked at Canon Cuthbert, fearing that he was about to be parted from his

41

charge. He would not have it so. Too much had happened for him to fail his calling now and pass his burden meekly to another.

'This child is mine,' he said, hugging it closer. 'I am his chosen guardian. He is my rightful godson according to the holy rite of baptism.'

Cuthbert noted the anxiety in his eyes. 'These facts are not disputed,' he assured him.

Simeon blinked a stinging wetness from his eyes. 'I will not give him up.'

'And none will ask it of you.' Cuthbert smiled in kindly understanding. 'Go now, my son. Have your wounds tended and sleep while you still may. We will all have need of an active body and a vigorous mind before this night is far behind us.'

Trusting the word and authority of his canon, Simeon allowed the helpers to take him by the arms and lead him away. He turned back once, his handsome face made gaunt by the strain he had endured. The child was a soft dark mound against his chest.

'Father Cuthbert . . ?'

'What is it, Simeon?'

'Father . . .' His throat was stopped and there was a look of anguish in his eyes.

When he saw that look the older man felt a rush of compassion that caused his heart to quicken. Feeling old and incompetent in the face of these strange events, he patted the young priest's shoulder and looked closely into his troubled face. Like Simeon he had been shaken to his soul this night and like him he perceived all this to be a beginning, not an end, of something neither of them could hope, as yet, to comprehend.

'I know,' he would have said, had he the words. 'I know, my son, I know.'

CHAPTER SIX

Father Cyrus de Figham, his dark eyes turned to glittering black in the shadow of his hood, stepped from his quiet niche as the group of priests began to pick their way across the rubble toward the north door. He too had witnessed that astonishing scene. He too had seen the mysterious hooded figure cross the Minster to St Peter's altar and drop from sight as if some unseen force had sucked it underground. He had seen, but then, such eerie play of light and shadow as found its way into a church in dead of night would suffice to make a miracle out of nothing. Something peculiar, even extraordinary had taken place here, but Cyrus de Figham was no God-fearing simpleton to be taken in by any kind of trickery. Show him a profit, a gain in gold, position or reputation, and he would believe in that wholeheartedly, but so-called miracles were a different matter. There had been a spectacular explosion when the great east wall collapsed, and a man with imagination could colour the rest as he saw fit to paint. Cyrus would reserve his judgment until he heard what others said about it. Then he would take up and confirm the story best suited to his personal interests.

Stepping over a pile of rubble he shook a shower of fine masonry dust from the folds of his dark brown cloak. It powdered his hands, and in the candles' light he saw the

43

creases on his palms etched in the dark stain of a dead man's blood. He picked his way to the high altar, intending to cleanse his hands in the holy water kept there in a stone bowl for the officiating priests. As he reached the recess and stooped towards the bowl, he saw a face reflected in its dark, quicksilver depths and he drew back, for an instant startled. A fragment of coloured glass had been flung there from the shattered window, a portion of some saintly painted face. It seemed somehow accusing in its bland innocence.

Cyrus looked towards the east end of the church where a gaping, jagged hole revealed a sky no longer savaged by the storm but calm and decorated with a thousand glittering stars. The great east window was gone, all but a few twisted fragments of it strewn around the church in chunks of masonry, thick wedges and shards of glass, slivers of lead contorted into bizarre shapes. Between the virtually demolished pillars of the choir those priests who had survived were singing as if oblivious to the devastation lying all around them. Cyrus fixed them with his coldest stare, contemptuous of their misplaced piety, then glanced again at the saint's face shimmering darkly in the bowl of holy water. With a growl he snatched up the segment of glass and flung it away from him. Then he plunged his hands inside the recess and rubbed his palms together until the water there was tinted a coppery red.

'Help us, holy Father.'

A woman had crawled on her belly through the debris to touch the hem of his robes. She was bleeding from many wounds, so much a victim of the night's horrors that he could not tell if she was young or old. She held a small coin between her thumb and finger, hoping to buy her way into a more merciful afterlife. The body of an infant hung across her shoulder, its head askew because its neck was broken.

'Help us, holy Father,' she wailed, dribbling and choking on the words. 'Heal us, protect us, give us your holy blessing.'

Cyrus grimaced in distaste and backed away, yanking at his robes in an effort to free them from her grasp. There was a stink about the poor that tainted the air and made him want to vomit. He despised them for their poverty and their ignorance, and most of all he despised them for the way they bred, as fertile as cockroaches. And now this filthy, miserable creature was slithering after him, grovelling and persistent, as he backed away.

'Have pity. Help us, holy Father, help us.'

'Get away from me.' He stooped to hiss the words into her face.

'Your blessing, father . . .'

'Filth! Get away from me.'

A man's voice, close at hand, caused him to start. 'Oh, God be praised! It's Father Cyrus! Look there, by the shrine, it's Father Cyrus!'

He turned his head to see two dusty and dishevelled men, a reader and an acolyte, staggering towards him from the direction of the old chapter house stair. One of them stumbled and almost fell headlong as the carved arch of a canopy to which he clung for support gave way under his weight and crashed to the ground. His companion, himself unsteady and stained with blood, offered what help he could.

'Father Cyrus, praise God for your safety.'

'And for yours, brother!' He returned the greeting solemnly.

'Father . . .' With a groan the woman cringing at his feet fell sideways against the rubble, silenced by exhaustion. Under the pretext of improving his balance on the jagged debris, Cyrus tugged at his robe until her enfeebled hands could grip the cloth no longer. Then he stood back and, muttering a prayer for her redemption, made the sign of the cross over her. In the presence of others his face had undergone a transformation. Its look of disgust had become an expression of tender compassion. It was an instant, much-practised alchemy.

'How many dead?' he asked, his eyes wide with concern.

The younger of the two priests shook his head. 'Who can imagine the number? All this . . .' He spread his hands to

45

include the bloody chaos all around them. 'All this and so much more. There was a terrible flood below ground, just one of many, I suspect, since every culvert and waterway in the city has burst its confines. A wall beneath the chapter house collapsed, its underground supports washed clean away. The main part of the crypt is flooded to roof-level and the door is jammed. Eighteen were sheltering there. *Eighteen.*' He wrung his hands, his face a mirror for his inner suffering. 'They are all drowned. No miracle came to save them.'

Cyrus nodded and touched a hand to his forehead. 'And in the choir? What damage there?'

The first priest hung his head and his companion stepped forward to answer in his stead. This one was younger, little more than a boy, with a bright purple birth-stain that marred the left side of his face from scalp to neck. He was trembling and his smooth crown shone with perspiration. 'I fear our numbers must at least be halved,' he said. 'Poor Father Paul was struck by flying glass. I saw it for myself, a slender piece no longer and no wider than my finger. It pierced his skull. He died without a sound.'

'And Father Bruce? What news of my dear friend, Father Bruce of York?'

The young man winced as if the question pained him. 'His legs were severed in a fall of stone. We tried ... dear Christ alone knows how we tried ... but we could not stop the bleeding, the terrible bleeding.'

Cyrus signed the cross and lowered his head. There was a sudden brightness in his eyes that he would prefer to keep concealed from them. He had recalled the body of Canon Bernard, lying as if struck down by a fall of stone. With Bernard dead the prebend of St Martin, or what remained of it when the rubble had been cleared, would fall vacant. Cyrus wanted it, and because he was not well liked by his superiors he must find an edge, a special circumstance to raise him up and give him priority over his many equals in this matter. He scowled in sudden animosity. Already such an opportunity had been snatched from him, for how could he compete with all this talk of *miracles*? When the Provost and his Canons met to discuss this night's events it would be Simeon's name, not Cyrus's, that coloured their conversation.

'God rest his soul,' he muttered, but his thoughts raced on, seeking a profitable course. He needed to save a worthy life or in some very public and dramatic fashion appear to risk his own. He must become a hero, an undisputed leader of lesser men. He must find a way to make himself worthy of recognition and, by due process, suitable reward. His narrowed eyes cast about in all directions in search of inspiration. In all that confusion there must be something to influence those canons, something a clever man might use to manipulate old men to his own advantage.

'Father Cyrus? Father Cyrus, are you injured?'

He realised then that he was leaning heavily against the high altar, gripping its rough stone edges so tightly that the knuckles of his hands had grown white and bloodless. He felt the deep nerves pulsating in his cheek.

'I have been dragging bodies from the rubble,' he said as if speaking to some inquisitor within the altar itself. He lied with practised skill and an easy conscience. 'I have clawed away stones with my bare hands, helping the injured, comforting the dying, blessing the dead ... oh God, there are so many.'

The two young men reached out to support him as his legs appeared to tremble and give way beneath him. They thought him to be on the verge of collapse and feared the jagged stones and glass that would do him injury if he should lose his balance there.

'Forgive me,' he begged, feigning a show of courage. 'I will recover my senses in a moment. Leave me here if you will with these stones for my support. Look to your comrades in the choir arches and I will come to assist you as soon as I am able.'

The disfigured young priest held back. 'Perhaps we should see you safely to the infirmary, Father Cyrus?' he suggested. 'On your own admission you have already done more than your share to help these poor unfortunates.'

47

Warming to his theme, Father Cyrus grasped the young man roughly by the shoulder. 'How can it be enough?' he demanded passionately. 'How can I rest or think of my own comforts while even one man still wants for my assistance, or one dead body wants of my prayers for its passing?'

'But you are injured, Father,' they protested.

'Indeed, but neither injury nor fatigue will persuade me to close an eye until the very least among us is accounted for. Go now where you are most needed, to the choir. I will come when I can ...' He paused to touch his elegant fingers to his folded brow, swaying a little. '... In a moment, just give me a moment.'

They went reluctantly, impressed by his courage, moved by his dedication, doubting no word of his story. Smiling now at their backs, Cyrus marvelled at their simple-minded trust in the higher orders of their Mother Church. The seed was sown in fertile, obedient ground. He would be a prince among men before this night was over.

Across the south chancel by the simple altar of St Mark, a figure loomed, huge and dark, into the candlelight. It had been crouched, well-hidden behind the altar, and Cyrus knew Wulfric de Morthlund at a glance. Here was a choral priest fortuitously elevated to higher status by the prolonged absence of his Canon. His personal wealth was a matter of much speculation, for he had come to the church a ruined man save for his price of entry to holy orders, and in a few short years had acquired the life-style of a wealthy knight. None who knew him well would harbour a moment's doubt that he had advanced himself by less than honest means. By his Canon's default he now had at his disposal the fine prebendary house in Minster Moorgate, and by sheer arrogance and clever manipulation of church affairs he wore that canon's stature as his own. He hid his excesses behind a facade of piety, his immoralities beneath a showman's mask, and all around him hung a veil of lies, deceits and clever manipulations of the truth: a veil that concealed his sins and protected him from censure. Those who doubted and might have spoken against him out of conscience were easily persuaded into silence, for he was a powerful and a dangerous man, and his close friends loved him no better than did his enemies.

Now Wulfric de Morthlund hoisted his priestly habit high around his waist and brazenly wiped his loins and inner thighs with a band of fine white linen, a maniple, one of the sacred vestments assumed while serving at the altar. While doing so he met Cyrus's unreadable stare with a look both triumphant and openly challenging. He was grinning broadly and his face was red, the blood raised in a hot flush to his cheeks by the effort of labouring for so long on his knees. His features were shaped in flabby folds of flesh, his eyes bright gems half-buried in the softness, his lips as full and sensuous as a woman's. He stepped back, laughing, and the movement caused his corpulent body to quiver from its several chins to its ankles.

Just then, as if suddenly sprung from a trap concealed in the darkness behind the altar, a dark-robed figure came scuttling into view. It moved on all fours, its face divided by a tightly knotted gag, its robe slashed at the back from waist to hem. Even from that distance and in the flickering candlelight, Cyrus saw the pale buttocks and genitals exposed, saw the glistening dark bloodstains on the young man's inner thighs. It was a fresh young student from the Minster's grammar school, an intelligent lad too plump and gentle-eyed to escape de Morthlund's lecherous attentions. He scrambled away like a terrified crab, scuttling over the debris of stone and glass or flesh and bone, not caring which was which. Reaching an arch that trapped him in its corner, he prised the gag from his face, threw back his head and howled his shame and outrage to the heavens.

Cyrus looked back at de Morthlund with his eyebrows raised. He felt neither revulsion nor pity, but he filed the scene away in his mind for possible future use. He too might have been as powerful as de Morthlund, had he the same detachment from his Canon and his scruples. And like a plump balloon that power could be deflated with a single prick if one or two men of similar mind were willing to breathe a word in the Archbishop's ear.

The fat man licked his lips and leered, then spread his hands and shrugged his fleshy shoulders, unconcerned. 'Each to his own,' his expression clearly said.

Cyrus offered no sign of judgment or recrimination. Instead he made a small formal bow and turned his attention to the task of making himself conspicuous in the choir stalls. If he would nurture the seeds of his own advancement, he must demonstrate how well he loved his fellows and how selflessly he was prepared to toil on their behalf. When he glanced back toward the altar of St Mark, de Morthlund had lumbered on his way, leaving his victim crouched, still howling, in a nearby corner.

Father Cyrus stepped over the body of a girl, pausing to peer into her startled face. Her skirts were hoisted high around her waist and if he were any judge of what he saw, a good many men had taken their turn between her skinny legs. Her eyes stared blindly at the highest arches and there was a glistening stain where a blade had slid across her throat. Even to him, with little affection for the lower orders, that seemed to have been an act of senseless violence.

'All mortal men are opportunists,' he muttered wryly to himself as he moved away. 'All thieves or murderers, sodomites, rapists, adulterers, according to the colour of the moment. Even the saints themselves, if they could be seen in a sharper, less mystic light, would bear the unsavoury stains of mortal men.'

'Father Cyrus! Can you help us, please? One of our brothers is trapped to his chest in rubble and we need more hands to shift the stones away.'

The voice was high-pitched with urgency and came from a throat burned dry by choking dust.

He hurried forward, compassion softening the dark glint in his eyes. He was wise enough to include himself in his cynical judgment of the human race. Father Cyrus was an opportunist to the core, and like all such men he was swift to calculate the gains against the losses in any situation in which he found himself.

The buried priest did not survive the rescue. Someone had jammed a crucifix between two stones so that it leaned so close to his face that his eyes were crossed when he focused his gaze on it. He prayed coherently for his own salvation while the diggers worked to free him from the rubble. He even smiled and blessed their efforts on his behalf. Courageous to the last, he swore he felt no pain and seemed unaware of the blood that dribbled from his nostrils and pumped in rapid little spurts from the corners of his mouth. It took four men, one heaving on each corner, to lift the final slab of stone from his chest, and when the weight was off he cried out once and died.

'Wasted effort,' Cyrus muttered under his breath, then commended the dead man's soul into the care of God and gently closed the lids over his eyes. He remained but briefly on his knees before moving off to direct the rescue in another area, leaving the others to light the candle, kneel around the body and recite the lengthy Litany of the Saints.

It was while he was working in the dusty chaos of the choir that he noticed a young man not of holy orders lurking in the area of the sacred shrine. A glance aroused his suspicions and a closer look confirmed them. This was no pilgrim kneeling at the shrine, no simple believer giving thanks to St John of Beverley. The man's dark hood had fallen back to reveal a matted mop of dark brown hair and a beard of proportionate substance. He was working on all fours in a nervous, furtive manner. He was a Beverley man, a carter by trade before he lost his living to the storm. He feared God and His church like any other, but an empty belly has no need of obedience, not when an easy profit lay glittering in the debris of the Minster's misfortune.

Cyrus took the reredos steps at a run and caught the man in the very act of desecration. He was a red-faced, broad-backed individual, wielding a hammer and a metal stake. Beside him on the tiled floor lay an open leather pouch into which he was dropping the precious gems hurriedly hammered and prised from their settings in the golden tomb. He leaped to his feet as Cyrus appeared in the little turret arch, instinctively lifting the hammer to his shoulder. Then he stopped, his first intentions hampered by confusion as he found himself confronted by a priest in holy orders.

'You'll swing for this,' Cyrus told him, watching his eyes for the measure of his intent. 'You'll swing, and after that your soul will burn in Hell for all eternity.'

The man winced as if stung by the words. He glanced down at the incriminating pig-skin pouch lying between himself and the priest, then at the tomb debased by his clumsy handiwork. He had damned himself in this world and the next. It occurred to him that here was his only witness, an unarmed man, a priest. He could kill him on the spot, make good his escape with the gems and live without challenge until such time as God, the ultimate judge, called him to account. He might even offer the gems to another church in exchange for dispensation for his sins. All this flashed through his mind as he met the hard encounter of the other's stare, and at the end of it he knew he could not strike a killer's blow against an innocent man of holy orders. Instead he threw the hammer down as if it burned his fingers, turned on his heels and fled.

'Come back here, you . . .'

Cyrus snatched up the pouch and fastened it by its leather cord to the girdle at his waist. Then he moved quickly to the exit stair and, yelling a loud alarm, gave calculated chase. Brother Andrew, one of the vicars choral, was in the south choir aisle, carrying water to the injured and the trapped. He was roughly brushed aside by the fleeing fugitive and saw him vanish into the dusty confusion beyond. Then Father Cyrus appeared from the reredos steps, waving his arms about, unsteady and dishevelled.

'Stop that man! Thief! Thief! Somebody stop that man!' Cyrus staggered forward, feigning breathlessness. 'He robbed the holy shrine,' he gasped. 'My God, that sacrilegious cur has robbed the holy shrine.'

'God's mercy on us,' Andrew exclaimed.

'The gems, he prised away the precious gems . . .'

'Watch out, Brother Cyrus. Here, let me help you. Take my

arm and lean on me. What happened? Are you badly hurt?'

'That wretch attacked me and beat me to the ground when I disturbed him.' Cyrus groaned and clutched at the other priest for support. 'He must be stopped. He robbed the holy shrine.'

Brother Andrew held him back. 'We are too late to catch him now,' he said. 'He is already gone.'

Allowing himself to be restrained, Cyrus hugged his head with both hands in a gesture of distress.

'Gone? Gone with those priceless jewels? Gone?'

'I fear it is so,' said Brother Andrew. 'The thief is already lost in the crowds. But you are hurt. Come, let me help you to the infirmary.'

Cyrus shook his head. 'There is too much to be done here for that,' he insisted. 'But first we must lock the reredos gates to seal off the steps so that nobody may approach close enough to touch the shrine.'

Brother Andrew looked aghast. 'Close off the shrine? But Father, I doubt if such a thing has ever been known.'

'I will accept full responsibility for the decision,' Cyrus assured him. 'At all costs we must protect St John from further harm.' He shook his head as if incredulous. 'Can you believe that anyone would do such a thing? My God, what sacrilege, what sacrilege.'

He allowed the priest to help him to a lower stair and there he sat with his head cradled in his hands, bemoaning the fact that he had been neither swift enough nor strong enough to apprehend the sinner. Despite the protests of Father Andrew, he soon insisted on disregarding his own discomforts in order to resume his rescue work. He returned to the task a happier man, acutely aware of the weighty pouch beneath his cloak and all the advantages those gems might purchase. It would go well for him if he sold them on, perhaps to Bathal, the Jew, who paid for such things in gold and silver coin. It might go even better for him if he chose a careful moment to return them, or a few of them at least, to the proper church authorities. Already the news was being passed along that Father Cyrus, injured and wearied by his tireless efforts on behalf of those in need, had bravely risked his life to prevent an armed and desperate man from desecrating the holy shrine of St John of Beverley.

CHAPTER SEVEN

Father Simeon did not close his eyes that night. Instead he watched the dawn from the battered timbers of the infirmary roof where he had climbed so that the sharp night air might cleanse the dust from his lungs. In the rafters above the long main room he kept a quiet vigil for the new day, much as a loyal servant watches at the deathbed of his master, fearing the worst yet praying for a miracle.

Simeon stood in the eaves where the roof lay open, one foot raised on a wide oak beam and his shoulder resting against one of the cross pieces. Beside him a beam as wide as a man's pelvis was broken at right angles in a jagged, splintered wound, split by the wind as easily as a twig might be snapped between strong fingers. He watched an insect scuttle across the exposed heart of the timber, testing with delicate feet the tender innards of the oak. This was but one of so many things that bedevilled his understanding, that the strong may be torn asunder while the weak survive.

Simeon was wearing a dark red cloak fully lined with squirrel fur, a hooded, wide-cut garment that reached his ankles and was long enough to envelop his body totally. Instead of doing so on that chilly night, it hung from his shoulders in a careless manner, its glossy lining soft against bruised skin and wrenched muscles, its open front revealing his naked chest. Under this he wore tight linen braes drawn in around his waist with a twisted cord with tasselled ends. The legs of his braes were tucked into soft leather boots that were intricately cross-bound from knee to ankle with thongs. From his right hand, suspended by its circlet of yellow braided silk, dangled the wooden cross that was the symbol of his office and his faith. It turned slow circles in the deeper shadows; its effigy of the murdered Christ, worn smooth and sleek by innumerable caresses, took on the subtle glow of nearby stars. He watched the night, aware of a soft voice quoting from the book of Nahum: 'The Lord hath His way in the whirlwind and in the storm, and the clouds are the dust of his feet.'

Simeon looked down, wincing as the gash on his neck rubbed against its dressing. Between his feet the broad oak beam that bore his weight formed a bridge across a void. Few sections of the ceiling covers remained, so that the bare rafters criss-crossed the room like webbing, and standing on the ground a man might count the stars. The infirmary had a chimney at each end, and in each one a fire burned and metal pots hung down from brackets swung out over the flames. The stink of boiling mutton, wood smoke, wet wool and sweating bodies reached him in the vapours curling upwards to the rafters. And from the fire at the lower end of the room came the kinder scents of herbs left simmering in the pot: catnip and comfrey root, betony, mallow and coltsfoot.

'He maketh the storm to calm so that the waves thereof are stilled.'

The voice belonged to a priest of St Catherine's chapel. He sat on a low stool with his legs wide apart and his shoulders hunched, while all around him the injured slept or writhed upon the ground, or on low wooden pallets, and one by one they died and were carried out. A handful of priests, some monks and an assortment of clerks tended the hurt and administered final unction to the dying. Those who were judged to be nearer to death than life were hastily stripped and lifted down to lie upon the bare stone floors, lest they

56

commit the sin of dying not humbly, as a true Christian should, but on a bed of worldly ease and comfort.

Simeon spread his hands on the beam above him and hung his head, watching the room below. The priest who quoted from the book of Nahum gradually allowed his voice to falter and his head to fall forward. Exhaustion had overwhelmed him. It stilled his tongue and bade him sleep where he sat, on a three-legged stool barely sturdy enough to support him. Close by sat other priests, all stooped with fatigue and wearing dirty, rain-sodden clothes that steamed in the heat from the nearby fire, giving their hunched dark shapes a misty, almost ghostly outline. Between them was set a half-barrel packed with a bedding of straw and hastily gathered chicken feathers loosely bound inside a linen sheet. On this lay a robe of fur that in the firelight had a fox-red glow, and in its folds the child, Peter of Beverley, was lost in the sleep of the innocent.

As he looked at the child, Simeon held his breath against a strange sensation that started behind his breastbone and travelled down the centre of his body. He would not have described it as a physical pain, and yet it drew a sigh from him that was almost a moan. He had felt it for the first time at the font, and again when the child first turned its gaze on him. It was as if the sight of that small figure touched him somewhere deep within the essence of himself, and because nothing in his life had ever touched him in quite that way before, he found the sensation unwelcome and disturbing.

Just then Brother Osric, the leathery infirmarian, led a hooded woman to the little group of priests and bade them make a space for her by the fire. He gave her a wooden bowl filled with mutton stew, a large wooden spoon and a half-loaf that was dense and darkly baked. Hunched on her stool, she fell upon the food and devoured it noisily. Brother Osric lifted his face to peer between the rafters. It was a thin grey face with eyes turned into hollow sockets by the shadows.

'Simeon?'

'I am here, my friend,' the priest replied softly.

'This woman comes from the hovels around St Mary's,'

57

Osric spoke into the darkness. 'She gave birth three days ago and watched the mite die in her arms before the storm came. She offers her milk in exchange for food and shelter, and begs a proper burial for her child.'

'Was it baptised?'

Osric shook his head. 'Her husband refused to pay the priest's fee, and neither the mother nor the midwife knew the holy words of baptism.'

'Such ignorance shames them both,' Simeon remarked sadly. 'Is the milk she offers good?'

'As far as I am able to ascertain. Some decent food, a bath, a good night's rest, and I think she will be fit to nurse the child.'

Simeon looked at the figure on the stool, a ragged woman, poorly nourished and filthy, with the smell of poverty on her. She was young, perhaps no more than twenty years. She wore a tattered gown that reached her calves, a short cloak with a hood attached to it, and her feet were bare. When the bowl of mutton stew was finished she used her grubby fingers to gather up every last smear of grease that remained. Then she wiped her sleeve across her mouth and looked around for more. He watched her with dismay, reluctant even to consider her as a wet-nurse for his godson. Those rags of hers might conceal any number of sores and blemishes. Few things, he knew, were more vulnerable than a suckling infant. What might her own child have swallowed with its milk, that it should perish so swiftly after entering the world?

'Will you come down?' Osric asked the shadows above him.

'I will,' Simeon nodded. 'Give me a moment, brother.'

He turned his attention back to the sky beyond the ravaged roof of the infirmary. To the south lay the marshes and the Humber estuary, to the east the sea and the ragged coastline winding its way up country. He thought of distant Whitby and the recently restored abbey high on the rocks above its little harbour. Those same monks who had laboured to raise the abbey from ruin carried their faith and fortitude to York, there to found the great abbey of St Mary.

And two of them, brothers in blood and name as well as in faith, had made a humble pilgrimage to the shrine of St John and died together that night in Beverley Minster.

'Sometimes death comes to find us,' he told the rafters. 'He hunts us down and picks us out from our fellows as easily as if we bore the mark of Cain upon our foreheads. And sometimes He summons us to our fate the way a pope calls bishops to Rome to answer for their misdemeanours. Either way, we go at *his* appointed time. Willing or not, He takes us at his leisure.'

He sighed and his train of thought carried him to York, lying another thirty miles inland. Despite the wealth and power of Beverley's Minster, despite its extensive acreage and the special rights that lay within its see, its Provost was subordinate first to York and then to Rome. York's powerful Archbishop was made sole lord over Beverley by Royal Charter, and so the matter had rested for two long centuries. And never had it been an easy alliance, for the delicate balance of power between the two dictated that the Provost and his Archbishop should ever be at odds, one with the other. Bishop John was Beverley's saint, and rightly so, but he had been York's Archbishop for thirty-three years, and such a loss was bitterly resented. York was the overlord, that much could not be denied, but the beast he owned had grown too strong to be mastered. Only careful give and take and wise men's bartering maintained the uneasy peace between them now.

Throughout the dark hours snippets of news had been brought to the infirmary, as many tragic stories to hear as there were men to tell them. A scribe with a broken wrist brought news that the grammar school, its libraries and its master's yard were left in shambles. The whole of the south-west corner of the Minster Yard, housing St Martin's chapel and many of the clergy buildings, had suffered most griev-ously in that awful tempest.

Simeon learned that the prebendary residence of St Stephen, a splendid timber house only recently renovated, had been struck down by a mighty ball of fire. Despite the uncommon volume of rain that fell, it burned to the ground in minutes with several unfortunate people trapped inside. It seemed to Simeon that few had escaped the anger of the storm. All but one of the prebendaries grouped around the Minster, St Martin, St Catherine, St Mary, St Stephen, St James and St Peter, were either extensively damaged or left in ruins. Only St Andrew's, that splendid house in Minster Moorgate, had survived intact. It was held in its canon's absence by Wulfric de Morthlund, and many might suppose that it had braved the storm so well because the Devil takes care of his own.

Simeon's beloved St Peter was one of the worst hit. When the bell and its tower fell, the roofs of the nave and chancel were badly damaged and the blessed altar crushed by fallen debris. The nearby kitchen building and the dovecot stood in ruins, the brewhouse was flattened, the dormitory crushed. Only the ovens and fractured brick chimney marked the spot where the bakery had once stood. The little storehouse and scriptorium where Simeon slept and worked was hidden behind a mountain of rubble and fallen trees. He tried not to dwell upon the months of tedious work that had been wasted, and on the priceless manuscripts, brought there for careful copying, that might be lost or ruined by the storm.

Twenty-three men and seven women had died within St Peter's prebendary walls. Their bodies were lying side by side along the outer wall of the infirmary, their faces hidden by their turned-down hoods for want of proper burial sheets. Another score lay injured inside the building while as many more, the terrified Father Willard among them, would never be found to be given a decent burial.

'Goodbye, my friend,' he whispered. 'And may God take to Himself your immortal soul.'

When he opened his eyes again the sky was streaked with silver and the stars, from the western horizon outward, were rapidly dissolving into the light. Now he could see the mist hung on the marshes. It mimicked a shroud, a pale burial cloth tossed haphazardly over the land. To his right the damaged east wall of the Minster loomed high in the sky, its magnificent stained-glass window replaced by a gaping black hole in the honey-coloured stone. To his left the broken chapel of St Peter seemed to have sunk to its knees in its own rubble, and it pained his heart to see it brought so low. For a while he closed his mind to the damage surrounding him and stared to the east as all true Christians should at dawn, giving silent thanks that the new day had begun.

'The dawn is coming,' he said, convinced at last that it was truly so.

'Did you doubt it would?'

He was surprised by the response, for he had believed himself alone with his thoughts. He looked down at Brother Osric and nodded gravely.

'Yes, Osric, I do confess I doubted it.'

The other tried to smile his reassurance. 'You were not alone, my friend, in your lack of faith.'

'You too?'

'Oh yes, I too have feared the worst.'

'And yet we both survived it,' Simeon said. 'For us a new day is already on its way, while for others, the faithful, the ones perhaps who did not doubt . . .'

'Swallow your words and be grateful,' Osric cut in. 'You were ever a man to question where there can be no answers. You must leave the Almighty to do His work as He so wills it, Simeon. Come down and speak to the woman.'

'Soon. I will come down soon.'

'She has a tale to tell, and a strange one, if her words are to be believed.'

'I have known enough horrors this night to last a lifetime,' Simeon groaned. 'Must I endure the next man's nightmare with my own? Must I add this woman's share of it to mine?'

'Fatigue and pain make you intolerant,' Osric told him sharply. 'And you do not wear intolerance well, my friend.'

Hearing them speak of her, the woman had risen from her stool and now came slowly forward, her face upturned to the unlit places in the infirmary roof. Her name was Elvira. She was eighteen years old and her mother had died at twenty. She lived in fear of hunger, of sickness and her husband's brutal temper. She also lived in terror of a God that would

61

cast a sinless new-born babe into the jaws of Hell for want of a worthy offering for His priest. She was taught that God was merciful and just, and that innocence would have its own reward. She was taught it, but she had not found it so. Between the church's teaching and its purse, there was an abyss that swallowed such as she.

She shuffled forward across the damp stone floor, encouraged by the fullness of her breasts and the pretty metal horse-crest hidden inside her clothes. She had something of her own to bargain with at last. That tiny bundle lying outside between two lifeless priests would have its place in Heaven, after all.

This woman had lost her child and seen her home blown away like so much matchwood, and while the windfall lasted she had lost her husband too, for he gave no thought to her when he was in profit. In one short hour the world had turned and cast her down, then turned again and set her on her feet. She had bread and mutton in her belly now, and a mother's precious milk swelling her breasts. With that milk, and with the shining horse-crest, she might yet strike a decent bargain with these priests.

As her eyes became accustomed to the gloom she saw a man up there, standing in the crossings of the rafters. He was a tall, broad-shouldered man dressed in a rich fur cloak and tight linen braes. She saw that he was handsome and was surprised at that, for she had assumed the infirmarian to be addressing his words to a fellow priest. This, she was sure, was no man of holy orders. This man had the strength and energy of a field-worker; she could see that much in the way he braced his legs and in the bulging muscles of his naked arms and chest. Soft hair the colour of corn curled round his ears, and when he moved his head into the growing light she saw a wide, strong mouth and deep blue eyes in a face too handsome to be anything but worldly. To Elvira he looked like royalty, a prince of noble blood and royal bearing. She felt a flush rise to her cheeks and closed her mouth on the words she had intended to speak. He watched her until she dropped her gaze, then spoke without unkindness.

'What is it, woman? Do you have something to say to me?'

'I saw the horse,' she offered, stealing a shy glance upward.

Simeon was puzzled. 'What horse is it you speak of?'

'The big horse,' she said. 'The horse that broke its heart to bring them here.'

'Them?'

She nodded. She liked the sound of his voice. It was deep and clear and lacked the coarseness she was used to hearing. 'I saw it fall and die as it reached the boundary. I heard the rider speak to it by name. I saw the babe.'

Simeon felt his scalp prickle and grow tight across his skull. He grasped the edges of his cloak and stepped into the air, and in an instant he was on the ground below. The woman shrank back a little as he dropped down. She was small, much shorter than himself, and pretty despite the ravages of hardship. Her eyes were very dark and her hair, caught up in a simple net of woven twine, seemed thick and raven black in colour. She was gaping at him now as if a spectre, not a man, had fallen from the rafters. He saw her gaze flicker from his face to his body and quickly closed his cloak. It was unseemly that this young woman should soften her gaze upon his nakedness.

'You say you saw the babe?' he asked.

She nodded. 'I did. It was swaddled in fur. The rider was all in black and taller than any man I ever saw. Are you a . . .'

'And you say the horse is dead?' he cut in. 'If that's the truth you will take me to where it lies.'

'I cannot do that,' she said. 'All trace of it will be gone by now.'

He scowled. 'Gone? How so?'

'Gone without a trace.' She nodded sadly. 'The butchers were on it even before the rider was out of sight. They cut it up where it lay, ready to sell the pieces on, and not so much as a drop of its blood was gone to waste. There's much to be got from a dead beast when folk are left homeless with their livestock gone and their cooking pots empty.'

'Describe the man then, the rider of the horse.'

'He was uncommonly tall, that's all I know, and dressed in black from head to foot. He wore a hood. I could not see his face.'

'The horse, then. Tell me about the horse.'

Elvira clasped her hands together and recalled how the great beast had loomed out of the darkness on the far bank of the ditch.

'Oh, it was an animal fit for a king to ride,' she exclaimed. 'It was a warrior-horse and *huge*, with hooves as large as shovel heads and a back much broader than that of any plough animal.'

'From which direction did it come?' he asked.

'From the coast, with that fearful tempest coming after it like hounds to the hunt. We watched them come. It was a nightmare sight. The storm was boiling and churning, but the horse was faster. When it reared up it pawed the sky, and when it galloped it tore up the earth with every stride. And then it fell at the boundary near the great ditch. Fell dead, it did, heart-crushed, driven too hard. But it brought them safely here. It was a brave, brave beast.'

He watched her face light with the memory and darken again as she retold the story. He wanted to see what she had seen, to plant the vision of it in his mind.

'What colour was it?'

'Brown, dark brown, with splashes of black and cream, and polished leathers and shining brasses fit for a noble mount. Its trappings were all taken from it except for ...' She bit back the words, then said again: '... except for...'

'Yes?'

Encouraged by his gentle manner Elvira dipped into the ragged folds of her gown and pulled out an item wrapped in a dirty cloth. When she looked at him again her brow was creased, and she could see bright torch-flame dancing in his eyes. 'Are you ... are you a priest?'

He bowed his head, revealing his shaven crown. 'I am Simeon.' He saw her dark eyes widen at the revelation and a look that might have been relief or disappointment, or a brief confusion of the two, invaded her features.

'I didn't think . . . I mean . . .'

'Just tell me what you have there,' he prompted gently.

'My husband refused to give me a share of the pickings,' she explained. 'But I managed to grab this to pay for my baby's blessing. He died without baptism, Father, and if I cannot buy the blessing for him, he'll go to Hell and burn there for ever. Will you bless him, Father Simeon? Will you bless my babe and let him go to Heaven?'

Simeon nodded. 'Of course I will. Woman, if you had come to me sooner . . .'

She made a haughty sound and tossed her head as if to say that all priests were the same and did not sell their precious blessings cheaply. Her manner saddened him. He wondered what worldly price could be fixed on the holy sacrament of baptism or the final rites for a child that had barely lived. A silver penny? A humble ear of corn? Better to ask what price a human soul if God's grace was to be purchased in the marketplace.

'Your child will have the sacrament,' he told her.

She nodded her head to thank him and he was surprised how readily her dark eyes filled with tears. On the heels of his surprise came anger at his lack of charity. She was a grieving mother, after all. She had carried a child inside her for nine long months, brought it forth in pain and distress, then held it to her breast while it slipped away, dead before its time. Sorrow was not the privilege of the wealthy. It stuck more often where the hearth was poorest and caused more heartache where the loss was already the greater. How easy it was, even for a compassionate man like Simeon, to separate the poor and illiterate from the finer aspects of human nature.

Elvira unwrapped her treasure and placed it in the priest's hands. He turned it over in his fingers, offering its burnished surfaces to the firelight, and he was deeply moved by the beauty revealed in it. He was holding the heavy forehead piece from the bridle of a horse, a magnificent crest not shaped in brass, as was the common way, but fashioned in finest gold with small gems incorporated into its design. It was a thing of symbols and holy marks. He saw the keys, the

65

church, the stone, the dove, but it was the centre mark that made him gasp. Embossed there was a single word, the animal's name, and reading it Simeon felt that same sensation behind his breastbone that made him want to groan out loud.

'*Cephas!*'

Now Brother Osric was standing at his shoulder. Simeon held out the glistening crest and watched his eyes.

'Cephas,' the older man said, reading the name.

'Aye, Cephas,' Simeon nodded. 'Another sign. Another strange coincidence to unravel. Cephas, the name of the beast that gave its life to bring them here, the very name Christ gave to Simon for his special calling. It means the same in Hebrew and in Greek. Cephas, The Rock, *Peter!*'

'The child's name,' Osric breathed.

'The name I gave to him,' Simeon nodded. 'Knowing nothing of this I gave the child the very name that was his own.'

He strode to the half-barrel where firelight flickered its warm copper lights across the fox-fur covering. The child was awake now and looked up at him as he bent over it. A tiny hand reached for the glittering horse-crest, grasping the way all newborns do, and the fingers closed around its polished rim. Watching its guardian's face through veiled blue eyes, the baby gurgled contentedly.

'I do not understand this,' Simeon whispered.

The baby watched him solemnly.

Simeon moved his arm so that the tiny hand might close itself around his forefinger. This infant already had him held so firmly by the heart-strings that he wondered, as he stared into its strange blue eyes, how much he really needed to understand.

'*There is no fear in love,*' he muttered, quoting the words of St John the Evangelist. He would have argued that. Right then he would have challenged the saint and insisted that love, touching a man too deep, the way love always must, brings with it a special vulnerability even the gods must dread.

CHAPTER EIGHT

In the stricken Minster voices were raised in song. While rescuers toiled and sweated in the dust and waste, those choral priests still capable of singing offered up Matins in anticipation of the night's conclusion. They were keeping the ancient Office of singing in the dawn, and their song would not be stilled until the new day was in. The sound brought cheer and renewed hope to all who heard it, for such prayer could lift the spirit and feed the soul. And these devotions served a far deeper purpose, for mortal men, in their most secret souls, believe blind faith and adoration sufficient in themselves to calm God's wrath. They hope that He, created in their image, is like themselves amenable to flattery.

Cyrus de Figham let the sound of strong male voices touch a chord of familiarity inside him.

'We call the dawn into existence,' he said aloud. 'We sing the sun up every day as if the stars and planets would grind to a halt within the Greater Scheme of things without our human voices to depend upon. Do we really believe God made a sun that is unable to rise up or down without our miserable assistance?' His smile was bitter but his eyes were merry. 'We are all the same,' he mused. 'Christian, Muslim, Pagan or Jew, we all build our pretty altars facing east and warble the new day in like little sparrows. All men are Heathens when the night has cowed them.'

Cyrus was watching for the dawn from a little corner window of the chapter house. He could see the morning star above the marshes, hanging low and still against the blue-black velvet of the sky. He stank of stale sweat and other people's misery. He had neither washed his body nor changed his clothes, and the blood of a dozen injured men and women was still on him. For once their grime was not offensive to him. Instead he viewed the filth with a sense of pride. It was appropriate that when the time came he should stand before his superiors wearing the battered vestments of his heroism.

Cyrus had toiled with the rescuers until his fingers bled and every muscle in his body ached. He was exhausted and bitterly resentful of the need to perform such degrading manual labour in his quest for personal advancement. It had been hard, but already his efforts were showing some reward. With his quick mind and authoritative manner he had made himself the leader of the pack. With leadership came prestige, and with prestige came power, and with power, profit. They spoke of him as if he were a hero. It was Cyrus who found the jewelled communion chalice and the altar plate, Cyrus who pulled out an injured child and had the presence of mind to blow the life back into its small lungs. And by his hand a well-loved priest, Father Paul of Cottam, was dragged from beneath a fall of rock and carried, still breathing, to the infirmary.

'A good night's work for me,' he smiled to himself. 'A good night's work and profitable . . . *profitable*.'

Just then a monk in a dark brown habit moved forward to offer him a cup of wine. He was not a Beverley man by birth but a traveller, a man of forests and hedgerows, a wandering pilgrim who offered his services wherever they were needed, and for his pains enjoyed a beggar's existence.

'Drink, Brother, and be refreshed.'

Cyrus eyed the cup suspiciously. It had a scent of hot cinders and scorched spices, and tiny tendrils of aromatic steam curled up from it.

'Drink. The wine is good. Can you not sleep, Brother Cyrus?'

He shook his head and sipped at the warming liquid. He hated monks. Their dusty piety unsettled him. 'No, *Brother*,' he said with uncivil emphasis. 'I cannot sleep.'

The monk looked at the priest and was unable to make out the colour of his eyes. They might have been brown or grey or blue. The hostility in them was not so indistinct.

'We are all brothers here,' he said passively. 'In times of such disaster, all of us must bend our backs to the same task.'

'Indeed we must,' Cyrus replied. He handed back the cup and held the other's gaze with his steady stare. The wine was good. It warmed and revived him but he would not condescend to thank the monk for it.

When the monk moved away to offer his aid elsewhere, Cyrus allowed himself to smile at the self-defeating folly of the man and his kind. They walked in the path of Jesus, so they believed, and by their misguided mimicry they placed themselves outside the common circle of respect. No man could trust a vagabond, for he had neither peers nor kin to censure his behaviour, nor goods that might fall forfeit in the event of his wrong-doing. Thus he became immune to and uncaring of punishment, a law unto himself and so beyond the rule of ordinary citizens.

As for the shepherds these monks professed to be, what man since the dawn of time would give one ounce of respect to a detested shepherd? He dealt in country practices and was skilled in the bloodstained arts of butchery. He was rightly despised by all God-fearing men, for like the leper he was tainted and depraved. He shunned the company of his kind and centred his meditations, so decent men believed, upon the vile hindquarters of his beasts.

'Three of a kind, these monks, lepers and keepers of woolbacks,' Cyrus muttered to himself.

It was a fact that England had three Sirs: Sir King, Sir Knight and Sir Priest. And if that were so then three kinds of men must likewise share the lowest level of the human orders, and they were undoubtedly the leper, the shepherd and the monk.

Cyrus turned from the window and peered about him. There were others crowded into the chapter house, exhausted priests and clerks brought there to rest. Many, like himself, were carried there by stronger hands after collapsing in their struggles to free the trapped. Licking torchlight illuminated their faces so that they were like masks hung in the darkness, each with its tale to tell of fear and pain, perplexity and loss.

Several young boys from the stricken grammar school were huddled together in quiet corners or stretched out amongst the rushes on the floor. Some of them had wept for hours after seeing their fellows crushed by falling stones or plucked up by the storm and carried away to their deaths. Somewhere a muffled voice cried out incessantly, sometimes in a sobbing whimper, sometimes a scream, but on and on, without cessation. Cyrus was sure he recognised the voice. He was told it had been howling thus for hours.

He shifted his position until he was looking to the north, beyond the churchyard and the half-demolished Fishmarket, on to Butcher Row, the corn market, the bull ring and the Bishop's palace near the market cross and, further yet, to the great North Bar where the ditch was deepest. The town was devastated. Smoke from untended fires belched out to hang with the mist that swirled in the greying dawn. Closer to hand, in Eastgate to his right, many houses lay crushed or burned while the debris of the storm was everywhere. And just as many buildings stood their ground, unaccountably disregarded by the tempest. The marshy moorland around the Minster had become a quagmire. Both under the ground and above it, the many waterways of Beverley had been swollen to several times their safe capacity. From the Westwood to Long Lane and the deeper drain, a distance of two miles or more, the ditch had overflowed its banks to dump its stinking waters everywhere. From the North Bar to the little beckside port, running a curved course east along Hellsgarth, its secondary fork spewed out the same filth as it travelled on its way.

'This town is little more than marshland hemmed in on all sides by sewers and ditches and streams,' Cyrus observed without affection. 'It floods in winter, stinks in summer and keeps a man's feet sodden all year round.'

He scowled as small movements beyond the window caught his eye. Furtive figures were darting here and there in the early morning light, creeping around the ruined houses and the market stalls. Looters were at their work. They came like slinking hyenas after carrion, sniffing out the misfortunes of their fellow men and hoping to fatten their bellies and purses on it. He saw a stooped man hammer at something on the ground before darting behind a shadowy pile of rubble, and it crossed his mind that he might be witness to a bloody murder. He guessed that the sins concealed by darkness were legion, for that night was one in which the wicked prospered while the godly fell. These hours were for thieves, cut-purses and violent men, for assassinations, spiteful blows and wily appropriations.

'And for a priest's advancement,' he whispered grimly, feeling no sorrow for a kindly old man bludgeoned to death by one of his fellow priests.

Once again Cyrus became aware of the voice that cried incessantly in some shadowed corner. He rounded on the monk who knelt nearby, hearing the gasped confession of a woman close to death.

'Will no one silence that irksome voice?' he demanded.

The monk lifted his head, his eyes a-glitter with reflected torchlight. 'You could offer the boy the benefit of your comfort, Brother Cyrus.'

Feeling himself slyly chastised, Cyrus bristled but kept his voice even as he said: 'Such lamenting smacks of self-indulgence. Someone should remind him that prayer is by far the better way.'

'He knew that once, but he is no more than a boy and his faith has been cruelly tested. He is struggling in the wilderness, brother Cyrus. He needs someone strong and firm in faith to guide him back. If you would help, if you will go to him ...'

71

Cyrus was furious. This upstart monk was actually reminding him of his priestly obligations to the sick and the needy, as if he had not already done far more for them than any had a right to expect of him.

'I have worked all night,' he said.

The monk nodded. 'Our calling is not an easy one. The Lord is merciful, but a hard task-master.'

The priest drew in a long, deep breath and forced himself to smile. No man, least of all a sanctimonious monk, must have cause to speak anything but good of him to the canons.

'If I am needed then I must go to him,' he quietly conceded, glancing upward to where the screams were at their loudest. 'Is he up there on the flat part of the roof?'

'He is, in the little alcove on the south side where the shadows are darkest. Thank you, brother.'

The monk bent his head then to the dying woman, placed his hands over hers and spoke a prayer acquitting her of blame. Confronted by that stooping back and lowered head, the priest was hard pressed to keep his anger checked. He had been dismissed, discharged from the shabby company of this vagrant monk. White-faced, he clenched his fists and turned away and carried his fury with him to the roof.

The boy was crouched in the corner the monk had described, his body folded and crushed into the angle of the walls as if he hoped the stones would close around him. It was the same boy he had seen before, scuttling on all fours from behind the altar of St Mark, his mouth gagged and his fresh young body defiled. As Cyrus approached his wails increased and he lifted his arms to defend himself while pressing his buttocks hard against the wall. In his shame and distress he had abandoned the power to distinguish one priest from another.

Without a moment's hesitation Cyrus reached down to fasten his fingers around the lad's throat and slowly squeezed off his air supply. As he did so he dragged him upward until he hung backwards over the roof's low parapet. The view from there was sobering, for it was a long way to the ground below. The screaming stopped abruptly. The lad's eyes bulged and swam with tears, and his soft, small hands clutched at the big man's wrists. His struggle for life was feeble but intense.

'Not another sound,' Cyrus hissed, venting his own ire on the helpless boy. 'Your weeping and wailing is driving me to distraction. Not another sound or I will choke the miserable life from your body and drop you over to the stones below.'

He watched the young face purple and the mouth become slack and fish-like in its search for air. He was tempted, sorely tempted, to test his strength upon that tender throat. When at last he released his grip the boy fell heavily to his knees and there remained, gasping and sobbing but quietly, for his windpipe and his courage were both half-crushed. The priest strode away without a backward glance, and when he stepped back inside the chapter house the wailing voice could no longer be heard.

'You have quietened him,' the monk said, smiling.

Cyrus shrugged his shoulders and answered modestly: 'I used a simple wisdom. He was ready enough to listen.'

'My thanks to you, Brother Cyrus.'

'I left him with instructions to recite the Creed, in Latin first and then in English.' The lie fell smoothly from his tongue. 'I believe the discipline will calm him and no doubt he will sleep a little after it.'

'Your efforts are much appreciated, Brother.'

'No more than are your own,' Cyrus replied.

'My name is Antony.'

'Antony. I will remember that.' He smiled. This monk was ambitious for some reward and Cyrus, being prudent, would see to it that he got what he deserved. 'And now I must return to the church, where my help is needed. As you observed, our calling is not an easy one.'

'God be with you, Brother Cyrus.'

'And with you, Antony.'

Feeling better for having vented his anger on the boy, and for having got the measure of the monk, Cyrus turned and headed for the door. As he picked a careful course between the bodies on the floor he wondered if his own face, like all

73

those others, danced grotesquely in the light from the torches. He hurried downstairs and instead of passing through into the Minster's north choir aisle, continued down to one of the outer doors.

The chapter house was a many angled, two-storey building with a flat roof and the slanting windows of a fortress. It was a solid wing of ancient stone built at the Minster's quiet north-eastern corner, a relic of the abbey that had once stood on that site. It rested on old, secure foundations in a sheltered spot, and so it had suffered little in the storm. Its outer doors gave access to the Minster graveyard looking east, and to the bustling Fishmarket, known as Hyegate, looking north. In Fishmonger Row there was a house he frequented, the home of Gervaise, the fishmonger and his family. It was a hovel, but it served his purpose.

The dust and backbreaking work had made him thirsty, and the wine that had quenched his thirst had turned to fire in his loins. He needed a woman. He had never embraced the extreme discipline of celibacy. Few sane men did. Only a fool would allow his tongue to make solemn vows his genitalia would not let him keep. It was Eugenius, in his short and turbulent reign as Pope, who decreed that no bishop, abbot, deacon, priest or monk should take unto himself a wife. And how Old Satan must have danced with glee at such a grandiose declaration of man's foolishness. To make a trespass of a natural instinct is to condemn good men to Hell in droves. And if sinful thought is merely a sin unhatched, all men are doomed but those who are castrated at their birth.

Cyrus's thoughts increased his need for relief, and the irony of that did not escape him. By his thoughts he had committed fornication, yet still his body hungered for the tangible, material fact of it. He needed a woman and he would have one, and neither Pope nor devil would tell him otherwise.

He lifted his hood and turned his step in the direction of the fishmonger's house. For the better part of his journey he was treading mud to his calves and reduced to shouldering his way through an army of grasping human parasites. Within the church walls the graveyard was a glistening bed of sludge. He held his sleeve to his nostrils and breathed through the heavy cloth to avoid the stench of putrid bodies disgorged by the waterlogged earth. Twice he almost lost his balance despite his careful steps. Once he threw out an arm to steady himself and found that he had grasped the naked buttocks of a man whose body had been folded double and rammed head downwards in the slime.

A river of mud had run from Walkergate to the adjacent churchyards of St Martin and St John, carrying corpses and storm debris as it came. The houses on each side of Fishmonger Row were at worst demolished and at best awash with stinking mud. The home of Gervaise stood on the left between two better houses, and so it had been protected from the worst of the wind and rain. It was a one-roomed house with a single centre beam and a large brick fireplace where the family's meals were cooked. Cursing the sludge that sucked at his legs, Cyrus ducked to avoid the eaves and stepped inside.

'Father Cyrus, bless you for coming.'

He scowled and squinted in the semi-darkness. 'What? Did you send for me?'

'Some hours ago,' the man nodded, apologetically. 'I sent my eldest lad in search of you. I was beginning to fear you might be dead.'

'I received no message,' Cyrus told him, wondering if his death would have proved a blessing or a curse to this unwashed dullard.

'My wife,' the fishmonger said. 'There was a tree, an oak, ripped up and carried by the storm. It punctured the roof like a spear and my poor dear Maud was hit. It was the mud that killed her, though, not the tree. It drowned her where she fell while we were running about in the pitch darkness, saving ourselves. Rain put the fire out, you see, and the torches too. We had no light to see by.'

Cyrus stared about him in the gloom. There were several pigs and chickens in a corner. Two goats were tethered to a metal spike and a barrel of fish-heads, crawling with flies and maggots, stood open against a wall. Six of the dead woman's children were gathered around her corpse, which had been stripped of its clothes and covered with a makeshift shroud. It lay on a wooden board raised up on bricks to prevent it from sinking into the layer of slime that covered the dirt floor ankle deep. The eldest child, also named Maud like her mother, lowered her head and would not meet his gaze. He had never seen her smile. She was a girl of fourteen years, quite plain of feature but with a decent body. It was convenient for him to have her here, within sight of the Minster and not too far from his own small church at Figham. He could reach her here whenever the need came upon him, and to this end he had the fishmonger firmly in his debt for services rendered. He kept the man from ruin just so long as the girl was made available to him. A few paltry shillings left owing were neither here nor there to a man like Cyrus, but to this illiterate fishmonger they marked the dividing line between survival and disaster.

'Do you have the fee?' He asked the question simply out of curiosity. He was there to have the girl, not bless the mother.

'Alas ...' the fishmonger spread his hands and shook his head. He was reluctant to part with so much as a brace of fish unless the levy was demanded of him. He saw no reason to settle his debts in kind or coin while his daughter held the fee between her legs.

'No matter,' Cyrus told him. 'Bring me the girl.'

He moved to the low pallet in the alcove where the fishmonger slept. It was covered by dirty sacking, a few handfuls of straw and a roll of filthy cloth to make a pillow. A chicken sat there in comfort on the straw, while insects scuttled and fed upon the bedding. When Cyrus surveyed all this his upper lip curled in a grimace of distaste. There had been not the slightest improvement since his last visit to the house. The fishmonger's bed was too unsavoury a place for any decent man to lay his head. Weary though he was, he would rather take his pleasure standing upright.

At a signal from her father Maud came to the priest without a sign of protest, paddling through the mud from her place beside the corpse. She had exchanged her mother's winter hood for her own, which had grown short and threadbare after years of use. Being but half the dead woman's height and girth, she was enveloped in the dark cloth from neck to calf. Her hair was loose and reached her waist, but there was little comeliness in it. It had no definite colour and was matted with dirt and grime, and her fingers were constantly scratching at her scalp.

The priest looked down at her with unconcealed disgust, and just as he had known it would, that which repulsed him also served to heighten his desire. He licked his lips and felt the fires rising in his loins. He dipped his hands into the front of her clothes, found that the cloth restricted their freedom of movement and ripped the garment open with impatient fingers. Finding her firm young breasts, he fondled them as roughly as his mood dictated, pulling and squeezing the nipples until she winced. Then he began to hoist his habit up.

'Lift your skirts and bend over,' he ordered, gripping his penis in urgent readiness. 'Come girl, don't keep me here all night. Bend forward and let me get this over with. There's work to be done and I have no wish to linger here a moment longer than is necessary. Further ... bend over further ... take hold of the bed ... a little wider now ... oh yes, now I can reach you with both hands while I ... oh yes ... oh yes ...'

It was over in minutes, for there was scant enjoyment to be savoured in his encounter with this wretched girl. She whimpered as he withdrew from her and remained stooped over, her arms folded across her body as if she were in pain. Indifferent, he dropped his robes and settled his cloak more comfortably on his shoulders, then made his way to the centre of the room. The other children were watching him without embarrassment while the fishmonger smiled and lifted his shoulders as if to apologise for the inferior quality of his hospitality.

Now eager to be gone from that stinking hovel, Cyrus made the sign of the cross and mumbled a hasty prayer for the departed soul of Maud, the fishmonger's wife. This ritual, too, he performed in record time before leaving the house with a curt nod for his host. Neither man was any less satisfied than he had hoped to be. That their basic mutual needs had been fulfilled was all that concerned them.

Retracing his steps through the squelching slime, he felt no conflict between the outer man and the inner, between the man his church knew and the fishmonger's guest. If challenged he would have smiled his slow, lop-sided, cynic's smile and claimed neither weight nor stain upon his conscience. He would have asked how many great saints deserved one tenth of the virtue and humility their followers, with all their good intentions, heaped so hastily upon them. Even the famous hairshirt of St Thomas Becket, so men whispered, had secretly been lined with purest silk to keep his skin from chafing under it. What then if Cyrus de Figham was just a man, no more than he professed to be, if saints themselves were the same as he beneath hypocrisy's pretensions?

CHAPTER NINE

Only with the greatest reluctance did Simeon prepare to leave the infirmary shortly after dawn. He would have chosen to remain there had not his canon, Father Cuthbert, sent urgent word for him to come without delay. His wish to linger there in that sheltered place was barely influenced by the discomfort of his injuries. These were, for the most part, blessedly superficial. His bruises had been soothed and cooled with chervil leaves to bring the colour and the pain to the surface. His cuts and abrasions were smeared with an ointment containing Indian aloe, which helped wounds heal more rapidly by encouraging them to scab over. The deep gash on his forearm had been tightly bound, the cut on his neck loosely covered to keep out dirt and give protection from the chill December winds.

The crown of his head, within the circle of thick blond hair shaping his tonsure, sported a swollen, fierce-looking bruise slashed open at its centre. Dried blood turned the slash to glistening black until it resembled, according to Father Osric, the ragged fissure of a spent volcano.

With the assistance of his dedicated helper, Brother William, Osric the infirmarian had removed a dozen shards of glass from Simeon's back and shoulders, probing each gash so that no risk of poison should be left behind. Then he smoothed the whole area with Indian aloe and bound strips of white linen around his patient's body. Simeon was a strong young man well acquainted with physical pain, so it was neither his injuries nor fatigue that had kept him sitting by the fireside or standing in the rafters, shunning sleep. That tiny figure lying in the half-barrel was the compelling force that kept him there.

Two lesser priests had come to fetch him immediately after the Office of Lauds was over and the dawn was in. One was an ostiary dressed in a plain black cassock, the other an exorcist in scarlet and white. They were both mud-spattered, their eyes red-rimmed and their faces drawn with weariness. They had come to St Peter's to make a record of the dead and injured, and to summon Simeon to an urgent gathering in the canons' hall. He could not refuse to attend and would not disappoint his canon by sending his excuses, but he went unwillingly.

'You have your duties to attend to,' Brother Osric reminded him.

'My duty now is to the child,' Simeon corrected, his voice as even-toned as ever but now with a more authoritative edge.

'The child is safe enough with us. No harm will come to him in your absence, Simeon.'

'I should remain here ...' He glanced at the ostiary and the exorcist, who in their lesser orders looked to such as Simeon for demonstrations of obedience. '... but since I have been summoned ...'

'The child is safe with us,' Father Osric repeated. 'Go now. Obey your Canon. Brother William will accompany you for safety's sake, and when you have attended to your duties you may return to us here.'

Simeon nodded and sat down on a stool so that young William could lace his boots with thongs about his legs. The boots were unequal in shape and size, for one must accommodate the rigidity that had set Simeon's ankle bones after a childhood accident, creating the flaw that robbed him of a father's love and so marked him out for holy orders. Now

80

Brother William grasped the extra folds of leather in his fingers and looked up at Father Osric with a silent question. The two were so close that a glance was all it took to still his tongue. Without a word he bound up the boot's soft folds, empty and superfluous, with the rest. He watched Simeon as he strode around the makeshift crib, gathering his long dark cloak around his shoulders, then the young man gaped at the infirmarian and mouthed the words:

'*His foot!*'

Father Osric shook his head in warning, but his eyes were troubled and doubt was clearly etched upon his features. He signed the cross and whispered: 'Merciful God, go with our Brother for his protection and his guidance.'

As the messengers took their leave to go in search of other priests, Father Simeon stooped to touch his fingers very gently to the child's small forehead. He looked into its blue-veiled eyes and felt that special, shifting ache behind his breastbone.

'God keep and guard you,' he whispered, then turned on his heels and strode away.

Outside he made his way to the narrow iron gate and stepped gingerly on to the little bridge that spanned the ditch beyond St Peter's wall. The beds of earth into which its ends were set were awash with mud, and the bridge itself, a single oaken beam, was rendered treacherous by the slime still clinging to its surface.

Now Simeon negotiated the narrow timber with special care, leaping the last two strides in order to avoid the quagmire where it met the bank. His thoughts were still with the child. As yet he had made no firm decision about the woman's milk. He was loath to have his precious godson swaddled in that unsavoury embrace where another babe had died only hours before. He might have argued, as Osric did, that supernatural forces were at work to provide this little stranger with a substitute mother, and that the death of one child was pre-ordained to benefit the other. It was a seductive argument that slotted with ease into the night's events, but Simeon was not so easily convinced. Even as his fingers closed around the golden headpiece in his pocket, he knew he must not allow strange happenstance to sweep aside his better judgment. Honeyed cow's milk must suffice, for his godchild would not be put in haste to the very nipple where a dead babe had suckled.

On Simeon's instructions the would-be wet-nurse, Elvira the ditcher's wife, had been taken to the little convent of St Anne lying just outside the Keldgate Bar. There she would be bathed and cleaned of lice, closely examined for sores and rashes and, if considered suitable to nurse, dressed in clean linen and returned to him. Only then would he decide.

'God's blessing be on you, Brother.'

'And may His love sustain you,' Simeon responded.

The other knew his voice. 'Brother Simeon? Can that be you, Brother Simeon?'

'It is indeed.' He threw back his hood and looked into the face of the man who had greeted him.

Father James was carrying a holy water pot and a silver-handled aspersoir with which to asperse the injured he encountered. He had stopped where the churchyard wall curved itself into Eastgate, where a sorry group of sufferers awaited the administrations of a priest. His greeting had been directed to a passing priest and the words were out before he recognised that one as Simeon. Now he peered into the familiar, strong-boned face, into the intense blue eyes, and for a moment he experienced an odd sensation that made him want to bow his head and bend his knee in humble supplication. Here was his friend and fellow priest, Simeon the lame scribe, the same and yet no longer quite the same.

'What is it, Brother James? Do you not recognise me?'

'You seem . . . changed,' the other man remarked.

Simeon placed a hand on James's shoulder. There was new strength and certainty in his grip.

'This night has surely changed us all,' he said.

'But you are . . . you have been . . .'

'Through Hell,' Simeon offered. 'I have been through Hell and out the other side.'

He squeezed the softer flesh beneath his hand, then turned and strode away. He was a tall man, but now he seemed much taller than before. His shoulders were wide and squared beneath the enveloping folds of his fur-lined cloak and there was an extra boldness in his stature. Father James stared after him, seeing a friend who had surely now been separated from his kind. With the handle of his aspersoir he signed himself with the holy cross of Christ.

'He does not know,' he whispered to himself in disbelief. 'Dear God, you have touched our Brother with a miracle and as yet he is unaware of it.'

Following some way behind, Brother William noted the response of Father James and knew that many other men would find the scribe both physically changed and subtly altered. He wanted to be a part of this, to be present at the moment of truth, when Simeon looked to himself and saw the miracle.

Oblivious to the speculation he left in his wake, Father Simeon strode on towards the Provost's hall. His head was slightly bowed as he watched for pitfalls, his mind still on the child placed in his keeping. He saw as if at a distance the ruin of the storm, the fallen walls, the flattened timber buildings. He felt detached from the hordes of hurt and homeless people huddling together, listless in the cold light of the morning, exhausted by the trials of the night.

Beyond the wreckage of St Martin's church, lying in moated grounds on the south side of the Minster, sprawled the extensive grounds surrounding the Provost's Hall. Before going on in that direction Simeon paused to rest his hand on one of the shattered buttresses of St Martin's. As yet untouched by the rising sun and still glistening with winter rain, those pale, coarse-textured limestone walls were warm beneath his palm. He felt a sadness deep within himself. The loss of this little parish church was a tragedy. Through a gap in the stones he could see the many looters swarming there, moving like hungry rodents over the debris, looking for treasures cast down by the storm. The old font was still standing, draped in a shroud of fallen masonry. It looked as if the whole weight of the stricken church was held upon its shoulders, as if it bore a very special burden.

'Peter. I name him Peter.'

The sound of his own voice rang in Simeon's ears and a shiver ran through him as he recalled that extraordinary baptism. He decided then that the font must be lifted free of the rubble and set down in the Minster church itself. It would be safe there from the hands of thieves, and would remain intact when the masons took St Martin's stones, as they most surely would, and used them to repair the damaged minster.

He turned his head to survey the moated lands laid out ahead of him. The massive drawbridge had stood its ground despite the efforts of the swollen moat to undermine its foundations, but the other, smaller bridges all were gone. The entire area had become a muddy lake. The gardens and orchards were submerged, the buildings flooded, the wooded areas flattened. Now little flat-bottomed boats were struggling there, carrying priests to the Great Hall, labouring through the litter-strewn water and pools of thick black mud.

News had already reached Simeon that the Provost's Court, where cases were heard and sentences passed by the Provost himself, had suffered extensive damage in the storm. Five prisoners, one a boy of ten, were crushed to death inside their cells when the walls caved in. The priests who tried to save them were drowned when a solid wall of flood-water cut off their only means of escape from the subterranean prison. The eastern end of the same building, being a recent extension constructed over a culvert, collapsed and compressed itself upon its own foundations, killing the priests who had gathered there for shelter.

A little flag still flew on the roof of the Provost's house, telling the people of Beverley that old Geoffrey, with his sick lungs and his wandering senses, had not perished in the storm.

'God be thanked for his survival,' Simeon muttered, then shook his head as if to cancel out the automatic response. He had spoken the words with no clear thought behind them. The death of Geoffrey would have been a blessing. Why spare a sick and sad old man to face this devastation?

Poor Geoffrey would be hard-pressed by his canons now to decide upon important new appointments. His precentor, who was in charge of choir and song-school, had survived. His sacrist, who was responsible for services, books and valuables, would recover from his injuries, given time and a good deal of care. But Geoffrey was yet to be informed that Father Aidan, his closest friend and trusted chancellor, had perished in the ruin of the grammar school where he had been *ex officio* head. There would be little time to grieve upon his losses, for there were ambitious men still living, all of them eager to join the rush for new appointments.

Simeon sighed and wondered how many here would bless the old man for his resolute grip on life. The benefice of Provost, which Geoffrey had held for twelve long years, was extremely lucrative and much sought-after. Those self-serving men of York who had the Archbishop's ear had staked their various claims on it some years ago, when Geoffrey's illness first became apparent. It was a position of wealth, prestige and power, first held by Thomas the Younger, nephew of Archbishop Thomas de Bayeux. After him came many notables, not least among them the martyr, St Thomas Becket, who had also held the prebend of St Michael. Poor Geoffrey's canons were not so eager to bury him while the Archbishop still had no man of Beverley measured for those lordly vestments. It was their wish to leave their many extra comforts and privileges unscrutinised by the critical eyes of strangers. Better to enjoy a pliant, unremarkable master than suffer the tight-pursed patronage of one set firmly in the Archbishop's pocket.

Simeon looked at the sky. In the early morning light its grey-black clouds were edged with polished brass, soft-toned and unthreatening. The moon was still visible as a pale and distant reflection of itself, sinking towards the brightening horizon. The morning sky was calm and still and beautiful. It hung above him, impervious, remote, and in its blue indifference he detected something more than the simple daily miracle most men dared take for granted. In that day's first glimpse of infinity he almost felt the presence of his God.

Two men were watching Simeon from a distance. One was the simple-hearted Brother William, hovering several paces behind, reluctant to walk beside a man whose thoughts were fierce and whose person had been touched by the Almighty. William knew his place and was content to remain in it. He knew that some men were destined to be rulers of other men, that some were singled out for fame or martyrdom. Many were called upon to be the Lord's special instruments, but for the rest obscurity must suffice. William knew what every Christian was meant to know, that he was duty-bound to remain in the place God-given at his birth. To aspire above it was to commit the sins of ingratitude and pride; to fall below it was to reject God's gift and walk in shame. For Simeon there had never been such conflict, for he had been born to wealth and power and God had brought him low by laming him. Now God had relented, and His change of heart would elevate Simeon to His intended level.

Brother William watched the handsome, blue-eyed priest lift up his head to the early morning sky, and as he watched the breath caught in his throat. Father Simeon's face was beautiful. The morning sun touched his tonsure with a sheen of gold, giving the circlet of thick, curly hair the look of a royal crown. His profile was strong and aristocratic in structure, with a fine jaw and even, well-balanced features. In his huge cloak, reaching to his ankles, the tall man had assumed the stature of a giant.

Even as Brother William looked on in wonder, the man who was the focus of his attention turned his blue gaze briefly upon him and smiled the sad, small smile of the separated. Then Father Simeon swung away, springing lightly over an area strewn with rubble until he reached more level ground, there to stride off in the direction of the Provost's enclosure.

Another man had been watching from the shadows. Cyrus de Figham narrowed his night-dark eyes and squared his shoulders. Returning from the fishmonger's house, he too had stopped to survey the pile of rubble that had been St Martin's church. Ruin or no, he was determined to have that prebend for his own. He would rebuild it on a grander scale. He would make of it a bigger and better parish church than it had ever been, and for every penny that went into the making of it, two more would find their way into his own purse. And there was no measured dishonesty in his plans, for he considered it a fair exchange. St Martin's would be his, along with all the extra work and parish responsibilities, and in return he would make that mediocre little church the prince of Beverley, second only to its monarch, the mighty Minster.

'Brother William, a moment, if you please.'

The sound of that unexpected voice caused Brother William to start. He gathered up his woollen cloak and hurried across to where the priest was standing.

'God's blessing, Father Cyrus.'

Cyrus did not return the greeting. Instead he scowled and asked: 'What is happening here?'

'Oh Father, have you not heard?'

'I have heard only babble and foolish speculation,' Cyrus answered.

'But you were there in the church,' Brother William said, as if the fact had only now occurred to him. 'I saw you there. You were a witness to the holy baptism. And after that you followed them to the Minster and that's what saved you, for every witness who came survived the storm, and those who stayed were either killed or maimed.'

'Nonsense.'

'Forgive me, Father. I know it to be so.'

Cyrus would not admit to his presence at the font of St Martin's. He would not assist that upstart Simeon to a position of high repute. 'Who owns the child?' he demanded. 'Who sired it and who brought it here amid all this destruction? Where is the woman that bore it?'

'Father Cyrus, I can answer none of these questions.'

'Then I will assume it to be Simeon's child,' Cyrus declared. 'He has sired a bastard.'

'Father Cyrus!' William was horrified by the base assumption that a priest of Simeon's calibre had fallen into sin. 'Father Simeon has taken a vow of chastity.'

'And so aspires to sainthood,' Cyrus scoffed, 'unlike the rest of us, who willingly admit that we are mortal men, and so make no rash promises of virtue. But even would-be saints fall short of perfection and succumb to earthly vices when they must.'

'Not he. Not Simeon,' William insisted.

'He is a man like any other.'

'He took a voluntary oath for reasons other men might fail to understand.'

'Aye, so you say,' Cyrus agreed, unable to keep the sarcasm from his voice. 'But I understand this much, William, my naive little brother. No glib movement of the lips, however noble and sanctimonious, will stop up the fires of lust in a young man's loins. Tell me the truth. Be honest. Is it his child?'

Brother William met the intimidating stare with a courage he did not feel. 'No, Father, it is not,' he said. 'The child was brought here on horseback from the eastern coast. There were witnesses to its coming . . . the woman who will be its wet-nurse and the man who is her husband. Its guardian wore a hood that hid his face, and he was steadfast in his purpose, to have the child baptised in the Lord and offered at the shrine of St John of Beverley. And as for Father Simeon, it was no quirk of circumstance that placed him there to receive the child into his keeping. The guardian came for him. It called him by name. He was . . .' The younger man paused, sucked in his breath and glanced at the fur-clad figure standing in the distance with his hand raised up to bless a stooping man. '. . . *He was chosen!*'

Cyrus scowled at that. He did not like the way things were shaping themselves in Father Simeon's favour. He had worked his fingers to the bone that night to make himself the hero of the storm, the name on every grateful tongue, the man of the moment. It was imperative that he attract the gainful light of favourable attention. He would not stand in the shadow of some crippled scribe who lacked self-interest and true ambition but stood to snatch St Martin's for himself.

'And has this mystery child been carried back whence it came?' he asked, folding his heavy brows over narrowed eyes. 'Is that bizarre baptism now a matter of speculation, a tale to be told and retold around the cooking pot, to be embellished and inflated out of all proportion so that simple-minded men might dream they saw a miracle?'

Brother William felt the man's arm on his shoulder and realised that Father Cyrus, for reasons that were his own, was deeply resentful of the situation. He found himself babbling what details he could recall, eager to speak of it and then be gone. He had, after all, been sent to protect Father Simeon from the attentions of thieves and cut-purses. He watched the grey-black eyes close into slits as he spoke, felt the bony hand grip painfully at his flesh. Filled with the need to defend a good man from censure that was surely undeserved, he finished his story with a statement in defence of Simeon's chastity.

'Peter is Father Simeon's godson, his to protect and nurture, his own yet not of his own loins. Father Simeon remains true to the solemn vows he made. He was chosen, Father Cyrus. You saw for yourself how it was at the baptism. *Simeon was chosen.*'

Cyrus's reply was ground through tightly clenched teeth. 'What foolish talk is this? I saw no baptism. I witnessed nothing.'

'But Father, you were *there!*'

'Nonsense, The man is a liar in search of personal advancement, and in these troubled times he preys upon the gullibility of fools.'

'Father Cyrus, you cannot believe that to be so!'

'Don't take me for a simpleton,' Cyrus spat.

'But you were *there!*'

'I saw no baptism, I tell you, and as for that poor, crippled . . .'

The harsh words died in Cyrus's throat and suddenly his

face grew ashen. He had seen and yet not fully seen the change in Simeon, and now his eyes were widening in disbelief. He turned his head. In the distance the fur-clad figure of the priest could be seen near a cart that had been dashed to pieces against the housing of the drawbridge. He was helping to shift the wreckage.

Brother William stood back and said, with a hint of satisfaction in his voice: 'Ah, *now* you can see the miracle, Father Cyrus.'

'By Heaven,' Cyrus breathed, 'the cripple walks as straight as any man.'

'And does not know it, yet,' Brother William smiled. 'He is too preoccupied with these events even to notice his own good fortune.'

Cyrus gaped at the scribe who had been lame and now walked on two healthy, balanced feet. He could feel his own advantage slipping away from him. How could a man compete with this, a miraculous cure for everyone to see, a miracle associated with the mysterious arrival of a new-born in the midst of a malignant tempest? It had an appeal of Biblical engineering. That quiet man, that undistinguished innocent, was about to rob Cyrus de Figham of his hard-won advantage.

'My God,' he growled, his fists clenched on his fury. 'My God. My God.'

'He is healed of his affliction, as you see, and yet he does not . . .'

Brother William broke off before the words were out. He could see Father Simeon moving now with his head lowered and his cloak held out on either side of him. He turned slow circles, stepping from one foot to the other, dancing and capering while his cloak billowed in dark waves all about him. Then he ran a few sure steps, leapt high into the air and landed nimbly, and from where they stood they heard his half-delirious whoop of joy. And just as suddenly as it began the joyful prancing stopped and Simeon was struck by the enormity of what had befallen him. For a moment he seemed to hang, quite still, upon the startling truth of it. Then his muscular body buckled like a broken thing and he fell to his knees on the ground and hung his head, weeping like a creature in despair.

'Oh God, he knows it now,' Brother William said with an ache of compassion in his heart. 'He knows it now.'

CHAPTER TEN

The Archbishop of York's men were on the streets before the bell for Terce was rung at 9 am. They came on horseback, led by Sir Hugh de Burton, a powerful local knight with several manors in the region. He came on a fine black destrier, armed from top to toe, with a shield on his arm and carrying a lance with his knight's pennon fluttering from its point. He wore a long-sleeved, hooded holberc to defend his body, and a heavy iron helmet with a nasal guard. Over his common braes his legs were bound with strips of leather and his boots, rising almost to his knees, sported a fancy padded guard, his own invention, to protect his shinbones. A simple sling and a wide-bladed short-sword hung from his jewelled girdle.

Sir Hugh de Burton had ridden hard to grasp what plunder or prestige were waiting to be harvested in Beverley. He reached the town before the sun came up, but floods across the wetlands kept him out. Like all the little water towns in its manor, Beverley was hemmed in by swamp and flood for much of the year, and now the storm had cut it off completely. He managed to procure a number of sturdy, flat-bottomed boats much favoured by the locals, but there were far fewer available than the large number his men required. It was reported that he lost a third of his force to those treacherous wetlands, yet still he came with more than a hundred and thirty fighting men under his command.

Beside Sir Hugh rode his four legitimate sons, his pride and joy and personal men-at-arms. They too were splendid in their armoury. Behind them rode his younger brothers, Guy and Stephen, equally grand and flanked by their five sons, and they in turn were supported by forty mounted men. They brought three score of foot soldiers, some in their leather jerkins and close-fitting skull caps, others in coats of mail and iron caps that glittered dully in the feeble sunlight. At least one half were armed with pikes and lances, while others carried bows or knives or clubs. Swarming at their backs were bands of ruffians and thieves rushing to join the affray, all armed with whatever stick or stone had come to hand, all eager for the action and the profit. It was a sight to strike cold fear into the hearts of men, for by the very nature of the beast, an army is a terrible thing to loose on any town.

With a company thus fashioned from his various manors, Sir Hugh de Burton rode into Beverley as captain of the troop, heading the force he was bound to furnish for his King and, on this chilly morning, for his lord Archbishop of York.

The screams of bewildered and weary people whipped into fresh panic brought Father Simeon and some others to the window of the Provost's Hall. They watched the knight's men clearing the streets by force, striking at random with club and lance and spear, riding their horses at a pace that caught the injured and exhausted unawares.

'Clear the streets! Clear the streets! Be off, you dogs! Clear the streets in the name of the Archbishop of York. Clear the streets! Clear the streets!'

Sir Hugh de Burton was an ambitious man, a clever angler for his Archbishop's friendship and his monarch's favour. He was here to keep the peace at Beverley, to protect the sacred shrine of St John, and to pluck some personal distinction from the debris. His Archbishop was in the capital with King Henry. Sir Hugh had dispatched an urgent message there, with a solemn undertaking to quell the riots rumoured to be taking place at Beverley. The man who carried the message had been carefully schooled in the weight and colour of his story and would be generously rewarded when Sir Hugh was credited with deeds well executed in the name of York. And should the messenger be proved a liar, Sir Hugh would walk away unscathed, regretting the over-zealous imagination of his servant.

The clatter of the horses' hooves rang out above the cries of those who found themselves at the mercy of the soldiers. The troops came on in two waves now, dividing at the Fishmarket to form two lesser armies, one to approach the Minster via Eastgate, the other, behind Hugh's pennant, flowing down Hyegate. This proud knight had taken up the growing vogue of carrying a fixed device for his identity. Not for Sir Hugh the fanciful, symbolic markings of yesteryear's knights and warriors. His personal motif was a pair of hawks guarding a castle, with bars and bells to symbolise the family of Burton. He wore it for his vanity and his growing reputation, so that all men, illiterate or learned, might know him at a glance as he rode by.

'This is preposterous,' bellowed the Provost's clerk. 'That knight has set his sights on ruling Beverley like a monarch. Riots, he speaks of, *riots!* Does he think we brought this ruin upon ourselves? How dare he come here leading an army and wielding a short-sword when the people are in need of bread and shelter?'

'He seeks advancement,' Father Cuthbert said, too long resigned to the ways of men to be astonished by the actions of one ambitious knight. He had once walked in the early morning over the public pasture land at Tonge, where the Archbishop claimed for himself all straying animals. And while the Archbishop's demands promised easy profit, few men were content to sit upon their hopes, waiting for mindless beasts to wander here or there, this way or that, in search of sweeter pasture. There had been a modest herd left in the care of a man who slept too long in a hollow in the ground and awoke to find the Archbishop's men driving his beasts away. At the sound of his alarm other men rushed to the scene and a noisy furore rapidly ensued. The animals rushed about in a frenzy of confusion and alarm, while yelling men drove them first in one direction, then in another, in the quest for possession. Between the Archbishop's men, the rightful owners, the peasants and the thieves, no beast would know his master until the dust settled. Father Cuthbert recognised the same principle practised now in the wake of the tempest. An Act of God had taken place here, setting the laws of ownership in disarray. In the scramble for profit, favour and advantage, the choicest meat would go to the stronger master. And if the poor were only cattle of a different colour, it might be argued that they cared not who should wield the master's whip.

'It is advancement Hugh de Burton seeks,' Cuthbert repeated.

'And he will have it, one way or another,' Simeon remarked.

'By quelling "riots" of his own imagining?' The clerk demanded.

'Even of his own *engineering*,' Simeon said coldly. 'If that would better serve his ends.'

These three were gathered at one end of the Provost's long and narrow meeting room, where several broken windows had been hung with cloths to keep the chill at bay. For light and warmth some torches still flickered on their metal sconces. Their flames deepened the many shadowed recesses where priests bent their heads in whispered conversation, prayed in hushed tones or merely sat in contemplative silence.

Priests who had looked like muddy beggars following the storm were now resplendent in their finest apparel, their bodies washed, their feet and sandals cleaned. There was to be a procession through the streets in which all clergy, the lesser and the higher orders, would take part. Solemn masses must be said for the dead, unction offered to the sick and injured, hope returned to the bereaved and the homeless. Beverley was in desperate need of the Good Lord's blessing, and so His servants of every rank would parade through the stricken streets, bestowing His benediction. Now that the town had suffered the divine wrath, every lost altar candle must be relit so that the survivors might receive the holy sacrament.

The great procession would also be a show of Church authority to convince the masses that God still ruled, that the Devil had not yet conquered Beverley. But first the troops must be given time to tire of their pilfering and bullying. It must not be thought that Church and Army stood on opposing sides like rivals bickering over the spoils of war. When the clash of steel and the crude profanities were gone, the voices of the choral priests would fill the streets, rising up like the morning sun itself, sure and inevitable. The people must be reassured that while mighty armies come and go, while seasons pass and tempests rage and die, the Church endures.

The Provost's Hall held scores of men all dressed in readiness for the procession. Father Simeon, his Canon and the Provost's clerk were at the narrow eastern end where an undamaged window caught the morning sun and shed it, pale and golden-toned, across the floor. The men seated or squatting around the walls were mostly silent, watching and listening from their shadowed places. Word had been passed around of Simeon's cure, and most were determined to walk close to him and the venerable Cuthbert in procession. Among them were Brother Michael and Brother Mark, who would lead the procession bearing the aspersoir and holy water.

'The troops are gathered at the drawbridge now,' Simeon said, still watching from the window. 'They are holding back, and rightly so, for York has no authority here. While our Provost lives his rights are sacrosanct and well the Archbishop knows it.' He peered hard across the distance and his brows puckered in a frown.

'What is it, Simeon? What else can you see?'

'I can see Father Wulfric standing with two young knights, Sir Hugh de Burton's sons, I think, and there is Father Cyrus in conversation with another.'

'Wulfric and Cyrus? Well, well. Perhaps the crow would

preach a sermon to the vulture?' Father Cuthbert's voice was lowered so that Simeon alone might hear his cutting words.

'Or else they conspire to divide the spoils in equal portions between them,' Simeon whispered in reply.

Just then two priests were brought into the room, each bearing the marks of heavy blows about their heads and faces. One collapsed in a corner and was given water by the Provost's clerk. The other, a sub-deacon newly established in his post, was at pains to explain their situation. They and several companion priests had been carrying food to ease the needs of the poor, and holy water to perform the blessings, and they had met with soldiers in the Minster Yard.

'They were stealing from the poor,' he said, distressed by the events he had witnessed. His name was Vincent and he was a man who despised all levels of injustice. 'When we tried to intervene we were attacked with clubs and sticks. They even spat on our heads when we prayed for their redemption. They stole the bread and meat and ate it while the hungry looked on. One man, a brute in a skull cap and stinking leathers, snatched up the holy water, *the blessed water*, and drained the pot to quench his heathen thirst.'

'May he repent that sacrilege,' Simeon muttered. 'Have they taken the Minster?'

Brother Vincent shook his head and wiped a bloodstain from his cheek with the sleeve of his surplice. 'I doubt they will dare go as far as that. Sir Hugh is keeping all but a few of his troops outside the doors, but while he struts like a lord at the High Altar, his men run wild around the town, behaving exactly as they please. What is to be done?'

'Done?' Father Cuthbert asked gently. He looked at the younger man with sadness in his eyes. 'My Brother, I fear that nothing is to be done. Where might becomes right, will priests dare stand against it?'

'But these soldiers are striking down men and violating helpless women in the streets,' Brother Vincent protested.

'I know, my son. They count such sport in their wages.'

'And there are many others, thieves and vagabonds, drunkards and evil-doers who follow in the army's wake,

97

picking over what the soldiers toss aside.'

Father Cuthbert smiled sadly. 'Alas, it is the way of the world, my son. The opportunist, too, must have his profit.'

The Provost's clerk stepped forward and dared to take the Canon by his sleeve. 'Father Cuthbert, surely we cannot stand by and do *nothing.*'

Father Cuthbert smiled his quiet smile and patted the priest's arm. 'Do not distress yourself unnecessarily, my Brother. Like the storm that brought it here, this misfortune too will run its course.'

'But the people might read our inaction as consent,' the clerk protested.

'Then so be it. We cannot take up swords against an army, especially when that army claims to act in the name of our own lord of Beverley, the Archbishop himself.'

The men were silent then and leaden-hearted.

Simeon leaned into the niche and stared from the window. 'They come like a plague of hungry locusts to a corn field,' he said, and there was rage, not sorrow, in his voice. 'They call themselves keepers of the Archbishop's peace, yet in truth they are nothing more than a band of thieves and scavengers picking over our dead.'

'When was it ever otherwise?' Father Cuthbert asked, grim-faced. 'Of the nine daughters of Satan, was it not Pillage he wedded to the knights?'

'Aye, and Sacrilege to the peasantry,' Simeon said, re-calling the news that St John's shrine had been violated and several of its precious stones removed. He had been watching a mounted man hand something down to Cyrus de Figham, and the dark priest fasten it firmly to his girdle. Now Simeon turned from the window to look into the gentle eyes of his canon. 'And to the clergy, Simony,' he added bitterly, 'the buying and selling of church offices, the traffic in sacred things. Cuthbert, my friend, sometimes the crux of human nature sickens me.'

Cuthbert nodded his grey head. 'As indeed it must. Man is a poor, base creature, but think what a soul he has, Simeon.' The old eyes lit with quiet wonder. 'Think what a soul he has that can embrace a God like ours.'

Simeon smiled. 'Cuthbert, your goodness looks for its echo in everything.'

'And yours does not, my son?'

Simeon held the wise old gaze for a moment, then sighed and turned his face once again to the sunny window. Father Cuthbert always seemed to see far more in him than Simeon saw in himself. He saw beyond the anger and the doubt, just as he had seen beyond the crippled foot all those many years ago. If Simeon had ever harboured true ambition, it was to become, in time, what that dear man believed him now to be.

Brother Vincent was standing to one side nursing his cuts and bruises and seething with indignation at the presence of the soldiers. For several minutes he had noted the easy movements of Father Simeon, the even placing of his feet, the balanced strides, the unimpeded stance. And now the truth came to him in a flash of understanding. He almost stumbled forward and his voice rang out much louder than he intended.

'Father Simeon, your foot ... *your foot!*'

'Father Simeon's foot has been healed by the grace of God and the Divine intervention of St John of Beverley.' The Provost's clerk signed the cross in acknowledgement of the miracle. 'It happened at the shrine when he brought the newly baptised child before the Saint.'

The priest's face blanched. He stared again at Simeon's foot and Simeon, feeling awkward, walked a few unfaltering strides to convince him that the once-cemented joints of his left foot had been unfastened.

'Your foot is healed?'

'Yes, Brother Vincent, completely healed, though still a little painful,' Simeon smiled.

'God be praised!' He signed the cross with trembling fingers. 'Oh, God be praised ... a miraculous healing.'

Brother Vincent's voice had risen to a girlish squeak. He stared at Simeon, searching his eyes as if to read some deeper mystery hidden there. Then he got down without a word and prostrated himself, touching each of Simeon's boots in turn, gripping his ankles, grasping and kissing the hem of his robe. His lips shaped the words of the prophet Isaiah: *'The eyes of the blind shall be opened. The ears of the deaf shall be unstopped.'*

Simeon was shocked. He looked to Father Cuthbert, whose soft blue eyes were misted with tears and filled with a kind of pity, but which of his priests he pitied Simeon could not tell.

The man at Simeon's feet now clutched the embroidered panel stitched to the hem of his under-robe. He kissed it several times without noticing that the delicate stitching tore away beneath his trembling fingers.

Simeon was at once touched and unsettled by the demonstration of devotion. 'Stand up, brother. I am not deserving. You must not prostrate yourself before me.'

'*Then shall the lame one leap up . . .*'

'Come, brother, please raise yourself.'

'*. . . and the tongues of the dumb shall sing . . .*'

'Vincent, this is unseemly.'

'*. . . and the ransomed of the Lord shall be redeemed.*'

'Enough!' Simeon's voice maintained its calm and soothing pitch but now there was a firmer edge to it. 'Have done with this. Come, let me assist you to your feet.' He stooped to help the other up and felt the border of his under-robe torn free by the grasping hands. He took hold of the trembling fingers, trying to still their shaking. 'It is to God you owe your tribute, Brother Vincent, not to me.'

Brother Vincent hung his head and drew up his hands to kiss Father Simeon's fingers. Hot tears fell from his eyes and his heart was swelled to bursting. If Simeon had been chosen, and surely none could doubt that it was so, then he, a mere sub-deacon, had been similarly marked. It must be so, for he felt the call distinctly. He had been shown a miracle and now he must bear witness to the fact.

He looked up through his tears to see the figure of Simeon framed in the little pointed window. Simeon was smiling and with the light behind him his dark blond tonsure took on a golden, halo-like sheen. He was vested as a priest for mass, in finely embellished amys and tunic of white linen, his stole crossed over in front and fastened with a decorated girdle. As he signed the cross and spoke the blessing, Brother Vincent gaped at him with eyes so round and startled that it seemed they must burst right out of their sockets. Then he cried out as if in terror, turned on his heels and fled.

Bewildered, Simeon watched him elbow his way across the room and vanish through a curtained door beyond the press of priests. He looked to Cuthbert and was surprised to find the old man kneeling in prayer. He looked to the clerk, who stared back at him as if he were a stranger.

'What is it, man? Why do you gape at me like that?'

'The sun ... the sun is behind you at the window,' the clerk stammered at last.

'Yes?'

'It ... it gives you a look of ...'

'Yes?' Simeon repeated.

'Your hair is golden. There is a growth of whisker on your chin and cheeks, and the morning sun is shining on it. Your vestments are gold on white with much embellishment. And your eyes ... your eyes are so ... so *blue*.'

'An illusion of the sunlight,' Simeon said sharply. He stepped to one side, out of the light, and glowered at the clerk. 'Look at me now. *Look at me now.*'

'I cannot ...'

Exasperated, Simeon turned and strode to the tiny altar in the corner where a candle burned. He bent his knees in a deep bow and signed the cross, then stood with his head lowered and his hands tightly clenched together. All around him priests were slipping to their knees to pray. They followed like mindless sheep, as if one man's error would infect them all.

Simeon stared at the altar light. He was afraid. He could not accept what was being thrust upon him. He had done nothing to earn the acclaim of his fellow priests. He had been healed, as others had before him, a miracle, yes, but commonplace, *commonplace*. The possibility that he had truly been touched by the hand of God struck cold fear into his soul. He did not welcome it, for the Almighty asked too much of ordinary men. He did not want to one day be required, like poor Jesus, to drink the bitter and deadly cup of God's patronage.

Outside in the corridor Brother Vincent paused to press the torn portion of Simeon's tunic to his cheek. It was a piece of decorated cloth as wide as his hand and almost as long as his forearm. Like all such vestments it had been stitched with crimson, blue and purple silk, with silver and silver-gilt, with copper and with gold. Light touched upon the delicate embroidery, giving it warmth and life. To Brother Vincent, a true believer, the glory of the miracle was in it. He carried it to one of the nearby rooms, found an altar cloth and placed the piece upon it. Then he folded the edges and the corners over, rolled the cloth from one end to the other and knotted the finished bundle into his girdle-cloth. A portion of God's divine power was now in his possession, and with it he would heal and cure and save in Simeon's name. And if ever he should doubt his part in it, he would recall that mended foot and the soul-shrinking sight of Father Simeon trapped in the window-niche and turned to shimmering gold by the hand of God.

'Brother Vincent, may I come with you?'

He turned to find Brother William hovering in the shadows. 'Were you there? Did you see?'

Brother William nodded earnestly. 'And there is more,' he said. 'There is much you do not know, about the child, the baptism, and when it all is added up together...'

'Do you believe?' Brother Vincent asked earnestly, grasping the other's arm with urgent fingers. 'Do you believe that you and I have seen a Saint in the making?'

'I do, Brother. Oh, indeed I do. I believe what I have seen with my own two eyes.'

'Then come with me, my Brother,' Vincent declared, 'for now we are duty-bound to speak of what we know.'

They left the building together, arm in arm, each clinging to the other for support.

Father Cuthbert was helped to his feet by a priest. He moved to the little altar where Simeon still stood, quite

102

motionless and with his shoulders stooped. He laid a trembling hand upon one burdened shoulder, wishing he knew which words to say and which were better left unsaid.

He had known this young man for a decade, had taught him his Latin grammar, given him the freedom of his own library, raised him from a novice to a scholar of distinction. They had spoken, so many times, all through the night and into morning, debating some point of ecclesiastical teaching, quoting the great philosophers, seeking together their personal truths. With Simeon he had probed afresh the writings of Plato, Aristotle, and Abelardus. They had re-examined the Evangelists, sifted the words of Popes, argued at length on matters of philosophy and theology. Here was the man he loved as a son, and now he must watch that son set down the burden of his physical disability and take up a burden of a far weightier kind. He knew this for a certainty, for he had seen and recognised the look in Brother Vincent's eyes: it was the impassioned look of the disciple.

CHAPTER ELEVEN

St Thomas's chapel outside the Keldgate Bar was built on lands belonging to the prebend of St Michael, the same that was held by St Thomas Becket when he was Provost of Beverley in 1154. The chapel was more frequented now that he was recognised as a martyr. It had gained a congregation more in keeping with the great man's reputation, though not one soul in Beverley could recall ever having seen that man in person. For the most part he had been an absent holder of the office. His ambitions were too closely linked with those of Henry, King of England, and his sights too firmly set on the bigger catch at Canterbury.

St Thomas's had been spared the savage temper of the storm, as had the nearby convent of St Anne. Between them they had lost only one man and two women, drowned when the town ditch broke its banks and carried a tide of mud into the cellars. A few roofs were gone, cellars flooded and trees uprooted, and many livestock had been lost; but thankful praise was given up that, all things considered, God had been merciful to them.

Elvira the ditcher's wife placed a lighted candle on the altar of St Anne, a candle dedicated to the babe that had died in her arms. On the altar of St Thomas she placed another, this one for the blue-eyed priest, for Simeon.

Under the watchful gazes of the merciful Sisters of St Anne, Elvira had been scrubbed and soaped, her body scoured for lice, her hair so closely and so fiercely combed that in places her scalp had bled. Then her long tresses had been braided and enclosed in a soft white net that held the flattering coils against her head and neck. The grime of many years had been scraped from beneath her fingernails, the yellowed tallow from her teeth, the hardened skin from the soles of her feet. Then the sisters had dressed her in the vestments of a nun, in an under-robe of white, a dove-grey over-robe, a long dark hood with a lining of white silk.

'From gutter to cloister in a single hour,' one of the merciful sisters commented with a bitter smile. 'No fee to pay, no vows to make, no prayers to learn or tedious duties to perform to the point of exhaustion.'

'Indeed,' her elderly companion agreed. 'Elvira the ditcher's wife has shrugged off the coarse wool of her old life and found the new life lined with softest silk.'

'She is to be envied,' another sister, young and plump, agreed.

'Unless her fee is to be paid in kind, poor thing,' the old one remarked.

'Poor thing indeed,' the second sister sighed, and there was a wishful, envious gleam in her eye.

The sentiments behind the women's words were wasted on Elvira. Thrust into their closed world of devotion, she was too overawed by the ritualistic splendours kept within the walls, and too astonished by the transformation in herself, to note such subtlety of attitude. In the little chapel window she had seen her own reflection and experienced the heady taste of long-lost vanity. No words of theirs could dampen her spirits after that.

Now it was daylight and Elvira had been put to rest on a blanket in a corner of the room where men were gathered around a fireplace hung with pots and ablaze with crackling logs. Their conversation ebbed and flowed, leaving little impression on her understanding. She knew that one of them was Robert de Clare, an important man of the church who was there to take over the provostry of Beverley, should the need arise. He was a Canon of York and had travelled hard from there on hearing of the night's events at Beverley. His journey had ended, much to his disappointment, at St Anne's hearth. Gaunt-faced and still in his out-door cloak and boots, he stared into the crackling flames and waited for the messenger to come with news of Geoffrey's death. He must take up the reins the instant his predecessor set them down, and before Sir Hugh de Burton could set his youngest son, his bastard, in his place. Robert had a better and firmer claim, but whichever man was beaten there and forced to beg the Archbishop's intervention might rightly call the matter lost to him. The Archbishop of York was loath to raise his voice against a man already firmly set in place, so any knight or priest with half a claim could have the office if he got there first.

Elvira stirred on her blanket, wishing the soldiers would leave the town so that the sisters from the convent could take her back to the infirmary. She held a folded napkin to her full and swollen breasts. Unless she were allowed to suckle the child, the milk in her breasts might sour and turn to mould and she would die of a terrible fever. She closed her eyes and felt a stab of sorrow for her poor dead babe. Its tiny face, so grey and still, was impossible to conjure in the dark behind her lids, and yet the image of the golden-haired priest came to her with a sinful clarity.

Lulled at last by the crackle of the fire in the grate and the low-toned drone of masculine conversation, she turned her face to the wall and slept without dreaming.

In the prebendary house in Moorgate which he rented from his absent Canon, Wulfric de Morthlund paced the floor of his sumptuously furnished chambers. He was dressed in white with an over-robe of blue, all edged with a border of brilliantly coloured embroidery. His stole crossed over his body to meet a girdle of enviable splendour, worked in copper and gold and with a pair of tasselled knobs hung down in front. His silk-lined amys was trimmed with sable and caught at the shoulder with a jewelled brooch. He had not shaved his face for several days, and the smooth, dark whiskers growing there gave promise of a splendid beard and moustaches. His Archbishop, of course, would not approve the growth, but Wulfric cared little for even an archbishop's whims and preferences. As yet the Pope had made no direct ruling on the matter of priestly whiskers, so Wulfric would grow his beard until it suited him to shave it off, and no Archbishop of York would tell him otherwise.

He smiled to himself as he paced the room with his generously cut robes billowing about him. It seemed to him that certain enemies were pre-ordained: their imperious majesties the King of England and the Pope in Rome, that discontented duo York and Canterbury, and those other obstinate rivals, the great Minsters of York and Beverley. He might argue, then, that he was merely conforming to the natural order of things by pushing one more thorn, however trivial, into the imperious side of York.

'Your thoughts amuse you, Wulfric?'

He turned his head and winked an eye at his priestly clerk, a young man with a noble nose and pretty eyes, whose long, aristocratic features had earned him the nick-name 'Hawk'. When Brother Daniel Hawk took holy office he was not yet fifteen years of age, a clever, sharp-witted lad whose visible commitment to the church could not be faulted. The Archbishop himself had named him for a saint, as was the custom, and supervised the shaving of his crown. Within three months the novice had found a generous master in Wulfric, and since that time no blade of any kind had touched his head, and no tongue had called him by his saintly name. Young Daniel was twenty now and coldly wise, for his master had found in him a willing pupil. And if he did not rise within the ranks of his church as swiftly as it seemed at first he might, it was because his ambitions had taken a different course.

'I was thinking of York,' Wulfric confessed. 'He would make Beverley his cringing servant, if he could.'

'Aye, but not while we have St John and the good King Henry in our favour.'

'And Beverley's wealth,' Wulfric added.

'And the Minster's power,' Daniel grinned. 'In us he has a tiger by the tail and well he knows it. Whichever way he pulls he will be bitten, and should he loose his grip ...' He spread his hands in an expressive gesture. 'We will never be subservient to York.'

'You will make a Canon yet, my friend.' Wulfric came close and touched the young man's face with the backs of his fingers. He licked his lips and smiled into the other's eyes. His voice had softened when he added: 'Aye, lad, we'll make a Canon of you yet.'

'If God so wills it,' Daniel replied.

Wulfric threw back his head and guffawed. 'And what has the Almighty to do with it?' he asked. 'Dear heart, you would be wise to leave the shifting of oceans and mountains to Him and trust the rest to me. You'll be a Canon because I will it, lad, *because I will it*. Now, did you send word to Simeon?'

'I did. He is with Father Cuthbert and the others in the Provost's Hall and will see us presently. Logs and faggots are being laid down to make a ramp across the quagmire so the procession may pass without distress. We should join them directly this temporary path meets with the door. I believe they are impatient to begin.

'The soldiers plunder and the church laments,' Wulfric smiled. 'Fond prayers for empty bellies. Words for meat. The body may perish but the soul will prosper.'

'A note of bitterness, my lord?'

Wulfric's laughter bellowed and his dark eyes twinkled. He slapped Daniel so heartily on the shoulder that the young man winced. 'Bitterness be damned. What you hear is cynicism, lad, good, honest cynicism. Now what of that handsome devil Cyrus de Figham? Where is he?'

'Still here, attending to his vestments. He has sent to St Andrew's for a brooch and sandals.'

'Why should he make such effort for himself when I have placed my entire wardrobe at his disposal?'

'I think he owns more pride than you are willing to allow,' Daniel replied. 'He must be seen to be his own man. He will not have your items recognised in the streets so that other men may say he is handsomely vested at Wulfric de Morthlund's personal expense.'

'Such vanity is wasteful,' Wulfric commented. 'I believe he is too proud for his own good. Tell me, how went his meeting with the Canons and the Provost's clerks?'

Daniel grinned. 'Wonderfully well, so I am told.'

'Aye, I'll wager he gave a fine enough performance.'

'His finest yet,' Daniel agreed. 'It seems he was brought before them in a filthy state, reeking of sweat and blood, red-eyed and shaking with exhaustion. When the clerk completed the reading of all the virtuous and heroic acts attributed to him, de Figham flung himself face down on the ground and wept that he had managed to save so few.'

Wulfric tapped his forefinger against the bridge of his nose and smiled wryly. 'An ingenious ploy. Indeed, ingenious.'

Daniel nodded. 'And then he begged that his colleagues refrain from speaking of him as a hero. Neither his integrity as a priest nor his sense of fair play would allow him to receive such verbal praise while so many others, equally deserving, remained unsung.'

Father Wulfric laughed out loud. 'Oh yes, de Figham is a clever man. And silver-tongued. How those pious old crows must have loved him, as he well knew they would, for such a show of humility. How many did you pay to speak for him?'

'A dozen men, with others standing by.'

'So many?'

Daniel spread his hands and shrugged. 'I considered it politic to use them all, leaving the genuine witnesses to speak out in their own good time.'

'Good man. And we must not allow this saintly hero to forget that he is in our debt for this.'

'And we in turn must not forget that he is actually *entitled* to a certain measure of acclaim,' Daniel said, a little too defensively. 'It is no mere fabrication that he toiled the whole night through with barely a moment's rest.'

'Aye, but only for his own advancement.'

'Do motives matter, when the end result is for the good?

Father Paul of Cottam is not the only man who owes his life to Cyrus de Figham, however base his motives might have been.'

Wulfric nodded solemnly, then fixed Daniel with a cynical stare.

'Why lad, I do believe you admire that slate-eyed priest.'

The young man's features coloured with a tell-tale flush. 'You said it yourself, he is a clever man, and are not the more gifted among us to be admired?'

'A slippery answer, boy.'

'An honest one, my lord.'

Wulfric looked deep into the young man's eyes. 'Temper your generosity with care, my Little Hawk,' he warned. 'Lest you forget who holds the strings of that pretty silk purse of yours. Now, let us have done with talk of Cyrus de Figham. What of the girl from Swinemoor and her great bear of a father?'

'In the anteroom,' Daniel replied, nodding towards the nearby wall to indicate their proximity. He watched the sly smile crease his master's face. 'Do you intend to have her?'

'Can you think of one good reason why I shouldn't?'

Daniel shook his head but his features tightened. 'I cannot.'

'Well, then?'

Daniel shrugged. 'I wish you joy of her.'

'What have we here?' Wulfric stepped close again, his expression questioning. 'Well, well, do I see jealousy in those pretty eyes?'

'No, Wulfric,' was the stiff reply. 'I simply wish you every joy of her.'

'Don't suffer jealousy, Daniel. It is a woman's trait.'

Daniel bowed, his features grimly set. 'If you will excuse me, sir, I will attend to Father Cyrus.'

Wulfric nodded and watched the young man go out. He did not admire this tendency of Daniel's to harbour resentment for his master's pleasures. A jealous man is a potential enemy, and Wulfric preferred his enemies at a distance. Today the boy was his creature out of love. Tomorrow it might be hatred, want or fear that kept him sweet, and any one of these would serve his interests. Jealousy, though, was capricious in its nature. It rendered a man a stranger to himself, never knowing in which direction to jump.

Wulfric resumed his pacing in the quiet room. He was wearing the full canon's vestments, for he rarely did anything with half a heart. In the Canon's absence his priest was expected to stand for him in certain church activities, but the work of a humble servant had never been to Wulfric's taste. He chose instead to play the role to its glittering hilt, as if the office were already his. He sat with the canons proper, cast his vote for or against their rulings, raised his voice with theirs and counted himself as equal to them all. Wulfric de Morthlund was a powerful man who always took exactly what he wanted. Some might deplore his arrogance or hate him for his position of superiority, but any complaints fell short of the Archbishop's ears since Geoffrey, the Canon's first recourse, could no longer tell his canons from his clerks. Nor was Wulfric one to wield his power discreetly. His main advantage lay in one simple fact: there was barely a man who mattered that he could not repay two-fold for any grievance played against him.

He was rubbing thoughtfully at his chin when Daniel returned with a messenger from the convent of St Anne's. The man who bowed respectfully at the door was robed in a shabby hooded cloak that hid the better clothes beneath and sheltered the many purses fastened to his belt. His feet were muddy and his head unshaven. He had the boldness of a soldier and the common sense to know how tightly to rein that boldness in. Unfastening his girdle purses, he placed a jewelled casket on the table and uncovered a handsome pair of ornamented brooches for Wulfric's inspection. A purse of fine leather, jangling with coins, and a pair of beautifully decorated sandals came next, followed by a dagger sheathed in a glittering case.

'From my master Sir Robert de Clare, lately arrived from York,' the messenger announced, bowing low.

'Well, well, I am overwhelmed by these tokens of your

master's friendship,' Wulfric replied, returning the bow with equal formality. 'I can only hope that my tireless efforts on his behalf will soon prove worthy of his generosity.'

'Sir Robert believes it shall be so,' the man said carefully.

Wulfric nodded. 'Then perhaps our prayers, and a little dexterity, will *make* it so.'

'Sir Robert wishes you to sup with him this evening after Compline.'

'Does he have the table for it, at the convent?'

The messenger grinned. 'An excellent table has been set for him, and an excellent cellar placed at his disposal.'

'And an excellent profit slipped into the bottomless pit of the Reverend Mother's pocket,' Wulfric said behind his hand. He weighed the bulging coin-purse in his palm, bowed to the messenger and said: 'After Compline, then. Sir Robert may expect me.'

Daniel closed the door at the visitor's back, then crossed to the table and unsheathed the little dagger. It was an ornamental knife to be hung from a priestly girdle, as was the custom, though its blade would not prove wanting in a crisis. Daniel held it to the light and clicked his tongue to register his approval. The handle was gold, engraved and set with rubies. The case was decorated with strips of gold and patterned with rows of tiny, milky opals. A covetous glint was in his eyes. Wulfric saw it and responded on the instant.

'Do you like it, Daniel?'

'Like it? It is *magnificent*.'

'Then you must consider it yours.'

'What? Mine? But my lord, you cannot mean that.' Daniel was genuinely taken aback by the gesture. 'It is too rich, too splendid a gift. You cannot really intend for me to have it.'

'The dagger is yours,' Wulfric smiled, much gratified by the expression of pleasure on the young man's face. A clever lord may rule by many means, but in the end the swiftest way to a man's devotion is through his hunger to possess fine things.

'You could be Provost when the old man dies,' Daniel said at last, his eyes still on the jewelled hilt of the dagger as he turned it in his fingers almost lovingly. 'You have the means to purchase the Archbishop's special favour. Why grab the seat for Robert when it could as easily be yours?'

'What, and bog myself down with extra church duties and responsibilities while seven ambitious canons plot against me?' Wulfric scowled and shook his head emphatically. 'I would not be in Geoffrey's place, not while the likes of Wulfric de Morthlund and Cyrus de Figham live and breathe.'

'You count yourself amongst the Provost's enemies?'

'Among his manipulators,' Wulfric corrected.

'As Provost you would have power.'

'Power I have, and wealth too,' Wulfric reminded him. 'And more than that, I still have the freedom to use both as it best suits my own interests. Why should I lock myself away with all those books and cobwebs when I already have free access to the old man and the minions who serve him?'

'Then the seat will go to Sir Robert?'

'Aye, better him, with his counterfeit piety and market-place religion, than Sir Hugh de Burton's muddle-headed bastard. And besides ...' Wulfric grinned and with both hands adjusted the folds of Daniel's crimson-lined hood. 'Sir Robert has paid me well over the years to safeguard his interests here in Beverley. His ambition has helped make me a wealthy man. Let him have the seat when dear old Geoffrey dies, and I will have his gratitude and yet another puppet dancing on my strings.'

'Oh?' Daniel raised a brow in a fine arch over one eye. 'Are you so sure that he will dance, once he is Provost here?'

'He'll either dance for me or kneel for the Pope in Rome,' Wulfric said with a glint of malice in his eyes. 'I have the proofs to hang him, if it suits me.'

'And I believe you would do it, too,' Daniel said uneasily.

'Aye lad, I would, for power perhaps, for spite or revenge, or for the simple sport of it.' He gripped Daniel's face in his big hand and squeezed until the cheeks were flattened and the lips pursed in a fleshy pout. Then he leaned forward and kissed the young man firmly on the mouth. At the end of it

113

he grinned and said again: 'Aye lad, I would gladly hang a man for sport.'

The door burst open and Cyrus de Figham swept in wearing a purple cloak and a hood of crimson lined with yellow silk. His eyes were as black and glittering as was the huge onyx stone set in a bed of gold on his left hand. He paced the room, marching to and fro with his brows pulled down, tense and agitated.

'This Simeon will be the ruin of all our plans,' he growled, choosing to ignore the passionate kiss and young Daniel's embarrassment. 'How in Hell's name am I supposed to compete with this miracle of his?'

Wulfric waved his fingers elegantly as if to dismiss the threat. Then he said firmly: 'Calm yourself, Cyrus. This upstart priest will soon enough be lowered back into the obscurity whence he came.'

'Oh yes? And will it be done before or after his fame is carried first to the Archbishop of York and then to the Pope in Rome?'

'It will be done this very day, my friend.'

Cyrus halted his pacing and scowled into the fat man's face. 'Today?'

'*Today,*' Wulfric confirmed. 'First we must make a convincing show of concern for this mysterious godchild of his, then we will weep aloud with our dear Simeon when the child is lost. I have it on the best authority that timely grief sits high amongst your repertoire of skills.'

Cyrus merely glanced at Daniel and nodded.

'And the miracle?' he demanded of Wulfric. 'I have seen it for myself. It cannot be denied. The cripple walks as straight as any man, damn him to hell.'

'Such cures are two-a-penny,' Wulfric quipped.

'Oh yes? And will you convince the peasant and the gullible clerks of that when they inflate the significance of this particular cure beyond all sane proportions? My God, the tales will fly and gather strength until the Church feels honour-bound to elevate that dull, unambitious scribbler to a position of strength and power. They'll place him over us

114

and before we know it we will have the Archbishop himself sniffing around in search of a would-be saint to pull the pilgrims in. He'll make a . . .'

'Cyrus! My dear Cyrus!' Wulfric cut in. 'How little faith you have in me.' He placed an arm around Cyrus's shoulders and pulled him close against him. 'What has been done may just as easily be undone, remember that.'

'Undone? A miracle *undone*?'

'Aye even a miracle. If need demands it, I will have him bound and gagged and I will personally crush the bones of that disputed foot with an axe-head, and let the rabble call *that* a miracle.'

Their faces now were very close together. He could smell the wine and honeyed fruits on Cyrus's breath and see the glistening layer of saliva on his lips. He smiled and his dark eyes twinkled with amusement. 'Wulfric de Morthlund,' he warned without drawing back, 'if you intend to kiss me as you did your priest just now . . .'

Wulfric guffawed. 'One day, perhaps,' he offered. 'One day I'll catch you off your guard and then . . .'

'. . . and then I will be obliged to kill you,' Cyrus said with a small, malicious smile.

For a moment the two were caught in confrontation, with neither quite sure how much of it was jest. Then Wulfric laughed and the two slapped each other heartily on the back.

Watching them from across the room, Daniel Hawk took careful note of the encounter. Six years in holy orders had taught him never to judge a man by his words alone, for the tongue is merely a fleshy organ with neither conscience nor integrity. It was the eyes that mattered: they spoke for the soul and never lied. When Wulfric said, 'I'll catch you unawares,' had there been threat or invitation lying in his eyes? When Cyrus spoke of murder had his eyes declared it no more than the moment's banter, or did their inky depths impart a deadly warning against intended trespass? Daniel wished he had the true measure of these two, for he was accountable to one while holding the other man in high esteem. He watched them laughing together and mistrusted their show of easy brotherhood. These two were ambitious to the very core, and true ambition bowed not to friendship's mannerly restrictions. When power is in the balance, even the jackals will fight amongst themselves.

CHAPTER TWELVE

The priests were assembling now for the great procession. In addition to the masses for the dead, there was to be a ritual blessing of holy places, beginning with the stricken Minster and the devastated parish church nearby. While their numbers were gathering they sang the psalms, their voices rising and falling in glorious harmony. Every window and door was open to the morning, every room and corridor filled with vested priests, the higher and the lesser orders standing shoulder to shoulder and sending their voices and their praises up. Across the town a hush began to fall as the sound of their singing drifted on the sharp, cold air. It was the morning of the fourteenth of December, Sunday, the Sabbath day.

The Minster bells were ringing still, as they had rung without cease throughout the storm. It has ever been believed that the sound of bells could turn away thunder and drive the lightning back. They had rung the chimes for the holy offices, for the passing, for the dead, for the tempest's coming and the tempest's end, and now they rang to the glory of God and to call the faithful in. And in their echoes could be heard the chimes of lesser bells as every church and chapel added its voice to theirs. And wherever a bell still rang the long procession of chanting priests would perform the

117

special ritual to bless and purify the altars.

Simeon took a deep breath and held it in his lungs before expelling it in a long, deep sigh. There was a smell of frankincense on the air. It mingled with the scent of powdered catmint and lavender and pounded calamus root, used to protect the precious church vestments from winter's damp and the grubs of hungry insects. With every swish of over-robe and tunic, the splendidly attired priests gave off a perfume fit for angels' nostrils. A man might suffocate in such a smell and never want for purer air. The tombs of saints were said to be filled with it. Just six years earlier, King Henry II went in a filthy hairshirt and a pilgrim's cloak to do penance at the tomb of the martyred Becket. He knelt there, scourged and bleeding, amongst a forest of miracle-candles in the crypt at Canterbury, and witnesses swore that the odour of Becket's goodness left him stupefied.

Sweet scent of angels, play upon my senses
And guide my hungry spirit to thy door.

Simeon closed his eyes and breathed more deeply. The rich and vibrant voices of the priests rang in his ears and sent waves of sound pulsating through his body. He could almost *feel* their singing. He was a part of it, a tiny portion taken up and carried skyward on the praises of the many. And yet his feet remained firmly on the ground while others, he had reason to suspect, were lifted to a higher and purer state. There were times when the distinction blurred between religious experience and the exaltation of the worldly senses. Simeon had never abandoned himself completely to that tidal wave of fervour so often induced when the senses are overwhelmed by pomp and ritual and scented air. There were times when he wondered if God would have it otherwise. Perhaps His plan was not to elevate simple men to the lofty realm of angels. Perhaps a man's best, however short of perfection it might fall, was all He ever asked of anyone.

'You are not singing with the others, my son?'

The voice of his Canon reached him through the chanting

of the plainsong. He turned, and for a moment his thoughts were clearly written in his eyes. Cuthbert smiled and gently nodded his grizzled head. He touched Simeon's large, strong hand with his own dry palm and envied the younger man his little seed of faith. That faith was small but constant and scrupulously honest. It was a faith for greater men to envy, for it sustained the young priest where one of gaudier colours and more eloquent expression might have failed. He dared to reach out to the Almighty in anger as well as in love, with misgivings as well as with defence. With his humble seed of faith this Simeon knew his God, and there were lofty popes and cardinals who had not come to that.

Cuthbert sighed and closed his eyes, letting the music bear his thoughts away. He knew that every man or woman fit to work had been given meat and bread and special dispensation to labour in God's name on His Sabbath day. Now they were almost at the door of the Hall. They had carried logs and fallen timbers, broken carts and wind-torn trees across the swollen moat to lay down a pathway for the priests to tread upon. The breaths of a hundred toiling Christians blew in white gusts upon the frosty air, and their freezing perspiration twinkled like crystal gems upon their skin. Some collapsed, exhausted by the heavy work, and were left to recover or not where they had fallen. Women worked beside their men. Some carried on alone because their men were lost. Several had infants fastened to their backs or babes bound to their bosoms, small bodies warmed by mother's sweat while she shivered in the freezing mud. The laying of the pathway grew more urgent as the morning progressed, for there were many souls in dire need of the holy sacrament.

He thought of the Provost, Geoffrey, lifted from his sickbed to be dressed in his finest vestments and carried to the tiny chapel off the hall. The poor man barely knew what coloured his life from one day to the next, but he was needed here and so he came, for appearances' sake, not of his own volition.

The singing ebbed away and then the priests began

another hymn of praise. Father Cuthbert bent his head to hear the whispered words of a clerk whose hands were torn and bloodied from his labours in the rubble. Then he turned to Simeon with a smile.

'The clerk has come from the infirmary at St Peter's. He tells me that young Peter has had his fill of milk and is sleeping peacefully.'

'God be praised,' Simeon smiled. 'How many are with him?'

'Enough,' Cuthbert assured him. 'He has enough protection for his needs. That boy of yours will be well-loved, you can be sure of that.'

Simeon nodded and watched as the old man added his thin, small voice to those of the singing priests. Simeon's thoughts were elsewhere, so that the words evaded him from time to time and he was left struggling, several notes behind. He was particularly saddened by reports that the people had resorted to driving sharpened wooden stakes through the hearts of their dead. Small bands of hooded men, brazenly calling themselves 'stakers,' were searching the town with spikes and hammers concealed beneath their cloaks. This was an ancient practice more commonly reserved for murderers and suicides, those who were buried in unconsecrated ground, usually where two or more roads or pathways converged. The stake was meant to hold the unholy soul in check, to prevent the spirit of the dead from wandering free and vengeful amongst the living. The people tortured their minds by imagining that those who died in violence and without absolution would grow weary of lying in mud or rubble and rise up to torment the living with madness and disease. In such a climate the stakers claimed their modest fees and crept from corpse to corpse, emptying pockets and driving wooden stakes into dead men's hearts.

Such heathen practices sickened Simeon. He had been asked to pray for Edric, the one-eyed carter, who was pinned by the legs and hips when his fully-laden cart was flipped on to its side by the wind. He lay trapped for several hours before the stakers came. They found him half-buried and unconscious and, taking him for dead, proceeded with their grisly work. His screams, they said, could be heard from Tonge to the Westwood, for the stakers were so alarmed that they fled without offering the unfortunate man the mercy of a second blow. In his agony he pulled out the stake and cursed to Hell the men who drove it home, until his heart, crushed by the broken fragments of his ribs, lurched to a halt.

On hearing this gruesome story, Simeon had at once sent news of it to St Peter's so that guards could be set to watch the bodies of the priests and servants who had lost their lives there.

'If the Almighty turns His back for a moment the people are as good as lost,' Father Cuthbert had observed. 'They revert to the Paganism ingrained within the very marrow of their bones. And who can blame them for that when we ourselves, God's priests and helpers, offer them so little?'

'They are hurt and frightened,' said a priest who was standing nearby. 'They are like drowning men in need of a lifeline. What does it matter what raft they cling to in their desperation, so long as they survive?'

Simeon and his canon had exchanged glances, and both were reminded that often the Devil seemed more diligent than God Himself in his endless quest for souls.

'It matters,' Simeon told the priest. 'Believe with all your heart, my friend, or you are lost. *It matters.*'

With only three psalms left to be sung before the procession started on its way, Simeon was called into one of the smaller chambers leading off the main hall. Inside the room the atmosphere was thick with the smell of incense and rain-sodden wool. Several people were waiting for him there. Cyrus de Figham had with him the young exorcist, John, who was his regular attendant in church matters. This man had been for a while a palmer at the grammar school, employed to beat the palms of pupils for each mistake they made in their exercises. It soon became apparent that he carried his work to extremes by beating boys in private and with undue severity. His Chancellor, an understanding man who hoped

121

to put the palmer out of temptation's way, gave him the duties and status of an exorcist. To Simeon's certain knowledge the change had failed to modify the man's unpleasant habits. At every opportunity he palmed young boys for real or imagined transgressions, and almost all such palmings culminated in an act of gross brutality.

Also in the room was Wulfric de Morthlund, wearing the full vestments of a canon. He was lounging on a high-backed couch with his companion-priest, the hawk-faced Daniel, hovering at his elbow. Wulfric was holding a little jewelled box in his lap while he picked between his strong white teeth with an ivory tooth-pick. Nero himself could not have appeared more fleshy and self-satisfied than he. His lazy glance went to the visitor's mended foot, then to his face in search of other changes.

'God's blessing be on you, Brother Simeon.'

'And with you always,' Simeon responded with deliberate courtesy.

He had no liking for the fat man, Wulfric. He thought him a boastful, arrogant individual who lacked the humility to temper his excesses with discretion.

If the rumours from Rome were to be believed, moves were afoot to encumber all secular priests with solemn oaths of allegiance and obedience to the Church. Where now a man might style his hair, his clothes and beard, his life-style and his character as he saw fit, in due course he would find these vanities restricted by the powerful yoke of Rome. Such sobering oaths, if they could be enforced, would help loose the hold corruption had on the church and those who claimed to serve it.

Throughout his reign, King Henry Plantagenet had been beset by malcontents and troublemakers who set their robes and shaven crowns between their misdeeds and their monarch's will. Too many thieves and murderers claimed benefit of clergy. Too many traitors to the crown of England took their protection from the crown of Rome. King Henry would have these felonious priests stripped of their church immunity and tried as laymen in the common courts. No priest faced loss of property, nor could he be hanged, burned or mutilated as a poor man might for a fraction of the crime. King Henry was keen to set the balance right, for he was aggravated at every turn by unscrupulous priests who thumbed their noses at his royal authority from the safe under-skirts of the Mother Church. Becket had stood against him, as he must, for such reforms as Henry sought were not in Becket's interests. And there were those who argued now that a sword, well placed, was worth far more than all the laws of kings and popes alike. The proud, unbending Becket was murdered at his own holy altar in Canterbury cathedral. Nobody won the day. No laws were altered. Monarch and Pope remained as rival princes, and so the corruption, safely protected, prospered.

'Will you take a little wine?' Wulfric offered, the way a spider might offer its hospitality to a fly.

'Thank you, no,' Simeon declined.

His thoughts were still with Becket and the King. Few friendships ever reached such heights or plummeted to such cruel depths as that between the King and his Archbishop. Rome had also stood firm against Henry's attempts to re-shape holy law. The chastisement of a priest must not be double-edged, with exclusion from holy orders leaving him exposed to further punishment by the crown. All popes would have their priests obedient to Rome, without denying them full benefit of clergy. Rome's interests were better served by priests and bishops who would keep the holy laws while maintaining a united stand against the King of England's interference. Thus all would be accountable to Rome who would not, through their own convictions, render themselves accountable to God. For thirty years and more the arguments had waxed and waned according to the flavour of the day. No honest man could deny that the Church was in need of such solemn and binding oaths as might produce a middle way and breed a worthier calibre of priest. Too many criminals shaved their crowns and shed their responsibilities for a surplice. And there were too many like Wulfric de Morthlund, living as pampered, self-indulgent lords, growing fat and wealthy with the Church's blessing. The King could see it plain enough. Only on pain of extreme loss and humiliation would such powerful men as these be persuaded to curtail their grand excesses.

Simeon was brought back to the present by the sound of a man clearing his throat in the manner of a gentleman. From across the room Cyrus de Figham inclined his head politely while holding Simeon's gaze with his own.

'God's blessing be on you, Brother Simeon,' he said, his lips curving slightly as if he were amused by the other's solemn expression.

'And with you always, Brother Cyrus,' Simeon responded.

The two men watched each other without warmth. This de Figham had the strangest eyes. They were dark grey in colour, much like the sea in winter with its murky depths and shifting undertows. And yet they might be blue or vapour-grey, and in poor light those same eyes turned to black. Now they were midnight-toned, and lit with coppery glints that might have been echoes of the colours in his gold and crimson hood. Those eyes were like the skin of a chameleon, designed to mimic and to deceive. Cyrus's face, strong-boned and handsome in its way, could show a whole range of expressions on demand, but not so his grey eyes. Simeon had watched those eyes for many years, and had never seen compassion or goodness in them.

'The night has been a long one,' Cyrus said.

'Too short for some,' Simeon replied, wondering how many dead were still uncounted.

Cyrus conceded the point with another small bow. He was guarded, mistrustful of Simeon's talent for assessing a man's true nature and intent with just a glance. Simeon in turn was wary of Cyrus's determination not to be so easily inter-preted.

There was one other man present in the room. He had travelled from Swinemoor with his only child, a little girl with tangles in her hair. He wore a good lambskin hood with the fur dressed on the outside, a leather cloak tied loosely on one shoulder, and a tunic of some heavy, sombre-coloured stuff.

His feet were bare and filthy to the knee, and the lower hems of his garments were stiffened and caked with mud. A giant of a man, he stood a full head taller than most others. He lived by petty crime and felt no shame in it, that much was clear to any with eyes to see. Both ears were missing, marking him as a thief, and yet he wore no skullcap and he cut his hair too short to hide the branding.

This was Ulred the tiler, passably skilled in his chosen craft and also a conniving and resourceful man. He knew which priest would pay the most for this or that perquisite, and who would offer the best price for a rumour or a secret overheard. The Church was wealthy and its priests were generous, especially when an inventive man could tempt them with whatever tidbit their appetites demanded. At present he owned a little patch of land the Archbishop coveted, and he was determined to turn it to a handsome profit before his betters conspired to relieve him of it.

The girl, his daughter, was tiny and very young, and had he not been certain of his facts, Simeon would have doubted that she was old enough to have borne and lost an infant of her own. She had the look of innocence still, that simple shyness so pleasing in the young. She was dressed without embellishment, her feet and ankles bare, her hair hanging loose about her face, her tunic ungirdled. In every respect she was so much a child that Simeon felt himself moved to pity on her account. Nature dictated that girls became women with their first loss of blood, but the master of the house, be he relative or employer, dictated when that woman should become a mother.

'Here is the girl I spoke to you about,' Wulfric said. 'She gave birth to a stillborn brat four days ago and the midwife who delivered her of it swears it was a healthy birth and that her milk is untainted. It is our wish that your godson has the very best of care.'

'Oh?' Simeon smiled. 'Does my godson's welfare concern you, Brother Wulfric?'

'It concerns us all,' Cyrus de Figham cut in. 'We are all brothers with a common purpose. We must assist each other as we may.'

'And the dowry you spoke of?'

'She comes with the patch of land close by St Mary's.' Wulfric smiled. 'The one that touches the Archbishop's land near the market cross. Ulred feels, and we are inclined to agree with him, that the land would better prosper in the Minster's holding.'

Simeon nodded. He knew that Ulred was under great pressure from York to part with his land, and that the Archbishop's men harassed him at every turn, making it impossible for him to have safe use of the property. The Archbishop had halved his price now that the owner was robbed of his living from it, but the crafty tiler still angled for a better deal. By offering his land and his daughter to the Minster he would make a handsome profit and a safe new living beyond the reach of the Archbishop's retaliation.

'The land will, of course, be sold initially to Brother Cyrus,' Wulfric added.

'Ah, of course,' Simeon nodded, unable to keep the irony from his voice.

'Why yes, it must be so,' Wulfric insisted. 'Our first consideration is our Provost. We cannot allow it to be said that Geoffrey craftily undercut the Archbishop just when he was about to acquire the land for York.'

Simeon smiled. 'In that case, the loss to York represents a personal gain for our brother Cyrus and no real profit for the Minster Church.'

Cyrus met the candid blue gaze with his own dark stare.

'Brother Simeon, I fear you have misread my intentions in the matter. The land will be gifted to Provost Geoffrey at a later date, when none can accuse him of having a personal interest in its acquisition.'

'A noble gesture, and a selfless one, to be sure,' Simeon said. He could not resist adding, to demonstrate his perception of the man: 'Provost Geoffrey might be persuaded to recommend you for a canon's office in lieu of such a gift.'

The dark eyes narrowed into slits and sudden hostility glinted there. Simeon met the coldness with a smile, and on the instant Cyrus, the sly chameleon, was also smiling.

'You read me correctly, Simeon,' he conceded. 'For myself an offering to the Church and for you a wet-nurse to suckle your godson. The matter is jointly profitable, I believe.'

Simeon looked at Wulfric and raised an eyebrow. 'And you, Brother Wulfric? How will you gain by this?'

With a smile Wulfric spread his hands, palms uppermost, and shook his head. By sign he denied his part in the transaction, but keener eyes had already seen the lie.

Simeon rubbed his chin and scowled a little, feeling himself drawn into the conspiracy. He turned his attention to the girl and struggled to disregard the personalities and politics involved in the transaction. His godson's interests must be placed ahead of any other's. Peter would not survive for long on watered cow's milk with some honey added. The child needed a mother's milk to help it live and thrive. He remembered Elvira, the ditcher's wife, grimy and clothed in rags and barely fit to nurse such a precious child.

'She's very young,' he said. 'Are you sure her milk is good?'

Without a moment's hesitation the tiler dipped his huge hand into his daughter's clothing and scooped out a breast that was full and over-large for one of such tender years. He rolled the flesh between his dirty fingers and the nipple leaked its thick, pale fluid over his calloused skin.

'The best a bairn ever sucked,' he grinned, then licked his fingers one by one to clean the milk away.

Wulfric de Morthlund sat forward in his seat and licked his fleshy lips. His gaze was fixed on the girl's glistening breast, still hanging from the scooped neck of her tunic. Her father grinned and made such a slow, deliberate job of covering his daughter's modesty that his movements seemed designed to titillate. In that brief scene Simeon saw the truth of it. He noted the father's blatant familiarity with the child's nakedness, de Morthlund's lustful stare, Daniel's resentment and de Figham's disdain. Even the exorcist was moved to strike his own palm repeatedly with the wooden crucifix hanging from his girdle. And in the girl there was a compliance born of resignation. Young though she was, the basic facts of life had not escaped her. She was as much a chattel as was her father's milking cow, to be sold or hired or used as he dictated.

Simeon glanced at de Morthlund and guessed what profit the fat man was hoping to secure for himself. Then he looked directly into the tiler's eyes and demanded:

'Who sired your daughter's child?'

The tiler flinched at so direct a question. His gaze flickered to de Morthlund and back again. He seemed about to challenge Simeon, then changed his mind and shrugged his massive shoulders. 'Who knows? She will not say.'

'I think you know it well enough.'

Ulred shrugged again. 'Some local lad, I reckon, or else a neighbour's son or a passing journeyman.' He spread his hands as if the mystery defeated him.

'A little closer to home, I think,' the priest said coldly.

'Eh? And just what do you mean by that?'

'You take my meaning well enough.'

'Eh? Me? Are you saying it was me?'

'Do you deny it?'

'I do. I do. It was not me what done it.' The man glanced about him, blustering.

Simeon persisted. 'And would you dare deny it at the holy altar, in the presence of God?'

The man clasped his hands together and looked to the heavens with an expression of righteous indignation on his face. He seemed about to weep in his own defence, and yet with every word his voice rang false.

'As He is my judge, I never done it,' he wailed. 'Not I, Father. Not on my own daughter, and her such a young 'un. That's the truth, I swear to it, the truth. Let Heaven strike me down right where I stand if ever I laid a hand on that poor motherless child. Why, if any man even dares to say that I . . .'

Simeon raised his hands to halt the flow of words. The tiler's garbled denials spoke out as eloquently as did the faked virtue lying across his features. What man protests his innocence half so loudly or so brazenly as the guilty?

It was Cyrus who moved forward to fill the silence.

'Well, Brother? Will you have her?' he asked, and there was a guileful glint in his slate-grey eyes.

'I will have her taken to St Anne's for examination,' Simeon replied carefully. 'And if she is judged more suitable than the other, she will be employed as wet-nurse for my godson.'

'We strive to please,' Cyrus told him with a smile.

'And she will be given the protection of St Peter.'

Cyrus glanced at Wulfric, saw him shrug. 'If you insist, Brother.'

'I do insist on it. I want no *local lad* given access to her while she is forbidden to men by virtue of her milk.' He looked at them all in turn. 'Will it be so?'

'So be it,' Cyrus smiled.

The hawk-faced Daniel leaned forward to lend his arm when Wulfric began to hoist himself from the couch. The big man stood with his feet apart, magnificent in his colourful robes and glittering jewellery.

'They tell me you have been restored to health by divine intervention, Simeon. Can this be true? Have you received the *blessed touch*?'

Simeon squared his shoulders. 'My health is as you see, Brother Wulfric.'

'No more the cripple.' The statement was made with a smile that failed to rob it of its scorn.

'No more the cripple,' Simeon said coldly.

'And this friend of yours, this tall man in the hooded robes who hides his face so carefully from others. Where is he now? What has he to say of these strange events?'

Simeon tensed. 'He was a stranger and now he is gone from here,' he said.

'But he must have a name, at least.'

'If so, he chose to keep it to himself.'

Now Cyrus cut in, impatient to have his say. 'Why you?' he demanded. 'Why do you suppose these things have been engineered according to *your* particular convenience? Do you seek advancement, Brother Simeon? Notoriety, perhaps? Or do you merely seek to conceal the fact that you have sired a

129

bastard on some common whore or grubby serving wench?'

The man was mocking him and Simeon, wise to the fact, would not be drawn.

'No words of yours can change one single fact,' he said quietly.

'Games,' Cyrus hissed, his eyes as cold as steel above his smile. 'I suspect you play games with us, my friend.'

'And I care nothing for your suspicions,' Simeon told him. He met the hard encounter of those near-black eyes and neither spoke again nor even blinked until Cyrus was forced to turn his gaze away. Then Simeon bowed stiffly, declared, 'God be with you,' and strode from the room.

Outside in the main hall a mass of bodies were crushed together in their finery, shuffling into position according to the hierarchy of the church. The room was stiflingly hot despite its open windows, and the sweet smell of herbs and incense had become suffocating.

Simeon pushed his way to the rear of the hall where Father Cuthbert, flanked by two loyal priests for his protection, was waiting for the procession to begin. Simeon caught his eye and smiled to reassure the old man that all was well, but in his heart he was uneasy. It did not please him to have such men as de Morthlund and de Figham and their dubious minions offering him their favour. Nor did it please him to see young children passed like cattle from one owner to another. If the girl proved suitable for nursing he would find a way to keep her from de Morthlund while she did her work. If not, he would have her permanently sheltered by the sisters at the convent.

'You step unharmed from the company of scorpions,' Father Cuthbert observed.

Simeon smiled at that. 'I dance more lightly now my foot is healed.'

'Be wary, Simeon. The scorpion's sting can be fatal.'

'I will take every care,' Simeon assured him. And so he would, for while de Morthlund and de Figham smiled and offered favours, his instincts were warning him to watch his back.

CHAPTER THIRTEEN

Sir Hugh de Burton received a message to say that Robert de Clare of York, who had been promised the provostry of Beverley, had installed himself at the convent of St Anne to await the outcome of Provost Geoffrey's latest lapse into ill-health. He immediately dispatched one of his own men to the convent to inform the lady Abbess that he and his sons would make use of the apartments adjacent to Sir Robert's. The convent had a spacious gatehouse where his men could lodge, and there was wealth enough in that holy place to provide a decent table and good barrels for a hundred men or more. He had no qualms about the imposition, for a wealthy man may take liberties and demand favours where he will. While none could yet know the outcome of the battle, the best of hospitality must be offered to both contenders. The modest convent of St Anne could ill afford to offend the future Provost of Beverley. And besides, the lady Constance who was Abbess there could put a Jew to shame when there was profit to be had. If anyone was to gain from this it would be her, for she was shrewd enough to offer a lavish welcome to her guests and still come out the richer in the bargain.

'Get all these pilfering curs together and bring them into line. We leave at once for St Anne's.'

Sir Hugh barked the order from the saddle, and a burning

contempt for the lower ranks of his army was in his voice.

His strategy in installing himself at the convent was a sound one, for by placing himself so close at hand he could observe his rival's every manoeuvre in the race for the Provost's seat. No word would reach St Anne's to which he was not also privy. No secret guard would carry this Robert of York to the Provost's house where he could bar the doors against all comers until his friend the Archbishop confirmed his seat. For Hugh the race was almost run. He had already bought his youngest son, his only bastard, Hubert, the office of sub-deacon of the church at York. Hubert was a charming, likable young man but highly volatile and not to be trusted far beyond the watchful eye of his father. He wanted authority and showy status, and he craved the submission of better men to his own will. The seat at Beverley would suit him well, but Sir Hugh would be the power behind the throne. He was familiar with the thrust and parry, the subtle give-and-take of politics. He knew how to play upon the ancient rift between the Minsters of York and Beverley, and how to profit handsomely in the process. He would be content to place himself firmly in the Archbishop's pocket, so long as the Archbishop was prepared to return the favour to the letter. Besides, he had already offered a thousand marks for the Provost's seat. Let Canon Robert match that sum if he could.

The soldiers clattered along Keldgate towards the Bar, the prancing horses trailing a rabble of foot-soldiers in their wake. To a man they were weighted down by loops of cloth knotted to their girdles or thrown across their shoulders, and in the folds such spoils as they had managed to plunder from the stricken town. Some carried sticks hung with rabbits or cuts of beef. Others carried bundles of chickens, strings of fish, even the bulky carcasses of swine and sheep. One had a sack containing several cats whose flesh would be roasted and eaten before the skins were prepared to make a lining for his hood. The fur of cats was soft and warm and passably attractive. For poor men who could not afford to wear sable, beaver or fox, the fur of the cat was adequate and considered far superior to the common lambskins.

132

In the prebendary house of St Andrew in Minster Moorgate, Cyrus de Figham adjusted his amys with the help of a small looking glass held by his exorcist. This house was set aside by the church for the sole use of the Canon of St Andrew's, and in his absence Wulfric de Morthlund, his priest, had taken up residence. The house was magnificent; heavily panelled and draped, richly furnished, equal in every way to Cyrus's own. And there he had the edge on Wulfric de Morthlund, for the house at Figham was his own by rightful inheritance, and neither absent canon nor church authority could relieve him of it.

Cyrus de Figham's was the hand that penned the secret message to Sir Hugh de Burton, warning him of his rival's presence at the convent. Now word had come that the knight and his soldiers were making haste for St Anne's, just as the cunning priest had anticipated. Cyrus was impatient for the procession of priests to begin so that it might be over in time for Nones and the midday meal. He was also anxious that it should not cross paths with that uncouth band of men calling themselves an army. He favoured Robert of York as Beverley's Provost, not the bastard son of a man who sought to bring church matters under his own jurisdiction. In due course he would cast his vote accordingly, but the seat was not yet vacant and the soldiers were a nuisance in the town. Better a skirmish between the two contenders at the convent, safely contained within those high stone walls, than a public confrontation between a force of lusty ruffians and a parade of priests. Until his mark was entered for the voting, Cyrus felt entitled to lend his assistance and his promises to whichever side might better accommodate his immediate requirements.

Cyrus's short-sword hung flat against his right hip, discreetly concealed when that side of his amys was lowered. He wore it on a leather strap that crossed his body from left shoulder to right hip underneath his priestly stole, and all who saw him took him to be unarmed. Thus he avoided the risk of hasty challenge and, being left-handed, took double advantage of the small illusion. Despite the changes this Plantagenet king sought to force upon the church, it was still a priest's prerogative to carry a baselard or dagger at his belt. Cyrus preferred the short-sword, and kept his dagger well hidden for extra protection.

Just then the leather curtain across the doorway was lifted by a servant and Wulfric de Morthlund strode into the room, closely followed by the handsome Daniel Hawk bearing his master's folded cloak in his arms.

'Are you ready, Brother Cyrus?' he asked with a flourish.

'I am as you see,' Cyrus replied, scowling.

The big man planted himself in the very centre of the room with his legs braced wide apart and his fists clenched on his hips. It was a pompous, regal stance, and he remained thus while his favourite set the great cloak about his massive shoulders. The cloth was dyed a rich, deep purple, lined with glossy, near-black sable, topped off with a luxurious red fox hood. Its lower edge was weighted with a broad panel of intricately worked embroidery, and from the crown of the hood a long gold tassel hung, marking the centre back from shoulder-blade to ankle.

'Well?' he asked, arching his brows.

'I suppose I am ready,' Cyrus conceded, 'though I must confess I find this whole matter of pomp and show quite tedious.'

Wulfric laughed out loud and set the dagger he always wore more comfortably against his rounded hip. His girdle was broad and barred with silver, a huge, bejewelled thing that shone as it bounced and quivered with his laughter.

'Tedious, yes, but necessary, my friend. When all is said and done the Church must be prepared to show its strength and re-establish its authority. Those peasants out there must know that all remains the way it was before the tempest struck. And we must show these bothersome monks just who is master here, before they have the whole populace in their pockets.'

'My bones ache with fatigue,' Cyrus confessed. 'Right now I would rather be snoring in my bed than parading through the streets of Beverley for beggars and thieves and fools to gape at.'

Wulfric strode to and fro to test the flow of his wide cloak, speaking as he moved. 'Believe me, my friend, your absence would be noted. Your fame is spreading, Cyrus. My clerks have repeated on your behalf such tales of heroism as would cause a warrior-king to weep with envy. Why, even as we speak your praises are being sung and lauded in the hearing of our Provost. By the time the Archbishop gets here there will be no more for him to do than confirm your office with the usual blessing.'

'Aye,' Cyrus said bitterly. 'Unless this Simeon's fame flies swifter than my own.'

'Trust me,' the fat man declared. 'Take the glower from that dark brow of yours and trust me. No word of Simeon will reach the Provost or the ears of York unless at my instruction, on that you may rest assured.'

'I wish I could be certain of that, but while his hooded accomplice remains at large and unidentified . . .'

'Even now my men are scouring the streets for him. He will be found. He is too distinctly tall to avoid detection, and when he is found he will be swiftly silenced.'

Even as he nodded his approval, Cyrus's scowl deepened and his eyes were cold. 'And what of the child, this mysterious infant the whole town is babbling about?'

Wulfric halted in his pacing and turned to Cyrus with his palms turned up and his face a mask of puzzlement.

'Child? And what child is it you speak of, my friend?' he asked, all innocence.

'Why, the newborn that . . .'

'Newborn?' Cyrus cut in. 'I have no knowledge of a newly born child connected with any of our priests. Brother Daniel? Brother John? Do either of you know anything of this?'

Both lesser priests replied with smiles and guiltless faces. 'No, my lord, we know nothing of any child.'

Cyrus's dark eyes glittered. 'Nothing?'

'Nothing, my lord.'

'And the miracle?'

'What miracle?' Wulfric asked, and the shrug of his shoulders spoke louder than his words. With a grin he stroked the backs of his fingers across the well-defined cheekbone of his favourite priest, his Little Hawk. 'Come lad, take up that fancy cloak of yours and let us be off to join our fellow peacocks.'

Brother Daniel grinned and did as he was bidden. His outer cloak was hardly less grand than was his master's, being of moss-green cloth and lined with beaver and quilted silk. This had been his master's gift to him, and one by one, in moments of generosity, de Morthlund had added the extra embellishments: the golden tassel, the decorative panels, the sable hood and the great jewelled brooch at his throat. The young man wore it proudly over his simpler vestments, careful to hook back the front edge so that his newly acquired jewelled dagger and his splendid girdle were not concealed from view.

In complete contrast to this display of quality, Brother John took up his plain cloth hood and pulled it grudgingly over his tonsured head. His eyes were hooded, but they glowed with envy. An eloquent glance from Wulfric alerted Cyrus to the fact that this envious young man was privy to his plans and could, by malice or default, undo them. He snapped his fingers into the air as if a thought had only now occurred to him.

'God damn my careless memory,' he exclaimed. 'Brother John, forgive me. I fully intended to offer you my second cloak, the one with the sable trim and beaver hood.'

'You did?' The young man coloured.

'Indeed I did, but due to my neglect it still lies in my black leather chest at Figham.'

'But Father Cyrus, you have been much preoccupied with other matters,' John offered.

'That is true, quite true, but still I beg your forgiveness for the lapse. The cloak is yours, the red one with the gold embroidery and the fox-fur hood. Accept it as a token of my gratitude.'

'My lord, you are most generous.'

'And you are a good man, John. Your loyalty is much appreciated.'

John bowed his head, his face bright with pleasure. 'Father Cyrus, you have placed me in your debt.'

'I sincerely hope so.' Cyrus smiled but his eyes were hard. He was irritated by the oversight. A poor man's loyalty came cheaply to a man of greater means, but it was just as easily withdrawn and sold elsewhere. He must never again overlook the settling of such obligations as they fell due. 'Quickly now. Send runners for the cloak and wear it in the procession so that none will doubt your advancement in my service. And take for yourself the embroidered sandals sent by the Archbishop's clerk a month ago. I believe you will find them suitable for your needs.'

'Father, I am overwhelmed.'

Cyrus nodded, his lips still curved into a smile. He was in no doubt that the young man was well satisfied, but for how long could he rely on such simple gratitude? A man with ambition must always look to the next rung of the ladder, and even while he pranced in his new attire, this little exorcist would be looking to place his feet on a higher step.

Cyrus had first met the exorcist in confession. It was the practice for ambitious men to advertise their talents so that the higher clergy might make use of them. Likewise a priest in need of some exclusive skill or vice would judge a man's confession as he might an item in the marketplace. To certain individuals the confessional served a mutual purpose above and beyond the give-and-take of penances and the absolving of sins. It allowed one man to buy another discreetly, or to sell himself without risk of exposure. Under the sacred seal of confession, mortal sins and ruinous vices might be bartered with impunity. All senior priests selected their minions following these soul-baring revelations, the devout as surely as his more worldly brother. Few priests would be so unwise as to take into their personal service a man about whom they had no private knowledge.

By this long-held tradition Cyrus might once have secured

the special services of Brother Daniel. They had an honest
liking for each other, and he had been the first to hear the
Little Hawk's confession. Even then, at barely fourteen years
of age, the lad had possessed a repertoire of talents as yet
unhampered by the bonds of conscience. Cyrus had been
sorely tempted to take him on until he saw the lad's eyes lock
with Wulfric's and the mutual recognition that passed
between them. He saw in that instant the one vice a man like
de Morthlund could put to better use than any other: the boy
was a sodomite – untried as yet perhaps but without doubt,
as Wulfric knew at once, a sodomite. A second confession
and the boy was his, and six years later de Morthlund still
claimed exclusive use of his handsome Little Hawk. No man
could honestly dispute that the Devil too made use of Holy
Sacrament. A clever priest assessed the faults confessed and
guessed the rest, and with competent handling mastered the
lesser man.

'Remember me at the altar,' Wulfric said.

Cyrus shook his head. 'Remember yourself, brother. I have
other matters more pressing than your dubious salvation.'

'Then stay conspicuous in the procession and count your
problems solved,' Wulfric smiled. He lowered his voice then,
as if their personal clerks could not be trusted with the
confidence. 'By the time we reach St Peter's it will be done.'

'Both parts of it?'

'Both parts,' Wulfric confirmed.

Cyrus made a sweeping bow without taking his eyes from
Wulfric's face.

'Then perhaps I will speak for you at the altar after all,
Brother Wulfric.'

'Damned hypocrite,' Wulfric spat, and went out laughing.

A group of tonsured clerks was sent ahead of the procession.
They wore their surplices over plain black cassocks and their
hoods were modestly lined in plain-coloured linen. At their
belts were hung the symbols of their office, the penner and
inkhorn, and they carried small handbells to ring the way
clear for their more exalted brothers. They kept the pathways

free of beggars and with their own weight tested the planks newly laid across the mud.

After the clerks came three young parish clerks, three *aqua bajalus* in their ritual albs, all carrying water pots and aspersoirs and sprinkling holy water. Behind them walked the cross-bearer in his cassock and surplice, a strong man by necessity, for the great cross, a thing of solid gold encrusted with the best of gems, was no trivial burden for a man to carry. Bright yellow sunshine touched upon it, lighting the tragic figure hanging there and giving the whole a fiery, molten appearance.

The holy cross was followed by a multitude of robed and tonsured students and scribes, copyists and illuminators, and after them the ostiaries bearing the precious keys of their various churches. Then came the solemn readers, the exorcists with their books of exorcisms, the acolytes with their pitchers and taper staffs. Then followed, walking one behind the other, the subdeacon of the Minster in his alb and maniple, the deacon in his brilliant stole and carrying the Book of Gospels, the treasurer, the cellarer, the precentor in his choir habit of white embroidered surplice and fur amys. With them walked the gaudily attired priest who represented the chancellor, one of the storm's many victims.

The canons numbered seven, though one in fact was dead, one missing after the storm and two more permanently absent from their duties in Beverley. Like Wulfric de Morthlund, the priests who stood for them were vested now in the best their lords could offer. Their robes were vivid and they all wore canon's caps and carried their fur amys hung over one arm. Then came the mass of priests in their sacerdotal vestments, and after them a bewildering array of followers, high clerks and priests and clergy of every level. Each man was accompanied by the clerks and lesser clerks, the servants, students and many followers of his office. Their numbers ran into the hundreds, creating a sight to take the breath away, for every priest from every church was gathered there.

Moving towards the rear of the procession, Simeon of Beverley held his own cloak over his arm as he stepped from the Provost's Hall into the frosty morning air. It was a clear, bright morning with the smell of winter on it. A mist still hung on the flat lands in the distance, and while the priests sang out their sacred words their voices were visible as frosted gusts puffing about their faces.

In one movement Simeon unfurled his cloak and swept it about his shoulders. It was warm and light and comfortably familiar. The outer cloth was the colour of deep red wine, and the whole was lined with squirrel-fur that glowed like burnished copper when it caught the light. It had a narrow border of dark red stitching with a fine thread of silver added, and a clasp of beaten copper at the throat. Though fine enough for many men his cloak was considered modest by canons' standards. And yet Brother Simeon would not have changed that precious hooded garment for all the sables and beavers in Christendom, for it had come to him as a gift from Father Cuthbert when he took his holy orders.

Stepping with extreme caution, the magnificent procession of priests and canons made slow progress from the Provost's Hall. The hastily erected ramps offered dry but uncertain footing over the muddy river that was the Hall Garth enclosure. In those places sheltered from the winter sunshine, a delicate layer of ice lay atop each shallow pool of mud and water. Where a foot fell, shattering the film of ice, a crystal pattern emerged to mark its passing. A stricken tree lay broken by the main stone well, its branches white with hoar-frost.

Simeon blew ghostly breaths and watched them fade to nothing on the air. He saw a spider's web set in the angle of a gate. The rain and dew had hung the threads with beads of moisture for the cold to whiten, and now the web was a mesh of hoar-frost beads with the spider set like an alabaster jewel at its centre. And all about him ruined buildings pointed accusing fingers at the sky, their jagged outlines sharp and crude against the soft blue background. He sighed and was strangely moved by what he saw. He had not expected to find such beauty in it.

The procession was halted for several minutes when it

reached the drawbridge. A man had been hanged there as the sun came up, his body hoisted over the lifting gear that drew the drawbridge up and lowered it down. His feet were only inches from the ground, but the drop had been enough to break his neck. One hand was an ugly stump in his tunic's sleeve, his ears were missing and his nose was clipped. Nobody knew what crime he had committed or who had hanged him there. Rough justice this, to hang a man while he still had a good hand and two whole feet to give as forfeit for his crimes.

Two men were paid to cut the body down and cart it to the rubbish tip beyond the nearest Bar. It did not reach its intended destination, for as the procession moved on the two men dumped their burden in the nearest ditch with a small coin in its pocket for the stakers.

'May God have mercy on your soul,' Simeon whispered sadly as he passed the discarded body.

'And if the dead man was a thief, a murderer, a suicide?' Father Cuthbert asked, always eager for debate. 'What then?'

'God is merciful,' Simeon replied, then qualified the statement by adding: 'So I believe.'

'Even to these, the ones we have rejected?'

Simeon shrugged and took the old priest's arm to guide him safely over a slippery portion of the pathway. 'Who are we to reject God's work and dare to curse men in His stead?'

'Thou shalt not kill, nor shalt thou steal,' Cuthbert quoted from the scriptures. 'The rules were laid down in antiquity.'

'Then let all men honour them who can,' Simeon answered dryly. He had seen enough of life to know that some are mercilessly tested while others are sheltered from the worst temptations. The theories were all so fine and noble, but the flesh was not. He shook his head and added softly: 'For good or ill, the hanged man has my blessing. God will decide if he should benefit from it.'

Old Cuthbert chuckled and offered no reply. His argument had been no more than words, since he had also muttered a simple blessing for the corpse.

The townspeople were hurrying forward now to gather in

141

jostling groups along the route. They streamed from streets that were blocked by debris, houses that were wrecked, piles of rubble that had been coaxed into makeshift shelters. They came in their hundreds and their thousands, travelling from all the nearby parishes, bringing the many scores of foreign pilgrims with them.

The great parade of priests soon reached the shattered parish church of St Martin, where figures still were huddled among the stones. No stop was made here, for the first mass was to be held in the Minster church itself. Already the candles and tapers had been gathered, the water blessed, the sacred oils prepared, the incense packed and lit within the censers. The holy office of Terce was barely over, and those few priests who kept the office in the choir were moved to sing the louder as the glittering procession at last approached.

As they passed St Martin's, Simeon could see that nothing had been done, as yet, to remove the rubble tossed down by the storm. The sturdy Norman font was still entombed beneath the fallen roof and arches. The windows all were out, the doors ripped from their hinges and thrown down with the fallen stones. He turned his head away and held his breath as he passed the open graves around the church. Scavenging dogs had done their worst here, lifting what bones the storm had not exposed. Today their bellies bulged with human meat, but tomorrow those dogs would be food for hungry men.

'Father Simeon! Father Simeon!'

He looked up then and saw the girl. She was running along through the muddy Minster Yard, weaving an erratic pathway between the mass of people gathered there. She was dressed in a nun's white habit and silk-lined hood, a striking, dark-eyed girl with glossy hair and a brightness in her face to match the quickness of her movements.

'Elvira?' He spoke the name aloud in disbelief, doubting that this could be the same low creature who had hoped to nurse his godson.

She met his gaze and her face lit with bright laughter.

'Elvira?' he said again.

She nodded, laughing, and the sun touched on her hair as on the bluey-blackness of a jackdaw's wing, lifting its colours up. She darted forward as he was carried on by the press of men around him, and for a moment his gaze would not remove itself from hers. He felt a movement deep within himself, as if she had reached out across that crowded place to touch his innards with a soft caress.

A moment later the girl was gone, pulled away by the two Sisters of Mercy who had pursued her to the rear of the procession. Simeon stared after her with a peculiar sense of loss or longing stirring itself inside him. Then he fixed his gaze on the great north doors of Beverley's Minster Church and forced himself to sing the words of the psalm the choral priests were chanting. His voice, like his footsteps, were moved by force of habit, for in his head his thoughts were in confusion. He must not think of Elvira – she was a married woman and he a priest. And yet he could not deny that she had moved him, had reminded him of his forsaken manhood.

CHAPTER FOURTEEN

A man shoved himself into the moving mass of priests and reached almost reverently for Simeon's sleeve. His eyes were fever-bright and his face streaked with blood. One arm hung limply at his side, one leg was tightly bound with a dirty cloth to close a gaping wound that split the thigh almost from hip to knee. He thrust the other priests aside to get to Simeon, and spoke after a brief but violent fit of coughing.

'Bless me, Father. Save me with your blessing.'

'You have my blessing.' Simeon reached out to steady the man and found himself held fast.

'I am dying, Father. Save me.'

'*In nomine Domini*,' Simeon said, freeing one hand to make the sign of the cross. 'Now go in peace.'

The man pressed his lips to Simeon's sleeve and sobbed his thanks. Then he was caught roughly from behind by two angry clerks.

'Be off with you!' the bigger man insisted. 'How dare you touch a man of the holy church?'

Despite his injuries they did not handle him with gentleness. They shoved him so hard that he fell to the rubble with a sob of pain, and when he spat to clear his throat the stuff had much blood in it. Simeon stepped forward to help him to his feet.

'Forgive them, brother,' he said. 'They feared for my safety.'

The man coughed into his sleeve, then turned to Simeon with a haunted look.

'Are you truly the one who was healed?' he asked, grasping at the priest's hands. 'Are you the cripple who was healed? Are you he?'

'I am he.'

'Healed? Healed by a miracle?'

'As you see, I am not as I once was, lamed at the ankle.'

'Then I am saved,' the man exclaimed. 'The surgeon swears this wound will be the death of me before the lung-rot does its vile work, but you have saved me, Father. You have saved me.'

'Not I . . . it is not I . . .'

'Come away, Father Simeon. This wretch is consumptive. Come away.'

The man held on to the priest's hands as he was drawn away. He mouthed his thanks, smiling despite his many wounds and the disease that wracked his chest in painful spasms. Simeon's heart went out to a man whose faith survived against such odds.

Simeon felt himself drawn back by his fellow priests until he was swallowed into the slowly moving throng. Once again he was walking beside his canon and mentor, and he took the old man's arm so that he would not stumble.

'So, it begins,' Cuthbert said.

'Not I,' Simeon repeated. 'This cure was not my doing.'

'Try telling that to them,' the old man said.

He saw that there were others then, men and women who reached to catch his eye or touch his garments with their fingers as he went by them. He heard his name passed from one to the other ahead of him, their many voices pleading: 'Heal me, touch me, cure me, bless me,' and once again Simeon was afraid.

At the doors of the Minster, Father Cuthbert drew Simeon's attention to a tight knot of people gathered amongst the graves near the church wall. Brother Vincent was standing in their midst, holding a piece of embroidered linen upon an altar cloth. He was blessing the sick and injured in Simeon's name and they, sharing his faith, clamoured to touch that fragment of the miracle.

'He must not do this,' Simeon protested.

'Can he refuse if the people ask it of him?'

'But he is mistaken . . . what he does is wrong.'

'Simeon, can you be sure of that?'

He frowned, discomforted. 'What he believed he saw was nothing but the trickery of light on glass and shadow.'

'A man sees what he *thinks* he sees,' Father Cuthbert reminded him. 'And who are we to tell him otherwise, when we ourselves can only see as our own faith, our hopes and our experiences teach us? Brother Vincent sees the truth, if it is truth to him.'

'But you saw for yourself . . .'

Father Cuthbert looked at him through the outer corners of his eyes, lifting his head sideways and up with difficulty. Their gazes met and locked, but it was conflict, not understanding, that passed between them.

'I did,' the old man said firmly. 'I saw it for myself.'

Simeon turned away and groaned aloud. He felt himself eased forward from behind as that part of the procession moved to the open Minster doors. Two small steps up brought him to the rows of slender columns supporting each side of the arched entry. The heavy oaken doors stood wide, the windows above them glittering in the sunlight.

For a moment the warmth and brightness of the sun was lost to them as they stepped inside, then from the low arch of the doors the stones swept upward to meet the sunlight streaming in from all the upper windows. Two rows of massive columns supported the lofty arches that were the centre cross-piece of the church. They made a high grotto of the greater transept, drawing the gaze from north to south in one breathtaking sweep. At the far extreme, above the round-headed arches of the south facade, the multi-coloured windows were intact. Shafts of bright sunlight slanted through them, making long beams from light to shade where particles of golden dust were dancing.

All the little stone seats built into the outer walls were occupied by those men and women bold enough to have staked a firm claim upon them. At the doors the common folk were being turned away to make more space for the slow-moving company of priests, but that did not prevent them creeping in through every crack and opening. They huddled together, the sound of their small, uncertain prayers overwhelmed by the grander harmonies of the priests. Some clerks were pushing through the crowds to clear a way, angrily trying to keep the crippled, the old, the blind and the infirm from falling beneath the greater press of people.

'The weak to the wall,' they shouted, pushing through. 'Let the weak go to the wall for their protection. You there! Give up your seats for those in need! Make way! Let the weak go to the wall!'

The task was a futile one, for the ancient seating provided for the feeble was not to be so readily surrendered by the hale and hearty. Unless a clerk be stronger than its present occupant, or willing to part with a coin sufficient for its hire, not a stone was yielded up. And wherever a clerk was successful in his purpose, the weaker man or woman was thrown back into the crowd the moment his back was turned.

The procession veered to the left and slowed its pace to squeeze between the pillars of the central arch. Here was the stricken choir, the high altar, the site of St John's tomb and, towering above and beyond them all, the pale and elegant skeleton of the great east window, stripped of its fine adornments. No colours here for the light to play upon, just one enormous, sculptured hole that seemed to hold fast the risen sun within its empty tracery. From that angle the precious tomb stood above the gold-shrouded altar, and the gleaming cross with its figure of the hanged Christ both fronted and embraced the two. The sight was one of lustrous gold and fire, enough to bedazzle even the Heathen's eye.

'Beautiful,' Simeon breathed. 'Beautiful.'

'To the glory of God,' Cuthbert nodded, signing the cross.

147

At the altar Provost Geoffrey stood trembling in his finest robes, supported by his closest servants and a guard of stronger priests who had carried him in a litter from his sick bed. The special mass for the dead and the blessing of the high altar must be attended by no lesser dignitary than he. It was expected of him. Only in times of ease was the ailing Geoffrey permitted to lie abed and nurse his failing health. In times of need he was compelled to show himself.

Watching him now, Simeon saw that he was unsteady on his feet and, when his face was lifted, seemed bewildered. Today the duties of his office were beyond his comprehension, so those who loved and respected him would help him through it, step by step. There were some who would hasten Geoffrey to an early grave, and their spies would be watching here from every corner. For this reason every critic's eye must see the Provost fully in control of all his faculties. It was a fair and justified deception, for there was much at stake.

The priests were singing the hymn of praise, the *Te Deum*, and in the brilliant sunlight Simeon stared around at the rapt, upturned faces and the eyes that could barely open in the glare. He saw row upon row of priests, all open-mouthed, soul-lifted with the song. Their vestments and their faces shone, illuminated by the sun, and for a moment he was lost with them in the devotions. Then something jarred in him and his vision cleared. Wulfric de Morthlund was watching him from the far side of the choir. He glanced to his left and picked out Cyrus de Figham from a sea of other faces, looking through narrowed eyes in his direction. He saw the clerks too, the hawk-faced Daniel and the ambitious John, both watching him. Seeing them all, his flesh crawled and he shivered. Their faces had seemed to leap at him from within the throng of priests, as if some voice or hand had marked them out for his attention.

'Simeon?' His grip had tightened on the old man's skinny arm. Cuthbert winced a little at the strength of it. 'What is it, Simeon? Are you ill?'

Straining his stiffened neck, he looked up to see that Simeon's face was deathly pale with beads of perspiration glistening on the surface of his skin. His eyes were wide and bright. The wound on his head had opened in one spot to allow a trickle of crimson blood to draw a line down his crown to the gold-blond circlet of his tonsure. The tension in his body was electric.

'Simeon? Are you ill?'

The voice of Father Cuthbert reached Simeon's ears with an oddly distorted quality. He licked his lips, they were parchment-dry, and tried to offer Cuthbert a reply, but no words came. He was staring now at the shrine beyond the altar, for in the glaring golden light he fancied he had glimpsed a dark-clad, hooded figure there. He shivered again and suddenly became aware that he was trapped, hemmed in on every side by priests whose voices were too loud, who stood too close and made him want to gag upon their cloying scents. He needed air.

'Simeon? What ails you, my son?' Father Cuthbert tried to prise the fingers off that gripped his forearm like steel bands biting into his elderly flesh. 'What ails you?'

'I must go out.'

'Not now. You are needed here.'

'I cannot breathe . . . I must have air . . .'

'But the roof is open to the elements and most of the windows are gone,' Cuthbert protested. 'The air in here is fresh and cool. Breathe deeply, Simeon. Recite the *Jesus Prayer*. It will calm you.'

'No . . . I must go out . .' Simeon cast about him for an avenue of escape and, finding none, looked desperate. 'I must go out. I am choking . . . I must . . . go out . . .'

With that he began to elbow a pathway through the crowds to reach the north transept doors. It seemed the whole of Beverley was standing in his path, for every man and woman who could find a space had crowded into the Minster behind the priests. He shoved and shouldered his way through them. His voice, like his manner, was harsh.

'Make way! Make way! I must get out of here! Make way!'

At last he found himself outside on the Minster steps, and there he slumped against the wall and gulped fresh air into his lungs in noisy gasps. He was perspiring, yet his skin was cool. His heart was pounding violently, yet his legs were weak. He threw back the heavy edges of his cloak and leaned his shoulders against the wall, not knowing what had driven him from the church.

'May the hand that healed our brother heal you also.'

Simeon turned his head at the sound of a familiar voice. Brother Vincent was still at his place by the Minster wall, blessing the many who were unable to find standing room inside the Minster. He looked at Simeon across the heads of those eager believers and his face was clear and open, as if he knew precisely what he did.

Simeon closed his eyes and shook his head. He did not want this. He had prayed long and hard, over the years, that he might be made whole like other men. His prayers were answered now but at what cost? What price might yet be asked of him for the simple privilege of walking straight?

'*Simeon!*'

He came alert on the instant. He knew the voice, the peculiar depth and resonance of it. It came at once from inside his head and out, and he could not tell if others heard it too. He searched for but could not find that familiar hooded shape. All he saw was the crowded Minster Yard and beyond it the ancient wall around St Peter's. All he saw was the little broken church drawn sharp against the skyline, and the storm-crushed buildings where his friends had died.

With a sudden gasp of understanding Simeon straightened up, his body tensed and his blue eyes widening. The name escaped his lips in a ragged whisper: '*Peter!*'

It was the child. Peter was the lure that had pulled him from the church, the cause of that sudden, suffocating sense of dread. He knew it now as surely as he knew he lived and breathed. It was the child.

With a loud cry he flung himself from the church steps and across the Minster Yard to Eastgate. His cloak billowed behind him and he ran now as he had never dreamed he would. He leaped effortlessly over obstacles, sprinted over mounds of rubble, weaving this way and that in a crooked course while keeping the iron gate of St Peter's enclosure in his sights. He reached the ditch and raced across the slippery bridge to find the gate locked fast from the inside. Barely pausing in his stride, he scaled it with an ease he would not have thought possible for any man, and dropped into a crouch on its inner side. From the great Minster at his back came the joyful harmonies of the choral priests, but from St Peter's infirmary came more forbidding sounds: the cries of men and women and the clash of steel on steel.

Simeon leaped to his feet and sprinted across the rear grounds where the mud and waste were thickest. He plunged into the tunnel-like gap between the store-house and the infirmary where he and Father Willard had taken shelter. Moments later he was out the other side and running along the front wall of the infirmary, stepping lightly between the shrouded bodies still lying there. He could hear the sounds of battle from within, the clash of swords, the screams, the shouts of triumph.

The only door leading into the infirmary was set at the lower end, beneath the eaves. Some horses were tethered there, cropping the bits of winter grass that poked up through the mud. He saw a soldier lolling against the roof support, his head thrown back and a skin of wine held to his lips. Much of the wine spilled down his leather jerkin as he drank, and he snorted like a hungry animal as he gulped the rest. He never knew what struck him from behind. A blow between his shoulder-blades sent him crashing into the wall. A second blow, this time to the back of his head, rendered him senseless.

Simeon grabbed the soldier's short-sword from its harness and, gripping it with both hands, ducked beneath the eaves and through the infirmary door. For a moment he was blinded by the gloom, then his vision cleared and he was able to take in the situation at a glance. The battle was already won, the poorly armed priests defeated. Several of them had been herded into a corner and were held there by a single soldier with his dagger and his short-sword bared. Two more armed men were venting their lust upon a naked woman and

151

a girl whose wrists and ankles had been bound. Two priests lay dead, two others had been wounded, and Brother Osric, who had obviously fought a manly struggle, was now pinned on his back on the ground with a sword-point at his throat.

Simeon's eyes went to the makeshift cradle. A soldier was sprawled across it with his face turned up. The blade of a tree-felling axe had made a channel down his head from crown to upper lip, dividing his face so that his brains were spilled. His bloody sword was still gripped in his hand. Nearby a young monk sat upright in a corner, hugging himself to keep his innards from falling through the dark hole in his belly.

The two standing soldiers, one holding the priests at bay, the other straddling brother Osric, were startled by the sudden appearance of an armed man in the doorway. They turned their weapons on him as he bellowed with rage and rushed to the attack. Simeon swung the short-sword and felt the blade slice cleanly through the first man's neck. The other was caught in the return swing as he lumbered into the fray. Coming on at speed, he encountered the blade held fast in Simeon's double-handed grip and was skewered on it like a piece of meat upon a spit.

Osric leaped to his feet and his voice rang out in warning.

'Look out behind you!'

Simeon responded instantly. He swung his body down and sideways, turning on his heels to swing the sword, and in that movement neatly deflected what would surely have been a lethal strike. Before the soldier could recover, Osric swung a blow to his throat that sent him reeling backwards. He came to rest with his back against the wall, the hilt of a priest's knife jutting from his throat, his eyes like glassy beads in his startled face.

The fight was clean and brief. Seeing his men cut down like scythed corn, the last soldier made a grab for his weapon, only to find it pinned to the ground by a sandalled foot. His braes unlaced, his legs unsteady, he drew his knife and turned on Simeon. The young priest's sword-arm was a match for any. Before the soldier had his dagger fully raised, the short-sword touched its point against his groin and slid

152

inside, slitting the skin like cheese before a wire. The loins that had spent their lust a moment ago now spent their life's-blood into the dirty rushes on the floor. The man toppled forward, silent and surprised, and breathed his last before his upper body touched the ground.

With another roar Simeon spun on his heels, sword raised, to meet a movement at his back. Two figures were framed in the open doorway, their faces white, their arms raised in alarm. One shrank almost to his knees and cried out:

'*Peace, Father Simeon, peace!*'

'We are friends,' the other hastily added. 'We are here to help, on Father Cuthbert's orders.'

A hand touched Simeon's arm. 'Put up your sword, my friend. Put up your sword.'

Simeon stood his ground but Osric's voice cut through the burning rage still heating his blood. He gripped his arm more tightly and repeated: 'Put up your sword. The fight is done.'

Still staring at the huddled shapes in the doorway, Simeon lowered the sword and let it clatter to the ground.

'They came for the boy,' Osric told him. 'It seems incredible, but they actually came here for the boy. And they meant to kill him, Simeon. They meant to *kill* him.'

Brought back to his senses by the words, Simeon strode to the stove and dropped to his knees beside the barrel that had been his godson's cradle. The cleaved face of the soldier stared up at him, a blank mask glistening pale and crimson in the firelight. He flung the body of the man aside and saw that the cot was empty. The child was gone. The bed where it had lain was filled with glistening blood, freshly spilled, but the child was gone.

'Where is he?' Simeon's voice was icy cold. 'Where is he?'

He looked all about him, his eyes bulging. Men shook their heads at him, their faces blank. He jumped to his feet and grabbed Brother Osric by the folds of his yellow hood. He stared into his face as if he saw a stranger.

'Where is my godson,' he snarled, his eyes as hard as flint. 'Where is the boy?'

Osric shook his head and glanced at the cot, bewildered.

'He was here ... I do not know...'

'You *must* know. You must have seen,' Simeon growled and held his friend as if he meant to throttle him. 'You were here when the soldiers came. Where is the boy?'

'Unhand me, Simeon. If I knew the truth, do you think I would keep it from you?'

'Osric, for pity's sake ...'

'*I tell you I do not know,*' Osric bellowed. 'They burst in on us while we were at prayer. There were soldiers everywhere, demanding that we give the child up to them. There was panic. People were screaming and running everywhere. I killed one with my axe when he drew his dagger on the child, but after that ...'

A priest stooped down behind the stove and then approached the others to show what he had found. The cover of fur in his hands was a coppery red in colour, soft and rich and heavily stained with blood. He stared at Simeon and declared in a whisper: 'Dear God, I think they have killed him.'

Simeon stared at the fur, reached out a hand and touched it, drew back his fingers and shook his head from side to side as if he would deny that he knew it. The flush on his face, raised by the heat of battle, now drained away, leaving a greyness behind. Dismay had rooted his feet to the spot where he stood. Nobody spoke, fearing that shock might turn to fury in him. At last he lifted up his head and uttered a cry that made the blood run cold in the veins of all who heard it.

'*No! In the name of God! No!*'

His anguished cry seemed to echo in the rafters. It was the roar of an injured animal, or of a man bereaved. The others shrank back, not daring to approach him. He looked like a fire-eyed warrior standing there amongst the soldiers he had slain, his cloak flung back, his bloodstained sword discarded at his feet.

Simeon lashed out with his foot to kick over the half-barrel of fur and chicken feathers where the child had slept. Then he clenched his fists and lifted them to heaven and roared again that anguished denial:

'*No!*'

CHAPTER FIFTEEN

As the last echo of his cry died away they heard another, smaller sound fall on its tail. It came from the rafters where the roof was open, from the deep shadows where the eaves sloped down. For a moment no man dared breathe. Simeon's face turned sideways, grimly handsome, the blue eyes narrowed and the nostrils flaring. Every nerve and sinew in his body was tensed as he willed the shadows to release the sound again. The song of the choral priests drifted on the morning air, the fire crackled, a woman sobbed, some groaned in pain and others bit back their suffering. But no man spoke and no man moved; they simply stood and listened.

The sound reached them again soon after, and this time there could be no doubt as to its source. It was the soft wailing of a new-born child.

'*Peter!*'

Now Osric and Simeon moved as if they knew each other's minds. One rushed to grab the overturned barrel while the other bent his weight against the heavy table where the infirmary priests sat down to eat. Willing hands cleared a path and helped Simeon shift the table to the centre of the room, beneath the square-shaped opening in the beams. Even as Osric slammed the barrel down upon it, Simeon was

156

springing up as lightly as a cat toward the roof. His big hands gripped the upper beams, and with no more than a small grunt of effort he had swung his body up and vanished into the darkness above their heads.

'Simeon, wait!'

Osric snatched a dagger from the girdle of a priest who stood nearby and, holding it by the blade, flung it upwards into the gloom above him. He nodded grimly when it did not fall back.

In the rafters Simeon caught the knife with ease. He looked down into a dozen upturned, anxious faces, then turned his gaze to the shadows all around him. There was no blackness here, only a murky greyness lit by the harsh glare of sunlight streaming through holes in the damaged roof. The shadows were impenetrable. He could make nothing of them, no rounded human shapes amongst the angular outlines of the great oak beams. He closed his eyes, made useless by the gloom, and strained to bring his ears to peak efficiency. One by one he identified and discarded the noises from below, the singing of the choral priests in the Minster, the crackle of the two infirmary fires. And having rejected them he strained to pick out other, more important sounds. As motionless as a statue he crouched there on the rafters, stretching his senses into every cleft and crevice of that angled place.

At last he heard a rustle of cloth, a soft intake of breath. Someone was there, in the farthest corner where the roof sloped down to meet the outer wall. Simeon turned his face, willing the sound to come to him again, and when it did his eyes snapped open and he had his quarry in his sights. Keeping his gaze fixed on those murky shadows, he moved across the beams with infinite care, for he had seen the damage here, the gaping holes, the splintered timbers and the shifted props. As he stood in the sunlight it occurred to him that he was vulnerable, a lighted target for a cross-bow or a lance. The thought came briefly and left no real impression on him, for as he approached the shadow shrank away. Whoever was lurking there had no intention of standing up to fight. His senses told him that the figure in the corner was sick with fear.

He reached the slopes and dropped into a crouch to ease his body through the narrowing space. Between him and the cowering shadow was a hole made by the falling roof and a loose beam left precariously balanced. Glancing down, he could see the room below, the stove, the door, the bodies still lying where they had fallen in that brief and bloody affray.

Now Simeon heard a whimper, a quiet sob, and he turned his attention back to that narrow corner in the eaves. Someone had pinned some leathers in the roof-space, hoping to keep the worst of the weather out. He reached out and pulled one down to allow the sun to stream in and light the gloom between the rafters. The figure shrank back, let out another sob and peered at him with terror in its eyes. He saw a mass of glossy hair, an oval face, a mouth that only recently had greeted him with smiles.

'Elvira!'

She sobbed again and clutched her hood to her body, and that was when he saw the tiny hand protruding from the folds of cloth lying across her breast. His eyes closed on a sickening wave of relief. The boy was safe. His prayers were answered and the boy was safe. Slowly, he held out his hands across the hole and whispered:

'You know me, Elvira. I am Father Simeon and I am here to help you. Hand me the boy.'

She stared at him, too terrified to move.

'You have no cause to fear me. Give me the boy.' His voice was low and reassuring. He shifted his position on the beams and stretched out further, until his fingertips were only inches from the child. Elvira's eyes were wide and she began to tremble. She glanced down at the hole and tried to move away from it, and as she did so a shower of splintered wood and dust fell down.

'Don't move!' he told her sharply, then lowered his voice and added, 'Sit still, Elvira. The boards here are unsafe. Will you pass the boy to me?'

She shook her head, clutching the baby to her breast. He

could see a wisp of sun-kissed fair hair and that tiny, grasping hand, and he ached inside.

'You have saved his life,' he told her. 'Now give him up, Elvira. Let me have him. Let me have the boy.'

Elvira watched his eyes. His voice was calming and his face was gentle, and in his cloak and priestly robes, caught in that dusty sunshine and framed by slanting timbers, he looked magnificent. How could she disobey a man like this, a man they said was touched by God Himself? Her fear gave way to humility and the tears in her eyes spilled over.

Her slightest movement caused loose dust and bits of stone to fall. She clutched at the child as if it would hold her back from the hole. Men were moving about in the room below, dragging the table back, throwing their cloaks and hoods upon it, reaching up their arms to help save her if she fell. She shook her head and felt the fear rise in her once again.

'Do not look down,' she heard the priest say. 'Look at me, Elvira. *Look at me.*'

She lifted her head. He smiled and she was grateful.

'Now, lean your body forward from the waist. Yes, yes. A little more.'

'I cannot.'

'Yes, you can, Elvira.'

'No . . . the hole . . .'

'Forget the hole, Elvira. Watch my eyes. Lean out a little more . . . Now pass the child.'

Again she shook her head, her eyes dark pools of fear.

'Do not look down, Elvira,' he said softly. 'Just pass the child. Steady now . . . slowly . . . pass the boy to me.'

Her gaze was locked with his as she began to extend her arms across the gap, easing the tiny shape towards him.

'That's good, Elvira. A little further . . . further . . .'

He felt the bundle brush against his hands, closed his fingers round it, and for a moment the child hung above the hole where many hands reached up into the gloom. Then he drew back and leaned against the rafters, pulling the infant close against his chest. Its tiny face was still, its eyes wide open and looking into his.

159

'Dear God in Heaven, I thought I had lost you, boy,' he whispered into the veiled blue eyes. 'I thought you lost ... I thought you lost ...'

For long moments he held the little body against his broad chest and tried to keep himself from breaking down and weeping. The strength of his own reactions, the crushing extremes of despair and relief, had all but overwhelmed him. For a time he could do no more than rock his body to and fro and hold the child and wait for the tidal wave of emotion to ebb away. Then he became aware that Elvira was speaking, her voice high-pitched and tinged with hysteria.

'... and so I came directly here to nurse him,' she was saying in a broken voice, '... to a quiet corner for privacy, and then the soldiers came ...'

'It's all right,' he told her. 'Those animals are gone. You are safe now.'

'... and they took the Sisters who brought me here,' she said, as if unable to halt the flow of words. 'They stripped them both and bound the younger one hand and foot and then ... and then ...' She stopped to weep into her hands, then lifted her face and continued. 'A man in a robe, a monk, lifted me up into the roof and tossed the child up after me ... just threw it up for me to catch or not ... there was no time for him to judge the distance. Then he tried to help the Sisters ... oh God, their screams were terrible. The soldiers killed him.'

Simeon rocked his godson against his chest, watching the woman, waiting for her distracted outburst to end. At last her voice tailed off into helpless silence. Her eyes were huge and dark in her ashen face. Tears spilled out and ran down her cheeks and she, it seemed, was unaware of them.

'You saved my godson's life,' he said at last.

She shook her head, scattering tears that caught the sunlight and briefly shone like gems.

'I will always be in your debt, Elvira.'

She stared at him, then, confused. A nameless monk had hoisted her to safety before he died. The child was saved because that monk had the presence of mind to throw it into the roof-space after her. She had done nothing but catch the mite before he fell back into the room below. Surely his survival owed nothing to any act of courage on her part? And yet she had held him to her bosom and crawled with him into the darkest corner of the roof-space. She had given him her nipple to suck upon lest his crying betray their presence to the soldiers. This much was true; she had watched her own babe die but kept another safe, and that must count for something.

'I will always be in your debt, Elvira.' She tested his words in the privacy of her mind, and they were somehow precious, like silver coins or gold.

Simeon made a hammock of the hood in which Elvira had wrapped the child. He signed the cross, kissed his fingers and pressed them to the small forehead, then he grasped the corners of the hood firmly in his hand and leaned into the hole to pass it down. He watched Osric take it gently to himself and carry it to the barrel by the fire. Then Simeon stood up as far as he was able, held out a hand and called Elvira to him.

'Stand up, Elvira,' he told her.

She obeyed him slowly, clutching at the rafters for support.

'Don't look down, Elvira. Watch my eyes and do not look down. Now jump . . . *jump!*'

To his surprise she did not hesitate but leaped lightly across the hole to the safer, firmer beams where he was standing. Her small foot placed itself between his own. Her body made contact with his but lightly, and she clutched at him with both hands. Holding on to an overhead beam to steady himself, Simeon grabbed her in his free arm and swung her back to safety.

'Safe now,' he said with a reassuring smile. 'Safe now, Elvira.'

He closed his cloak around her, felt her shiver as the warm fur touched her skin. She was small and light in his arms, a warm, unfamiliar softness pressing itself against him. The breath caught unexpectedly in his throat and he held it

161

there, hearing her heartbeat flutter against his chest and her little gasps of breath puff hot and dry against his skin. A thousand sensations invaded his flesh, and for a moment his senses reeled. It was as if her presence had touched him so deeply that his soul was shifted.

'Elvira . . .'

As she clung to him her gently rounded belly pressed against that part of him that rose now in sudden, forceful eagerness to meet her. She lifted her head, brushing his throat with her lips, and her fingers melted into his flesh as if no layers of skin or cloth were set between them.

'Elvira . . .' He held her from him, shocked by the intensity of the emotions she aroused in him. He had believed those fires to be dead, those needs suppressed. Her eyes looked into his and saw his need of her, and there was no hint of conquest in her knowing.

It was the voice of Brother Osric that broke the spell. It sliced between them like a sword, dividing them. They both drew back, unwilling and uncertain.

'Is the woman safe?' the voice called out.

Simeon licked his lips, for they were dry and tight, and spoke with his gaze still locked with hers.

'She is safe.'

'Then hand her down to us.' Osric said. 'The danger is over now.'

Elvira was the first to move. She turned away abruptly, gathered her skirts about her calves and crouched above the hole. Then she held out her hands to Simeon and when he took them, dropped into the space. For a moment she hung suspended with her arms above her head and her face lifted up, while he stood braced above her with her whole weight hanging from his hands. Then he lowered her down to where Osric and the others waited. Somebody threw a cloak about her shoulders. She glanced back briefly, and in the dark glow of her eyes her heart lay open, like his own.

Simeon stood in the rafters for several minutes after Elvira was gone from view. Slowly the burning need in him subsided to a smouldering warmth that he suspected would erupt again if the woman so much as looked at him. He did not think of sin or guilt, only of the strength, the sudden potency that had coursed through his body to fill him with a desperate, heady sense of being alive. Not a temptation, this, but a blessed healing. He was a man of flesh and blood like any other man, and he believed his vow of chastity would survive this harsh reminder of the fact. Should the day ever come when he set that vow aside, it would not be in the adulterous bed of a ditcher's wife.

Much later he climbed down to sit by the fire with Peter cradled in his arms. The bodies all were shifted now and fresh rushes had been scattered on the floor. A pan of costmary leaves was stewing in a pot, yielding its perfume up to cleanse the air. He was aware that Elvira watched him from a stool in the corner, and that several others eyed him with concern, for he was silent and withdrawn.

The diminishing voices of the choral priests told him that the procession was moving north into the town, perhaps to the little Saxon chapel of St Mary, to bless the altar there. He knew he should join them but he was unwilling to do so, even for Cuthbert's sake. And suppose his Canon asked how he had known, with such chilling certainty, that Peter needed him? How would he answer that?

He looked down at the child and felt the smile in his heart spread up to his face and lips. He had suspected from the start that the weight of his lameness had only been lifted so that another burden might be given in its stead. Now he understood the truth of it. He loved this child, and love was a burden that could break a man. When he had seen that bloodstained cover of fur, when he had thought the little one lost forever, his grief had struck him like a mortal blow. Love is rarely, if ever, given freely. It comes with its own particular pains and torments, its nagging dread that the object of that love might be snatched away. And in return for all that it makes a man feel whole, as God intended.

'I fear you do not come cheaply into my life,' he whispered now, watching the child and feeling his heart expand to accommodate the new thing growing in it. 'But if there is a price to pay then I will and never, ever grudge the cost.'

He could not know then what the true price would be, what it would cost him to love this innocent. Nor could he have refused him if he had.

When Osric and Simeon left the infirmary together later in the day, the singing of the priests had become a distant sound, lifting and sinking the way a graceful bird floats on the warmer zephyrs of a summer's day. The Minster bells were ringing still, their deep, full-throated chimes echoed by the lesser bells of other churches.

'Is there no doubt?' Simeon asked at last.

'No doubt at all,' Osric told him grimly. 'They came for the boy. They meant to kill him, Simeon, and had they found you there at the infirmary...'

'They found me soon enough,' Simeon growled.

'But had they found you sooner...'

'... then they would have died more speedily, that is all.'

Osric halted in his stride, caught Simeon's arm and forced him to meet his gaze.

'This was no isolated skirmish, Simeon. They made their intentions clear enough, and were it not for the twin distractions of the women and the wine, they might well have succeeded in their vile objective. There is a clear warning here, my friend. Do not make light of it.'

'Light?' Simeon echoed. '*Light?* My God, four men have died at my hands, the infirmary has become a slaughter-house, and you believe I take the matter lightly?'

'I merely ask you to accept the warning in its fullest sense. If those men were hired for coin then others may just as easily be sent here in their place. You too were their target, Simeon. You too are in danger.'

'You can not be sure of that.'

'I know it. They boasted of their plans for you.'

'So, they would kill a priest as well as butcher an innocent child?'

Osric shook his head. His face was thin and lined and his eyes were keen. He had been a soldier once, campaigning for

164

the King, before he was injured by a falling horse and forced to settle for an easier life in holy orders. He was a good man and loyal, and quickly grasped the measure of an enemy.

'They came to lame you, Simeon.'

The blue eyes were over-shadowed by a frown and Father Simeon turned his head at an angle, as if to listen more closely to the words. 'To do what?'

'They were specific,' Osric replied, tight-lipped. 'They meant to place your foot, your *left* foot, in a vice and throw their weight against it until every bone was shattered. They came to lame you, not to take your life.'

Simeon stared long and hard into Osric's face.

'I have enemies then,' he said at last, as if it were the last thing he could imagine of himself.

'Of course you have enemies. It is only to be expected when men are simply men, not saints. You have two miracles in your charge, two mysteries: the child and the healed affliction. Someone out there resents your altered state and intends to rob you of both, to put you back the way you were before the storm came.'

'Someone?'

Osric curved his lips into a bitter smile. 'Think on it long and hard, my friend. However blind we pretend to be, our enemies are always know to us. They are the ones who hunger while we eat, who seek improvement while we are advanced, who are overlooked while we are singled out for favour.'

'But what do I have that others should covet to the point of murder? A child? I doubt they would envy me for that. Two healthy legs? Most men have those already.'

'Perhaps it is your new-found fame they envy?'

Simeon laughed at that. 'Then they may have it from me with my blessing,' he declared, 'If any believe I thrive on men's applause then either they are mad or they do not know me.'

'And how those ambitious men must despise you for that,' Osric countered acidly. 'Look at this matter from their view-point, Simeon. Would they not make better capital of it in your place, and doesn't that fact alone make them more deserving of the gift?'

Simeon scowled at that. 'I am as I am. I will not be persuaded to make capital of these events.'

'Then you will gather enemies at every turn.'

Simeon looked down at his feet. 'To lame me, you say?'

'Aye, Simeon, they came to cripple you afresh.'

'Would they dare destroy what God Himself has healed?'

'They dare,' Osric said fiercely.

'And would they murder the infant out of envy?'

'Simeon, you know men's natures as well as I. You know they would.'

They strode on together, each grim-faced with his thoughts, and soon reached a low stone building set against an earth-mound near the orchard. The rubble left by the storm had been cleared away to reveal that the structural damage to the building was less than they had feared. They put their shoulders to the door and after a struggle forced their way inside.

This was the room where Simeon had been working when the storm blew up, standing at a wooden lectern with candles set in its top to light the pages he was working on. The room was large enough to accommodate several scribes and copyists whose benches and candle-brackets were set around the walls. An illuminator's desk was in one corner where two high windows met. There were some tables and a centre stove, low couches against the side wall and a ground-latrine set in a deep angle at the rear. Also in the room was an ancient well-shaft covered by an iron grid clamped shut with rusty locks. The sound of water rushing along subterranean waterways sent echoes up into the room, for the well was dry and it drew those lost sounds to itself.

A wooden ladder stood against a low roofing beam, giving access to the limited space above. Up there was Simeon's mattress and his books, his washing bowl and the pegs that held his clothes.

High winds invading the roof-space had tossed the contents of the room about, but this sturdy place had suffered

166

little damage in the storm. In the empty fireplace were scattered some items from Simeon's little writing box: a lump of pumice for cleaning the parchment, a goat's tooth used to polish it, a ruler, a rubber and an inkwell. The scattered manuscripts were gathered up and found to be undamaged, and most of the rushes on the floor were dry.

This small scriptorium was a safe place where the precious manuscripts left for copying were well protected. On either side of the arched main door were two huge brackets of metal driven deep into the masonry. A stout wooden beam dropped across it and held by the brackets would keep an army out. The windows were small and shuttered from the inside. There was no other means of entry.

Elvira waited quietly by the lectern. Simeon approached her without meeting her watchful gaze, then reached out to brush Peter's cheek with his forefinger.

'Take care of him,' he said.

'Yes, Father.'

He frowned and dared to look into her eyes. They were dark and luminous, and something in them touched his senses.

'My name is Simeon,' he said very softly. 'You know that.'

'Yes, Father Simeon.'

She turned from him abruptly and moved across the room, rocking the child in her arms and singing softly. He watched her go, noting the narrowness of her shoulders and the way her long hair parted in the nape of her neck when she bent her head. Then he gripped Osric's hand in his own, nodded his trust in him and walked away.

CHAPTER SIXTEEN

The body of Father Bernard, elderly canon and holder of the prebend of St Martin, was found shortly before noon. A young man employed to help with the clearing of rubble from the choir had gone there to relieve himself. He came away sickened and shaken to the core, for he had known the old canon and loved him, as most who knew him did.

Young Richard came from nearby Weel and after six months still knew himself to be a stranger in Beverley. He was a novice attached to the church of St Nicholas beside the beck. He had come to St John's on an errand for his vicar, and after the storm, cut off by flood-water and other obstacles, had stayed to render assistance where he could.

Richard was wearing a short brown hood over the simple everyday habit of a clerk. His crown was shaved but his face was not, and the coarse brown beard that grew there was a secret source of pride to him. He had toiled for many hours in the Minster, content to spill his sweat and split his hands alongside priests and monks, pilgrims and townsmen for the church's sake. And he was not alone in his sentiments. He had watched a man drag stones away with bleeding hands, then lie on his belly over a hole to keep a priest's face clear of dust until the others could dig his body out. And when the priest, a stranger to him, was found to be crushed to death, his rescuer had wept as if a friend was lost. Richard had witnessed the scene with his own eyes. It proved to him that men really could be brothers beneath their chosen vestments. The dead man had been a priest of the Church of Rome; his would-be rescuer was a local and a Jew.

It was nearing noon when Richard's need to relieve his bladder became urgent. Some stragglers from the priests' procession were already returning from the great parade: the older men who tired more quickly than their younger companions, and the Provost's party, bearing poor Geoffrey home. The others would soon be following on their heels, for the time of Nones was near and the smell of roasting meat would lure them back in search of their midday meal.

Reluctant to go outside the church where beggars and looters still picked amongst the stones, Richard found the little pointed door under an arch in the side-chapel adjoining the shorter south-east transept. He ducked his head as he opened the door just far enough to allow him access to the stairwell. The darkness closed in behind him. Here was a space only one man's height in depth and barely twice that in width. It narrowed to a chimney's-width above his head, drawing the old stone staircase up like a twist of smoke. Looking up, he saw a narrow window cut like a slash into the ancient wall. It let the sunlight in, a golden shaft of light that might have burned its passage through the stones to startle the darkness from the upper stairs.

He spent his urine in a noisy flow, the steam coming to touch his nostrils with his own particular manly scent. As his eyes became accustomed to the gloom he saw that a nearby step had one of its tread-stones missing. It was the thick tread near the newel stone, and its absence left a clean, pale wound behind.

His gaze turned downward now, and in the darkness all around his feet he saw the figure of a man.

'*Holy Mother of God!*'

He started in alarm and the words were out before he could check himself. He fumbled for the door and flung it

169

back to let the light pour in. A priest was lying face-down in the dirt, an elderly man whose profile was familiar. His clothes were blue and red and heavily embroidered, and beneath them was a stained white surplice. His fallen hood was a brilliant green, with the little trims and markings of a canon. On the shaved crown of his head was a terrible wound. Blood had seeped from it and congealed into a thick, dark pool around his head. Beneath his body his hands were clasped in an attitude of prayer, as if some force had struck him down even while he communed with the Almighty. From the lower part of his surplice and his sandalled feet the steam of Richard's urine still rose up. The young man dropped to his knees beside the body.

'Dear, gentle man, forgive me,' he pleaded in a whisper. 'Forgive this desecration.'

He pulled off his hood and with it wiped his urine from the dead man's robes and feet, muttering all the while: 'Forgive me Father Bernard. Forgive me.'

The bells were ringing for Nones when Simeon left his place at the little altar of St Peter's. He had taken part in the solemn mass and had left an altar candle burning there for every man who had perished in its shadow. Outside he placed a single lighted candle near the bridge, for Father Willard. Someone had thrown a row of logs across the ditch, all lashed together and held in place by rocks. It was a temporary bridge but adequate. Simeon squatted there and watched the water rushing underground.

'God rest you, Willard,' he whispered into it.

In the scriptorium near the orchard Elvira and the boy were safe from harm. A group of Sisters and two old monks had come from St Anne's to help prepare food and nurse the sick and send the dead from this world to the next unburdened by their sins. The woman and the boy would not be left alone and vulnerable. The priests were armed now, ready to fight off any man who came to St Peter's with less than good intentions.

Simeon's church was one of the last to be attended by the

priests and canons. The procession had taken a figure-of-eight course through the town so that St Peter's, although lying within a stone's throw of the Minster itself, was left unvisited until the homeward twist of the journey. Now what remained of the parade was singing the mass at the small church of St Nicholas, dedicated to the sailor's patron saint and standing near the port at the head of Beverley Beck. There was still no news of Thorald, who had been the parish priest of St Nicholas now for twenty years. One rumour said that he was killed when the roof of his church collapsed before the wind, another that he was drowned when the nave was flooded. A man who came by boat to Eastgate swore he had seen the holy Father standing waist-deep in mud, blessing the injured at the crippled port. These inconsistencies were grounds for hope that Thorald had survived the tempest.

A priest and a bearded clerk were waiting for Simeon at the main gate. The priest signed the cross and smiled. 'God's blessing be on you, Father Simeon.'

'And may His love sustain you.' Simeon responded.

'I am Thomas, from St Catherine's. And here is my good clerk, Robert.'

The clerk inclined his tonsured head, his hands clasped tightly over his rosary.

Flanked by the two, Simeon made his way to one of the college buildings just beyond St Martin's, a building he scarcely recognised since the storm had left its cruel mark on it. Upwards of two score young men and boys had lived here, working and learning in the lower rooms, sleeping above, washing or copying, reading or praying in the little chambers set around the outer walls. Now the roof and upper floor were in ruins, but the ground floor was intact and had been lined with pallets to take the sick and injured.

A young man had been placed for his own safety in a locked chamber next to the chapel alcove. He had a bench to sleep on, a chair and a table, a urine pot and some handwritten pages copied from the Holy Scriptures. There was a single window in the room and a wooden cross pinned to the

171

centre rafter for his comfort. He had crammed himself into a corner, and in his distress rocked forward and back on his haunches, muttering through his sobs.

'He seems unharmed,' the priest told Simeon gravely. 'And yet he sobs and screams as if in pain. I fear the poor boy may have lost his sanity.'

'Or else he is possessed,' his bearded companion said.

'Has he not spoken to anyone?' Simeon asked.

Both men shook their heads. Brother Thomas said: 'Nobody knows what happened to him. He was brought by force to the chapter house, kicking and screaming and in a state of abject terror. He escaped his escorts and spent the whole night huddled on the roof. Father Cyrus managed to quieten him for a short time but then ...'

'Cyrus? What has he to do with this?'

'He was with the monk Antony in the old chapter house,' the priest explained. 'The boy had been screaming almost without pause for hours, and Cyrus went up to the roof to calm him with prayer. Perhaps he managed to sleep a little, but later he became so agitated that it was feared he might fling himself from the roof, so he was brought to us.'

'Again by force?'

The bearded clerk, Robert, nodded his head and said: 'I'm afraid there was no other way.'

'And he speaks to no one?'

'Not a word,' the priest said. 'We thought of you, Father Simeon. If you could lay your hands upon him perhaps he will be healed of this mysterious affliction.'

Simeon looked at him sharply. 'I have no magic powers to heal a man by touch,' he said coldly.

'But Father, I was given to understand by Brother Vincent that ...'

Simeon silenced him with a scowl. 'Listen to me,' he insisted. 'On Brother Osric's advice I can give the lad valerian to calm his hysteria and to help him sleep. I have comfrey and betony to knit his bones, aloe and agrimony to heal his wounds. And in God's name I can offer words of comfort and the healing force of prayer. Beyond these things

172

I can do nothing. I am a priest, young man. I am a priest and nothing more.'

'But Father, we believe . . .' the clerk began, only to leave the statement unfinished before the flash of anger in Simeon's eyes.

'I will hear no more of this,' Simeon warned. 'You have brought me to this place for a purpose. Now, where is the boy?'

They found him easily enough. Young Stephen was crouched in the darkest corner of his chamber, trapped between the wall and the wooden bench. As they approached he shrank away, shaking his head and moaning. His face was white and his eyes were filled with pain.

Simeon waved the others back, handed the clerk a small phial and indicated that a few drops were to be added to a cup of wine. Then he stepped forward a little way and dropped into a crouch.

'You know me, Stephen,' he said, very softly. 'I am Father Simeon of St Peter's. You helped me clear the ditches out last summer. We worked together in the scriptorium too. Do you remember?'

The boy rocked to and fro, hugging his knees. He gave no sign that he had heard the words.

Simeon accepted the silver cup from the clerk and took it to the boy. He prised the fingers open and let them close again around the cup, lifted it to the trembling lips and coerced the boy to drink. The youthful face was bruised and stained with tears. There was a mark like a burn on either cheek, as if brute force had been employed to gag his screams. He choked on the wine and rattled his teeth on the edge of the cup, but enough of the valerian was swallowed for it to do its calming work.

Simeon returned to his place and squatted on his haunches as before. He unfastened the crucifix from his girdle and placed it on the ground between them. Then he began to speak again, his voice pitched low and very deep as he quoted from the Holy Book of Proverbs: '*Trust in the Lord with all your heart and lean not on your own small understanding.*'

173

The words sprang to his mind as the most appropriate for the youngster's needs. It seemed to him that Stephen had either suffered or had witnessed with his innocent young eyes some horror that went beyond his comprehension. He must be reminded that God had not abandoned him in his hour of need. For a long time Simeon squatted there, a patient, softly spoken figure, coaxing and pacifying. And all the while he spoke in soothing, reassuring tones, and by degrees the terrible tension in Stephen's body began to ease.

'*Despise not the chastening of the Lord,*' Simeon quoted, infinitely patient. '*Nor be weary of His correction.*'

Simeon's voice was deep, his tone hypnotic, and as he continued he saw the boy's anguished gaze turn down and focus upon the holy crucifix. A trembling hand began to move as if it might reach out to touch that symbol of his faith.

'*Fear not the dreadful thing,*' Simeon recited. '*Live not in terror of the storm.*'

The boy moved with an aching slowness, as vulnerable and as fearful as a small, weak animal emerging from its winter sleep with few recourses left for its survival. At last the words had reached him in the remote place where he had fled from hurt. He trusted the priest, and from that trust came courage. Simeon had held a candle up within the darkness, and by its light that troubled boy would find his strength returned.

'Take up the cross, Stephen,' he softly coaxed. 'Take up the cross and let our Lord Jesus lead you into the light.'

Then Simeon heard the door open and close and a scuffle of movement behind him, the rustle of fine cloth and the impatient clearing of a man's throat. Stephen heard it too. With his fingers hovering just above the crucifix he turned his glance upward, staring first at Simeon and then beyond him. His bruised face twisted into an ugly grimace, he loosed an ear-splitting scream and in a sudden state of panic scrambled into the narrow gap beneath the bench, hugging the hard earth floor. There he cringed, trembling and sobbing, lost again.

'By all that is holy!'

Exasperated, Simeon turned to glare at the figure standing behind him, lifting his gaze upwards from the intruder's feet, watching from the corners of his eyes. He knew at once the elaborately embroidered sandals, the lavish robes, the glittering silver girdle, the purple cloak with its lining of soft black sables. Wulfric de Morthlund filled the doorway with his great bulk and his splendid attire. The priest and the clerk had fled their posts outside the door, scuttling away at sight of this glowering countenance, for the mountainous man in canon's garb was noted for his quick and vindictive temper.

'Has the boy spoken?' he demanded. 'Has he said anything?'

'I believe he was about to,' Simeon answered coldly. 'I had begun to gain his trust. Now he is as you see.'

'Because of me?' Wulfric looked crestfallen.

'Because of you,' Simeon confirmed, rising slowly to his feet.

The fat man stared first at Simeon, then at the quivering shape beneath the bench. He spread his hands, contrition in his face.

'Then I do sincerely beg your forgiveness, Father Simeon. Believe me, I had no idea. Perhaps I might make amends by sitting with him for a while?'

Simeon shook his head at the suggestion. 'No, Wulfric, you saw his reaction to the sight of you. He fears everyone.'

'Except yourself, it seems.'

'He fears me too. I have been here for some time now, trying to coax him out.'

'And but for my careless entry you would have succeeded, would you not?'

Simeon nodded. 'I do believe so.'

'Then I humbly beg your forgiveness, Brother.'

'And you shall have it. Come, let us leave the boy to his dark hole. The draught I gave him will soon take effect and he will sleep for several hours. Perhaps then I will be able to draw him out, when he is rested and can distance himself from his experience.'

'I am sure you will,' Wulfric replied, pulling the door closed behind them. 'I am sure you will.'

Wulfric did not attend the midday meal. A large number of those priests entitled to eat in the canons' hall were seated on the floor for want of stools and benches. Low pallets were brought for the older men, folded blankets and clean straw to soften the ground for brittle bones. The platters of food were brought up by a small army of servants and set on tables at one end of the room. Here were freshwater fish: pike, roach and bream, and roasted fowl and rabbit, smoked pig and cheese. Servants in pairs carried baskets of bread between them, or metal trays piled high with skewered wild birds roasted on open spits. There was a soup of mutton simmered with leeks and shallots, and cold blood pudding made from the best local pigs. It was a makeshift feast hastily prepared, but feast it was and all gave thanks for it.

In his lush apartments Wulfric de Morthlund dined upon pigeon and wine and delicate pastries dipped in melted butter. A plump cat had been stuffed with herbs and roasted, so tender that it ran with golden juices when the flesh was lifted off the bone. When the meal was over he had the table cleared away and rested for less than an hour, dozing a little as he drank his wine. Then he was on his feet, refreshed and ready to put his plan into action.

Daniel helped him remove his robes until he was standing in his silk undershirt. The young man thought, but did not say, how much the stature of the man depended on his vestments. In his undershirt, scratching the band of flesh around his middle where the decorated girdle had chafed his skin, he was nothing but an ordinary man grown bloated on his vices. It was the cloth-of-gold, the silk and fur and precious thread, that sumptuous representation of the power of the Church, that gave him glory.

'I will enjoy this,' Wulfric said, burping the remnants of his meal away. 'I will play the tormented penitent. I will grovel at his feet and beg his blessing on my worthless soul, and thus I will have that priest bow to my will.'

Daniel smiled. 'Are you so certain that he will play the

game according to your wishes?'

'This time he will. Be sure of that.'

'He has already thwarted you today. The child still lives. They say he fought like a man possessed to save it.'

Wulfric narrowed his eyes in response to the reminder. 'This is another matter,' he said. 'And this time I will test his weakness, not his strength.'

Daniel laughed at that. 'Aye, if he has one.'

'All men can be seduced,' Wulfric insisted. 'Even the haughty Simeon.'

'Seduced?' Daniel issued a guffaw of laughter, though behind the mirth he was mindful of his master's unpredictable temper. '*Seduced*, you say? Ye gods, I fancy we will see the rampant bull seduce the gentle dove before we have that Simeon bending to *your* persuasions.'

'Laugh all you will, my pretty Little Hawk,' Wulfric smiled, patting the young man's cheek with the palm of his hand. 'All men can be seduced ... *all* men, for each has his private measure of the seven human weaknesses.' He named a finger for each one in turn to emphasise his point. 'Fear, ambition, lust, vanity, malice, guilt and compassion. Touch one of these and you shall own the man.'

'It is to be compassion, then,' he guessed.

Wulfric lowered his head and screwed his features into a pouting grimace. When he raised it up again the skin was hotly flushed and tears had sprung to his eyes. His whole face had become a mask of abject misery.

'Aye, compassion, I think,' he said, his lower lip trembling.

Daniel smiled and shook his head. He had seen the forlorn repentant's act before, had even been taken in by the performance once or twice. When this Wulfric de Morthlund wept real tears and begged a man's forgiveness on his knees, none but the cruel of heart failed to be moved.

'A wise choice, my lord.'

'But of course, it is,' de Wulfric chuckled. 'My wisdom, dear heart, has never been in doubt.'

As Daniel settled the hairshirt over Wulfric's shoulders, the fat man winced and looked to where it touched his skin, prickling the tender flesh with its stiff fibres. The skin around his neck and shoulders had been rubbed with an ointment made from ground brimstone flowers and the soldier's woundwort, yarrow. It was a common cure, rather than a preventative, but Wulfric hoped its healing qualities would prevent the hairshirt from causing too much damage. Already the soft white skin had turned to pink where it met the prickly horse-hair. He was content with that, for a sign of his physical discomfort suited his purpose. What he dreaded was the 'good man's rash', that morbid condition of the skin that defied all remedy and caused an itching fierce enough to drive a man to distraction.

Over the hairshirt Daniel hung a woollen surplice, a plain dark brown in colour, simply cut and without embellishment. He dampened his fingers with water and ran them through his master's hair, setting it all askew. Then he stood back and viewed his handiwork.

'I am convinced,' he said, nodding his head gravely. 'The man of great pride and arrogance has suffered a dramatic change of heart. I know you better than any man, and even I am taken in by it.'

'Good, good,' Wulfric nodded. 'Go now and fetch the priest. Do you have your story firmly fixed in your mind?'

'I have.'

'Then tell it, Daniel, and be convincing when you do, for I must seal that priest's lips before he can take young Stephen's accusations to a higher authority.'

Daniel shrugged. 'At the end of the day, what would it really matter? You know as well as I do that the church does not call sodomy with either man or boy a mortal sin. It would be considered far more serious if your partner in the act had been a woman or a beast.'

'And it would have been far *less* serious had the lad been willing,' Wulfric snapped. 'And then there is the little matter of St Martin's altar.'

'Ah yes, I had overlooked the desecration,' Daniel conceded. 'Perhaps you are right. In this particular case, confession seems to be the better part of valour.'

'Of course I am right, my boy. Another word against me whispered into the Archbishop's ear and he will be obliged to act on it. I have more than my share of enemies, and too many men are jostling for recognition now that the leadership of our chapter is in question. Men like Cyrus de Figham and Simeon de Beverley are setting themselves up as saintly creatures deserving of special notice. Already we have Antony the monk, Osric the infirmarian, even that insufferable Thorald of the Holme Church, all gathering notice for their good deeds and dedication to the needs of others.'

'A hundred heroes,' Daniel mused. 'This town is choked with would-be saints, it seems.'

'And ahead of them runs that yellow-haired, sky-eyed priest who owns more charm and easy persuasion than the serpent who tempted Eve to ruin Adam. Simeon. God damn that pious priest to hell.'

'Take care your curses are not overheard, my lord,' Daniel warned, glancing toward the door. 'He and his good men are much in favour in the present climate.'

'And what of Wulfric de Morthlund, eh? What will the Archbishop hear of Wulfric de Morthlund in the midst of all this *goodness*? My God, no crippled priest will make me the black against which the white is measured.'

The fat man's face had coloured to purple and he waved his arms about so that the hairshirt rubbed against his fleshy neck.

'Silence him, then,' Daniel said quietly. 'Silence him before the Archbishop gets here. Do it by the sword or by the seal, but silence him.'

'As God is my judge, you may depend upon it.' Wulfric waved him out and continued scowling at his thoughts. 'By seal or by sword,' he growled, preoccupied, 'you may depend upon it.'

CHAPTER SEVENTEEN

Daniel Hawk found Simeon in the chapter house, helping a tired-looking monk to lift a dying man on to the floor. The priest and the monk, an incongruous pair, then knelt on the ground on either side of the man and held his hands as if he were a friend and not a stranger from another town. Their heads were lowered close to his ashen face, their voices a united, deep-toned whisper as they prayed him on his way to a better place. In Simeon's free hand was a silver cross, polished and set with gems so that it shone or softly glowed but would be seen by even the smallest light. It was the most a priest could offer in comfort, that a man might die within sight of the holy cross of Christ.

The monk was in his middle years and short in stature, a tough little man much weathered by his long years on the road. Daniel knew him by sight and reputation. He was Antony, a scribe and scholar of high repute who spoke so many different languages that rarely a pilgrim crossed his path who did not receive a greeting in his native tongue. For his namesake he wore the *tau cross*, the Cross of St Antony of Egypt, on a sturdy thong around his neck, and it was known that, apart from the dagger at his belt, that cross was his only possession. Brother Antony's mother had been a Flemish woman and his father a Spaniard, hence his swarthy features and his lank black hair. They said he was a good man, generous to a fault and caring of all men's comforts before his own. He stank of his endless toil and had the scent of hunger on him, so men despised him for his poverty even as they loved him for his charity and many acts of mercy. Daniel spoke out rarely on such matters, for he had learned that men remembered other men's opinions long after they forgot their own, and nurtured resentments when the climate altered. But he was watchful and astute and, having weighed each fact against another, had come to wonder if such striving to become a *good man* was but a vice masquerading as a virtue.

The young man stepped from the shadows now and injected a note of agitation into his voice as he stooped to pluck at Simeon's sleeve. He shrank back a little when the priest's face turned to fix that deep blue gaze on him. It seemed to look too closely, to see too much.

'Sir, you are needed urgently. My master is ill.'

'Father Wulfric?'

Daniel nodded and wrung his hands, avoiding Simeon's eyes. 'He rants and raves and screams for a priest to hear his confession before God strikes him down for his sins. He is in torment.'

Simeon rose to his feet with some effort, for he had not slept for many hours and by now his weariness was beginning to weigh him down.

'Father Wulfric?' he repeated. He stared into the young man's face and Daniel, once again confronted by that intense blue gaze, looked down and began to wring his hands as if beset by agitation.

'Yes, sir, the same,' he muttered.

'What ails him?' Simeon demanded. 'Is he poisoned? Did he eat bad meat or swallow tainted wine?'

'No, sir, he is not poisoned.'

'Did you send for Osric, the infirmarian?'

'No, sir, it is your name he calls upon. He says you know what ails him. He is distracted, babbling. He is in great spiritual pain, but he refuses to be comforted.'

'I saw him at the college at midday,' Simeon said. 'We spoke together. He was himself. What has befallen him since then?'

Daniel tugged at the priest's sleeve, urging him toward the door of the chapter house. His sharply handsome features were twisted now with concern, his gaze casting about as if he feared that others might overhear their conversation. When he spoke again it was with renewed urgency.

'Father, I cannot answer that,' he admitted, brokenly. 'I had hoped that you might be able to explain it, since you were the last person to speak to him before this ... this *transformation* came upon him.'

Simeon drew the young man aside, detached his sleeve from his grip and handed him a little cup of wine.

'Here, drink this and calm yourself, Daniel. Come now, I insist you drain the cup. Now tell me, slowly and clearly. What ails your master?'

'Thank you, Father. He told me you would listen.' He sipped the wine. It was sour and not to his taste but he made no complaint. 'He is convinced that you, and only you, will understand and look on him with compassion. I know he is a difficult man, at times overbearing, even insensitive ... such faults have earned him many enemies ...'

'We are not here to judge his conduct, Daniel,' Simeon interjected. 'If I am to help your master, as indeed I am obliged to do, I need to know what manner of illness has befallen him.'

Daniel nodded and set down his empty cup. He glanced at the priest and quickly looked away, began to speak but choked upon the words. The wine had stung his throat and soured his tongue, but he was not unaware that his reaction to it might well have been caused by a surfeit of emotion. Simeon gave him a moment to recover.

'Forgive me, Father,' he begged at last. 'Such weakness is unmanly.'

'Compassion is no disgrace,' Simeon told him gently. 'We are not shamed by the tears we shed on behalf of those we love.'

182

Even as he spoke those words, Simeon felt himself divided from the true meaning they were intended to convey. The love this Daniel had for Wulfric de Morthlund exceeded the love of clerk for priest or novitiate for master. Whether it went beyond devotion or fell far short of it he could not tell. He only knew that he, deeply offended by its implications, was both unable and unwilling to comprehend it.

'Thank you, Father,' Daniel said, clearing his throat against the back of his hand and seeming to pull himself together with an effort. 'I am recovered now.'

'Then speak out, Daniel.'

'I hardly know where to begin. My master was in a state of agitation when he returned to the house from the college shortly after midday. You say you saw him there and he was himself, yet when he reached the house he most certainly was not. He was distressed, *extremely* distressed. He swore that he despised himself, for he had been measured against the humblest of God's priests and found to be lacking. I brought his midday meal but he refused it, crying out that he was unworthy to receive so much as a crust of bread or a thimbleful of water.'

'Wulfric de Morthlund said all this?'

'Yes, Sir, and there is more. He sent for a flagellator to scourge his flesh. He tore the fine vestments from his back and tossed his valuables to the poor and needy by the handful. Then he took up the hairshirt and flung himself, barefooted and bleeding from the flagellator's stripes, into the chapel. Since then he has prayed and wept and constantly called for you by name. He wishes to make confession. You must come to him at once.'

'Why me?'

'Because he asks for you.'

'But I am not his confessor,' Simeon reminded him.

Daniel was insistent. 'How can that matter now? It is you my master calls for in his anguish, *you* who must hear his most solemn confession. In God's name help him, Father Simeon. He has been brought so low that even his close friends might not recognise him. You would not hesitate to come if only you had seen him as I did, weeping and tearing at his own flesh ... then you would pity him and raise him up in the name of God Almighty. I fear for him, Father ... I fear for his sanity.'

Simeon felt compassion stir in him. The young man's shoulders sagged and now he hung his head and wiped his sleeve across his face. He had been proud but love had made a frightened boy of him, and if that love was an abomination in the sight of God, then it was overdue by many years for its divine chastisement. Perhaps an end had come of it at last. God worked His will in ways that were mysterious to men, and even de Morthlund, at the end, must bow to it. All this was clear in Simeon's mind, yet still he held back, asking the question silently: *Why me?*

'He believes your influence brought him to this,' Daniel said as if reading the priest's thoughts. 'And because of that conviction he will bare his soul to no other priest but you. He was most adamant upon that point. Only you can save him.'

Simeon nodded. 'Then I will come,' he said, despite the doubts, and Daniel, the ever self-confident Little Hawk, fell to one knee and kissed the folds of his robe and stammered his thanks.

So it was that Father Simeon went to the little altar underneath the canon's house to find Wulfric de Morthlund, that pompous, worldly, cockerel of a man, grovelling in the dirty rushes, weeping and distraught. The floor was muddy here and very cold, and the fat man lay face down with his arms outstretched, sobbing into the sparsely scattered rushes. It was a sight to move the heart of any man, for he was clearly in much spiritual pain, dishevelled and stripped of all his grand pretensions. His remorse was shown in the livid marks around his neck and shoulders where the hairshirt chafed, the tear-stained cheeks, the tender undersides of feet rarely exposed to anything more harsh than silken hose and smooth leather boot or sandal.

'Wulfric de Morthlund, are you prepared to make full confession of your sins before God?'

'I am, I am.' The fat man sobbed and beat at the rushes with his fists. 'Forgive me Father. Forgive me, for my sins are heinous and my soul is darkly grieved.'

Simeon signed the cross and swallowed down the barrier of his own misgivings. He believed he knew the reason for this confession, and if that were so then he would sooner face de Morthlund on his own terms, not with a crucifix but with a sword. With a great effort of will he reminded himself that he was God's instrument, called upon to help reunite a sinner with his conscience, to lead an erring soul towards salvation. It was a privilege never to be misused, an authority not to be over-stepped or coloured by the personal prejudices of individual priests. Standing as he now did between a penitent and his God, he must not create a stumbling block out of his own misgivings.

At this point Daniel Hawk, his features grave and his gaze still reluctant to meet with that of the priest, slid quietly from the room and closed the door beyond him. He climbed the crooked stairway to the entrance hall, and from there the grander stairway to his master's splendid apartments. Only when the double doors with their rich hangings had closed at his back did he shake his fine young head and allow a smile to spread across his features. As always, Wulfric had accurately judged his prey, for never had Daniel seen compassion sit so openly on the face of any man. It branded Simeon susceptible to manipulation, for tender hearts and gullible minds were the fare on which de Morthlund had grown fat.

In the tiny room below the hall de Morthlund was kneeling now to embrace Father Simeon's feet, his body quivering with cold and wracked by fits of uncontrollable sobbing.

'I saw it in your eyes,' he managed to gasp. 'When I disturbed you as you spoke to Stephen. I saw it then and knew I must repent and make confession of my sins.'

'Saw what? What did you see?'

'God's will,' de Morthlund said. 'I saw God's will.'

'In me?' Simeon gasped. 'You saw His will in me?'

'I swear it.'

Simeon closed his eyes and felt a shudder pass through his

body. It was as if the hand of doom had touched him. For a moment he was tempted to fling this snivelling man aside and dismiss his words as lies. For his own sake he did not want this, but for the sake of de Morthlund's immortal soul he knew he must accept what God demanded of him.

'There is a higher authority here than mine,' he ventured, as a last resort. 'Perhaps your own confessor...?'

'It must be you,' de Morthlund said, and turned his tear-stained face up so that Simeon could clearly see his pain. 'It must be you, friend Simeon. You were there ... you saw it all ... the storm ... the evil ... oh God, what have I done?'

'Speak out then. Before God and with an open heart. Admit your sins and repent of them.' In a harsher tone he asked: 'Do you confess to sending armed men to St Peter's with orders to kill my godson?'

Wulfric's mouth sagged open and he drew away as if the priest had struck him in the face.

'*What?*'

'Confess it, man. Is this not the reason I am here? Confess it.'

'Never! Not I! It was not I!'

'But you had a part in it?'

'No part,' Wulfric protested. 'I swear I know nothing ...'

'Then why...?' Simeon checked himself. He recalled the voice that had spoken his name from nowhere, the way de Morthlund's face, and others, had leapt at him from the sea of faces gathered in the Minster. '... but I was warned ... I thought...'

'Please, Father ... I beg you,' the fat man sobbed. '... add no more sins to those already crushing me beneath their weight. I am guilty of much, I know, but not this.'

As Wulfric's voice rose in a fresh wail of anguish, Simeon put out his hands to still the fingers clutching at his robes. The other man's flesh was soft and plump and, even in that chilly place, damp with perspiration. Simeon drew his own hands away and touched the shaved patch on the lowered head, shaping with his thumb the sign of the cross. It took much effort to push his grievances aside.

186

'You who have sinned, confess and repent before God.'

'I repent. I repent. Can I be saved ...? Oh God, will I be damned to Hell for this?'

'Confess!'

'It was the storm ... the storm was terrifying. I thought I would die. I had a friend with me and we were almost struck by falling masonry. Terror overwhelmed me ... I became possessed ... oh God, it was beyond my control ... beyond my control ...'

As Wulfric choked on the words Simeon felt a sense of foreboding crawl along his spine. 'Go on,' he prompted, wishing himself elsewhere.

'Oh God, the awful shame of it. We fled for refuge behind the sacred altar of St Martin and we ... oh, forgive me, Father ... forgive me for I have sinned ... I have sinned most grievously.'

Thus Father Simeon heard the faltering confession of Wulfric de Morthlund, heard it and struggled inwardly to keep disgust from clouding his judgment of the penitent's sincerity.

'Who was your partner in this offence?' he asked at last.

The fat man raised his head. His face was very red and stained with tears, and his eyes were hidden behind a watery sheen. He shook his head and his lower lip trembled. 'I cannot, Father. I cannot say his name.'

'You know you must,' Simeon pressed.

'Please, Father, let him come forward of his own accord. Let his repentance not be on the orders of a priest but offered freely and without duress. Let him be saved, as I was, not brought to you by force. He will come. I know he will come, in his own time.'

'So be it,' Simeon nodded. He had guessed, as he was meant to guess, the name of de Morthlund's abettor to the crime. One half of that unholy partnership had seen the error of his ways at last. In time, by the grace of God, his Little Hawk would follow his example.

'You must know I cannot absolve you of this sin.'

'But you must! For pity's sake, you must. Am I to be cast

187

aside with my sins unforgiven? You must absolve me, Father. I heard God speak to me. I swear he said your name . . .'

'This is a reserved sin,' Simeon reminded him, moved by a disturbing cocktail of pity and repugnance. 'You know a mere priest cannot absolve you of it. Only the Archbishop can help you, Wulfric. You must go to him at once.'

The fat man's hands grasped at his robes and his body was a soft weight against Simeon's legs. 'Forgive me, Father, for I have sinned,' he pleaded. 'Absolve me. Absolve me.'

'I cannot,' repeated Simeon, 'and there the matter rests. Such sins as you confess are beyond my small authority. I cannot give you absolution.'

And so indeed the matter rested. Simeon prayed with Wulfric until the other man grew calm and resigned. He left him on his knees before the altar, the marks of the hairshirt livid across his neck, and as the door divided them Simeon closed his eyes and rested his head against the outer wall. The interview had sickened him. More than that, he knew he must now bear the burden of his knowledge without the healing satisfaction of knowing he had cleansed a sinner of his grave transgressions.

He touched his head and breast and then his shoulders, marking himself with the sign of the sacred cross. It did not ease the throbbing in his head.

Wulfric de Morthlund did not leave the chapel until a servant came to inform him that Father Simeon had left the house. Then he hurried upstairs to his rooms, ripped the hairshirt from his body and flung it across the room with a snort of contempt.

'There are men who wear such hateful things from choice,' he snorted. 'And those who do deserve the ever-lasting scorn of decent human beings.'

'Even a humble hairshirt has its place within the Greater Scheme of things,' Daniel reminded him, bringing a cloak to cover his master's nakedness. 'Did it serve its purpose?'

'Of course it did. Did you believe for a moment that my plan would fail?'

Daniel shrugged, pouring wine. 'This Simeon is a strange

one. Those eyes of his, they search a man too keenly, they see too much.'

'Rubbish! When it comes to the point he is just as blind as the next man. And just as dishonest, in his way. He sees what he wants to see and nothing more.'

'You convinced him, then?'

'He convinced himself.' The fat man took the goblet of wine and drained it quickly, then handed it back to be refilled while he settled himself on a couch and pushed his chilly feet beneath a cushion. 'How many believers can resist the possibility that God has set a particular task for them and them alone? What man is not overawed by the prospect of being singled out by the Almighty? I convinced the fool that God, through him, had touched my wicked conscience. And that was all I had to do, for his own vanity was content to do the rest.'

'You are too modest,' Daniel smiled. 'I am sure you gave a magnificent performance.'

Wulfric chuckled and sipped his wine. 'I am sure I did.'

Mindful of his master's needs, Daniel eased the folds of the cloak aside and proceeded to smooth a creamy white ointment into the inflamed skin. His fingers were firm but gentle. These were practised fingers, skilled in their ministrations.

'And now?' he asked.

Wulfric grinned, moving his shoulders to meet the soothing caresses of Daniel's hands. 'And now, dear heart, I believe we can relax. Whatever that cringing Stephen says to Simeon might just as well remain unsaid. Simeon heard my confession. His lips are sealed.'

'But he did not offer absolution?'

'Of course he did not. How could he for such a sin? Nevertheless, I have him. He may not repeat one word he hears against me now, lest by doing so he offend the sacred laws of the confessional. Nor can he ever, by hint or sign or innuendo, seek to connect me to the crime confessed. It is done as I intended. Simeon's lips are sealed.'

CHAPTER EIGHTEEN

The vesper bells were ringing. Men were carrying lanterns in the streets and fires were burning here and there where the homeless were gathered, huddled against the cold. Light flakes of snow blew on the wind and the ground already crunched underfoot, promising a frosty night. Families gathered at the smithy wall and around the homes of bakers, claiming a place against the warm chimney-bricks before the night closed in.

The Minster's doors were to be locked at nightfall. Only the sick, the very old, all nursing mothers and the very young were to be given shelter there, for space was at a premium while half the population of Beverley was clamouring for a place to lay its head. The church could only do so much. Many of its priests were homeless too and desperately in need of rest. If they were to succour and lead their flock as God intended, they must be given first priority.

Simeon stood in the little side chapel in the south-east transept where a dozen priests intended to spend the night. Near the altar lay the body of Father Bernard, shrouded and covered by an altar-cloth. Gold thread and fringing glinted in the light, and the candles at his head and feet supported yellow flames that danced and smoked a little in every movement of air. Father Bernard would be missed, for he had been much loved by those who knew him.

'You sent for me, Father Simeon?'

He turned from his thoughts to find young Richard, clerk to the vicar of St Nicholas, standing behind him. His face was pale and drawn behind the neat brown beard, and the dull fabric of his hood hung limp and dust-stained on his shoulders. Simeon offered a sympathetic smile and the young man immediately dropped his gaze, ashamed.

'You have been found blameless in the matter,' Simeon reminded him. 'If that is not enough then you must take solemn confession and seek absolution for any sin you fear you have committed.'

'And if that is not enough?' the young man asked with quiet passion. He lifted his face to show eyes that were red-rimmed with weeping.

Simeon placed a hand on his shoulder. 'If that is not enough, my friend, then you will place yourself in much graver error. Do you believe in a forgiving God?'

'Yes, Father, of course I do.'

'Well then, if God Himself freely forgives, may we withhold that same forgiveness, even from ourselves?'

Richard peered steadily at the priest as he took the words and held them to himself to wring what comfort he could from them. He swallowed with difficulty, for a hard lump had shaped itself in his throat all those hours ago and would not be shifted, neither dissolved nor coughed away.

'I loved him,' he said, not knowing what else to say.

'I know. We all did.'

'And God knows I didn't mean to . . .'

Simeon raised a hand to halt the words. 'Aye, God knows and so do we. It was unfortunate, but kinder than leaving him to lie undiscovered for days, or even weeks, in that dark place. Why else might you have gone there, Brother Richard?'

'Why else? I can think of no other reason, Father. I was afraid to meet with looters outside the church and unwilling to relieve myself where I stood. I went because I had to, that is all.'

'Then perhaps God, in His superior wisdom, knew exactly

what he was doing when He directed you there,' Simeon suggested.

Richard's eyes opened wide and a little glimmer of hope sprang in their depths. His lips moved as if he might speak, but for several moments no sound came out. He nodded thoughtfully, frowned and nodded again, the tack and turn of his thoughts clearly reflected in his features.

'Of course He did,' he declared at last, and his relief was shining in his eyes. 'Of course. It was God's will. He used me as His instrument.'

Simeon smiled. 'And now that you have seen the truth of it, will you be content to bear the burden bravely?'

'Yes, Father, I will.' Richard squared his shoulders and tried again to clear his throat. This time the obstruction did not seem quite so large. He met Simeon's steady gaze and, still nodding his head, repeated: 'Yes, sir, I will.'

'I am glad to hear it. Now, will you be so good as to show me where you found Father Bernard?'

Richard's face clouded over. He glanced at the pointed door set into the transept wall. 'In there,' he said.

'I would like you to show me, Richard.'

'Must I, Father?'

Simeon nodded. 'For your sake and for his. I do not ask it of you lightly. Believe me when I say that I would not scratch an open wound merely to satisfy my curiosity.'

He pulled a half-candle from his pouch and held it over the flame that danced at Father Bernard's feet. The flame divided into two and Simeon took his share. It spluttered as it fed upon the wick, flared up and settled. He signed the cross, his thoughts an unworded prayer of thanks for the precious gift of light. That single flame could split itself a thousand times to feed a thousand hungry wicks, and still his portion of it would remain. So too the flame of God's own love: sufficient to light the darkness of every man, were he but willing to hold his candle up.

He cupped the flame with his free hand and indicated that Richard should go ahead of him through the turret door. The lad went bravely, stepped over the low stone seat and stood in the darkness where the old canon had fallen.

'Is this exactly how it was?' Simeon asked. 'Think hard before you speak, Richard. I need to know, is this *exactly* as it was?'

Richard nodded. 'Exactly. Father Bernard was lying right here, face down and with his head turned toward the door. He looked so peaceful, lying there, as if he had fallen asleep over his prayers. His hands were still clasped beneath him with his rosary held fast between his fingers.'

'He had been praying, then?'

'I do believe so, yes.'

'And the rock that struck him down?'

'Still there where I first saw it.'

'And the candle stub?'

'Still lying where it was.'

Simeon handed the lighted candle to Richard and squatted down with his elbows on his knees. For a while he remained there, his palms together and his thumbs against his lips, preoccupied. Then he rose up and crossed to the steps to examine the broken tread-stone and, on a higher step, the fresh marks where the candle-stub had recently been placed.

'Hand me the light,' he said, and when he had it, held it into the shadows above his head. Then he went up, vanishing into the twisted stairway, pushing the shadows back with his flickering flame. When he came down again it was sit on a stair above the narrow window, his features shifting and changing in the oscillating light. Richard's face was below him, looking up. Between the beard and the shadows, what remained of his features appeared so gaunt and hollow-eyed they might have belonged to a dead man. Simeon handed him the candle.

'Set it down and show me how Father Bernard was lying when you discovered him,' he said.

'Show you? You mean ...?'

Simeon nodded. His voice was low and coaxing. 'I would like you to get down on your belly and show me exactly ... *exactly* how he was lying. Come, lad, there is no danger in the act, no risk, no sacrilege.'

'But why . . .?'

'Richard, please do as I ask.'

The young man hesitated for a moment, then set aside the candle and stretched himself out on the ground. He arranged his limbs carefully, judging their precise position according to the placing of the dead priest's candle, the rock that killed him and the glistening pool of urine that had stained his legs. He closed his eyes and breathed a prayer. His heart was pounding. He could not have felt worse had he been lying in the dead man's coffin. Long minutes passed and still he lay without moving while Simeon sat on the curved steps, staring down. And slowly it came to him that Father Simeon was questioning the circumstances surrounding the Canon's death. He raised himself up until he could see the other's eyes glinting brightly in the half-light.

'You doubt?' he asked, and he watched the big shoulders rise and fall with a sigh as the clear blue eyes looked steadily back at him.

'Yes, Richard. I doubt.'

'But it was an accident, a fall of rock.'

'From where?'

'The roof, the upper steps,' Richard protested.

'The stones up there are all intact. He was struck from behind, and the rock that killed him came from the step right there beside you, where the tread-stone is shattered. Pick up the rock that killed him, Richard. Go ahead. Now replace it. See how perfectly it fits there? See how clean the edges are where the piece was torn away?'

'There is your answer, then,' Richard offered, relieved but still uncertain. 'A simple accident. The tread-stone fell.'

'Fell? Measure the distance, Richard. Judge it for yourself. Whether standing, sitting, or kneeling on the ground, Father Bernard could not have been struck down by fortune's hand. Oh, the tread-stone killed him, there can be no doubt of that, but it did not fall. It was lifted.'

'*Lifted?*' Richard hurriedly crossed himself and glanced heavenward. '*Lifted?*'

'How else would it produce a killer blow? That broken step

is less than four feet from the ground. The worst it could have done, without assistance, was stub his toe.' He paused, drew in a breath and continued speaking. 'And how did the candle fall from here, by the window where its marks are clearly visible, to the farthest corner of the turret-space? And how did that heavy tread-stone, having opened the old man's skull, come to rest so far from its killing wound? I say again, the tread-stone was lifted, and Bernard, the best of priests and the sweetest of men, was struck down from behind by someone who had been sitting here before this very window.'

'Attacked?' Richard said in a failing voice. 'Killed? *Murdered?*'

'Do not believe it simply because I say it, Richard. Sit down and gather your thoughts together. Sift the facts. Consider all that you have seen and heard. When you have the answer you may correct me if you can. Tell me how it might have been done otherwise.'

In the silence that followed, Simeon closed his eyes and in his mind's eye saw the amiable old Canon resting on the stair. He might have been ushered there for his own protection while the storm was at its height, perhaps even by a friend. He would have prayed against the danger. He would have lowered his head and clasped his hands, a frail old man who saw no ill in anyone, while at his back a killer waited.

Simeon shuddered and his eyes snapped open. Men killed in passion, whether that passion be hatred or fear, revenge or jealousy. Or else they killed for gain. Father Bernard had been a simple and a pious man unlikely to arouse strong passions in others. And who would benefit by killing someone who had so little of worldly value to call his own? He had stockpiled no riches, cultivated no enemies, known no women, turned no beggar from his door. He was a poor man in the worldly sense.

'Passion or gain,' Simeon said aloud, and his words pulled Richard from his reverie.

'I fear you are right, Father Simeon,' he said, his voice tight with emotion. 'It could have been no accident, unless the stone fell upwards and the candle moved itself.'

'God's mercy,' Simeon muttered, and crossed himself. 'Of all men, who would want to kill poor Bernard? I see no motive for this crime. Am I missing something, Richard? Am I letting his goodness blind me to the truth? Was there something in him that was capable of inspiring hatred, something I was too blinkered to acknowledge?'

'No!' Richard said firmly, shaking his head in the half-light. 'Father Bernard was a good man. A *good man.*'

'And men are ever envious of the goodness they see in others, but how many are sufficiently inflamed by it to kill?'

Again the young man shook his head. 'He loved all men as equal to himself, even the beggars and the ragged children. And for himself he valued but one thing after God. His church.'

Simeon felt his scalp prickle. 'His church?'

'Aye, his church. St Martin's lies in ruins now, but he was still the Canon there. He would have wept for its loss and then rebuilt it, stone for stone. And the people would have loved him all the better for it.'

'Of course. St Martin's.' Simeon snapped his fingers in the air, a crack of sound that echoed against the stones. 'The passion was envy, and the motive gain. He was murdered for the prebend of St Martin's.'

'Father, if that be so then his own priest, the man who was closer to him than any other, must be the first upon whom suspicion falls. No, no, better to die by the hand of a stranger than to be struck down by a trusted fellow priest.'

'Why would a stranger harm him?' Simeon asked.

'Why indeed? But a *priest!*'

'His own priest,' Simeon agreed, his voice a whisper.

It was Richard who spoke the name. 'Cyrus de Figham.'

'We need the Archbishop here. He was sent for at first light, but heaven knows when he will get here, *if* he gets here.'

'He will come, Simeon.'

'Aye, if King Henry gives him leave.'

'He will come,' old Cuthbert nodded.

'He must. We are in dire and urgent need. The Archbishop should be here.'

Simeon had come from the turret-hole to the side-chapel where his Canon waited. He had sworn the boy to secrecy and Richard, kneeling to kiss his fingers and beg his blessing, had sworn to serve him loyally and without question.

Now Simeon paced a figure-of-eight, as restless as an animal, unable to rest his weary body because his thoughts ran deep and turbulent. The tiny side chapel, even with its doors thrown back, was meagre confinement for his disquietude. He seemed too big for it, as if the walls must fall back from their foundations to accommodate him.

The light was fading more rapidly now, pulling the shadows out of their cracks and corners, stretching them out like stains across the walls. A large crow spread its wings and stepped into the air from the arch where it had been resting. Lazily flapping, blue-black and with its eyes aglint, it swept above the choir and the reredos and vanished into the darkening sky beyond the skeletal remains of the great east window. Its passing was as an omen, darkly sinister.

'We need the Archbishop,' Simeon repeated.

Cuthbert nodded his agreement yet again, his chin rubbing gently against the plain bronze fastening on his chest. He had been dozing when Simeon came to the chapel, content to keep the long night's vigil at the deathbed of his friend. It was his habit now to snatch what sleep he needed in manageable parcels sectioned from the interminable hours of the day. The nights, especially, were longer now. He spent them lying on his bed, sliding helplessly in and out of sleep, his body aching and his mind fogged by fatigue. In the night his doubts came thick and fast upon him, testing his fear of death with visions of an afterlife too terrible for any Christian mind to contemplate. Sometimes he shunned his solitary bed and sat out the long night hours on the hard stone of his seat in the choir stalls, cold and stiff in his old joints but comforted by the voices of the choral priests. Their faith sustained him when his own might falter. He did not mind that they smiled at him for his eccentricities, and he believed that no-one guessed, except perhaps his beloved Simeon, that he was afraid of dying all alone.

As the office of vespers drew towards its conclusion, the gathered priests were beginning to think of supper. The scents of cooking food drifted tantalisingly on the late afternoon air. On every campfire in the streets some meat or fish was roasting. No opportunity had been wasted. Cats and dogs had been caught in makeshift snares, skinned and skewered on spits above the flames. Beasts found wandering free or trapped half-dead in the mud had been sectioned and divided for family pots. Pigs had been snatched from their owners, fowl from their hooks or cages. Even the bloated bodies of drowned beasts, already half-devoured by other animals, were claimed by the poor and homeless who cut and cooked the beasts where they had fallen.

'I must sleep,' Simeon said at last, as if the idea had only now occurred to him. His pacing halted suddenly and his shoulders drooped. 'God's mercy, I am tired beyond endurance. I must sleep.'

'Will you go to St Peter's?' Richard asked eagerly, and when Simeon nodded, added: 'May I come with you?'

'If you wish.' He turned to the old man. 'Father Cuthbert? Will you come with us?'

The old man raised a hand and waved it feebly in the air. It was long and threaded with thick blue veins, the fingers bony and tipped with yellowed nails. The skin was thin and almost transparent in the candles' light. 'I will stay here, my son. Go on without me, I shall not be alone.'

'You will send word to me when the Archbishop arrives?'

'It is too soon for him to come, unless our riders met him on the way.'

'But if he does?'

'Then I will send for you, my boy.'

'And if I am needed for any other reason?'

'Then you will be sent for, Simeon,' the old man repeated. 'Go now and sleep. I fear tomorrow will be no less demanding than today. You need your strength. We *all* have need of it.'

Simeon touched the old man's shoulder and whispered: 'God's peace be with you.'

'And with you also, Simeon.'

They left him nodding at the candle-lit altar, his chin on his chest and his frail hands folded in his lap.

'You did not tell him,' Richard said, when they were outside the church and picking a way through the multitude gathered in the Minster Yard. 'You did not tell him what we know about . . .'

Simeon glanced at him sharply. 'No careless words,' he warned, and as he walked he signed the cross and muttered: 'God be with you,' or 'Go in peace,' to those who begged a blessing.

'Should he not be informed?' Richard insisted. 'Should all the canons not be informed of this without delay?'

'To what end?' Simeon demanded. 'So that they might tremble in their beds and fear to turn their backs on each other lest they too are struck down from behind?'

'But surely they should be warned?'

'Against what? Against whom? Your word and mine, Richard, that is all we have. Nothing more. No proof, no witnesses, just your word and mine against the safe and comfortable assumption that Father Bernard died in a tragic accident.'

'But the *church*,' Richard persisted. 'You yourself have declared that the church must be reconsecrated, yet the services go ahead as if no crime has been committed. Mass has been said there, Simeon. *Mass has been said there.*'

'I know, I know.'

'Well then?'

Simeon stopped and reached out to grasp the young man by the shoulders. He shook him a little, willing him to understand.

'We wait for the Archbishop,' he said. 'I can do nothing more before he comes. If we speak our doubts the consequences will run beyond our control. Would you condemn a man without fair trial? Would you close the church at our time of greatest need?'

'Then we do nothing?' Richard answered flatly. 'We know that Father Bernard was murdered and we do *nothing*?'

'My hands are tied, Richard. I have no authority to remove the Blessed Sacrament and declare the Minster Church of St John desecrated. And even if I had ... to clear the altar and withhold the services at a time like this when the town is in ruins and the people dependent upon on us ...' He dropped his hands to his sides and shook his head. 'What can I do? My hands are tied.'

'So, we remain silent until we can speak to the Archbishop personally. We simply wait.' Richard was already nodding his acceptance of the decision.

Simeon turned his face in the direction of St Peter's.

'We wait,' he said. 'And with God's help, we sleep.'

CHAPTER NINETEEN

The scriptorium was warm and welcoming, its shadows softened by the glow from a crackling fire. Wood-smoke curled upwards to the heavy rafters, there to hang like a dark blue mist about the slopes and angles of the great oak beams. On that side of the room where the roof space made a sleeping area, drapes had been hung to ensure the privacy of visiting nuns. Their voices were sweet and distant as they praised their Lord at the going down of the sun. Fresh straw had been spread on the floor and piled against the walls to make soft beds or seats for weary bodies. Torches burned in sconces around the room, all set at ground level to avoid the risk of fire. Their flickering flames made monsters of men's shadows, leading them off in a grotesque dance, distorted and deformed.

The soft hum of conversation and prayer was stilled by a sudden rapping at the door. Osric the infirmarian set down his plate of food and crossed the room to check that the heavy beam was safely settled in its iron brackets across the door. Then he took out his knife and struck the handle twice upon the wood. The answering signal replaced his grim expression with a smile. He thrust the beam aside and flung the door back on its hinges.

'Welcome, my friend. Welcome.'

As Simeon ducked through the doorway into his friend's embrace, he met the dark gaze of Elvira, who had been sitting on a low stool by the fire. She leaped to her feet, then checked herself and greeted the priest with a curtsy and a small, self-conscious smile. He had seen the quick happiness in her face and guessed that she had watched the door for hours, willing him to appear there. He was neither joyful nor relieved to see her, for his weariness robbed him now of all such feeling. What struck him, though, was a clear impression that he had known this woman all his life, that she had never been a stranger to him. She searched his face and might have read his thoughts, for her smile grew wider and she dropped her gaze, and he saw a sudden flush invade her cheeks.

Simeon unbuckled his heavy cloak and shrugged it from his shoulders into Osric's waiting hands.

'The boy, how is the boy?'

'Content,' the infirmarian nodded. 'The woman Elvira cares for him as if he were her own.'

'And the other? The younger girl? Was she unsuitable, after all de Morthlund's and de Figham's bartering?'

'Who knows?' Osric scowled and lowered his voice for privacy. 'She never reached the convent of St Anne's. One rumour says the tiler was attacked and the girl carried off by soldiers. Another says her father resold her for a purse of gold, then fled the district before the priests could chastise him for his double-dealing. Which story is true I cannot say, but the girl has not been seen since she left the prebendary house with her father.'

'So, all parties prosper in the deal,' Simeon muttered. 'Cyrus de Figham gets his patch of land to offer as sweetener for the Archbishop's favour, Ulred the tiler gets his purse of gold and the girl is kept from Wulfric's lecherous clutches.'

'Aye, though I doubt she'll fare much better, wherever she is taken.'

Simeon shook his head sadly. 'Perhaps the tiler never intended to keep his side of the bargain,' he suggested. 'I liked him little and trusted him far less, but I had hoped to

202

give the girl the protection of our church. God knows she needed it.'

'Look at you. Half dead on your feet and hollow-eyed for want of sleep. Go in and greet your godson. I'll bring a plate of food and lay you abed.'

'And do as much for my young friend Richard, who has been of good service to me.'

'Indeed?' Osric turned his scowl upon the hovering young man, then grinned and slapped him cheerily on the shoulder. 'Then we are right happy to have you with us, lad. Where are you from?'

'From St Nicholas, Sir.'

'Ah, Thorald's man.'

'I am indeed. My home is at Weel, but I have lodged at the church these six months past.'

'And now you will lodge with us. Come, eat your fill and claim a place to rest your head.'

As he led the young man to the fire where meat was simmering in the pot, Osric was watchful of his friend Simeon. The priest was offering words of comfort to those who shared the hospitality of the scriptorium. Men touched his hands and women reached out to handle his cloak or his sleeve, and those who knew him looked to his feet and crossed themselves at the miracle of his healing.

Elvira felt the fiery flush return to her cheeks as Simeon moved towards her. She stooped to lift the sleeping infant from its bed and hand it gently into Simeon's arms. She glanced up at him and then away lest he read her thoughts too clearly. He looked exhausted and she ached to rest his head upon her breast and hold him while he slept, and she was not sure if she would have him know as much.

Simeon bent his head over the child and breathed its sweet, clean baby-smell into his nostrils. He stood thus for a moment, savouring the quiet relief of their reunion. Fatigue could not dull the cutting edge of these emotions. He pressed his lips to the little forehead and his eyes met Elvira's over the folds of fur in which the child was cradled.

'God kept you safe,' she whispered.

'Aye, He did.'

'I have prayed for you.'

He smiled. 'Then once again I am in your debt, Elvira.'

Simeon looked at his tiny godson sleeping peacefully in his arms and felt a warm rush of love invade his senses. Then he handed the bundle to Elvira and accepted a large silver platter on which his supper had been set. Hunger shifted in his empty belly as he stared at the roasted carcasses of wild birds smothered in golden sauce, at the nuts and fruit, fresh bread and hard, strong cheese, and at the leather goblet frothing with ale.

'Simeon? Father Simeon?'

He heard her voice as if across a distance. His gaze had gone beyond the tray of food to the wooden bench against the far wall where Osric had already spread his cloak. The soft fur was to be his mattress, the squirrel-lined hood a pillow for his head. Now the exhaustion his will had held so long at bay came rushing in to close his mind to everything but that. He neither saw nor heard nor spoke as every fibre of his body stretched out to reach the bench before he did. Without a word or a sideways glance he handed the platter back, the food untouched, and strode blindly to the rear of the room. When he reached the bed he fell face-down upon it and moved neither limb nor muscle after his body met the familiar comfort of his cloak. He was fast asleep on the instant, unaware that loving hands drew the warm cloak over him and touched him lightly, lovingly on the brow.

Near the fireplace Osric scowled at his dark thoughts. The woman was transparent. Her feelings for the priest were plain for any eye to see, for she lacked the arts required to keep them hidden. But it was Simeon's response that troubled him, the softening of his features when he saw her, the tender way his eyes looked into hers. The woman had a quiet beauty and the priest was vulnerable. Lust he could cope with, for he had learned to master that particular beast even before he took his voluntary vow of chastity. Nor would he confound one sin over another by falling prey to the charms of another man's wife. Not lust but *love* would be

Simeon's stumbling block. If such a man were to give his heart, his defences would crumble one by one until love stripped him naked of them all.

'And what of your solemn vows then, my friend?' Osric asked the sleeping figure on the bench. 'What of your vows then?'

The monk Antony was admitted to the prebendary house in Moorgate and shown into a lower room that was hung with glorious tapestries and embroidered drapes. An elaborately carved table dominated the room, with six high-backed chairs on each side of it and two great armed chairs, carved and studded and cushioned, stationed like thrones at either end. Heavy drapes with silken fringes adorned the windows and kept the winter draughts at bay, while tapestries hung on rods against the walls and heavy leathers guarded every door. This room was where the canons often met, where Wulfric de Morthlund entertained or chaired religious debates or offered some newly imported wine for criticism. It was where the fat man deployed his subtle powers of manipulation, where he kept his superiors sweet and pliable. Here he became the learned priest, the generous and devoted man of God. Lulled by good food, fine wine and strong debate, innocent good men of the church took bribery and trusted it to friendship.

Antony approached a heavy chest at the far end of the room where a magnificent candelabra had been set. It had been cast from gold, with twelve curving arms and a stepped base set with figures of the saints. The candles in it all were lit, and the candelabra glinted with fiery lights as it turned a dozen flames into a hundred flickering reflections. He reached out to touch the precious metal, felt its warmth, its strength beneath his fingers. This metal had the power to move men's souls. It was a beautiful and a dangerous thing.

'Brother Antony.'

He looked up with his hand still on the gold. His face was calm, as always.

'God's blessing, Brother Wulfric. How can I help you?'

Wulfric de Morthlund had flung back a leather flap to fill the open doorway with his bulk. He was simply dressed in a plain white cassock and a simple hood. He had seen the monk fingering the candelabra and judged him to be covetous of wealth, for Wulfric did not believe that any man could mark a precious object for its beauty and not burn in his soul to possess it.

'These are ill times for Beverley, my friend,' he said, stepping into the room. 'I hear the injured outnumber the dead by many hundreds.'

Antony nodded grimly. 'And the homeless outnumber both by many thousands. At least two thirds of our townspeople are destitute, while the other third ...' He let the statement hang, unfinished, while he watched the fat man's face. He would rather illustrate the fault than speak of it.

Wulfric allowed his gaze to travel over the other man, taking in the coarse woollen habit with its many stains, the filthy sandals and the threadbare hood. He too had learned to convey much outside the use of words.

'You disappoint me, Antony of Flanders,' he said at last. 'You travelling monks elect to live in hardship and poverty and then despise all those who choose not to follow your example. It is a narrow view.'

'And you misjudge me, sir. I despise no man but he who prospers at the expense of others. The scraps from your supper bowl would draw back a starving man from the edge of the abyss. The fancy cloths that serve no purpose here but to decorate the walls would keep the chill of death from those out there who have neither food nor warmth nor shelter. That golden candelabra alone could raise the means to preserve a hundred lives.'

'And what then?' de Morthlund asked mildly. 'You say that we who are more fortunate should fling open our doors to all-comers, empty our coffers, sell our gold, hand over our food and share the rabble's lot, and I say, *for what*? So that more can come, and more, and still more? So that they can swarm like sewer rats over everything decent, leaving it picked to the barest bone and every man no better than themselves?'

'And should those who are also created in God's image be allowed to die for want of bread?'

'The poor are with you always,' Wulfric quoted smugly.

'And so must be provided for,' Antony countered. 'A crust in the bowl today is not enough, nor can we discharge our human obligations with the isolated prick of a conscience followed by a moment's generosity. Our Lord was martyred on the cross not for the privileged few but *for all men*. Indeed, the poor are with us always, and so too is our responsibility to them.'

'We are not Christs,' de Morthlund smiled. 'We cannot feed a stricken town on five loaves of bread and a brace of fish.'

'We could, if others followed our example.'

'And there you have it,' Wulfric grinned in satisfaction. 'So tell me, Antony of Flanders, where are the ones who follow *your* example? Where are the ones who will add their bit to yours until the multitude is satisfied? It seems to me, my friend, that when you surrender your supper to the needy, you merely elect to go hungry in his stead. The balance is maintained, but never altered.'

'They would follow a man like you,' Antony declared. 'Give but a fraction of your wealth to those in need, feed the hungry from your own table, clothe the naked, and every priest of any substance here will follow your example.'

Wulfric's laugh was bitter. 'I envy you your faith in our fellow-man. In truth these priests would scoff at my back and pray for my hasty decline into poverty.'

'And so you are justified in doing nothing?'

Wulfric shrugged his great shoulders but was prevented from making his reply by the sound of a loud commotion in the hall. There was a crash and the sound of breaking glass, followed by several voices calling for assistance. The monk and the priest hurried out together, and in the large hall found Cyrus de Figham collapsed on the floor amid a noisy gathering of clerks and servants.

'Stand back from him,' de Morthlund bellowed. 'Give the man air and space enough to breathe. And why is he still here? My instructions were that he should be given private rooms and left there to rest until he is fully recovered from his labours. The man is exhausted.'

Antony dropped to his knees and moved his hands rapidly over the fallen man's face and chest. He found the skin cool and dry, the heartbeat strong, and when he lifted one of the closed lids it was to reveal a healthy eye only a little reddened by fatigue and masonry dust. He sat back on his heels, convinced that the priest was conscious and well aware of his surroundings.

'The purse ... for the monk ... for Antony ... the purse ...'

On Wulfric de Morthlund's instructions the collapsed man was lifted up and carried towards the main staircase leading to the upper rooms. One man was set to clear the fallen dishes from the floor, another sent at a run to fetch fresh herbs and a sleeping draught from the Minster's infirmarian. Antony was left to hover in the background, sufficiently wise in the subtleties of men to suspect that this performance was entirely for his benefit.

When at last the fat man returned his full attention to his guest, he carried with him two jewelled goblets brimming with wine, one of which he offered to the monk. Antony licked his lips but declined the offer with a gesture of thanks. He liked his wine no less than the next man, but he preferred to keep a clear head and a sharp mind in his dealings with these elusive secular priests.

Wulfric de Morthlund set the goblet aside and eyed his visitor as he sipped his own wine. The monk was in no way discomforted by his stare. This swarthy little man was a hard one to intimidate, but he had his weaknesses, and Wulfric knew them. With a flourish he loosed a soft leather pouch from his girdle and shook it until the contents jingled.

'This is the purse our brother Cyrus was so concerned about,' he said, tipping the contents out upon the table. His fingers touched upon a pile of silver marks, and one by one he picked them up and dropped them back into the purse, counting. 'He wants your dedicated and very admirable work rewarded. As you saw for yourself, the poor man could not rest until he knew it would be so.'

'A generous offer,' Antony said cautiously.

'Eleven, twelve, thirteen . . .'

'And yet an offer I feel I must refuse.'

'. . . nineteen, twenty. Cyrus was most insistent.'

'I work for God, not gain,' Antony insisted, then watched the coins as they were counted one by one on to the table.

'. . . twenty-seven, twenty-eight . . . so I believe . . . twenty-nine, thirty.' Wulfric jerked the thong that closed the neck, then held the bulging leather in his palm.

'And I may accept no payment in coin for my labours,' Antony reminded him.

'Then take it for your paupers and vagabonds.'

'It is food we need,' Antony reminded him. 'And medicines and blankets and water that is fit for men to drink. We have no use for silver coin in a town where nothing remains to buy and sell.'

Wulfric allowed his jaw to drop. He found the mild arrogance of this wiry little monk quite remarkable.

'Am I to understand that you reject this more than generous gift?'

'I do not refuse it,' Antony insisted. 'I merely ask that it be traded here, at its source, for the things we can no longer purchase on the streets.'

Wulfric considered that. 'It will be done as you request,' he said at last. 'And here is another small donation to your commendable cause.'

'A key?'

'It is,' Wulfric smiled, holding a large, ornate object between his finger and thumb. 'And it unlocks the door of the prebendary house in Keldgate where Sir Guy de Burton kept his daughter after the birth of her illegitimate child. The house has survived the storm with only superficial damage. You may consider it yours.'

'Mine? But that house is intended for the personal use of the Canons of St Martin's.'

'And not for a decade or more has any such canon put claim on it.'

'But now that Canon Bernard is dead, another man will claim it soon enough.'

Wulfric smiled. 'Cyrus de Figham will be old Bernard's successor, and he has little need of such a house. Besides, I hold the lease for two more years, paid for in gold.'

'And are you so sure that Father Cyrus will be elected Canon?' the monk asked.

Wulfric spread his hands and watched the other man's dark features. 'Trust me.'

Antony suppressed a wry comment in reply and said instead: 'You know we monks own nothing of our own, Father Wulfric. Why do you offer such a gift when I can neither turn it to profit nor take it for my personal comfort?'

The fat man shrugged. 'According to your preference, Brother Antony. What keeps one man in comfort and prosperity might well support a hundred with more frugal handling. Is that not what you teach?'

'I know it to be so.' Antony agreed, lifting his fingers briefly to remind the fat man of their lush surroundings.

'Well then, take possession of that fine old house for their sake.' He placed the key with the coins on the table and used one podgy finger to push them away from him. 'Shelter your homeless. Feed your poor. You have surely earned that privilege by your tireless dedication to their cause.'

'My lord, I am overwhelmed,' Antony said carefully, making a small formal bow and biting back the question uppermost in his mind. He knew this ambitious priest too well to suppose the gift was offered without terms.

'Consider this merely a beginning,' Wulfric smiled. 'Such stuff as you require to stock your house will be sent to you without delay and paid for by the Church. My good friend Cyrus and I insist upon it. You have earned the favour of powerful men, Antony of Flanders. From this day you have only to make known your needs and they will be fulfilled at our expense.'

'My lord, you are too kind.'

In spite of his misgivings, Antony's quick mind began to calculate the numbers he would be able to accommodate in

such a spacious house, the poor he would feed, the sick and
dying he would succour. He prayed he had erred in his hasty
criticism of these showy priests. It mattered not to a starving
man if his meal was offered in ostentatious fashion: all that
concerned him was the sustenance in the bowl.

'Well, man? What do you say? Have you swallowed your
tongue?'

'God bless you for the gift,' Antony said, signing the cross.

'And you for earning it,' de Morthlund responded. He
scowled and sucked thoughtfully on his lower lip. '... er,
there is just one small matter...'

'Oh?' Antony was instantly on his guard. The purse and
key had been pushed towards him across the gleaming top of
the table. Now the fat man drew them back a little way and
kept his hand poised above them, as if he were uncertain
whether to offer or reclaim the gift.

'I believe you have the ear of our lord Archbishop of
York?'

'I know him well.' Antony said truthfully.

'Are you aware he has been sent for?'

'What, out of Henry's court? I doubt the King will give him
leave to come.'

'But come he will, sooner or later, and he will want to know
what happened here.'

Antony smiled wryly. 'I believe there will be no scarcity of
reports.'

'But some he will trust more readily than others.'

'That may be so,' Antony agreed. 'He is a cautious man.'

Wulfric paused to push the purse and key a little closer to
the monk. If he had judged the man correctly, he was already
bought and paid for.

'Cyrus de Figham has proved himself a saintly man,
champion amongst his peers. I believe you can bear witness
to the fact.'

Antony drew back. 'I know what I have heard of him, no
more. Should I be challenged, I can but repeat what other
men are saying.'

'Oh come now,' Wulfric insisted. 'You know as well as I do

that a few well-chosen words from a man of character carry more weight than a thousand tales repeated by less trusted men. We need a record of events for the Archbishop and his clerks. And would you not agree that brother Cyrus deserves some small reward for his endeavours?'

'Christ taught that our reward shall be in Heaven,' Antony said carefully.

The purse moved back an inch or two, the fingers hovering. 'Indeed, but some of us deserve a little comfort on account.' The purse inched forward.

'I only know what I have heard from others. I can speak of very little at first-hand.'

One fat, pale finger moved the purse towards Antony. 'Cyrus de Figham toiled like a man possessed throughout the night.'

'So they say.'

'He saved the life of Father Paul when he dragged him from the rubble in the Minster.'

'To the fact there are witnesses,' Antony confirmed, 'though I was not amongst them.'

'And now he has collapsed under the strain of his good works.'

'So it would appear.'

'You saw as much just now with your own eyes.'

Antony held Wulfric's stare. 'I saw what I was meant to see.'

The purse moved a little closer. 'That same saintly man has sent this bag of silver for the benefit of the poor.'

Antony raised an eyebrow, matching Wulfric's gaze. 'If this is truly a gift, be sure the Archbishop will hear of it,' he said, reluctant to name the bribe for what it was.

'A gift for services rendered,' Wulfric smiled. 'A little comfort on account, for the good of those who look to you for their salvation. Have you the right to turn aside such generosity on their behalf? And one more thing ...'

'Can there be more?' Antony asked, unable to keep the sarcasm from his voice.

'For thirty marks and a house with well-stocked cellars?

Indeed there can be more, my friend. This priest of St Peter's, this crippled scribe, this *Simeon!*'

'No more the cripple,' Antony said. 'He is healed.'

'He is a liar and a charlatan.'

'By whose surmising?' Antony demanded hotly. 'Who dares to call him so? Who dares deny a truth as plain to see as the healing of that once-crippled foot?'

Wulfric de Morthlund placed both fists upon the table and leaned the great bulk of his upper body forward. Standing thus, his reflection lying across the wood's bright surface, he showed himself a giant force for any man to reckon with.

'*I* do!'

There was both challenge and malice in the statement. They stood this way for several moments, the big priest towering over the tough little monk, and the massive table, with its bulky leather purse and metal key, marking the chasm of differences between them. Antony believed that he now had the truth, the bitter kernel of the matter. The bag of silver, the fine old manor house, the guaranteed provisions, all these were merely bait with which to snare a man whose word and judgment were known to be respected by the Archbishop of York. Not much was asked of him. All he was required to do was speak out for one man and renounce the other, and upon his decision rested the lives and well-being of the poor.

'You strike a savage bargain, Wulfric de Morthlund,' he said bitterly.

'Needs must, since the poor are with you always,' Wulfric replied with a smile.

Antony nodded his full understanding of the bargain. 'Be warned that I will not be influenced to bear false witness, neither against a man nor in his favour. I speak the truth or else I choose to hold my words unspoken.'

'So be it,' Wulfric declared. 'We do not ask for lies, only that you select your words and measure your silences with the utmost care. Cyrus de Figham must become the golden face of the coin, Simeon de Beverley its tarnished underside. And be sure that the same coin, given into the hands of our lord

Archbishop of York, will purchase a dependable living for your hungry hoards.'

'You challenge my integrity...'

'Not so. I make you an honest offer, nothing more. You remain quite free to shape and colour your precious integrity as you think most prudent.'

Antony smiled grimly at that. 'Integrity, sir, is not a thing to be trimmed to fit the moment.'

'When the Good Lord bestowed free will upon his creation, He gave man leave to bridle the tyranny of his conscience,' Wulfric countered. 'Only the Saints are the helpless serfs of their own integrity. Real men are masters of it.' His smile was mocking. 'Or do you aspire to be counted amongst the Saints, Brother Antony?'

'If so, it would be an honourable aim.'

'And the grateful poor would lift you up while the sick sang out your praises,' Wulfric grinned. 'And let us not forget the many lepers you have protected, the children you have saved from harm, the faithless you have brought back to God. Ah yes, yours is the stuff true saints are made of.'

'You misjudge me, sir. I work in God's service, to do as he intended. I seek no personal advancement.'

'A saint indeed.'

Antony shook his head. 'God knows my heart.'

'Then who am I to doubt it?' Wulfric conceded. He brought the monk's attention back to the money lying on the table. 'You must decide this matter at your leisure, my friend. Inspect the manor house for yourself. List your needs in food and wine, furniture, blankets and medicines.' He spread his hands to indicate that the gift was limitless. 'See for yourself how generous Cyrus de Figham and I can be to those in our service.'

'In your service?' Antony echoed. He knew he had it all now, every subtle shade and nuance of the deal. Wulfric de Morthlund had set a price on need, and with that price he would buy himself a man.

Wulfric scooped up the purse and tossed it across the table. Its contents jangled as it struck the monk's chest and his thin hands came up to grab it. The priest believed the contract as good as sealed, for greed was far more powerful than compassion, and few men could resist temptation once it actually rested in their fingers.

'Take your time,' he smiled. 'Come back tomorrow or the next day with your final decision, then we will fix the terms and establish exactly what you are to say, and not to say, to my lord Archbishop when he arrives in Beverley. God's blessing, Brother Antony.'

The dismissal was abrupt. The fat man bowed and waddled from the room.

'God's blessing,' Antony muttered at his back.

Left alone in the room, the monk stared down at the ornate key and weighed the bulging purse of silver in the palm of his hand. The ways of men must sometimes be enough to make God hang His head and weep with disappointment. The world turned, the seasons blossomed and faded according to their long established cycles, and a thousand years after Jesus Christ's betrayal a man could still be bought and sold for thirty pieces of silver.

CHAPTER TWENTY

The priests of St Peter's buried their dead in hallowed ground behind the stricken church, in the narrow strip between the rear wall and the boundary ditch. The bodies were set down shoulder to shoulder in the narrow trench, a total of thirty-seven corpses interred in a single hasty ceremony. Here lay the drowned, the crushed, the suffocated, those who were victims of the disaster and those who had died by the sword in the infirmary. Here the priest lay down beside the humble servant, the monk beside the pastry cook, the servant with the tradesman. There were no markings to note the names of those who rested together in the trench. Such things would be added at another time, when the grave was no longer at risk of desecration by stakers.

The Sister of Mercy murdered by the soldiers had been carried back to her convent on a handcart, her violated body shrouded in clean white linen. The nun who had shared her ordeal went with the cart, silent and dry-eyed as she limped behind, the burden of her degradation heavy on her shoulders. When the little party reached the convent gates she was no longer following in their footsteps. Somewhere between the Fishmarket and Keldgate Bar she had simply altered course and walked away. In the aftermath of the storm, when every street and alleyway was clogged with fallen rubble and lawless scavengers, no lives were risked in going after her.

In a quiet corner behind St Peter's was a tiny grave, unmarked and well concealed in the shaded angle of the walls. Here rested the body of Elvira's son, baptised and buried as the church required. She named him with his father's name and did not uncover his face before she laid him in the ground with her own hands. Then she placed a candle for him on the damaged altar of St Peter. She asked the saint to carry her child to Heaven. She shed no tears: the time for tears was past.

'I kept my promise, child,' was all she told him. 'I paid the fee. God will accept you now.'

When she left the grave it was, for her, a final parting. Her child was gone and the living had no right to encroach upon those places given over to the dead. He had shared her world for the briefest of times before slipping away to a place where she could not follow after him. Their worlds were different now: she would not visit the little grave again.

Osric the infirmarian came to Elvira while she knelt before the altar of St Peter. Two priests were standing off at a discreet distance, watchful of her safety. She knelt upon the rubble as if uncaring of its roughness, her head lowered and her lips moving silently in prayer. One end of the altar had been destroyed when the great bronze bell was thrown down in the storm. Now only a single portion of the main slab remained, balanced upon a mound of broken stones and roofing timbers, marking the place where seven good men had died.

Osric touched Elvira's arm. 'A man has come in search of you. He waits in the infirmary.'

'What man?'

'He gave his name as Erik, and by the width of his back and the deep scars on his forearms I would guess he is a ditcher. He claims to be your lawful husband and asks if you are here. Two clerks are with him, ready to bear witness to your safe return to the man who is your lord and master.'

'Send him away.'

217

'Think carefully on it, woman,' Osric cautioned.

'I will not go with him.' There was neither doubt nor defiance in her voice. Her face was calm, her huge dark eyes untroubled, and she allowed no space for argument when she said again: 'I will not go with him.'

'So be it,' Osric nodded, and moved away, leaving her to her privacy at the altar. He had hoped it would not come to this. He had wished the ditcher lost in the storm, or else content to count his missing wife amongst the dead. Now he must swear that Elvira was unknown to him, for the truth, like her, was better kept behind closed doors, lest it provoke the ditcher to claim his rights more forcefully, or to carry his grievance to a higher authority. Osric was forced to seek the calmer course. He could hardly confess Elvira's presence here at St Peter's, and then deny the man all access to her, for such a stand would represent a challenge that must be met.

Erik the ditcher was not uncommon in appearance: of middle height and stocky, well-muscled as his work demanded, with a broad, intelligent face beneath his thatch of red-brown hair. He wore strong braes, bound up from knee to ankle, and leathers that had worn thin in several places, but there was a handsome girdle at his waist, a good warm cloak about his shoulders and the smell of expensive liquor on his breath. He turned to his two companions when Osric had firmly closed the door upon his polite enquiry.

'You said I would find her here,' he complained.

The tallest of the two clerks took a small pouch from his cloak and handed it to the young man. 'Not so, my friend. We merely suggested that you ask for her here.'

Erik took the pouch and shook it until the coins inside were jangling. The sound brought first a smile and then a dryness to his lips, for he had more passion for his cups that ever he had for his wife. 'She is not here,' he said, and shrugged his shoulders.

'No matter,' the clerk said lightly, turning up his cowl and drawing his arms into the folds of his cloak. 'We will bring you back in a day or two to ask for her again. Good day to you, master ditcher.'

They turned their backs and walked away, and did not notice the grey-clad woman who, flanked by two tall priests, left the little church with her head still bowed and crossed the grounds to the door of the scriptorium.

The days after the tempest revealed the town of Beverley at its worst. Overnight this bustling centre of trade and commerce had become a place of ruin. Where once it had risen proudly from the marshes, now it was left half-drowned and humiliated. With their senses dulled in the after-shock, Beverley's survivors stumbled blindly through the debris of their lives. Such swift and meaningless destruction was beyond their understanding. They feared that they were at the mercy of a wrathful God, the helpless victims of such divine retribution as could call up the very elements against them. They cringed and grovelled before such wrath, hastening to confess their sins and bare their souls that they might continue to be spared. And in their fear they left themselves exposed to more worldly dangers. There is a law of Nature dictating that out of despair, pestilence or disaster, those of least need shall reap the greatest succour: the weak are rendered subject to the strong. For a time this natural order of things prevailed in Beverley, giving the ruthless and the wicked the ruling hand. Respectable men shook off the constraints of honesty. Petty thieves stepped lightly into the ways of murderers, cut-purses looked for flesh to whet their blades, bullies became tyrants and these, in their turn, moved on to higher things. Women armed themselves with knives and swords, metal spikes and clubs, and banded together in defensive groups. All through the perilous nights some kept keen watch over their sleeping companions, waiting their own turn to lie secure beneath the blanket.

The priests' procession had marked the turning point. Little by little, reassured, the town began to reassert itself. Rough justice then became the order of the day. A band of stakers, caught at their grisly practices, were hanged in Butcher Row and their bodies left to rot there as a deterrent to those who shared their work. Looters were beaten with sticks or slashed with knives, while thieves and cut-purses risked losing their fingers or their noses to the vigilante's blade.

At St Anne's convent outside the Keldgate Bar a state of open hostility existed between Sir Hugh de Burton and Robert de Clare of York. The Archbishop's man was in control. His army of clerks dogged the movements of Burton's soldiers and maintained a written record of their activities, both at the convent and in the stricken town. At the same time he deployed his own small body of retainers as guards between the Sisters of Mercy and their uninvited guests, making his own men conspicuous protectors of the innocent. Every meal was costed, every candle noted, and in the stables even the keeping of the horses was scrupulously accounted for. Whatever the outcome of the present stalemate, Robert de Clare would sting this arrogant knight in his most tender places, his reputation and his purse. And in the privacy of her apartments, the Lady Abbess instructed her auditors and clerks to keep an equally detailed tally of the hospitality claimed by Sir Robert. Whichever way the final balance tipped, the convent would lose not a penny-worth of profit. Lady Constance was as shrewd as any man, and would not be the loser in their quarrels.

Between the two of them, these powerful enemies maintained a peace, of sorts, that was to Beverley's benefit. Both were on their best behaviour, since neither would willingly furnish the other with proof of his own imperfections. The Archbishop's favour was at stake, and through that favour the coveted Provost's seat. And so the soldiers were brought to heel and kept under strict control. They were put to work clearing the rubble of collapsed dwellings, made to unblock the streams and ditches choked by the debris of the storm and rebuild the humble shelters of the populace. As each man sought to ingratiate himself by stepping in to preserve the Archbishop's interests, those under his command were just as determined to curry favour with the common folk. When the master prospered, so too did his minions, and what was denied the soldiers at the convent could be

220

discreetly bought in any side street where a family had a daughter.

The Archbishop's house in the Cornmarket had suffered more damage from looters than from the elements. It stood overlooking the market cross, an imposing two-story house of local stone, with splendid painted windows and a great oak door that might have been carved for his Minster Church of St Peter itself in York. The door had not been breached, for who would dare attack those sculpted saints who were guardians of that place? The looters had entered by way of the lesser door through which the servants had fled when the storm was at its height. They had carried away what goods they could, and left untouched those items that, if discovered on their person, would brand them not only as looters but as desecrators. With an eye to his own advantage, Robert de Clare had set his men to repairing the damage and had arranged to restock the Archbishop's cellars at his own expense. Sir Hugh de Burton, not to be out-flanked, had responded by setting a force of men to guard the hall throughout the day and another to stand guard all night long. And so that the people of Beverley should know who did these things on behalf of their lord Archbishop, the pennants of the manors of de Clare and de Burton were fixed above those saintly figures carved in the great oak door.

Immediately after the office of Sect, the priests sat down to their main meal of the day, the noon-time meal, when refectory tables sagged beneath the weight of succulent meats and poultries, bulging pastries and generously stuffed puddings. Enough furniture had been salvaged from the rubble to seat them all in comfort, and in the midst of hardship every cup was filled. The monk, Antony, remarked to Wulfric de Morthlund that the poor stood off but a little way, hollow and empty in the midst of plenty.

'Should we be made to starve because they hunger?' Wulfric asked.

'Should they be made to starve because you don't?' Antony countered.

'God knows what He's about,' the fat man said, 'The rich are with you always, like the poor. Some would agree He strikes a healthy balance.'

'I do not doubt He would,' Antony conceded, 'if only his priests would let Him.'

Wulfric guffawed, but his eyes were cold. He looked along a double line of priests, some listening with half an ear to the exchange, others too intent upon their plates to note the impassioned opinions of a monk. Not half their number turned their heads as Wulfric de Morthlund hauled his richly robed body from the bench, reached over with both hands and took up the nearest dish of roasted starlings. A young clerk made a hasty grab to claim his share before the huge platter was handed to the monk.

'Take it,' de Morthlund said. 'You have the means to feed your wretches, Brother monk, if you are prepared to take from those you so despise.'

Antony looked into the dish. It contained at least a score of the little birds, all stuffed with a walnut paste and wrapped in well-browned pastry strips. In the base of the dish was a pool of golden juices, in itself sufficient nourishment to keep a starving man alive. Above the dish he met the glittering gaze of Wulfric de Morthlund. He had caught the double meaning in the offer, and would take the smiling fat man at his word. He reached for a basket laden with loaves of bread, tipped the warm contents into the dish with the starlings, took it with both hands and left the hall by its main doors. He heard the laughter following on his heels and thought it small cost indeed for such a feast.

Outside the refectory building ragged men and women were gathered, many with waif-like children in their tow, all drawn there by the tolling of the noon-time bell and the tantalising scent of roasting meat. They surged towards the little monk as he emerged from the refectory door. Thin, dirty hands like talons reached to snatch the food away, and in a moment nothing remained but the clay dish, scraped clean of grease and stain, lying in shattered pieces on the ground. Men snatched from their wives and women from their children, and those too small or too weak to snatch at all looked out through hollow and accusing eyes while others prospered. And when the food was gone not one of them was truly fed. Those first in line had tasted and gone short; those at the rear had tasted not at all.

Antony extricated himself from that place with difficulty, for the poor would have trailed behind him aimlessly but for the promise of scraps still to be had when the priests had eaten their fill. He had not seen Simeon in the main refectory and hoped to find him within the enclosure of his own church of St Peter. On his way there he noticed that a crowd was gathering at the lower end of Eastgate, between St Peter's wall and the Minster Yard. People were running from every direction to swell its numbers, from the Minster doors, from the Flemingate Bar and Moorgate, and from the other directions where the stricken markets lay. As he drew closer he saw a face he recognised, the two-toned, twin-sided face of Michael, the disfigured priest.

'What is it?' he demanded, grabbing the younger man by the arm. 'Do you know what's happening?'

Michael turned his head to squint at Antony through his misshaped left eye. That side of his mouth was also pulled and twisted by the cruel, violet-coloured stain on his face and neck. He spoke through it with difficulty, raising his voice above the shouts of the people all around him: 'A man is dead and a priest is trying to raise him. They say the priest is Simeon. They say a miracle is taking place. Let me go. I must see this.'

He was gone in a moment, plunging into the thicker part of the crowd and shouldering his way to the front for a better view of what was taking place. Now Antony, swept closer by the press of the crowd, could see that a man was lying on the ground, as still as death, with a cluster of curious onlookers mushrooming around him. Those who were closest to the source of interest speculated knowingly on his predicament.

'I heard he was struck down by a fall of rock,' a man said, confidently.

'Not so,' declared another. 'It was a slate from the Minster roof itself. An act of God, by any reckoning.'

'Nay, he was struck down by thieves is how I heard it. Robbed and left for dead,' a gruff voice said.

Only one thing did the watchers agree upon: that if Simeon could not save him, no man could.

Antony stood cautiously on the crowd's perimeter, jostled and elbowed by those who sought to gain a better view. He had glimpsed the fair-haired priest kneeling beside the fallen man, and had seen the ring of clerics holding back the press of curious townspeople. That young fanatic Vincent was among them, his face upraised and his hands tightly clasped as he called upon Almighty God to send down a miracle. He had a group of devotees now, those clerks and monks who hung upon his every word, sucked in by the persuasive forces of religious fervour. They were drawn to his passion like moths drawn to a flame, a dangerous attraction.

Only a short time earlier, Simeon had been at the grammar school, in the little beamed cell now permanently occupied by the distressed boy, Stephen. The priest had been sitting cross-legged on the floor, speaking in low and soothing tones as he tried to coax the lad out of the nightmare that still held him in its grip. For his part Stephen had kept to his tight, safe corner, his body crouched, his eyes staring at nothing, rocking to and fro upon his grief. Antony had stood in the doorway and watched them there, the big priest and the cowering boy, and he had seen more distance set between them than ever that little room could hope to accommodate.

Now the grim-faced monk began to circle the tighter knot of people that marked the inner circle of the crowd. He was a small man and tough enough to force his way between them. Those who were offended by the sharpness of his elbows stopped short of complaint when they saw his cowled monk's habit. At last he drew close enough to see the man who was lying on the ground, white-faced, unmoving, with a long wound on one side of his head that poured blood into his sandy-coloured hair. Whether minor hurt or mortal injury he could not tell, for the scalp, that thing of meagre substance, bleeds profusely when it is undone. He saw that Simeon's hands were on the young man's chest, directing the ribs to rise and fall so that the lungs inside might be filled and emptied at a steady rate. He worked thus while his companions held back the crowd, and all who watched him drew in and expelled their own breaths to the rhythm of his hands.

Antony had come in search of Simeon in the hope of setting his own troubled mind at ease. For days now he had been wrestling with his conscience, weighing his peace of mind, and Simeon's friendship, against his obligations to the poor. There were so many holding out their empty bowls, so many mouths to feed, bodies to heal and hearts to ease. Word had gone out ahead of him, if not on Wulfric de Morthlund's express instructions then certainly with his blessing, that food and shelter were to be had at the prebendary house in Keldgate. And so the poor had flocked there from all quarters of the town. They made their beds on the rushes, bringing their hopes and their empty bowls to him. Other monks, many of whom had journeyed to Beverley in response to news of the tragedy, hastened to locate the 'House of Antony' and place themselves at his disposal. And he in his turn was pressed to close the deal that would make him the rightful master of the house. If he refused de Morthlund, he would be obliged to take up those sorry remnants of humanity and return them, body by body, to the streets.

He stood now in the heart of the crowd in Eastgate, and he could feel the same ripple of anticipation that touched them all. With Simeon's help, the prostrate man was at last making some effort to raise his head. Dazed and confused, he moaned and cried out loudly for a priest, and as neatly as a company of soldiers under orders, the crowd stood back two paces and sucked in a collective gasp.

'Praise God in his mercy,' Antony breathed as he watched the priest sign the cross on forehead, lips and breast and then sit back on his heels with his eyes tightly closed in prayer.

The young man, seated now, held his blood-splattered

head in both his hands and moved it cautiously as if to test that it was still securely placed upon his neck.

'A miracle,' someone whispered.

'He raised a dead man,' a small, awed voice exclaimed. 'The priest has raised a dead man.'

A man behind Antony, a short man who was newly arrived on the scene and could not have witnessed anything at all, began to speak with urgency to those who stood closest to him.

'I saw it all,' he declared in his most authoritative tone. 'The man was dead. Quite dead. And now he lives. Just as Lazarus was raised from his tomb at Bethany by our Lord Christ, so this man here . . . what name does he go by . . .?'

'Thomas. He is Thomas, the salter's son,' a woman called out.

'. . . so this man here, this salter's son, Thomas, was snatched from death and returned to the living by our own priest, Simeon.'

'Simeon! Simeon! Simeon!'

The name of the priest was passed from lip to lip until it ran this way along Eastgate toward the town and that way to the open Minster doors.

'A miracle,' someone shouted.

'Lazarus raised again,' another cried.

'We all saw it. We all saw the dead man raised.'

'I too! I have seen the miracle!'

Their voices shrilled with wonder, bellowed belligerently, whispered in tones of awe, and everywhere the excitement and the speculation grew. It was Brother Vincent, clutching the strip of cloth from Simeon's robes and holding it like a precious trophy above his head, who reined in the crowd and brought the people to their knees in prayer. Only three men were left standing, three to tower above the crouched multitude with their rounded backs and lowered heads. Here was Vincent, his face lit with rapture as his voice rang out like a clear, strong peal of bells giving thanks for a man's deliverance. Here too was Simeon, pale and speechless, standing as if his clenched fists and tight features were all

226

that held him on his feet. And here was Antony the monk, who had seen and heard the swift play of falsehood over expectation turn the crowd from here to there with uncanny, almost sinister ease. Every man and woman gathered there was certain of what their eye had witnessed, and none with more conviction that those whose position in the crowd ensured that they had seen nothing.

The young man, Thomas, the salter's son, who had been struck down by a robber from behind, still sat on the ground, bewildered by it all. He knew only what his eyes and ears now told him, that he had been murdered and reclaimed, that by some miracle he had cheated death. He fell prostrate before the priest, clutched at his robes and kissed his sandals, sobbing his thanks for the gift of a second lifespan.

'*It is not so!*'

The voice of Simeon of Beverley was deep and carried far. It weighted the words with the emphasis of one who feels the sting of injustice to his very soul. No innocent man, wickedly accused of some horrendous crime, could have summed up such indignation in but four small words.

The short hairs at the nape of Antony's neck lifted up and his scalp turned prickly at the sound of it. He heard a shout and turned his head, and there was Osric with two other men coming at a run from St Peter's. They cut a rough way through the crouching bodies, reached Simeon's side and began to lead him, flanked for his own protection, back the way they had come.

'Not dead but stunned,' he heard the big priest say in protest. 'He was merely out of his senses for the moment. His breath was laboured and shallow, but the wound was light, the skull undamaged. As God is my judge, the man was only *stunned.*'

Antony sucked in his breath until it whistled sharply through his teeth. No words of Simeon's, however sincere, would keep this crowd contained. It was too late for that. Already the story was leaping from mouth to mouth, gathering embellishment the way a humming bird, passing from flower to flower, collects the nectar. Let any dare repeat those words of Simeon's, let any dare argue that the boy was not dead but stunned, and these believers might strike him down for his blasphemy.

A voice in his ear claimed the monk's attention. 'This will not please his enemies.'

Antony looked up into the sharply chiselled features of Daniel, companion-priest to the fat man, Wulfric de Morthlund. He did not trust this handsome Little Hawk, for any man bought for a penny might be traded again for two, and every word from a bought man's lips must be weighed and measured and even then might prove as hollow as a blown egg.

'This is a travesty,' Antony declared. 'Look at them. See for yourself what gullible fools they are. They look for a miracle and so they see one, and harm their own souls in the process. It is an unhappy business.'

'Aye,' Daniel nodded. 'And someone must contain it before it runs beyond control.'

Antony was unable to keep the irritation from his voice. 'If you are concerned to silence the voices that shout on Simeon's behalf, look first to the loudest one amongst them.' He lifted and extended his right arm to point out the figure of Brother Vincent brandishing its precious strip of embroidered cloth. 'He is the catalyst. He whips up the force by which the mob is moved. He so adores the man he serves that he is blind to the simple fact that he serves him not at all by his extreme behaviour. The cleric is in error here, not the priest.'

'The fault is his, perhaps, but the enemies are Simeon's.'

'Then let them look to the real culprit and silence that crowing tongue before it ...' He broke off abruptly, aware that his voice was thick with anger and his finger still pointing accusingly at Vincent. He drew back his hand and shook his head. No man deserved to be condemned for his dedication, however misguided the cause.

'Your words are duly noted, Brother,' Daniel said, and there was a certain smugness in his smile.

'Forgive me for speaking in haste and anger. My words

were in no way intended to . . .'

'Listen to me.' There was a sharpness now in Daniel's voice, and the smile had slid from his face to leave a hardness in its stead. 'When poppies grow too tall they lose their heads. You would be wise to remind your friend of that. If you would protect him from his enemies, curtail his growth before they feel the need to chop him down.'

As quickly as he had come, the Hawk was gone. The crowd that opened at his face closed swiftly at his back and he was swallowed up. Antony stood looking after him long after he was lost from sight. The warning was not for Vincent but for Simeon, who gained new height not from ambition or self-interest, but from being lifted, albeit against his will, above the commonplace: and either way he might well be in danger of losing his head.

CHAPTER TWENTY-ONE

In Latin the solemn voice intoned: 'We commend to thee, O Lord, the soul of thy Servant.'

Canon Bernard of St Martin's was buried in a muddy patch of ground in a quiet corner of the Provost's moated Garth. The makeshift walkways set atop the flood-water were still in place, though bearing now a layer of mud where the feet of many priests had pressed them down. The spot chosen to receive the body of the Canon lay at the rear of the Provost's house. It had for many years provided a retreat for the senior canons, a quiet corner where a man might go to look into his deeper thoughts, or merely to nod some time away. It was a small rectangular garth cut from the larger ground between the herb garden and the meadow. Its high stone walls were generously clad in creeping ivy, and at its open end a massive oak, said to have stood its ground for half a century, still spread its great trunk and limbs from wall to wall. Canon Bernard had sat beneath that very oak, well wrapped against the winter's chill, only the day before his savage death. He had favoured a wooden bench in the western corner, where he was wont to sit long hours away, content to contemplate the private worlds of thoughts and images behind his eyelids. Now he lay in a lead-lined coffin, his fine mind and his gentle tongue silenced forever.

'I must speak out for him,' Simeon whispered, and again, a little louder: 'I must speak out.'

Standing beside him, Brother Richard scowled and twisted the cord of his simple crucifix in and out between his fingers. He knew the dilemma tormenting Simeon. It kept the big priest awake at night, and today he had begged leave to abandon High Mass before the holy sacrament was ended. Now he had been summoned to give account of himself before the secular canons. Cuthbert himself had demanded it, for he was astute and wise to the many subtleties of ambitious men. His priest had become the victim of an insidious conspiracy, and in all innocence was playing himself into the hands of his enemies. Cuthbert could not stand idly by while such men as Wulfric de Morthlund and Cyrus de Figham, priests of no small authority in the absence of their canons, repeated such whispers from the gutters of Beverley as would paint a saint with the colours of a rogue. The least they said of Simeon now was that his conscience pricked, and by avoiding Mass he endorsed the lie. He would face the canons and hold himself to account, or Cuthbert himself would know the reason why. Such troubles as Simeon obviously bore might well be misinterpreted as guilt. It must be expunged, and soon, before vile rumour hung so many sins upon his shoulders that the good countenance of his peers was lost.

At the head of the grave the priest in his deep, clear tones cried out: '*Kyrie, eleison* . . . Lord, have mercy.'

And the choir and mourners responded: '*Christe eleison* . . . Christ have mercy.'

Richard looked down at his sandals and saw that they had sunk so far into the mud that what remained of his feet appeared grotesquely misshapen. His winter boots were hanging to dry in the current of warm air rising from one of the infirmary stoves. He had been helping to clear the network of waterways that crossed St Peter's grounds. He had found two bodies trapped in a culvert there, and in the process of dragging them out his boots had suffered at their stitched seam. And so he had been obliged to wear simple

231

sandals when he paid his last respects to Canon Bernard.

'I must, I must speak out,' Simeon muttered again.

Richard nodded grimly. To witness a good man wrestling, as Simeon now did, with a divided conscience and an uncertain heart, could pain a man as if the other's affliction were his own. He stared down at the mud-streaked stumps above his sunken feet. The chill of this place had penetrated to the very marrow of his bones. It saddened him to think of Father Bernard, that well-loved, gentle man, lying alone in such a lonely spot. Come summertime the garden would be planted bright and colourful, with wonderful scents and twittering birds and insects hanging on the hot, still air. But that was summer, still half a year away. For now the dear man's body was received into the bleakest of resting places.

Lost in his thoughts, he turned to leave with the others as the choir began to recite the long, hypnotic Litany of the Saints. With a start he remembered his sandalled feet firmly rooted in the mud and, too late to regain his shifted balance, pitched sideways with his arms askew. Simeon caught him fast and steadied him, his face creased and his eyes dark with concern.

'I'm stuck,' Richard explained in a rasping whisper, catching the stern edge of Canon Cuthbert's glance. 'My feet are held fast in the mud. I cannot move.'

'*Spiritus Sancte, Deus*,' the cantor recited, and those who were gathered replied: '*Miserere nobis*.'

Without breaking his own stride, Simeon grasped his friend and yanked him upward, freeing his feet from the cloying mud with a loud and lusty squelch.

They went from the burial ground directly to the Provost's Hall, where a low stone trough filled to its brim with water had been set outside the door. The priests were expected to paddle through the trough from end to end, rinsing away the mud before stepping, clean-shoed if not too comfortable, into the house. Those wearing boots thought nothing of the encounter. Those wearing sandals, as Richard did, were swift to learn that what ran in ran out again with equal ease, and that

232

skin already cold as ice became indifferent to secondary chills.

In the hall the seven Canons were duly represented, as was the absent Provost and his dead Chancellor. Lavishly garbed and splendid in their dignity, these very important men took their appropriate seats with much solemnity, marking their hierarchy by the careful placing of their ornate chairs. The Provost's seat was raised above the rest, with the high stools of his senior clerks set close behind him. Then came the Canons, St Martin's first, for that was the wealthiest prebend of them all and, being the parish church, the most significant. That position, left vacant by poor Bernard's untimely death, was represented now by Father Fabian, a priest already enjoying the fullest measure of his allotted three score years and ten. Though for the moment he graced St Martin's chair, no one supposed that he, semi-retired and already half-way into his dotage, was a serious candidate for such an office.

Wulfric de Morthlund and Cyrus de Figham were also highly placed among the Canons, for they were powerful men to whom the others were predisposed to acquiesce, preferring their goodwill to their animosity. If the prebends they represented fell a little lower in importance than did some of their neighbours, the men themselves, and the reach of their influence, did not.

Each canon had brought a priest or clerk to tally the small particulars of the meeting. They were informed that Father Cuthbert had requested the meeting on a serious matter, and serious indeed it must be, for they had been directed from the burial of Canon Bernard while the Litany and the last prayers were yet to be recited. Beyond the windows priests were still singing the old man to his rest. He would not miss the few who had left so early, and if he did he would forgive them for it: he was never a man to nurture a resentment.

Among the lesser notables were several Simeon knew: young Daniel Hawk, as elegant as always, and John, the exorcist, who gained in confidence with every gift with which his master sought to buy his loyalty.

The priest's attention soon rested upon that Nero among modern men, Wulfric de Morthlund. The man had changed tremendously since Simeon saw him last. Just days after his humiliation in that draughty chapel, he was no more the snivelling knave dressed in a prickly hairshirt. Instead, he was undoubtedly himself again, the true Wulfric de Morthlund, superbly attired, grand-posturing and arrogant. Simeon was only briefly astonished that the man's demeanour had undergone such a swift and dramatic reversal. From autocrat to penitent and back again within the week: he surely was a man of many facets. It did not come as any great surprise, for a man who was wont to turn his colours inside to outside on a sudden whim, was just as likely to turn them back again. Simeon had done his duty as was required of him. If de Morthlund defaulted now in seeking the higher authority recommended to him, if he preferred to discard the hairshirt for the silken vestments of borrowed office, then that was his God-given right and privilege. The soul hung out in jeopardy was his own: no man could know that better than himself.

Sitting quietly among the rustling robes and whispered voices, Simeon felt himself to be at a gathering of peacocks, and he wondered if he had been too long around common men and monks to appreciate this show of excellence. For the better part of a week he had toiled alongside dark-robed monks and priests and ragged workmen in the streets or within the confines of St Peter's enclosure. And so the untarnished finery of the church seemed garish now, as if it shone with the brightness of poor men's tears. Somehow the mud on Brother Richard's feet seemed noble by comparison.

When called upon to stand and give account of his actions during Mass, he told of the discovery of Father Bernard's body in the barest manner, unembellished by any additions of his own, until the end of it, when all that remained was for him to make his point.

'Every detail can be corroborated by Brother Richard here, an honest man who fears God as he should,' he said. 'As for myself, I am neither fanciful nor a fool. I see these cruel facts as speaking clearly for themselves. Canon Bernard was praying when he was struck down from behind by a heavy tread-stone loosened from the stair. That stone could not have shifted of its own accord, nor has a thing of any weight the power to fall upward, as it must if he were to be struck, as we at first suspected, by a fall of rock. He was not alone in the stair well, nor did he lose his life at the hands of Providence. However I wrestle to turn the fact aside, I am left with the unhappy truth that he was murdered.'

'*Murdered!*' The word passed through the room like a blast of unsavoury air. It left its mark on every face in turn. There was disbelief and anger written there, a sense of outrage and a hint of personal fear. How many of them had known as much, he wondered, but lacked the courage to give the knowledge voice. Now it was out at last, now he could set aside the burden that had never been his, by right, to struggle under. Now these worthy canons must decide what course, if any, was most appropriate to the circumstances. No neighbouring bishop would risk offence by stepping in to sanctify their altar, for all bishops were fiercely jealous of their territory, and Roger de Pont L'Evèque, Archbishop of York, was no exception. He would as soon make direct and bitter complaint to his Holiness the Pope as quarrel with a bordering bishop over rights of jurisdiction. His fury would fly to Rome and back again, feeding upon itself with every mile. It was a formidable weapon, that Archbishop's anger. It had been tested out on kings. Whatever else, the Canons recognised at once their true dilemma. If murder had been committed within their church, then the holy sacraments must be withheld until the altar could be properly reconsecrated. A bishop was needed here, but none would come, not to encroach upon Roger de Pont's dominion. Yet the law was clear and could not be avoided. The Holy Mass must not be said, for the altar was defiled.

Simeon held silent now while all those present whispered amongst themselves. For a moment he met his Canon's gaze and saw in Cuthbert's eyes that he had been correct in speaking out. Some distance away, Wulfric de Morthlund was shaking his head and smiling as if the matter were quite beyond all credence. And every man, from time to time, glanced back at Simeon's solemn face to mark what truths or untruths were written there. All men but one, for Cyrus de Figham kept his eyes averted. The man had remained quite motionless in his seat while Simeon spoke, his stare firmly fixed some inches from the ground. Despite his stillness, de Figham was on edge, as well he might be, for as Bernard's priest, close by him through the night offices, suspicion must first fall on him. Simeon had expected an open challenge from de Figham, but instead he found the slate-coloured eyes avoiding a confrontation. For reasons as yet between himself and God, Cyrus de Figham chose not to meet the eye of his accuser.

'Why have you maintained your silence all this time, Simeon of Beverley?' The ring of authority was in Cuthbert's voice. He would have his priest explain himself in full, before some other, self-interested party sought to do it for him, to his disadvantage.

Simeon looked steadily back at Father Cuthbert. He saw the old man's intention well enough, and with a movement of his head he silently thanked him for it.

'I kept my silence for the best of reasons,' he replied. 'I sought to spare poor Bernard's companions the knowledge that they might harbour a cruel killer in their midst. And I sought as well to spare the innocent people of our town. They have suffered a terrible tragedy here, with death and injury, loss and confusion at every turn. To bar the altar in the aftermath of that would have been to snatch the last hope from their reach. We all saw their desperate need of the Church, their unwavering trust in the blessings to be had here. I could not bring myself to instigate the barring of the altar merely on my own suspicions, not then, not when it seemed that all we had to do instead was wait, and the Archbishop would come to our aid.'

Now the Provost's representative, a clever, sharp-minded man of less than forty years, leaned forward in his seat to have his say. Jacob de Wold had been twelve years a secular priest, though of late he had come to prefer his orchards and his parks to the limitations of holy office. He watched Simeon closely, feeling that he had the measure of this blue-eyed priest, knowing him to be an honest man and stubborn to a fault. This Simeon had found favour with Cuthbert since the day his father handed him over to the Church: no mean achievement when Cuthbert, although compassionate to his fellow man, kept himself aloof from human closeness. Too much was being said of this priest, and all of it to extremes. For a mild-mannered man, a dedicated scribe who preferred to live in industrious isolation, this handsome young priest had the power to move men to excessive passion.

'Unfortunately, my lord Archbishop has been delayed,' Jacob announced. 'The king was good enough to grant him leave of absence from the royal court, and he was coming here in haste, so I believe. Then his party broke its journey at Roger's castle near Lincoln, and there he has been delayed on a pressing matter.'

'Pressing?' Simeon echoed. 'By all that's holy, what matter could be half so pressing as the one right here, on his own doorstep? We have hundreds of dead and injured, as many lost without trace, two thirds of the town made homeless at a stroke. Our churches are damaged or left in total ruin, our priests are dead, our altars desecrated. What place in the whole of Christendom could have more pressing need of him than this?'

Jacob spread his hands and shook his head. He had been told that Simeon of Beverley loved his God, his Church and his town with equal passion. Right then he was tempted to believe as much. He was unoffended by the young priest's outburst.

'My lord Archbishop has his trusted advisors,' he said, watching Simeon's eyes, surely the clearest, bluest eyes he had ever seen. 'His first report was that the town was safe in the hands of Hugh de Burton and his military forces. His second report declared that Robert de Clare of York was firmly in control. He has had news of damage repaired and riots quelled, of floods abated and of dangers passed. He

237

therefore believes there is little to concern him while his holdings here are in such worthy hands.'

'But this is not the way of it,' Simeon protested. 'Beverley has urgent need of him. If he believes his holdings in good hands, then he has been wickedly misinformed.'

'Indeed, but who will dare tell him so?'

'Why, any man with half a heart for truth.'

'Such as yourself, friend Simeon?'

'If needs demand it, yes.'

'I see.' The Provost's representative narrowed his eyes. 'You would declare Sir Hugh de Burton and Sir Robert de Clare, who share the Archbishop's friendship, let me add, two rogues and liars seeking to profit from our misfortune?'

'I would,' Simeon answered firmly. 'If it be truth then he deserves to hear it.'

Jacob de Wold sat back to survey the young priest at his leisure. Here was a rare thing indeed, a man who placed honour and truth above all other considerations.

'I do believe you would,' he said at last, and added, with a twinkle of admiration in his eye, 'whatever the consequences.'

Their exchange carried little weight save for the judging of one by the other. No man there was in any doubt that the Archbishop had scant affection for their town. He would rather see Beverley grovelling on her knees than rush to her assistance. He would collect her tolls and fees, claim her common lands and turbary as his own, and would try to bend her to the will of York at every opportunity; but as for love, that was another matter.

Among the Archbishop's richer holdings was a castle set in seven hundred acres close to the green heart of Lincolnshire. It was held in his absence by Sir Edmund Fyldes, a young knight crippled in a hunting accident only half a year into his marriage. The unfortunate invalid kept to his rooms now, bed-ridden and morose, while his beautiful bride Christiana ran his household and received his guests. It was said of her that she entertained an endless parade of lovers in her private chambers, and that she paid her servants handsomely for their silence. And if her doors were barred to other men while the Archbishop was in residence, it was neither modesty nor fear of censure that prompted her discretion. Her interests were best served by convincing Roger de Pont l'Evêque that he had sole access to her bed, for he was savagely jealous of his carnal pleasures. While he travelled between his monarch's business and his own, Hovard Castle provided such public hospitality and private entertainment as could delay a man for many weeks together. He would not see York or Beverley within the week. Indeed, those souls in gravest need of him were unlikely to see their lord Archbishop within another month.

'Why speak out now, today, this moment?' Wulfric de Morthlund suddenly asked of Simeon. He and de Figham had leaned their heads together in private conversation, and he had chosen a moment of thoughtful silence in which to introduce the question. 'I am puzzled, and others too, I'll warrant, as to why you should hold the matter so closely all this time before speaking out. Why not continue to hold your peace, now the unfortunate man is buried and the truth of which you speak just as illusive as ever it was?'

'A man must do as his conscience and his common sense dictate,' Simeon explained. 'The storm is over now and the people are beginning to recover, and since no loving archbishop rides to our aid in spite of what we suffer ...' he paused to swallow his anger on that score, 'I have no reason to keep the matter hidden. And to speak in fullest honesty, the weight of responsibility is more than I can bear. It steals my sleep and preys upon my peace of mind. I cannot do more, nor is it my place to try. The Canons must decide what is to be done.'

The Canons all were nodding now and Wulfric was loath to set himself against them. Even so, he intended to make his feelings known.

'I wonder if the matter of the Mass is truly in dispute here,' he said. 'After all, this is hardly another Canterbury, with a slain Archbishop's blood staining the very steps of the High Altar. Our Canon's death is regrettable, but since the body

239

was found in a stairwell in a side-chapel, it might well be argued that the High Altar has escaped desecration.'

'And it might well be argued that black is white, should it suit a man to do so.'

This comment came from Jacob de Wold, whose smile was amiable enough but did not reach his eyes. His dislike of de Morthlund was an open secret. 'The matter of reconsecration is to be decided in private chambers when the facts are before us in their entirety,' he declared. 'Such things may not be settled here, without due discussion.'

The fat man, smiling, half rose from his seat, inclined his great head in a bow to the Provost's representative, then turned to Simeon and demanded loudly: 'Then perhaps, since we are gathered here, we could discuss your part in other recent matters, friend Simeon?'

Simeon nodded calmly. He could see the animosity in Wulfric's face. He heard it clearly in his tone of voice and fully understood the reason for it. He had seen Wulfric at his worst, sobbing and pathetic, and for that he knew he may never be forgiven.

'No other matter is in dispute here,' Jacob de Wold cut in before Simeon could offer his own reply.

'But there is talk,' de Morthlund pressed.

'Rumour,' Cuthbert declared, suddenly and vehemently animated. 'Grubby tittle-tattle collected from the gutters. Such common talk has no place here, Wulfric de Morthlund, and well you know it.'

'Can there be smoke without fire?'

'Can there be truth in lies?' Cuthbert countered.

The fat man spread his hands and shrugged his shoulders. 'I stand corrected, sir. If the good name of your priest is of no consequence to you . . .'

'How dare you, sir?' Cuthbert demanded, indignation bringing him to his feet. 'This man's good name has never been in doubt.'

Again the fat man spread his hands, and his smile conveyed, as it was meant to do, an ill-disguised contempt for blind old men who saw no fault in favourites. When Jacob de

Wold waved him to his seat he quietly conceded, as well he might, for he had made his point. The seed was planted, ready to be nurtured.

Jacob addressed the meeting. 'We will adjourn now to discuss the matter of Father Bernard's death.' He turned to Simeon and said: 'My clerks here will require a detailed statement of the facts. It must be written down.'

'It has been done.'

Brother Richard stepped forward to hand the pages over. Simeon's bold hand stood proudly on the page, with every word of his own agreed upon by his faithful witness.

Jacob nodded thoughtfully, still watching Simeon. 'A copy will be dispatched at once to Hovard Castle. I think my lord Archbishop will come in haste, for this.'

'And the Mass?' Simeon ventured.

'It will be decided upon as a matter of dire urgency,' the man assured him. 'You took a weighty burden upon yourself, Simeon of Beverley. I believe I am not alone in thinking that you bore that burden well, and dispensed it in a timely and honourable manner.' He raised a hand to still the priest's response, then lowered his voice to add a parting comment: 'Return to your books and essays, scribe. Lower your head to the page while the wolves are running.'

Jacob de Wold turned with a swish of his crimson robes and left the hall ahead of his illustrious companions. Cuthbert hung back, too slow on his feet to seek the centre of the group, and Simeon and Brother Richard hurried to attend him. As the last two dignitaries made their slow way across the hall to the wide inner doors, Cyrus de Figham paused and turned his head. For the first time since the meeting began he looked at Simeon squarely and directly, and there was pure hatred in his slate-grey eyes.

241

CHAPTER TWENTY-TWO

The trusted friends of Simeon had agreed to meet in the privacy of the scriptorium immediately after Terce. The day was crisp and sharp and bejewelled with the glitter of scattered frost. The morning sun poured out of the east against a sapphire background, too thin to melt the ice from water-tubs or warm away the patterns etched on every pane of glass.

Simeon stood on the gentle slope of the little copse beyond St Peter's devastated orchard. There were no trees here now, not so much as a shrub left standing, for the storm had lifted out or flattened every one. To his right, the towering Minster stood in timeless splendour against a flawless sky: no stained and painted windows now to beautify its eastern wall, only the great hole and the twisted iron saddle-bars that once had kept the heavy glass in place. To his left, beyond the high enclosure wall, the flooded backlands glistened like a vast flat lake from the town ditch to the walls of St Nicholas and the Holme Church lane. At his back the crippled town was bravely struggling to regain its feet while here, inside St Peter's ancient walls, the broken church shimmered with the morning's frost and seemed to be in mourning for its dead.

Close by the Holme Church the little port was open now

and the navigable Beck, so recently blocked with the debris of dwellings, huts and stalls that once had lined its banks, ran free again. It brought the boats with their precious cargoes of wine and ale and foodstuff, and the ugly barges piled high with timber for building or for burning. Little makeshift craft were towed along behind, bringing more modest but no less important trade. And every vessel was required to exchange its load for an equal cargo of rubble or waste to be dumped somewhere downstream, away from the littered town. Father Thorald, for thirty years the priest of Holme Church, had personally overseen the clearing of the port, and it was to his credit that, between the sailors and the waiting carters, the quest for profit was not allowed to impede the flow of aid into the town. He gave the local farmers his protection, so that any man who hurried his winter crops and stores into the town went out again with coin enough to justify his efforts. An endless stream of flat-boats, rafts and handcarts choked the Beckside, and load by load the town began to right itself.

'In the shadow of death we are in life.' Simeon spoke the words aloud, and there was a certain reverence in his tone. 'Gods fall and Devils topple, but Man abides, and sometimes gods themselves might pause to wonder which is the greater force.'

He heard the familiar rumble of Osric's laughter. The man had come softly upon that quiet place, crunching the cold earth lightly beneath his feet.

'Heathen priest,' Osric declared affably. 'You voice your thoughts too loudly for your good.'

Simeon shrugged. 'I make no secret of it. I see the better part of God's work in the sheer resilience of mankind.'

'Aye, and the worst of it, too. Mankind has his blacker side, and he seems to wear it with greater comfort.'

'Made in God's image,' Simeon said flatly as he gathered up the loose folds of his cloak, 'and therefore God-like, whether we approve or not.'

Osric looked after him as he strode away to join his fellows waiting in the scriptorium. Then he shook his head and repeated, 'Heathen priest,' before he started after him.

Simeon rapped his signal at the scriptorium door and waited for it to open, then stooped his way into the gloom within. Elvira was crouching by the stove, her hair in fire-glow, patting and shaping oatcakes for the oven. She welcomed him briefly with her solemn gaze, then quickly lowered her head and turned away. He always knew on the instant where to find her, as if her eyes, and his, sought out some quick reassurance in the exchange.

A handful of trusted men were hunched together on the benches by the fire when Simeon, with Osric close behind, was admitted. They had broken their night's fast on sliced blood pudding and cold roast mutton, a dark, dense bread well sopped in ale, and a basket of hen's eggs to be added raw to the flagons. These men had come from their beds with the Matins bell, to work through the dark hours where they were most needed, all of them trying to cram the labours of three days into one. Old Cuthbert was present, determined to disregard his advancing years, and with him his elderly clerk, Henry Stockman, who loved his Canon unreservedly. Here too was the monk Antony, and the priest of St Nicholas, the fierce-looking Thorald, who in his time had sailed many oceans, toiled alongside slaves in foreign mines and skinned his knuckles in every seedy tavern in the western hemisphere; at fifty-three he could still down any fellow half his age in equal combat. Sitting next to him was his clerk, young Richard of Weel, and although their reunion was long since concluded, the big man slapped the other on the back from time to time and tugged him by his glossy beard with a manly show of affection.

'God's teeth, my boy,' he had said when he arrived. 'I gave you up for dead five days ago.'

'Then you could not have received my many messages,' Richard told him. 'Though I sent them quickly enough, when I heard that you had also survived the storm.'

'Not a one,' the big man declared, 'and little wonder at it, since thieves and cut-throats swarm the streets like rats. But here you are and in good hands with Simeon and these others. I am well satisfied, my boy, well satisfied.'

And so he was, for this bellowing brute of a man had much in life to be thankful for. He had survived unscathed, though his church was virtually levelled in the storm. Only its tiny chapel of St Dominic remained intact; well guarded by painted saints and living servants of the church, it now housed the precious altar plate and vestments, the sacred relics and the priceless books he brought from Rome and Normandy and Aquitaine. The priest himself had been buried under tons of fallen masonry when his church collapsed, and were it not for those who stayed to dig him out with their bare hands, he would have suffocated where he lay. They pulled him free unharmed, save for a hundred and one minor scratches, as many small bruises and an inconstant temper. His church was dedicated to St Nicholas, patron saint of sailors and tradesmen, and it was these, in great numbers, who saved him.

When Simeon asked that Richard be allowed to remain at St Peter's, Thorald consented with a shrug of his wide shoulders.

'I'm fond of the lad, and he's always given good value in my service, but for now his usefulness is in the strength of his hands and the broadness of his back, and those I can purchase on the streets, if I need them. If our Richard here is worth more to you than that, you shall keep him by you, and with my blessing.'

'I need him here,' Simeon nodded.

'Aye, that you do. I hear what's being said about the town, and I think you need every friend who can be trusted.' He paused to crack a raw egg into his ale. The blue-eyed priest was changed. He could see that much in his stature, in the way he held himself apart, like one who fears he has contracted a disease and will soon be discovered and cast from the bosom of his kith and kin. And he could see it in that mended foot. It pained a man to have a miracle stand so close. Scowling, Thorald, gulped the concoction down before he asked: 'What liking have you for my lord Cyrus de Figham?'

'Little enough,' Simeon admitted, and he recalled the hatred in that priest's eyes when the death of Father Bernard was revealed as unnatural.

'Then rejoice with me in knowing that his lands at Figham are made impassable by flood-water. His house was struck by lightning and the roof lifted clean off in the storm. Then the place was looted of everything of value that could be carried away in haste. His staff are either fled or killed and his livestock pilfered to feed the hungry.' He paused to smile and shake his grizzled head at the folly of ambitious men. 'While he twists and turns and bribes his way into the vestments of a saint, his property stands unprotected, an open invitation to those with empty bellies and no liking for the master of the house.'

Simeon shrugged. 'One way or another, he will manoeuvre the situation to his own advantage and the church will stand the cost for him. He wants St Martin's.'

'Does he indeed? And will he get it, now that his Canon is dead?'

'Better to ask if he would kill for it,' Richard offered grimly, and Thorald looked to them all in turn, his brows raised and his eyes a-glint.

'What, kill his Canon . . . *murder* his Canon?'

Richard shrugged. '*Someone* surely did.'

Thorald signed the cross and his scowl was savage. 'Old Bernard was a worthy man. When I heard of his death I gave thanks that he was taken while at prayer, quickly and without either pain or fear.' He shook his head, grim-faced. 'What animal would dare strike down a dedicated priest at the very moment when he is in communion with his God?'

'Someone with much at stake,' Richard suggested.

'And the blackest heart,' Thorald growled.

Here Cuthbert cut in to inform the group of the Canons' decision to close the High Altar and send news to the Archbishop that one of his Canons had been brutally murdered. The masses would now be said at St Mary's, which stood beyond the market cross and close behind the Archbishop's house in the marketplace. Simeon and the others

246

nodded their approval, for the pretty church of St Mary was held in high esteem, and its Canon was well respected. It seemed an irony that it should survive the storm to rise, surely the humblest phoenix, out of Beverley's sorrows. When Archbishop Thurston renewed a ruined Saxon chapel half a century ago, he could have had no thought that it would one day serve, albeit temporarily, as parish church in place of old St Martin's.

Their conversation ebbed and flowed over the murder, the terrible losses of the town, the absent Archbishop and the warring, would-be town protectors lodged at the convent close to the Keldgate Bar. News had reached them at St Peter's that Sir Hugh de Burton was kept to his bed with stomach cramps and violent vomiting. He blamed the filthy mud and water in which the whole town of Beverley wallowed, or else the bloated bodies of men and animals left stinking in every ditch. He also blamed the ambitions of Robert de Clare, suspecting poison dropped into his wine or smeared in melted butter on his mushrooms. And when the vomiting was at its worst he swore that holy magic was being worked against him. He did not trust these closed-faced priests with their wordy Latin rituals and closely guarded mysteries. The sooner his son was settled in the Provost's seat the better he would like it. He would make it his business, then, to keep a fast watch on their activities and a firm hand on their purses.

'As enemies, they do more good for Beverley than was ever their intention,' Thorald mused. 'Had they been friends, men of like mind and similar ambition, working side by side to their mutual advantage, they would have stripped her to the bone by now. As things stand, each jealously defends our town from the other's ownership, and in so doing, keeps it safe for us.'

'For how long?' Simeon asked. 'We are the spoils, to be divided out amongst them, each to have his share. For how long will our future hang upon this uneasy peace?'

Thorald smiled at Simeon. 'For just as long as it takes my lord Archbishop to see his property in dispute. The man is no

247

fool. Tell him his tolls at the port go unrecorded. Tell him his profits fall and his friends grow fat at his expense. For all this he will come. The fair flesh of a woman's thighs is no compensation for loss of revenue.'

As he spoke the woman, Elvira, dressed in the pale grey habit of a nun, and with her lustrous hair concealed by a white wimple, moved from the shadows into the fire's glow. She handed the swaddled child into Simeon's arms, and the glance that passed between her and the priest spoke volumes. Thorald's breath caught in his throat. For a moment the woman was quite extraordinarily beautiful. Some trick of the light gave her eyes an amber glow and her skin the pale, smooth look of sculpted marble. And Simeon's face, when he looked at her, had softened in feature, as if the masculine strength of him had yielded to her softness. The moment passed, severed by the lowering of the woman's lids over her huge dark eyes, and Thorald let out his breath in a sigh. Were the rumours true then? He looked at Osric, noted his warning scowl, and guessed the truth. The blue-eyed priest was no less innocent than ever he had been. He had yet to be truly tested in the matter, for he loved, that much was in his eyes, he loved and did not know it.

Thorald knew all there was to know about the mysterious child now nestling in the crook of Simeon's arms. He had heard from Osric how it came to Beverley with that terrible black tempest in pursuit, how Simeon was singled out to guard it, and how the soldiers came, like Herod's men of old, to slay the new-born in its cradle. He had even held the baby in his arms and felt its fierce lust for life, its ravenous hunger to survive.

A glance from Simeon brought the woman back to take the child away. The priest relinquished his godson with reluctance. He loved the boy, that much was clear to anyone with half an eye, and he would defend him with his life, if need be, and there was the pity of it.

The brief distraction at an end, their conversation resumed its easy flow. Before them all, confident in the company of trusted friends who would not judge him too

248

harshly, Antony openly confessed his present predicament.

'We have two hundred at the house,' he said, 'and more come by the hour in need of food, shelter and medicines. We have twenty orphans of six years old and younger, a handful of women close to their birthing-time, feeble old folk with none to care for them, young girls without protectors . . .' He leaned forward in his seat, his forearms on his knees, and fixed Simeon with his steady stare. 'What must I do? Must I turn them out into the streets and whip them from the door, as Wulfric de Morthlund surely will if I default on this?'

'The man has played you well, I think,' Simeon said gravely, and saw the others nodding at his words. 'Silver and gold you could resist, but succour for your poor and destitute? I think not. Two hundred, you say?'

Antony nodded. 'And unlimited stores with which to meet their needs.'

'All this for your denial of my friendship?'

'No more than that.'

'I fetch a good price then, in the marketplace?'

'I'm glad you see the humour of it, Simeon. I'm afraid I cannot, not while he seeks to make a Judas of me.'

'He gains but little in the transaction.'

'One voice the less to speak on your behalf.'

'And yet he must know you would never be persuaded to bear false witness against me,' Simeon said.

Antony looked mildly surprised. 'Can you yourself be sure of that?'

'I can.'

'Thank you, Simeon,' the monk smiled grimly. 'A man's trust is beyond price.'

When Simeon offered his hand Antony enclosed it in his small, strong fist and shook it warmly. They knew each other well, these two, for they were of a kind. They went by separate paths to reach the same door.

'Do as you must, my friend,' Simeon said at last. 'And know that you do it with my blessing. The needs of the poor outweigh my own in the matter. And besides . . .' He glanced first at his foot, then at the cradle where his godson lay. ' . . .

some things have no need of words. And now you must tell me all your news. What do the rumours say?'

Antony glanced round the little group and found himself elected as their spokesman.

'They say the child is yours, your flesh and blood.'

'It is no more than I expected.'

'And that you keep its mother at St Peter's as your mistress, in defiance of church law.'

'I see . . .' Simeon's gaze sought out Elvira. She was sitting close to Peter's cradle, felt the priest's eyes upon her and looked up, only to drop her gaze again as he repeated softly: 'I see.'

Now Cuthbert leaned forward in his seat and spoke to Simeon sharply.

'If the Canons do not ask you this the Archbishop surely will when he hears the stories. And make no mistake about it, he will hear them. Is the child your natural son? Is the woman his mother? Is she also your mistress?'

'You know the answer is no on all counts,' Simeon said mildly, his candid gaze unshadowed.

The old man held his gaze awhile and then sat back, satisfied, unsatisfied, certain and uncertain all at once. There was not a man among them who would dare to ask the question left unsaid. In honest truth, should it be demanded of him, could he swear he did not harbour affection for this ditcher's wife?

For days now, Simeon had had half a mind to send the woman away. She could be smuggled out at night, escorted to a safe house under guard, where her presence could no longer play upon his heart-strings. But where she went the suckling child must also go, and that was too much to ask of himself, for he was not yet prepared to be parted from his tiny charge.

To steer the subject elsewhere, Antony began to speak of the young boy, Stephen, still housed in his private cell at the damaged grammar school. By now his keepers were beginning to fear for his life. He would take no sustenance of any kind but seemed intent on starving himself to death. Nor had he uttered a single word beyond the hysterical babblings when he was first discovered, screaming, in the Minster church. He merely squatted in his corner, watchful of the door, nursing his hurts. Short of resorting to brute force, a recourse Simeon expressly forbade and Antony would not approve, they had not yet drawn close enough to tend his wounds. They had noted the bloodstains in his private piscina, but no matter how they pleaded and cajoled, the boy refused to allow any hand to touch him. It was if he had judged himself unworthy of all comfort, and demanded the ultimate punishment of himself.

Simeon brought his attention back to the group as Richard and Antony were discussing what might be done to help the boy. Something had jarred in him, something the monk had said.

'What was that you said about young Stephen?'

'Only that he remains unchanged, closed off from any comfort we could offer. No doubt his wounds will eventually heal of their own accord, for he is young and strong, but what of his spirit? Will it, too, heal without comfort?'

Now the monk had Simeon's full attention. 'What wounds do you speak of?'

'What wounds? Dear God, do you not know?'

'I know only what I have seen. All else is locked away in his silence.'

'His wounds are ... they are hidden,' Antony offered. 'I thought you knew all about them, Simeon. I thought that you, like the few others who know, had consented to help preserve the boy's reputation with your silence. And all this time you did not understand? All this time you sat beside him, offering prayer and comfort, and you did not know?'

'Antony of Flanders, the matter is righted easily enough,' Simeon said sharply, unwilling to prolong the mystery. 'Tell me now.'

Antony nodded and with some movements of his hand, indicated that he would speak to Simeon privately. The others left their seats and moved to the deeper shadows in a corner by the door. When they were alone and well beyond

251

the hearing of the others, the monk cleared his throat and spoke in lowered tones.

'The boy has been grossly misused,' he said gravely. 'It happened while the storm was at its worst, while he was praying at St Martin's altar.'

'St Martin's?' Simeon queried. He believed he had the answer then, the key to Stephen's suffering. That sensitive, pure-hearted boy had been made to witness an obscenity, a *reserved sin* committed at the very altar where he had knelt to worship. He had been the unwitting witness to Wulfric de Morthlund's act of fornication, and it had shocked him to his very soul. Simeon swallowed the lump that had risen in his throat and said at last. 'Go on, my friend.'

'It seems that someone grabbed him from behind, stopped up his screams with a gag and dragged him out of sight behind the altar, where none could mark the shameful act. There is no pretty way to describe depravity. The boy was raped, and seriously injured in the process.'

The truth struck Simeon like a blow. He leaned back against the roughness of the scriptorium wall, pressing his head against a knotted cross-beam. His eyes were tightly closed, his jaw so firmly set that his lips became compressed into a thin and bitter line. Not the witness then, that troubled, unreachable boy, not the witness but the victim of the deed. And now the priest knew why he had been singled out to hear Morthlund's confession: the *sacred seal*. He was bound and gagged by it, silenced as surely as if the tongue had been torn from his head. Not by word or gesture could he reveal to any living soul that which he knew, beyond all doubt, to be the truth. That farce enacted in de Morthlund's chapel had been performed according to the holy sacrament, and so the seal of confession could not be broken. The man was immune from all worldly punishment. No hand but God's could touch him now.

'Come with me to the grammar school,' Simeon said at last into the prolonged silence. 'I will speak to the boy again, and if he names his attacker, you will bear witness to the fact.'

They reached the grammar school as Brother Christopher

came running out by a side door. He saw them crossing the yard and changed his course, veering towards them over an area strewn with rubble from the storm-wrecked roof.

'Father Simeon! Father Simeon! Brother Antony!'

They halted in their stride and watched him come. He scrambled over the stones, his robes hitched up around his thighs, and threw himself at last upon them, babbling wildly.

'What could we have done to prevent it?' he wailed. 'What in God's name could we have done? Not one of us ever thought ... Oh God forgive him ...' He signed the cross three times in quick succession.

Simeon grabbed him by the shoulders and shook him roughly. 'Is it Stephen?' he demanded of the tear-stained face. 'Do you speak of Stephen?'

The young man nodded. The priest and the monk exchanged anxious glances, then both abandoned the younger man to his bletherings and rushed towards the school. They could hear the sound of voices praying long before they reached the cell, Simeon leading the monk by several strides. He stopped abruptly in the little doorway, and coming up behind him, Antony saw his shoulders sag and heard the heart-rending groan that escape his lips. Such sorrow, such abject pity was on his face that the monk understood, merely by looking at him, what had happened there. He moved to Simeon's side and together they signed the cross and whispered the simple words of the passing prayer. Then Simeon barked into the room, 'For God's sake, cut him down,' turned brusquely on his heels and strode away.

CHAPTER TWENTY-THREE

Simeon reached that part of the corridor that lay open to the elements now that the roof and much of the upper floor had been destroyed in the storm. There he slowed his pace, his footsteps hampered by uncleared rubble, his eyes stung by hot tears of outrage and frustration. He felt his belly heave as if bad food had settled there, but the spasms were unproductive and he knew that this particular sickness could not be coughed up at will and spat away. This ill was his to live with now. He closed his eyes upon the memory, only to see more clearly in his mind that limp young body hanging from the rafters, poor Stephen with his twisted neck and lolling tongue, gently turning on the rope to reveal, through his ripped habit, the shame that killed him.

The outer wall of the grammar school was holed where the central door and its little timber porch had been torn away by the tempest. Simeon stepped into the jagged opening and sucked the frosty air into his lungs, then blew it, clouded, back into the day. He clenched his fists and struck them several times against the rough stone wall, not hard enough to bloody his knuckles but with sufficient force to graze the skin and so give vent to his inner pain. If he had known the truth he might have found a way to reach Stephen in his despair. If he had been able to show him that he understood, that he shared his pain because he knew the cause of it, he might have been able to lead him by the hand from the edge of his self-destruction.

'Dear God, I let him down. I was his lifeline and I failed to save him. How will I learn to live with that?'

He growled the words against the wall, his teeth clenched and his eyes still closed as he pressed his forehead hard against the stones. Wulfric de Morthlund had played upon his vanity and he, convinced that God's hand was in the act, had given the fat man all the help he needed. And he had assumed, as he was meant to do, that Daniel Hawk was the willing partner in that sordid act, and so the connection between the evil-doer and his victim was never made, and Stephen had shouldered his burden all alone, until at last it crushed him.

He felt Antony's strong hand upon his arm. 'Stop this, Simeon. His death has shocked us all. I knew the truth, or some of it, these past few days, but nothing I could do or say would help him bear the shame of what he had suffered. Could you have done better, had you also known it?'

Simeon nodded. 'I believe I might have saved him.'

'Then the fault, if fault there is, must lie with me for keeping his secret too close. You must not blame yourself for this. God knows the truth of it.'

'But suicide,' Simeon groaned. 'Self-murder, the destruction of God's precious gift of life . . .'

'He will be forgiven.'

'Can we be sure of that?'

'Can *you* forgive him?' Antony demanded. 'In all honesty, my friend, can you forgive that hanged boy his ugly and premature death?'

'Yes. Oh yes, I do indeed forgive him.'

'Then God could hardly fashion to do less.'

Simeon nodded, still with his forehead resting against the wall. His warm breath met the frosty air in soft white gusts. He licked his lips and tasted salt where a tear had run.

'But not the man who killed him, Antony. I will see that one in Hell before I pardon him for this.'

He was gone before Antony could make reply, striding across the broken stones as if no obstacle, large or small, could impede his steps. He strode across to the Minster Yard and on beyond the church to the ditch that ran down Eastgate. Then he stepped over the narrow stone bridge and vanished through the iron gate set into the ancient wall of St Peter's enclosure. Only then did Antony turn back the way he had come, to the little beamed cell at the far end of the corridor, to so-called refuge where a troubled boy had died unshriven, by his own hand.

The scriptorium was quiet when Osric beckoned the woman to him and bade her sit beside him on the bench. At the far end of the long main room the priest still paced, prowling this way and that like some restless animal caged against his will. And those who marked his agitated steps were left to ponder the meaning of what they saw. Osric knew full well what he was seeing, however: the priest was unsettled and his thoughts were savage.

The woman sat down beside him on the bench. She was small and moved with a quiet grace and her grave dark eyes brought to her face an elfin, almost child-like beauty. She had come there dressed in dirty rags, hungry and hurt, but now that old life had been washed away, and she had emerged, as if baptised, into another. That week had changed them all. No man or woman spared the storm could know themselves alive and yet unchanged.

Elvira sat with her hands clasped in her lap, watching the deeply lined face of the infirmarian. She liked Osric. She admired his strength and his dour, rough-edged friendship. He rarely offered her a gentle word or a kindly smile, and yet she knew herself to be secure in his custody. He would defend her with his life if it were asked of him, and while she knew that such a sacrifice would be for Simeon's sake, not hers, she thanked him in her heart for watching over her. Now Osric followed Simeon with his scowl, marking his fretful progress to and fro across the room.

'He must be pacified,' he told Elvira at last. 'I know that

temper of his. It runs with deadly undercurrents. God help him if he yields control of it.'

'Does he blame himself for Stephen's death?' she asked.

'And more even than that,' Osric declared. 'Some factor of this business gnaws at him. He guards his silence and will not, or cannot, speak of it, but something frets him, something extra to Stephen's suicide. I fear some link in the sad chain of events leading up to it might well have been broken, and the boy's life saved, if only Simeon had recognised its weakness at the time. He sees it now, too late to help the boy.'

Elvira smiled sadly and glanced down at the pale hands resting neatly in her lap. 'We can all of us say *if only* when the deed is done.'

Osric nodded his agreement and judged her comment wise for one so lacking in formal teaching. She constantly surprised him with simple declarations that harnessed the kernel of the matter into a few brief words. She was not clever but she was wise, not taught by teachers yet learned in her own uncomplicated way. And she was hugely altered. She wore the nuns' habit but had now discarded the plain white wimple in favour of a simple net into which her thick dark hair had been neatly coiled. One slender tendril had escaped its confines to fall in a gentle curve across her cheek, and he felt himself moved to tenderness by the sight of her. Men carried such images with them into battle, or held them dear when far away from where they yearned to be. She had come from the gutter, yet she showed him now a vision of such beauty, innocence and patience as could lure a man back from half a world away.

'Osric?' She was looking up at him now, her eyes round and searching. 'Tell me what I must do. How can I help him?'

He brought himself back to the moment. 'You must distract him from his anger and his outrage. Show him the child, sit with him, engage him in conversation . . .' His voice trailed off into silence as he heard himself acknowledging that she, so lately come into their lives, might reach Simeon in his need where others, some with a lifetime's friendship to their credit, could not. He had admitted that Simeon's heart, closed off, might yield to Elvira's feminine persuasion. He shook his head and fixed her with a doubtful frown. She was a dangerous tool with which to mend a priest. To send her to him in his deepest need might be to set a lighted torch against the dry branches of a thirsting tree, the better to see what ailed it.

'Or perhaps he should be left alone,' he added lamely.

'As you wish, but you know his anger, and you fear it,' she reminded him.

'Aye, girl, I have seen it often enough for that. You saw it for yourself the day he thought the boy was killed by soldiers. Would you unleash a rage like that if you could keep it checked?'

She shook her head and light played across the glossy surface of her hair. She turned to watch the big priest as he paced, and in her face was all the love she tried to keep concealed within herself.

'He calls it murder. He says whoever attacked poor Stephen killed him as surely as if by the sword. That's where the real source of his rage lies, Osric. When the soldiers came he was able to fight, to draw his sword and strike the evil down, but now his hands are bound, he can do nothing. It must be torture for such as he, to be so angry and yet so helpless.'

'That's true enough, but nobody knows the identity of the boy's attacker,' Osric told her. 'And just as well, for with Simeon in this frame of mind, the man's life would be forfeit if his name were known.'

'He knows,' she whispered.

'Impossible. If Simeon knew, if he so much as suspected . . .'

'Then he would be as we now see him,' she cut in, and the gaze she turned on him was full of understanding. 'Believe me, friend Osric, he knows.'

'Not so,' he said indignantly. 'He would speak out.'

'Unless he were bound to silence.'

Osric shook his head. 'There is no oath that could persuade a man like Simeon to bite his tongue upon such as this.'

'Are you forgetting that he is first, before all else, a priest?'

'What?'

He looked at her long and hard, and his voice had shrunk to a whisper when he added: 'My God, what are you saying?'

He saw it now. The truth that had been hidden from him now stung like a splash of icy water in his face. She had spoken the words and set the whole thing neatly into place. That simmering rage went beyond compassion or anger at the sad waste of a human life cut cruelly short before it reached its prime. It was the frustrated, impotent rage of one who knows the truth and is forbidden to declare it, of one who must watch a vile killer go unchastised because his lips are sealed. What a burden of guilt had been placed at Simeon's door if this were true, to know the true identify of the killer and be forced to protect him with his priestly silence.

'How long have you suspected this?' he asked her.

'How can I answer that, friend Osric? I either understand a thing or I do not. How or why or when are of no importance. Watching him walk the floor in such anguish, and seeing that same anguish clouding his eyes, I simply feel it to be true. He knows but does not speak of it, and that can only be because he is first a priest and *then* an angry man.'

For a long time after she moved away to watch over the child, Osric brooded upon Elvira's words. He was ashamed that he had not read his friend so clearly as she did, and he was forced to remind himself that women are intuitive creatures endowed with what often appears to be an extra sense. They perceive what men are blinkered to, observe clear-eyed what blinds a man regardless of his intellect or military training.

He said as much to Father Cuthbert at St Peter's altar later in the day, and the old man shook his head and clicked his tongue over the time-honoured observation.

'What man since the dawn of time has managed to fathom

259

the mystery of woman?' he asked. 'Some have led lives of unsurpassed joy or total misery in that vain attempt, while as many more have taken up holy orders to be free of it. It is a futile quest, but a compulsive one, this sieving and sifting of the perplexities of Eve.'

Osric reached down to heave away one of the larger, heavier lumps of rock so that others might scoop the lighter pieces into manageable quantities. This smaller stuff was piled into shapeless sacks of leather, each with a double loop at its open end, and then man-handled away from the altar and from the church. As keen to help as any man despite his advancing years and failing health, old Canon Cuthbert waited to take his turn in passing the bulky bags from one man to the next.

'I have often looked at it this way.' Osric told him as they toiled together at the little altar. 'When God made the first man, perfect and unique in every way, the Devil was so incensed with jealously at His achievement that he immediately created woman to be man's downfall. And because the two were shaped by equal but opposing powers, man and woman must for all time pull against each other.'

'I have heard kinder ways of describing the imbalance of the two sexes,' Cuthbert said.

'Perhaps, but I never met the man who would disagree with me on it.'

'Nor a woman who would not swear it was the other way about?'

'Aye, true enough,' Osric agreed. 'But a woman would tell us anything, rather than be forced to admit that the Devil had a hand in her creation.'

Cuthbert nodded, watching him. The man was a soldier to the core, despite the years he had spent in the less adventurous service of the church. It was there in the weather-beaten face, lined and scarred with the mark of a thousand battles, and in the keen eyes that knew a potential enemy at a glance. And it was in the ungainly quickness of movement that remained after his pelvis, shattered beneath the weight of a fallen warhorse, had healed itself askew.

'I think you have never loved a woman, Osric.'

The other laughed at that. 'What, me? Well, Father, as God is the certain judge of it, I have lain with more women in my time than I would care to count.'

'You avoid my meaning, Osric. I speak of love, not lust. It springs from the heart of a man, not from his loins.'

Osric puckered his brow. 'Then yes, I must admit to loving a few.'

'A few?' Cuthbert pressed. 'A few?'

'All right, all right, since you insist, I shall confess it,' Osric declared, straightening up to scowl into the old canon's face. 'Yes, I have loved, once only, and the object of my affection was the purest and loveliest women who ever drew breath. I swear she was the *real* Eve, the first and only woman the good Lord ever made with His own two hands. Oh yes, I have loved, and the Devil must have wept with envy the day my precious Agnes was created.'

Cuthbert nodded his head and smiled at the conceits of mortal men. All things were as they ought to be, as God Himself had ordered in the Garden. When Adam first saw his Eve he knew it well enough, that any woman, when truly loved by any man, was elevated to the realm of angels.

They fell to silence then, each with his private thoughts. Osric lifted a leather-load of rubble and passed it into Cuthbert's waiting hands, and the old priest stumbled and gasped beneath the weight of it. From there it was handed to the next man in line, then onward and on, from each man to his neighbour, through a chain of thirty pairs of hands until it reached the door of St Peter's and the growing pile of waste laid out beyond. Thus, if a man be young or old, injured or blind, weak in body or already wearied by a full day's labour, still he could make his own small contribution to the clearing of St Peter's altar. And as Father Cuthbert, standing second in line to the strongest man among them, struggled bravely to pass each leather-load along the line, he was unaware that he handled but half the burden, and that Osric's brawny hands still bore the weight of every load.

Wulfric de Morthlund rose from his bed in time to prepare

himself for Vespers. For a while he sat on the edge of his mattress, where the soft padding sank beneath his weight and rose again in two high mounds, one on either side of his fleshy thighs. The Little Hawk was standing near the window, his naked body lean and long-limbed, every inch of it firm and tightly muscled. The afternoon was closing now, and the fading light softened the chiselled, aristocratic features to that his face was beautiful in profile. Wulfric's gaze travelled over the younger man, marking the narrowness of his hips, the rounded buttocks, the shapely back and shoulders. Sometimes he envied Daniel his youth and his slender beauty, but his envy, though it might sometimes burn, was cooled and tempered by the joy of ownership. The Little Hawk belonged to him in the same way that his magnificent robes, his jewelled sandals and all his other possessions belonged to him.

Daniel turned from the window to find the fat man watching him through narrowed eyes as if weighing and measuring his nakedness the way a cook might evaluate a pan of fish on a market stall. The two smiled at each other, but while one pondered the pleasures and rights of ownership, the other reflected that love and hate could become so tightly and so intricately interwoven that their edges blurred and each became indistinguishable from the other. They might be as vital to each other as the two sides of a coin, but they made unsavoury, often treacherous bedfellows.

A rapping at the doorframe sent the younger man padding barefoot across the room. He lifted the heavy tapestry and bent his head to listen intently to the whispered message of a serving man. Then he turned from the door and reached for his master's clothes.

'Father Simeon is on his way here. They say he strides out like a madman and wears a visage as black as thunder, and that he will not be turned away until he has spoken to Wulfric de Morthlund face to face.'

'Do they now?' Wulfric chuckled. 'Well, then, we must subdue this raging lion before his roars are heard too far afield for our comfort. Have him shown into the lower room and offer him our best wine. Then have the girl and the record-clerks brought down, but keep them in the anteroom until I call for them. Is Cyrus here?'

'He is.'

'Good, let him receive the priest and stay with him until I come down. I think I shall be a little tardy in my dressing. It will not harm the lion to pace a while.'

'May I advise caution?' Daniel added mildly. 'He is no little man, this Simeon. Perhaps it us unwise to test his anger.'

Wulfric had risen from the bed and stood now with his arms out-stretched to accept his under-robe. He let it fall over his shoulders in a soft white shroud that hid his naked flesh, then he reached out to pinch Daniel's cheek, cruelly hard, between his fingers and thumb.

'Question me not, Little Hawk,' he said. 'I like you better when you are submissive.'

'As you wish, my lord.'

'I wish it,' Wulfric hissed, then smiled and patted the discoloured welt his vicious pinch had raised on Daniel's cheek, and said more sweetly: 'I wish it.'

In the lower room Simeon prowled restlessly. He had brought Antony with him, not out of choice but because the monk had crossed his path, assessed his mood and insisted on accompanying him. Cyrus de Figham was seated in one of the great armed chairs, his elegant fingers caressing the twisted stem of a silver goblet, the fine embroidery on his clothes burnished by light from a dozen candles. He watched the priest range to and fro along the length of the room with an anger too large to be contained in so small a place.

Off to one side, in the shadows by a curtained window, hovered the exorcist, John, uncertain of the role he was expected to play. He had yet to acquire the full confidence of his office, and with it the arrogance of knowing that he served a powerful man. He stole sly glances at the steady, level strides of the pacing priest, and the sight of that once-crippled foot, now healed, caused him to shudder. He wondered how any ordinary man could live in comfort or sleep easy in his bed at night, knowing that God had singled him out in such a way as that.

Into this brittle silence Wulfric came at last, ushered in by Daniel to make his entrance with all the pomp and glittering flamboyance of an emperor. He did not descend all the steps into the room but stopped on the second tread, his fists placed on his hips, towering above the others in the room. And so they faced each other, the lion and the bull, the priest and the emperor.

'The boy is dead,' Simeon said flatly.

'Oh dear, and what boy do you speak of?'

'Stephen.'

'Stephen? The name is not familiar. Do I know him?'

'You know him,' Simeon said coldly.

Antony stepped forward and rested a restraining hand on Simeon's arm. 'Have a care, my friend.'

Simeon shook the hand free, his eyes fixed on de Morthlund's face. 'He hanged himself. He was driven to it.'

'Driven?' de Morthlund echoed. 'Driven?'

'St Martin's altar,' Simeon almost spat.

The reminder was a blunt one. Now the fat man stepped down into the room, his face a warning mask as he glared at the priest. He set his feet apart, his hands still on his hips, his shoulders raised, and the stance gave him more size, more space in the room, than any man of lesser bulk might claim.

'You would not dare,' he hissed.

'You think not?'

'The seal is my protection. You will not violate it.'

Now Simeon had drawn very close to de Morthlund. He was taller by several inches and used no clever devices to increase himself, for his anger was enough to make him a giant. His blue eyes were ablaze with fury, his fists so tightly clenched that his knuckles were bloodless.

'An innocent boy was murdered,' he growled into the fat man's face. 'And I can name his murderer.'

'How dare you threaten me, priest? I say again, you will not break the seal of confession.'

'If there is a way, be sure that I will find it.'

'Impossible. You are *unconditionally* bound to silence.'

'I was *duped!*'

'Then live with your gullibility, priest,' the fat man sneered.

The two men faced each other with a chasm of rage between them, then Simeon, seeing his purpose defeated, turned and strode for the door. He had almost reached it when de Morthlund bellowed after him.

'Hold up a moment if you please, Simeon of Beverley. You too, Antony of Flanders. If you are determined to set yourselves against me, then be prepared to do it on *my* terms. Your place is at St Peter's, priest, with your dusty books and your safe obscurity. And your place, monk, is with the human dregs you care so much about. There is too much power here for you to manage.'

With a flick of his fat fingers he gave Daniel Hawk a signal, and a moment later a small inner door was opened to admit a girl dressed in a cotton shift that reached her ankles. This was the daughter of Ulred the tiler, the same unfortunate girl who had been lost on her way to the convent, or taken away by soldiers, or resold by her father at a handsome profit to himself. She had been bathed and cleanly dressed, with sandals on her feet and a pretty net about her hair. Before Simeon could recover from the shock of seeing her there, in de Morthlund's home, she took her cue from her benefactor and pointed an accusing finger into Simeon's face.

'That be him,' she screamed. 'That be the one that lay with me for money and planted his bairn in me. That be the one, the father of my dead bairn. I swear to God and all His Saints, that priest be the one.'

Simeon shrank back from her accusations as if he had been struck a blow to the face. He heard Antony at his elbow say: 'Sweet Jesus Christ preserve us.' Then Wulfric de Morthlund stepped forward and shoved the girl aside with one sweep of his great left palm.

'Her father has left sworn statements with my clerks,' he said, his voice thick with triumph. 'He accuses you of paying him handsomely over the past year to bed this child, his only daughter.'

Simeon, white-faced with shock and rage, merely shook his

head from side to side, bereft of words. Close by them Cyrus de Figham was leaning forward in his seat, his slate eyes bright with malice as he watched the scene unfold before him. Even the little exorcist had drifted from the shadows and was hugging his prayer book tight against his chest, his eyes wide and his mouth hung open. Only Daniel Hawk remained aloof. What he saw and heard, if it impressed him at all, produced no outward sign upon his face.

'That be the one,' the girl cried again, pointing at Simeon, and when she was pushed aside by de Morthlund, repeated sullenly: 'I swear to God that be the one.'

'You see how the land lies, priest?'

'But this is ludicrous,' Simeon protested. 'You know well that I am celibate, Wulfric de Morthlund.'

'Tell that to my lord Archbishop when he arrives.'

'She lies. The girl lies.'

'But there is so much more,' de Morthlund spat. 'A young ditcher known as Erik swears on oath that you have made his wife Elvira your mistress, that you keep her under lock and key on church property, and that you have stolen his son from him ...'

'His son? *His son?*' Simeon almost yelled the words. 'His child is dead. He *knows* his child is dead.'

'He swears upon his soul that it still lives, and that you have stolen both his wife and his first-born from him.'

'Lies ... wicked lies ...'

'Indeed? So you say there is no new-born boy kept at the scriptorium attached to St Peter's?'

'There is. You know there is. He is my godson. *My godson!* The ditcher's son is dead.'

Wulfric de Morthlund smiled maliciously. 'Tell that, too, to my lord Archbishop.'

'I will. As God is my judge, I will.'

'And will you deny, on oath, that you keep the woman Elvira under lock and key?'

'For her own safety,' Simeon protested.

'And will you deny, under oath, that she sleeps in your own bed?'

266

'She does, but I do not.'

'And will you deny, before your Archbishop and your God, that Erik the ditcher has been refused all access to his wife and son?'

'His son is dead, I tell you . . . *dead!*'

The fat man snatched up the sheets of neatly written statements and wafted them in Simeon's face. 'Sworn statements, priest. Genuine grievances. Witnesses ready to swear upon their souls that you have wronged them.'

'*This is an outrage!*' Simeon bellowed the words, his eyes ablaze with fury, and de Morthlund smiled broadly, well satisfied by his response.

'Tell that to the Archbishop, priest.'

Simeon felt Antony's hand at his elbow, drawing him back, and his calm voice insisting: 'Come away. Do not play further into his hands. Come away, Simeon.'

And so he went, choking on his rage as he allowed himself to be drawn towards the door while every fibre of his being cried out to close that grinning, self-satisfied face with his fists. De Morthlund followed him out into the hall, where curious servants and clerks were gathering, eager to have their fair share of the drama.

'Mark me and mark me well,' the fat man shouted across the hall. 'I am not done with you, not by a long, hard way. You have declared yourself my enemy, and for that I will have your office from you, priest. I will have your woman and your bastard son, and let the Archbishop himself decide the rest.'

CHAPTER TWENTY-FOUR

'We saw the signs. We knew it, all of us.'

'Not I,' Cuthbert protested. 'I see the faults of men clearly enough, Osric, but I can swear that I saw none of this.'

'Osric is right,' Thorald agreed. 'We should have seen that it would come to this.'

Antony was nodding gravely. 'Ah yes, the signs were there all along, waiting to be interpreted, but we, with our backs bent to the grindstone on our town's behalf, have barely stopped to read them until now.'

'And who would hold us at fault for that,' Thorald demanded of the group, 'except ourselves?'

Antony continued as though there had been no interruption. The wiry monk was pacing, his face grave-set, his hands shaping expressive gestures as he spoke. 'Separately, individually, the signs mean very little. They speak of envy and petty spites, of this man fearing to stand in that man's shade, or of this one pricked with jealously over that one's altered fortunes. All scraps of unimportance in themselves, but together they show a more sinister picture, do they not?'

'Together they show us the works of a man spawned by the Devil.' Thorald declared. 'And if Stephen had lived long enough to . . .'

'Hush!' Antony brought up his hand as if to strike the priest of St Nicholas. It fell short of the older man's face, but the meaning behind the gesture was clear enough. All eyes were on him when he mouthed the words: 'The seal,' and all were thus reminded that, for Simeon's sake, some things must lay unsaid.

The last Angelus of the day had long since tolled the faithful to their nightly prayers, and from there to the welcome comfort of their beds. Those not weary enough to sleep shifted their stools and benches closer to the fire and bent their heads in earnest conversation. A week had passed since the storm first struck them down, and now the life-blood coursed once more through living veins as surely as the ditches flowed through Beverley.

Father Gilbert had joined them in the scriptorium, free for a time from his work at the Minster and his duties at the Provost's Hall. His was the hand that had penned the urgent message to his distant kinsman, the Archbishop of York, now lodged at his castle in Nottingham. Gilbert held out few hopes for Simeon's cause, though he himself had witnessed both the baptism and the dramatic events at the altar. The tempest had forced a terrible shift of power upon the church of Beverley. Ambitious men were fighting to grab control, or merely struggling to retain their former places, while all around them others fell to circumstance. Such men would not be distracted from their purpose, held back or shoved aside while the identity of a nameless child was decided. They would happily hand the child to the ditcher and rap the knuckles of the priest for his assumed transgressions, rather than sift for the truth while their own futures and fortunes hung upon the outcome.

'We must be prepared for the worst,' he told his grim-faced companions. 'They say the child is Elvira's, the only un-certainty lying in which man sired it, her husband or her priest. We can expect no help, I fear, from that quarter.'

'And is Wulfric de Morthlund likely to carry out his threats, even though Father Simeon has done him no personal wrong?' This was Brother Richard's question. Since

269

the murder of Canon Bernard he was learning to accept that all men, even those in holy orders, were capable of anything. Even so, the twists and turns and the subtle strategies that they employed against each other were new to him and, being unfamiliar, seemed mysterious.

Father Gilbert looked to Thorald, and when the priest nodded his head it was for them all. 'I think we can be certain of that one thing, lad. Wulfric will do as he intended from the start. He has been thorough in his evil work. He sets a trap of such fine mesh that not so much as an eel can wriggle through it.'

'And Simeon is the bait,' Antony added flatly. 'Wulfric de Morthlund will destroy him if he can, on that you may rely.'

They looked at Simeon, but he responded with nothing more than the lifting of his brow. He was sitting with his knees raised up and his back against the wall, his face half in, half out of shadow, his gaze on the sleeping infant in his lap. He had been sitting so for a lengthy stretch of time, his rage subdued but no less deadly for its slow-running depths. He marked the progress of the conversation without comment while the other men, each contributing what he knew, drew up a detailed picture of the trap that even now was closing in around him. He watched the child's face, still and soft in sleep, and he felt the deep ache within his breast, as if his heart was bound by metal fetters. He would not give him up. Not for the Provost, nor the Archbishop, nor even for the Pope himself would he surrender this child into the hands of Wulfric de Morthlund.

He knew now what the people said of him. They said he healed a hopeless case, a man whose lungs had rotted half away, that he raised a dead man and mended a child whose spine was broken clean in half. They said he was the subject of a miracle, that his crippled foot was made whole again, and that a young man of the Church, armed with a scrap of cloth from Simeon's robes, was healing the sick and the dying in his name. And they said that God had blessed him with a child that was not born of any women, an extraordinary, precious child that was to be the saviour of Beverley and the guardian of St John. All this they said of him, and they spoke his name as if he were to be counted among the saints.

And while these stories flew about the town, Wulfric de Morthlund harvested a crop of damning testimonies from greedy or frightened people who would condemn that same priest as a liar and a charlatan. They would make him a fornicator, a stealer of wives, a wicked seducer of poor men's daughters. These tongues would tell of so-called victims 'healed' of feigned afflictions, and of holy favours bought and sold in the aftermath of tragedy. There were even whispers that Simeon's crippled foot was never so, that it was part of a long conspiracy to make a martyr of an obscure priest. At least two men and a woman were willing to swear on holy oath that they had seen him walk and run and jump like any other man long before his so-called healing. Even God's miracle was to be turned to lies in the mouths of mortal men.

'Why do they do it?' Cuthbert had asked. 'These honest, simple men who let themselves be corrupted for coin, who damn their souls to hell for a penny-piece, why do they do it?'

'Because they are hungry,' Simeon had answered then, 'and hunger has no morals.'

'There is much gossip on the streets,' Antony was saying now. 'The place is teeming with journeymen and merchants, and the pilgrims still flock here by the score. They seek the blessing of St John and find instead a devastated town where the prayers for the dead can be heard at every hour, day and night.'

'And they continue on with stories of Hugh de Burton and Robert de Clare sacrificing their personal comforts and standing shoulder to shoulder for our protection,' Cuthbert said bitterly. 'And for once the lie serves ordinary men and women as neatly as it serves their masters. While those bitter enemies mark each other's every move, our beloved Beverley becomes the pampered property of York, where she might instead have been the spoils of war.'

'And so she was in the beginning,' Thorald reminded him.

'We have suffered more than our share of pillage and plunder, and not just the poor and hungry were guilty of it.'

There was a general nod of agreement from those around the fire. They had all heard stories of salters murdered for their loads, carters robbed of their animals, families looted of all they had managed to salvage from their wrecked homes.

'There are men here gathering information to pass back to Canterbury,' Antony then said. 'Archbishop Richard will pay well for news of us, for it is in his interests to know what befalls his rival Archbishop, Roger of York. And who would happily hang between those two, I wonder?' He saw the eyebrow raise itself again and knew that Simeon, despite his silence, was listening to his every word. 'Roger will try to snatch for York any fame coming out of Beverley, while Richard in his turn will try to grab for himself whatever belongs to York. Between York and Canterbury a priest in dispute is about as safe as a joint of meat between two snarling dogs.'

The men around the fire fell silent then. All knew they were unable to send Simeon's case direct to Rome, above the heads of Bishops and Papal legates. And if they did, no word of it would ever reach the Pontiff's ears, for lesser men than he would see a priest dead who could not be manipulated to their own advantage. They knew now that Simeon had dangerous enemies in Beverley: they had yet to discover how many waited for him outside the gates.

Osric was next to say his piece. He peered into every face in turn, then spoke the words that were uppermost in his mind.

'We must set the whole truth down on paper, and quickly, lest some ambitious canon decides to silence each one of us in turn. We must set it down and put our names to it, so that a record exists for all time of what has happened here in Beverley.'

'That much is being done already,' Cuthbert assured him. 'The two Sisters of Mercy from St Anne's who attend the wet-nurse are penning a detailed document during the long

272

hours spent shut up within these four walls. My clerks will study it on its completion, make any alterations or additions that might be necessary, then put it before us all for our approval.'

'Good, good.' Osric chewed his lower lip, then said: 'Those of us here who saw the *other* . . . the one who brought the child . . .'

He was suddenly at a loss for words. Not one of them had spoken about what he saw that night, though every description heard beyond St Peter's stood out in stark defiance of the next. Osric felt every eye upon him now.

'Some say he was St Peter,' he prompted. 'Others that he was St Anthony, or St Martin, or John the Baptist, or even Jesus Christ. I hear a different name from every mouth, and yet all insist they saw him in good light.'

'He wore a dark cowl,' Cuthbert said. 'Only when the lightning struck, or when he raised his head and cried out against the storm, only then were his features revealed.'

'You also saw his face clearly, did you not?'

'I did,' Cuthbert admitted. 'But he was none of those you have just named. He wore a beard . . .'

'No, he was clean-shaven,' Richard insisted.

'And a man of the East, according to his colouring,' Thorald said.

'But that is nonsense. He was fair, as blond as a Dane, I saw that for myself,' a clerk cut in.

'He was young, no more than thirty years at the most.'

'Not so,' Father Gilbert corrected. 'I had the distinct impression that he . . .'

'He was mature . . . his hair was grey as woodsmoke.'

'Please!' Cuthbert lifted his hands to stem the flow of protestations and contradictions passing between the men. 'Gentlemen, please! We must try not to disagree so heatedly amongst ourselves. Each man here knows in his heart of hearts exactly what, or who, he saw that night. Let us be satisfied with that.'

'And tell the Archbishop a dozen different stories?' Antony asked coldly. 'When he hears them all he will surely dismiss the whole thing as an insanity, as any one of us would do in his place.'

'That might well be so,' Cuthbert nodded. 'But I doubt if any man here will be persuaded to deny what he saw in favour of some other man's description. The only thing we can agree upon is this, that no man here saw what his neighbour saw.'

'And yet we all *heard* the same thing,' Antony offered. 'We heard him name the child *Peter, the Rock*, the guardian of the sacred shrine of St John, and we heard him name Simeon of Beverley as the babe's custodian.' He looked around and all men nodded, remembering. 'And this, then,' he added, 'is what we will tell the Archbishop when he comes.'

At the mention of his name, Simeon looked up to find Elvira watching him from a stool close to the rafter steps. She had set down her stitching to fix him with her solemn, thoughtful gaze, and he could detect a certain sadness in her eyes that had not been there before. He suspected that she blamed herself for the bigger part of his predicament. His enemies would use her as a weapon against him, for she was the ditcher's wife and neither she nor Simeon were able to say whose child it was she suckled at her breast. And where would they stand if they were brought before the Archbishop and asked, under holy oath, what manner of affection lay between them?

He lifted the child, such a tiny, helpless thing in his big hands, and Elvira came at once to take it from him. This time when her hands met his in the exchange she did not draw away but paused, holding the moment, and raised her eyes to his. Hers was the easiest of faces to interpret. There was no coy evasion or deliberate falsehood in it, for life had not yet taught her to veil her thoughts.

'I know.' He shaped the words in silence and they were enough for her. He saw the quick light jump into her eyes and the ghost of a smile spring to her lips. As she turned away, hugging the precious babe against her breast, he wondered at the sheer simplicity of love's rewards. One moment of simple joy was all it took to repay unnumbered hours of pain, and the closing of a tiny hand around a grown man's finger could reduce that man to helpless tears.

He felt a gentle touch on his shoulder, Cuthbert's hand, thin-skinned and deeply veined. He reached up to cover it briefly with his own, then sprang to his feet as lightly as a cat. Cuthbert looked closely into his deep blue eyes, then shook his head, despairing. 'Transparent,' he whispered. 'Dangerously so. I fear Wulfric de Morthlund will strip you naked and pick the flesh from your bones when the Archbishop comes.'

Simeon lifted his head sharply and looked down at his canon from the corners of his eyes. 'Perhaps you are right,' he conceded softly. 'But one thing he will never do while I still live: he will never put his hands on my godson. Believe in it, Father. He will never take that boy away from me.'

'I do believe it, Simeon. And we, your loyal friends, will help you keep that vow.'

'Thank you,' Simeon said. 'Thank you all. And now you must listen carefully to what I have to say, for I will not have my friends struck down or discredited within the church on my behalf. No man must speak for me unless the Archbishop calls him personally to account. No pleas must be made for my benefit, no statements drawn up in my interests.'

'What then, are you to stand alone in this?' Osric demanded.

'No, my friend, I will not stand alone, but if my enemies see that I seek no confrontation, that I make no claims and present no case to York, they might withdraw from the field and leave us all in peace. Forget the rest of it, the so-called miracles, the arguments, the lies and accusations. Think only on this, that I have been chosen to guard young Peter until such time as his purpose here is known.'

There was a murmur of assent. Simeon moved closer to the fire, the better to see the faces of his friends. He was wearing a robe of heavy cloth, thonged boots and a short red cloak. At his belt a dagger hung, for now he neither slept nor prayed without it. His handsome face was bronzed by the fire's glow, and the same soft light added sheen to his gold-blond hair.

'My first consideration must be for him,' he told them gravely. 'And then for Elvira, his nurse. They must be sent from here to a place of safety where the boy can grow and learn and be prepared for what his future holds.'

The others nodded. Only Father Cuthbert remained in any doubt.

'He was named Peter of Beverley,' he said firmly. 'Can he be raised elsewhere?'

'It must be so, at least for the present, if I am to ensure his safety,' Simeon explained. 'They came to kill him, Father. Like Herod's men they came for that little innocent with swords, and I doubt they will be content until they have him. And now de Morthlund declares him a ditcher's son, and if he has his way, as he intends, the Archbishop will uphold that claim. And what must I do then? Must I obey my lord Archbishop when he orders me to return Elvira and *my godson* to the ditchers' hovel? Must I give him up like a sacrificial lamb to be hunted and slaughtered by my enemies?'

'But to send him away when he was brought here at such cost,' Cuthbert insisted. 'To send him from the very place where he was brought with a raging tempest blowing at his heels. How can it be right, Simeon, how can it be?'

Simeon narrowed his eyes and made his answer through clenched teeth. 'Then find me a better way.'

To that one end they discussed the matter far into the night, until the moon was high and bright and slanted through the narrow windows in silvered shafts. Cuthbert was fast asleep by then, his old bones wrapped in Simeon's thick fur cloak and his body cushioned by a pallet of straw set in the warmest alcove by the stove. Elvira dozed on her mattress with the boy close by. It would sadden her to be parted from the priest, but so long as she nursed his godson she would share his life, and while she shared his life her own had purpose.

It was at last decided that the boy and his nurse would leave secretly for St Theodore's Rest, the Benedictine priory lying out beyond the marshland. They would be safe there until this present, man-made storm had passed, and if not they would be moved south, to the abbey at Meaux, or north-east to St Mary's at Whitby. When the climate altered, when men like Wulfric de Morthlund no longer threatened his well-being, the boy would be brought back to Beverley and St Peter's, where he was meant to be.

One by one the friends took to their beds or left the scriptorium by its well-guarded door. When Osric too had gone, for he was needed through the night at the nearby infirmary, Antony and Simeon kept vigil over the dying embers. Simeon leaned his elbows on his knees and stared into the fading fire.

'That girl,' he said, 'the tiler's daughter. I saw such anger in her face, such hatred in her eyes when she accused me. How will I deny her charges with any conviction, when she herself seems so convinced that I am guilty?'

'She has been well-rehearsed,' Antony murmured, blowing on the glowing coals until a spray of fiery sparks leaped upwards into the chimney. 'She will make a fine witness when she is brought before my lord Archbishop and his eminent assembly.'

'Then I am lost,' the priest said softly. 'She is a child, and pretty too, with the look of innocence still on her. Their hearts will melt at the very sight of her, and how could any fair-minded man, faced with such a performance as she gave today, fail to accept her story as the truth?'

Antony looked sideways and his gaze was steady. 'I did.'

'What, and never doubted?'

'Neither then nor now, not for an instant.'

'And yet, my friend, you have not heard me deny the accusation.'

'Make no denials on my account, Simeon. I know the truth without them.'

Still Simeon doubted. 'Are you that certain of my innocence?'

'I am,' Antony replied.

Just then there was a rustle of movement close to the rafter ladder. Yawning noisily, a figure stepped from the shadows and moved towards them, the fingers of both his hands scratching at the circle of hair around his shaved crown. As he stepped into the soft glow that the dying fire still cast about the hearth, light played on the purple stain that marred one side of his face.

'I fell asleep in the corner over there,' he confessed. 'I should have been gone some hours ago.'

'Go back to sleep while all is quiet, lad,' said Antony.

'Thank you, no,' the young man said, shaking his head as he righted his modest girdle and set his hood more squarely upon his shoulders. 'I must leave to prepare for Matins.'

'The Office will not begin for another hour, at least,' Simeon reminded him. 'And by that time several others will be leaving too. The streets are dangerous, Michael, and there is always safety in numbers. Wait with us here a while.'

'No, Father. My duties urge me to St John's without delay. But I will happily come again tomorrow, after Terce, if you'll allow it.'

'You will be welcome lad, but only if you can be spared from your other duties. The restoration of our little church of St Peter is not so high on some priorities as it is on ours. We must go first where we are most needed, remember that.'

'I will sir,' the young man said, bowing into the fireglow so that his features were at once made pleasing and ugly, his smile one-sided and his eyes so much unlike that they might have been looking out from different men. 'Father Simeon, if there is no work for me outside, I will be happy to guard the lady and the boy.'

'Do you have a sword?'

'No sir, but I can borrow one.'

Simeon nodded thoughtfully. Better to keep him separate from the rest, for church men were no less superstitious than their more worldly brethren, and this double-faced priest with his ill-shaped eye and lip, endeared himself to few, despite his efforts.

'So be it,' he said at last. 'Tomorrow you will take turn and turn about with Thomas as Elvira's guard, but only if your priest allows it, lad.'

'Thank you, Father, I will guard them well, you have my word on that.' He bowed again. 'God's blessing on you.'

It was Antony who took the young man to the door and dropped the weighted bar into place behind him. As he turned back to the fire he saw the woman's face above the ladder, her hair hung down as she leaned across the beam where her bed, once Simeon's bed, was set. Her face was small and pale amongst the shadows, and he had the distinct impression, before it vanished, that she would rather remain alone than have young Michael close by as her guard. He had seen her make the age-old sign against evil spirits when the lad came near, though she kept her hands against her gown so that neither Michael himself nor Simeon knew she did it.

Outside the scriptorium, Michael lifted his hood against the sharp night air and strode towards the main gate of the enclosure. A priest unlocked the gate to let him out, and he stepped with care over the bodies huddled together like penned sheep, hugging the gates and walls of St Peter's for want of proper shelter. From there he made his way along the short lane into Eastgate, and across to the eastern section of the Minster Yard. It was here that two men stepped from the shadows to place themselves on either side of him.

'You stayed a long time with your friends,' one of them said. 'You must have found much to talk about that kept you with them all this time.'

'The fellowship of friends is precious to us all,' Michael answered carefully.

'And tongues wag freely when the door is barred, eh lad?'

Now Michael stopped and, standing his ground, faced each of the men in turn. He knew them both, though one he could not name and the other he feared for his habit of inflicting pain upon others. He found no virtue in physical discomfort and he had no wish to be singled out by the palmer to be disciplined for some imagined fault.

'I am expected at the Provost's Hall,' he said.

'You are expected at my master's house,' the palmer corrected.

'But why? What could your master possibly want with me?'

'Your ears, lad,' the other told him with a sadistic leer. 'I believe he wants you for your ears.'

They took him by the arms and led him off and, hung like a twin-faced puppet between the two, Brother Michael prayed that God in His mercy, who surely knew his terrible dread of pain, would either deliver him from adversity or else forgive him his cowardice.

CHAPTER TWENTY-FIVE

At first light two willing men were sent by boat across the flooded marshlands, making their way with careful haste to a humble, isolated priory dependent on the abbey at Meaux. Although dedicated to the Blessed Virgin, the priory had been known as St Theodore's Rest since that one-time Archbishop of Canterbury had rested there when foul weather and failing health prevented him from reaching Beverley. He had been travelling to meet the then Archbishop of York, no less a personage than John of Beverley, in the days before either man was elevated to the company of Saints. The priory then was little more than a timber enclosure set on an island of higher ground within that low-lying and inhospitable marshland. Surrounded by a natural lake, it supported a mere handful of monks who scratched a living from the land and went hungry when their crops were washed away. It was a barren, neglected place that travellers avoided, for it rose in ghostly fashion from the marshes, floating upon a bed of mist as if no natural forces held it to the ground.

The legend said that Theodore's guards, his pack-horses and loaded carts, were all swallowed by the marshes when the night was at its darkest, and that the Archbishop and his priests were trapped by rising flood-water and a freezing, swirling fog that left them blinded. Guided by the tolling chapel bell, they managed to reach the priory on a makeshift raft, and there the ailing Theodore of Canterbury lay as if in the lap of death for many days, lovingly tended by the monks. They poulticed his ulcerated legs and eased the racking fever in his lungs, warmed his frail body with their wine and fed him simple food from their own plates. They prayed over him day and night without a pause; hour by hour, prayer by prayer, they drew the great man back from the shadowed place where Death had lured him. They saved his life, and in his gratitude the Archbishop dedicated an altar there and left what remained of his personal treasure for its support. And since that day, five centuries past, no crop had failed, no monk had perished in the lake or on the marsh, no animal had drowned there or become diseased. Pilgrims braved the treacherous journey to worship at the island's altar, and miracles were claimed in St Theodore's name, for the cloths that had bound his ulcers and cooled his fevered brow were still preserved in a silver cask bearing his crest and his eternal blessing. Even after the passing of five centuries, the cloths were said to be whole and white and imbued with powerful healing properties.

On that chilly morning Simeon stood on the edge of the backlands, just beyond the eastern boundary wall of St Peter's enclosure, stamping his feet to keep the cold away and blowing his breath in little white clouds about his face. When the time was appropriate he signed the cross and gave the messengers his blessing.

'Go with God and travel safely.'

'We will return before the day fades,' one man assured him.

'God grant it will be so,' his companion said grimly. 'I've heard men say the Devil himself runs loose across those marshes after dark.'

They took their leave and Simeon watched them go. Armed and well-cloaked against the bitter weather, they moved like phantoms into the murky distance, their dark shapes hovering for a while against the edges of the mist, then swallowed into its density like vanished things. Simeon peered after them, squinting through narrowed eyes until he could no longer identify the spot where they had stepped from his sight. Then he turned and walked back to the wall, slipped through the waist-high iron gate and locked it fast behind him. As he walked through the ruined orchard and the flattened copse, his steps were sure and even; for a while he dropped his gaze to watch his booted feet marking their steady passage across the ground. No more the cripple, his strides were those of a whole and healthy man, so confident and sure-footed that he might have been so, unlamed, for all his life. As he stared down his steps began to falter and his vision blurred. He halted, suddenly unable to continue, and when he lifted his face to the cold, grey dawn his cheeks were wet with tears. Once again the reminder of his altered state had struck him like a blow.

'I am healed,' he told the morning, 'God be praised, the cripple is truly healed.'

From the scriptorium window Elvira watched the big priest standing at the orchard's crest with his face upturned, and even before he sank to his knees on the frosty ground she knew that he was praying. He prayed not as a priest should, with his head lowered and his palms together, but with his clenched fists resting on his knees and his head raised up. He was not like the rest. While other men cringed before their God this Simeon met Him face to face and unafraid. It was neither the tonsure nor the robes that made this one a priest, but something deep and powerful inside himself. He was God's man not merely because he served a Heavenly master: in his soul was where the pact lay, in his *soul*, and Elvira ached to have it otherwise.

Across the great River Humber, the whole of Lincolnshire lay beneath a shroud of winter mist. It levelled the land by slicing the tops from towering trees and filling every dip and hollow so that everywhere was flat and soft and shapeless. And it was cold, bitterly so, this Arctic fog, that seeped through a man's clothes and into his bones, stiffening joints and twisting muscles.

The little party had ridden out from Hovard Castle reluctantly, too hastily gathered for comfort, since many of those who attended the Archbishop had been pulled from their beds at dawn to find their grooms already scuttling to the stables and their master fuming with ill-humour. They crossed the frozen lawns and meadows in a sorry line, their horse-fittings jangling, creaking and ringing, their mounts pawing the hard ground and snorting the cold, damp air from their lungs. For over an hour they traversed the castle grounds like dark phantoms, each figure hunched over a beast that trod flank-deep in the wet and freezing mist. They followed a course as erratic as their master's temper, unable to see the ground beneath their feet, and the very air they breathed served to increase the pale vapour hanging all about them.

The man who led the riders was a stout figure with a broad back and an impressive bearing. Heavily cloaked and hooded, he wore a copper warming flask strapped to his chest, thick quilted braes drawn tight at the waist and ankles, and fur-lined boots that reached above his knees. Only the inner circle of his face remained visible, showing a peevish frown and a fleshy mouth that drooped at its outer edges. Roger de Pont l'Evèque was no longer a young man. At sixty-four he sat a horse with little enthusiasm, though with a certain skill and poise that many half his age might envy. Now he was exasperated. His body still ached after the lengthy journey from the capital. He needed the comfort of his private hearth, a breathing space, a chance to recuperate before submitting once again to the heavy yoke of ecclesiastic duty. Instead he was being plagued by stories of tempests, miracles, murder and disorder, and all of them coming out of 'Beaver Lake', that water-logged town daring to rival York, that Beverley.

'*God's teeth!*'

At the sound of the angry ejaculation a man reigned closer to his master's horse. His face, made gaunt by long illness, was whitened now with hoarfrost where the wet mist clung in frozen droplets to his hair, beard and brows. His wife had begged him not to leave his sick-bed, but the arrival of the Archbishop's party three days past had forced him to forgo it. And this morning he had ridden out unprepared, at Roger of York's sudden bidding, and the sable cloak that would have kept the chill at bay still hung on its peg beside the gatehouse fire while its owner shivered and cursed its absence with every breath he took.

'My lord Archbishop?'

'God's teeth, if I'm not struck to the bone with this unearthly cold. What manner of day is this?'

'My lord?'

'And you, Melville, are you a mindless fool that you ride out on such a morning as this *uncloaked*? Your clothes are sodden and you look like death.' His eyes narrowed suspiciously as he peered into the face of the man who was his steward and kept his castle business running smoothly. 'Or is it that you seek to impress me with your powers of endurance? Or perhaps I am intended to note your piety, your humble trust in God's protection from the elements?'

The man's jaw dropped open, cracking the frost from his beard. His lips were tinged with blue and his teeth were chattering. 'My lord ... if you please ... it was certainly not my intention to ...'

'Don't bother to explain,' the Archbishop snapped, waving the man aside. 'But mark this, Master Melville. I am not so easily impressed as you might imagine. My friend the King of England has more vigour and energy than a score of ordinary men such as yourself, and if I need to be reminded that men suffer, I shall contemplate the mortal lives of Saints, not the antics of a fool who leaves his cloak behind when he rides out in winter.'

The Archbishop spurred his horse and pulled its head around so sharply that it pitched its body sideways, striking the other's mount a flank-to-flank blow that startled the second animal into a canter. Master Melville struggled to regain control with fingers that ached with cold on the leather reins. When at last his mount was calmed he trotted it back towards the group and fell obediently into step with his companions. He sat up stiffly in his saddle, trying to ignore the biting wind that cut right through his body, outlining every rib, back and front, and the spine and breastbone holding them in place. Injustice stung him no less than the cold. Four years of currying favour at Hovard Castle had just been lost, four years of bending his back in service wasted. Despite his efforts he had fallen foul of the Archbishop's bilious disposition, and in that brief, humiliating exchange his fate was surely sealed. Roger de Pont l'Evèque was an unforgiving man whose mind, once set upon a certain course, would not be shifted. Melville had left his cloak behind in order to heed his master's call on the instant, and by doing so had branded himself an imitator of kings, an aper of the humility of saints. The distortion was ludicrous, but one he could not put to rights, for he knew the peculiar loops and tangles of this old man's reasoning. They could make or break a man without compunction.

Roger de Pont l'Evèque had been Archbishop of York for twenty-six years. He had been consecrated to that high office in 1154, the year this second Henry took up the crown of England, the year the Englishman, Nicholas Brakespear, accepted the title Adrian IV and began his five years as the Roman Pontiff, His Holiness, the Pope. Another Pontiff, Alexander, served them now, and he would not bend before any monarch but God. King Henry would rest much easier in his bed if only he could curb his rebellious sons, master his barons, control his lovely Eleanor and see another Englishman in Rome. As for Roger de Pont l'Evèque, he had the friendship of both King and Pope, and trusted both no further than any bishop should ever dare trust either. Even great men were vulnerable to manipulation, of this fact Roger of York was well aware. He had encouraged Thomas Becket of Canterbury to test his powers against those greater forces, had secretly complained of him to the Pope, and had personally warned the King that he would know no peace while Becket lived. His part in Becket's downfall had taught him not to place his trust in popes and princes, not when proud bishops like Thomas and himself became mere pawns in the powerful games played out between the two.

He had left the castle in search of privacy, for walls themselves have eyes and ears and hanging tapestries too often gather secrets to carry to outsiders. He wanted privacy, but all he found outdoors was this cold, seeping silence that clung about his ears and carried a man's voice to any who cared to listen. Behind him lay a crackling fire, good wine and a superb table, while all around him lay a wasteland of frost and swirling fog. Little wonder his temper was soured. He would have this matter settled and his comfort restored, or else some fool would pay the full price for his discontent.

The Archbishop beckoned two men to follow him, signalled the others to wait behind, then heeled his horse and galloped towards the woodlands, marking a curving course to skirt the huge, flat disc that was the frozen lake. Roger de Pont l'Evèque brought his mount to a standstill near the woodland's edge and spoke out brusquely as the first man rode up to join him there.

'This is an imposition, sir. I will not be sent for, *summoned* to attend these Canons of Beverley. I am not obliged to hold myself at their disposal.'

Sir Matthew Turton nodded and added carefully: 'My lord, they insist their need is great.'

'Aye, great indeed,' the Archbishop snorted. He pulled a sheaf of papers from the inner folds of his cloak, shook them in the air and declared angrily: 'And yet they have Sir Hugh de Burton and Sir Robert de Clare to attend their needs. And while my back is turned they have the effrontery to muster their numbers into a grand procession, parading through the streets in a show of pomp that would rival York itself. They had no need of their lord Archbishop then, sir.'

'Father Gilbert writes that the High Altar of the Minster has been desecrated,' Sir Matthew said.

'Then let them use another.'

'But sir, they report that a canon was murdered there.'

'Then let them find the culprit and deal with him as they must. Their Provost has his own court, has he not? He does not require an Archbishop's help in bringing a murderer to justice.'

Sir Matthew's companion, a priest who bore the name of the first English martyr, Alban, had joined them now. He drew his cloak more tightly about his shoulders and leaned over his horse's neck to speak in lowered tones.

'There is the matter of the so-called "Beverley Miracles",' he reminded the Archbishop. 'Their fame is spreading. They cannot be ignored. They speak of a priest who was healed, the raising of the dead and the healing of the sick. And there is the child to consider, its origins and its future. What is the Church to make of these events? Without your intervention, His Holiness the Pope might think ...'

'Silence! No more of this,' Roger commanded. 'This matter will not go as far as Rome. As long as I remain Lord of Beverley, no word of this will reach the ears of the Pontiff.'

'Then you must make haste to Beverley,' Father Alban urged. 'Richard of Canterbury has a team of spies there, enough for some to watch and listen while others carry the news back to their bishop. The papal legate has sent messages to the Provost and expects to receive a detailed report without delay. If you are to regulate what comes out of Beverley, you must be seen to stand securely at its helm. Only then will your words be accepted above all others. Only then will the rumours and exaggerations be disregarded and the reports of profiteers such as Hugh de Burton and Robert de Clare be taken as the fatuous documents they are.'

'I want this matter settled,' the Archbishop growled.

'But settled to your own advantage, my lord, and to the greater benefit of the Mother Church. Men grab your glory while your back is turned. This priest, this Father Simeon, will have himself revered a saint, a maker and receiver of miracles, and his Holiness the Pope will chastise you, my lord Archbishop, for letting things get so far out of hand.'

'I will not have it.' Roger of York chewed on his lower lip and scowled into his priestly advisor's face. 'By royal decree I am sole Lord of that ungrateful town. If Beverley's fame is to reach as far as London, Canterbury and Rome, it must only do so as a chattel in the ownership of York. God's teeth, I am the *Archbishop*. I will not hold my fame in Beverley's wake.'

'Then you must take the helm, my lord,' Father Alban said quietly.

'Nor will the power of York be eclipsed by an unknown priest. This Simeon is ambitious.'

The priest shook his head. 'Some do accuse him of it, though others believe the child is his sole concern.'

'Ay yes, the mysterious *godson*. He is not the first priest to father a bastard child, nor will he be the last so long as men are made from flesh and blood and women live to tempt us.'

'My lord, if I might speak?' Sir Matthew Turton leaned forward now. 'This matter of the child is not so simple as you have been led to believe. The town is alive with speculation and divided as to whether it was brought there by forces outside the natural. Some say the tempest was sent by Satan to deter the will of God, which was specifically to place the child in the care of Simeon of Beverley. There were many hundreds of pilgrims there when the storm struck, so the stories are carried the length and breadth of England and beyond, and those who hear are rushing to Beverley to see this *miraculous* child for themselves.'

'A dangerous situation, my lord,' Father Alban cut in. 'How long before these pilgrims turn from the relics of a dead Saint to the living babe, who seems to have come to them like the new-born Christ Himself, against all odds and with divine intervention? And how long before those same pilgrims, flocking to Beverley like flies to honey, are persuaded to take their offerings and altar-gifts to Simeon, for the babe's sake?'

'*God's teeth!*' the Archbishop spat.

Across the frozen lake the others waited, standing half-buried in the mist and viewed now through a damp and chilling haze. The horses' necks were lowered and the riders sat with rounded backs and covered heads, bearing the weight of the fog upon their shoulders. The group made a spectral display, hanging in the nebulous distance with the swirling mist closing in around them.

For a long time the Archbishop watched the waiting men without sympathy. He was indifferent to their discomfort, for he had learned to carry the burden of his duties as he must, without complaint, and he expected other men to do the same. At last he gathered himself with a shrug and barked instructions to the men beside him.

'Take nothing more than is needed for the fastest journey and ride ahead of me to this upstart town. See that my house in the corn market is made ready for my arrival, and let the Provost of Beverley and his canons be prepared to wait upon me there with detailed reports of these events.'

Sir Matthew dared protest at that. 'My lord, perhaps the Provost's house would offer better protection from the rabble?'

'Indeed it would,' the Archbishop agreed, his voice weighted with sarcasm. 'And the rabble would then observe that the Archbishop of York makes humble haste to attend the Provost of Beverley. Prepare my own house as I have instructed. Let the people see for themselves which of us waits and which comes running on command. And there is one thing more . . .'

'My lord?'

'Under no circumstances is the woman to be brought before me. I will not have the soiled under-linen of some lecherous priest exhibited for all to see, nor will I lower myself to discuss these delicate matters with a ditcher's wife. See to it.'

'But my lord, she is to speak on the priest's behalf.'

'As well she might, while she suckles his child and sleeps between his sheets.'

'Not so, my lord,' Father Alban contradicted softly. 'She will swear on oath that he is blameless.'

'Would his mistress do otherwise?' Roger demanded. Once again he dipped into his clothes to pull out crumpled sheets of hand-written messages. 'These say that he is blameless, these others that he is a crafty charlatan. Am I to let the ditcher's wife decide the issue?'

'How can you deny her the right to speak, my lord?'

Roger scowled thoughtfully. 'I cannot, for that will leave me open to criticism, but to wait like a humble clerk upon her words would be to invite the ridicule of the people. The eyes of many will be upon me once I take my place as judge and overlord in this irksome matter; the King's, the Pope's, those of my dearest friends and bitterest enemies. Are you suggesting that I place my reputation at the disposal of this common ditcher's wife?'

Sir Matthew glanced at the priest by his side. 'Indeed no, your lordship, but how is it to be prevented?'

'Easily. You will deal with her before I arrive. Come now, don't gape at me like a pair of nervous wenches before an army. Have a clerk take down her words and let that be an end to it. I choose to believe that she is the priest's mistress and the child their bastard son. As you well know, this present pope of ours would have all priests avowed to celibacy. He will chastise all those who flaunt his wishes, especially those who keep their whores and bastards comfortably housed at the Church's expense. I have a mind to bind this rebel priest to a pilgrimage in the Holy Land for seven years or more. Such hardship should dampen his ambitions, if he survives it. As for the murdered canon, let the Provost deal with the matter as he will. My efforts will be fully occupied in making sure that my personal interests in Beverley are protected. Let any man beware who dares make profit of his lord's absence.'

'Indeed, my lord.'

'Be on your way within the hour and go in all haste. My company will follow at a slower pace when the carts are packed and this wretched fog begins to lift.'

'As you wish, my lord.'

The Archbishop heeled his horse forward, only to rein it back so sharply that the animal was forced to change direction mid-stride. 'And when I reach this *Beaver Lake*,' he growled, pronouncing the old name as if it were an insult, 'I expect the ditcher's wife and her whelp to be gone and their whereabouts unknown to any but yourselves.'

'But my lord,' Sir Matthew protested, 'we must know your wishes before we can act on this. What exactly is to be done?

The woman is under the close protection of her priest, and neither Father Alban nor I have the authority to override his guardianship, unless you intend that we gather a force of arms against him.'

Roger of York looked coldly at the two men, the priest and the knight, who hung in shared indecision upon their master's pleasure. He felt the way his monarch must have felt when all his princely power and prestige, his rage, his pleas, his threats, were not enough to bend one stubborn bishop to his will. He saw this priest of Beverley as a lesser Becket, a self-opinionated, ambitious man who would become untouchable unless expediency trimmed his hasty progress before he was allowed to outgrow himself. Now the Archbishop chose his words with care and spoke them clearly, so they could not be misinterpreted.

'God's teeth, will no one rid me of this turbulent priest?'

He saw both men blanch to hear King Henry's ill-fated words repeated for their benefit. Full responsibility had now been passed into their hands. He had simply ordered that the task be done: how they achieved it was their own affair. Having said his piece he wheeled his mount around, spurred it savagely and galloped back towards the castle.

'Rid him of the priest?' Father Alban repeated.

'That's what he said.'

His companion signed the cross, shaking his head. 'I want no part of this.'

'Nor I,' Sir Matthew said. 'I am not in the business of killing priests or cutting down women and babes.'

'But what is to be done? How will we escape what our lord the Archbishop expects of us?'

Sir Matthew scratched his chin and shrugged his shoulders inside his heavy cloak. 'We will ride to Beverley at once and we will repeat, word for word, what Roger of York has said on this matter.'

'Repeat to whom, an aging Provost who has but half his wits remaining? A company of canons who will take the words full circle, back to the Archbishop?' The priest was nervous. Despite the cold, a sudden sweat was glistening on his brow and upper lip. He was not shaped for intrigue and deception, and the memory of Becket's murder, though ten years old almost to the day, still had the power to make his stomach churn.

Now Sir Matthew Turton, made of sterner stuff and blessed with a more devious turn of mind, righted himself in the saddle and said decisively: 'Well then, friend Alban, if Roger of York can play so well the part of Henry Plantagenet, we two will assume the guise of Pontius Pilate. We will carry this burden as far as Beverley, and there we will wash our hands of the whole affair.'

'May such a thing be done without incurring the wrath of York?' the priest asked eagerly. 'If so then I will hear of it.'

'Then listen well and speak of it no more,' Sir Matthew told him. 'Thanks to Simeon's inquiry into the death of Canon Bernard, one Cyrus de Figham, a powerful and ambitious man, has been exposed to the worst kind of suspicion, that of murdering his Canon for personal gain. He will take up this burden of ours for he will, I am sure, be glad of a chance to serve his lord Archbishop at the expense of his accuser. He too might well be thinking at this moment: "Will no one rid me of this turbulent priest?"'

Together Father Alban and Sir Matthew urged their mounts to a gallop and followed the Archbishop across the frosty, hard-packed ground. The waiting group had already fallen in behind their master, grateful that the lengthy wait in the freezing cold was at last brought to an end. As they hastened off in a newly formed group towards the castle, one man who had been among them stayed behind. This was Master Joseph Melville, steward of his lordship's provisions, accounts and sundry holdings. Cloakless and hoodless, he sat bolt upright in the saddle, staring straight ahead, his face gaunt and his beard white with frost. Long after the others had gone in search of crackling hearths and frothing flagons of good strong mead, a steady drizzle of sleet began to fall. It blew in soft clouds across the open meadows, hiding the frozen lake behind a veil and shrouding the trees in white. From time to time Master Melville's mount shook its head and pawed at the ground, whinnying softly. When it heard no soothing sound and felt no comforting hand upon the bridle, it shook its head once more and began to walk towards the castle, bearing its master home.

CHAPTER TWENTY-SIX

For two more days a heavy mist surrounded Beverley, making the wetlands and marshes so treacherous that few dare venture out upon them. The messengers returned from St Theodore's Rest in the dead of night, both of them shivering and chilled to the bone, and with their souls unsettled by the eerie nature of those barren marshes. They brought the prior's welcome for Elvira and the child, and a list of items desperately needed by the monks. The storm had brought a high wind and several hours of torrential rain to the little priory. The waters of the surrounding lake had risen, as they always did at that time of the year, to flood the cellars and keeps and further disturb the priory's uncertain foundations. Being well used to the harshness of the winter months, the monks had lost no more than a few sacks of flour and some trays of dried herbs. Other than that, St Theodore's Rest remained as it had always been, a small oasis in a hostile sea, a place where a man, or a woman, might retreat from danger.

'They will leave when the fog lifts,' Simeon decided when he heard the news, and so it was to be, until the riders arrived from Lincoln to say that Roger de Pont l'Evèque was on his way. And after that he had a change of heart, for he began to think that the boy and his nurse might avoid the perilous journey and be sequestered much closer to home than was that isolated priory. With the Archbishop of York in residence at last, what safer place for them but under his very roof?

Father Alban left the prebendary house in Moorgate with a troubled mind and a heavy heart. He had been two hours in the company of Cyrus de Figham and Wulfric de Morthlund, two priests who wore their absent canons' rich attire with an almost unseemly ease. Father Alban and Sir Matthew had been splendidly served in a manner designed to rival many of the greater houses. They had dined on dressed pike and firm, fresh eels, three meats cooked on a spit and honey-glazed, and roasted pigeons stuffed with walnuts and chestnuts and swamped with honey and almond sauce. All this in a town half-devastated by the elements, and to wash this fine fare down, as much imported brandy wine as they could drink.

'Will no one rid me of this turbulent priest?'

Sir Matthew Turton's words had rung in that sumptuously furnished room: the Archbishop's words and once the King's, the very words that had, a decade since, condemned a sainted man to death at his own altar.

'Roger of York said that to you?' de Morthlund asked. 'In those same words?'

'The same.'

The fat man's gaze then rested on Father Alban. 'In those same words? Exactly?'

'Exactly,' Father Alban had heard himself confirm, and he did not think of himself as Pilate, washing his hands of an innocent man's destiny, but as Judas, passing that same man into the hands of his enemies.

'*Will no one rid me of this turbulent priest?*'

Cyrus de Figham had rolled the words around on his tongue, reciting them like poetry and savouring their sweetness. His coldly cultured voice made them sound like a sentence of death.

'Such careless words once sealed an Archbishop's fate,' Wulfric commented with an almost gleeful smile.

'Careless?' Cyrus asked. 'That meticulous King, who knew his knights so well he could read their minds? That sharp, conniving monarch who could judge the measure of any man with the accuracy of a craftsman? King Henry *careless*?' He shook his head and smiled, and his slate-grey eyes showed malicious amusement when he surveyed his guests. 'No more careless than was our own Archbishop when he repeated the words to you, Sir Matthew Turton, and no more than yourself in bringing them here, to us.'

Father Alban shivered now as he recalled that quicksilver gaze. A canon had been murdered and suspicion for the deed must first fall upon the man who had seen him last, even if that man had been his own priest. Father Alban had met that priest, Cyrus de Figham, only once, and was convinced that he was capable, if not actually guilty, of murder. He would be glad to reach the Archbishop's house in the Cornmarket, and there lay down his head and sleep away both the fatigues of the journey and the discomforts of that interview. But first he was to meet the aging Cuthbert, Canon of St Peter's, and the priest that some already called a saint, though they sinned against the Church itself by doing so.

In the Minster Church of St John, Father Alban saw the stripped, closed-off altar and the gloomy stairwell where the canon was murdered, the flooded crypts that would never be reopened, the awesome damage inflicted by the storm, the lesser, more sickening damage imposed by a thief upon the golden shrine of St John of Beverley. He heard the story of an infant's baptism at St Martin's font, of the subsequent destruction of that ancient parish church, and of the strange hooded figure that brought the new-born as a gift to Beverley. He saw young priests and hooded clerks tending the sick, feeding the hungry, comforting the dying, and doing all in Simeon's name, against the Church's teaching. Roger de Pont l'Evêque would not be pleased with all that awaited him in Beverley. The stories were many and various, but one fact shone as brightly and as clearly as the morning star upon each one of them: something had happened here.

However history, Popes or Archbishops chose to interpret it, something of great significance had happened here.

It was Cuthbert who brought Simeon from the grounds of St Peter's where he had been toiling to clear the waterways of debris. The younger man arched his back and lifted his arms to flex the aching muscles of his shoulders. His fingers were split in several places and his palms were calloused. His face was streaked with dust and sweat, yet from the midst of all that grime his eyes shone as blue and as clear as a cloudless sky. With a tired smile he took the older man firmly by the arm and together they walked amid flattened and uprooted trees towards the old scriptorium.

'You must think long and hard about your meeting with Roger of York,' Cuthbert said, breaking a lengthy silence.

'I have done little else but think of it,' Simeon admitted. 'And whichever way my mind turns I arrive, as I always must, at the same end. I can but offer him the simple truth. Will it be enough?'

'Enough?' Cuthbert asked. 'My son, I fear the simple truth, as you so naively name it, will be too much for our lord Archbishop.'

'He knows his duty,' Simeon said. 'They say he has never shirked it elsewhere, so I doubt he will do so here.'

'Your faith is touching, Simeon. Oh, he is a fine Archbishop, that much cannot be denied, but first he is an artful politician. Why else would Henry value him so highly? But duty, now that is another matter entirely.'

'Are you telling me that our lord Archbishop is something less than honest?'

'I am merely reminded you, Simeon, that a man who keeps so conspicuously well the laws of England and the laws of Rome is treading a precarious course. He serves two masters, determined to satisfy both and lose his seat for neither.'

'And hung between the two, the only master he really serves is himself,' Simeon conceded. 'Yet even then, the good he does along the way may far outweigh the bad, at the Last Reckoning.'

'Indeed. All I ask is that you see beyond your own clear

truth when you are brought before this one-time Provost of Beverley. Roger de Pont l'Evèque is the man who twice procured the dismissal of Thomas Becket, who played a dual-handed game, then cleverly took an oath of innocence to absolve him of his part in the Canterbury murder. For years he has been playing off his Pope against his monarch and vice versa, leaning to each, this way and that, according to which way the wind is blowing, and still he keeps his balance and his head. Do you hope that he will serve your interests any better?'

'I can only hope that he will recognise the truth when he hears it.'

Here Cuthbert stopped and shook his head, a stiff-necked, painful gesture. 'To what end, Simeon? How will it serve you if he does believe it? What have ambition and politics to do with truth? He will judge your story by how it can be used, no more than that, and he will not fail to sacrifice you and your *simple truth* for the greater good, if he judges it politic to do as much.'

'Well then, I fear he must lean in and out of whichever wind he chooses, but he will not see me twist and turn on this. I will neither deny nor embellish anything that has happened here.'

'I fear you may have to, Simeon, for the child's sake.' They had reached the scriptorium and slowed their steps. 'May we go in? A priest is here from Hovard Castle. His name is Alban, and he's an honest enough man despite his eagerness to see all sides of every argument, lest some higher authority bring him to account. He came to St Peter's in secret, to see the boy. I think you would be wise to hear what he has to say.'

'But not before he has been heard by Wulfric de Morthlund and Cyrus de Figham, it seems.' Simeon smiled.

'He has?'

'Indeed he has. Even we who toil in the muddy ditches hear our portion of town gossip. But yes, I will come inside with you to hear what this Alban has to say.'

In the scriptorium Father Alban set aside some hand-written pages reluctantly, for he had been enjoying the detailed history set out in perfect script on every sheet. He did not count himself amongst those scholars who would be remembered by posterity, but he recognised and appreciated translation of fine quality when he saw it. As a scribe this Simeon stood in a class of his own. He wrote three languages and had the hand of an artist, and such skills were surely wasted in this place. They might be put to better use at York or Durham or even Canterbury. If that could be arranged, the Archbishop would not need to waste such talents on fruitless pilgrimage to the Holy Land.

Alban was nervous when he met the priest. He was shocked to see that the hands which had produced those beautiful translations of the Latin text were bruised and bloodied. Today the hands of a scribe were the hands of a common labourer. He had not expected such a man as this, with the bearing of a nobleman and a physical presence that was overwhelming.

'This is Simeon of Beverley,' Cuthbert said, as if the tall, broad-shouldered, blue-eyed priest might not be recognised. 'He plans to seek Roger's protection for his godson and his nurse. What say you to that idea, Brother Alban?'

The small man shook his head and seemed uncertain. 'I came to see him with my own eyes,' he said, 'and I find he is a child like any other, and yet . . .' He shrugged and fell silent, finding no words to express his unease. Then he glanced about him nervously and looked unfalteringly into Simeon's face. Whispering now, he said: 'If you would keep him alive, send him away in secret to some place where no man or woman knows of him. And send the woman too, for she'll not be allowed to speak on your behalf. Do it now, at once, while there is yet time to save them. And trust no one. Your enemies, and theirs, are everywhere.'

Simeon scowled. He knew a frightened man when he saw one, and he recognised the truth when it rang this clearly in his ears. 'They are in certain danger, then?'

'From every source. Forgive me, I dare say no more than this: they will be taken long before Roger of York arrives in Beverley. And after them, yourself, friend Simeon. And now

I must make haste to the Archbishop's house. By your leave, sir.'

'But wait, hold up one moment, Brother Alban . . .'

Father Cuthbert's hand fell lightly on Simeon's arm. 'No, let him go. He has already put himself at risk by coming here.' He bowed and signed the cross for the benefit of their visitor. 'We are grateful to you, friend Alban. Go in peace, and may our Lord be with you.'

'And with you also,' Alban muttered, hastening to the door.

As Osric lifted back the heavy beam to let him out, the nervous priest turned his head for one last glance at Simeon. 'Nowhere is safe for them,' he repeated, 'nor for you, I fear.'

Osric bolted the door and strode into the room with a look of thunderous rage on his face. 'They have us trapped from every side,' he growled. 'His lordship prefers to sidestep an issue and so that issue is quietly removed. My God, this is the coward's way.'

'Or simply the more politic, depending on your point of view,' Simeon observed.

'Well, what is to be done? We cannot sit here waiting for the axe to fall.'

'Nor will we,' the big man said. 'We can make no move in darkness, so we must double the guard at the door and make everything ready for the journey to St Theodore's Rest tomorrow. Fog or no, they must leave here at first light.'

'As we first planned? The same way?' Osric asked, and Simeon nodded, trusting to the other's strategies.

'As we first planned,' he said.

Throughout the long night services, Simeon's mind was so preoccupied with the problem of Elvira's safe conduct with the boy to St Theodore's Rest that his prayers remained half-said and his singing of the Office frequently faltered. The Minster was bitterly cold. Its gaping eastern wall and damaged roof made it a haven for icy draughts that scuttled from every curve and corner and whistled through damaged masonry. Despite the shrouded, unlit altar where no masses could be said until reconsecration, a full complement of

301

sixty-three hooded figures braved the night air and the lowering hours to sing their splendid anthems to the glory of God. They huddled close together in the half-cleared choir, and all around them, in every arch and corner, around the pillars and altars and against the piles of rubble, the homeless clung to what meagre shelter they could find. Pilgrims from foreign parts slept shoulder to shoulder with their backs against the walls, their knees drawn up to provide a pillow, their hoods pulled down over their faces. It was a long, cold night, the twentieth day of December, seven days since the tempest came to Beverley.

Towards the end of Matins, while the sonorous voices swelled for the last *Te Deum*, the weary priests began to file from the choir, some staggering with fatigue and cold, some holding another's arms for their support. Wulfric de Morthlund was one of the first to leave, though he had slipped quietly into his place in the choir only minutes before the *Te Deum* was begun. It was his practice to show himself there from time to time, especially when the Archbishop was expected, but in truth, although he claimed the fee of fourpence for attending Matins and Vespers, he rarely came and never enjoyed the Office in its entirety. He swept out now ahead of the others, intent on reaching home before the night's chill could penetrate the warm fur linings of his fine attire.

Simeon left soon after, stamping his feet to force the cold away. Near the door he heard a deep voice speak his name.

'God's blessing, Brother Simeon.'

'May His love protect you,' Simeon responded, then turned to meet the dark gaze of Cyrus de Figham. The man had been standing by one of the great stone columns scrutinising the faces of the choral priests as they filed towards the door. Swathed in a splendid cloak and with his hands warmly gloved, he fell into step beside Simeon and bent his head to speak so that others might not overhear him.

'The Archbishop is on his way here. You have done what others could not do. You have lured him from his winter lay-

302

over at Hovard Castle, and now he hastens here at your beckoning. I am inclined to believe he will not thank you for it.'

'Or to hope he will not,' Simeon answered dryly. 'Nevertheless, he comes and that is good. We need him here.'

'And what will you tell him, priest, that will make sense?'

'The truth. No more, no less.'

Cyrus smiled without amusement. 'You and a hundred others.'

'The truth will out,' Simeon said, not quite convinced despite his confident tone.

Now Cyrus's smile was smug and his eyes danced with amusement as he surveyed Simeon with his head half-turned. 'We have arrested the man who murdered Canon Bernard.'

'What?'

'Ah, I was sure that piece of news would interest you. We have him at the Provost's house, locked in the keep for want of a prison cell that is not already occupied with gallons of mud and water. He is a likely murderer.'

'Indeed? Has he confessed to the crime?'

'Not yet, but he will. And even if he maintains his plea of innocence, who will believe him? He is a thief and a liar, and he made a brutal attack on a priest within the Minster itself. He was caught red-handed prising jewels from the sacred shrine, and though the authorities failed to apprehend him at the time, he has since been found with one of the jewels hidden in his hood, though he swears he has no idea how it got there.'

'Planted, perhaps, by someone with a vested interest in seeing him hanged for the murder of a canon?' Simeon suggested.

Cyrus shrugged his shoulders. 'His kind are as numerous and as inconsequential as sewer rats within God's Great Design. My lord Archbishop will enjoy chastising such a wretch.'

'Guilty or not?' Simeon asked.

Cyrus shrugged again. 'If he is not, I'm sure he will suffice.'

303

'Your prisoner is a scapegoat, then, to be punished in place of the real killer?'

Cyrus looked long and hard into Simeon's face, and even in the flickering candlelight his eyes were hard. He seemed to be holding his answer back for best effect.

'God's blessing on you, Brother,' he said at last, inclining his head in a small, curt bow before turning away and heading for the door, the satisfied smile still hanging upon his face.

As Simeon turned to take the other door he collided with a priest whose hood was pulled well down to hide his face. The other man made a grab for Simeon's hands and hastened to dismiss his polite apology.

'You do not know me. We have not spoken.'

'If you insist,' Simeon said, recognising immediately the distinctive voice and manner.

'Take this and beware,' the voice said urgently, and pressed a scrap of paper into Simeon's hand before hurrying away to join the line of priests picking their way through the eerie shadows of the Minster Church.

At the door leading from the north transept Simeon paused beside a flaming torch set in a metal sconce high on the wall. By its light he unrolled the narrow tube of paper in his fingers and saw the cryptic message written there. Three words, *you are betrayed*, was all it said.

They met on the higher slopes of St Peter's grounds, some distance from the scriptorium, in a spot where the earth was so hardened by frost that a footfall might be heard long before its owner could draw close enough to eavesdrop upon their whispered conversation. Thorald was here, Antony and the faithful Osric, young Richard and Simeon.

'Are you certain it was him?' Osric asked in a whisper.

Simeon nodded. 'Could any man here mistake the Little Hawk, even with his hood over his face?'

'It is a trick, then?'

'I doubt it,' Simeon said. 'If we are betrayed why warn us of it? Why not simply act upon the betrayal?'

'Unless our enemies want to force us into keeping the boy and his nurse right here, where they might be more easily reached by swordsmen.'

Thorald nodded and gave a grunt of agreement. 'That is a real possibility, Simeon. If the Archbishop himself demands access to the scriptorium, can you refuse him? And if he bids you remove them from Church property, as he is bound to do if only for appearance's sake, what then? You will be forced to comply, and where will that leave the woman and the boy?'

Simeon sucked air through his teeth with a hissing whistle, scowling at his thoughts.

'No, I believe the message to be genuine.'

'But why would he warn you?' Osric asked. 'Why would he defy his master by giving aid to you in such a serious matter?'

'Perhaps he seeks to prevent his master doing something unforgivable,' Simeon suggested. 'Perhaps by saving the boy and Elvira he saves his lord from the crime of harming them?'

Thorald scoffed at that. 'I doubt if one crime, more or less, would alter the measure of Wulfric de Morthlund's guilt.'

'Be that as it may,' Osric said, 'but either way, we gain by knowing that we are betrayed.'

'So, gentlemen, what is to be done?' Brother Antony asked, speaking for the first time.

All eyes were on Simeon when he said: 'We send a boat to St Theodore's Rest, as we first planned. We carry out our first plan to the letter. Are we agreed?'

'We are agreed,' all whispered, then the group divided into shadow and fog, each man slipping away as he had come, silent and furtive.

By dawn the mist had lifted so that it hung above their heads like fallen cloud. Its moisture had frozen on the ground so that their steps made noise that could not be avoided. The dawn was grey and murky, and here and there a slender shaft of sunlight filtered through, as if the sky above the fog was already clear and bright. Three mules had been prepared, each heavily laden with the monks' supplies, and with them would go five armed men to act as guards until the boat was loaded and away.

The scarred priest, Michael, had begged to be allowed to accompany the boy to the priory, and there remain for as long as he was needed. Simeon stared at him for a long time, hoping to read his guilt or innocence in his face. He saw no trace of either, yet someone had carried details of their plans beyond the walls of the scriptorium. Someone had put the boy's life at risk, and Simeon could not believe that Father Alban was the culprit. Even so, he saw no fault in this young man.

'May God go with you and keep you safe,' he said, signing the cross over the young priest's head. 'Guard your charges well, friend Michael.'

'With my life, if needs demand it,' Michael said.

'I'll pray it does not come to that,' Simeon answered grimly.

After receiving Simeon's blessing, Michael stood aside, watching the group make final preparations. He had been assured that his was no hazardous betrayal, that the woman and the boy would not be harmed but merely carried to a place of safety, a neutral place decided by the Archbishop. They would be taken from the boat when the other guards were gone, and Michael would carry the Archbishop's message back to Simeon, and there receive forgiveness for his part in it.

He watched the big priest stoop over the woman, adjust her hood well down over her face and bundle the child more closely into her arms. It was a brief farewell and then the little group started out, moving away from St Peter's and toward the wetlands lying beyond the beck. Michael, on foot and armed with a borrowed sword, brought up the rear, and try as he might he could not keep himself from turning at the gate to see the figure of the big priest watching after them.

'Forgive me, Father Simeon,' he muttered into the mist that hung between them. 'Forgive the lie, and know that I deliver your lady and your godson into safer hands than any humble priory could provide.'

And this, young Michael firmly believed, was the truth of it; had not two acting canons, Father Cyrus and Father Wulfric, told him so?

CHAPTER TWENTY-SEVEN

They made good time, for the dawn was barely in when they reached the marshes. Once there, they transferred the heavy sacks and boxes from the donkeys, left the animals in the charge of a jobbing boy and paddled their ungainly, flat-bottomed boats toward the open lake. The grunts and growls of their labours hung on the mist rising up from the marshes, and on several occasions the boats were slowed, or brought to a halt, by ice that had to be broken with their poles to allow free passage. Once into the deeper water of the lake they transferred their cargo to sturdier rowing vessels and gave their final instructions to the priest who was to row the lead boat out, with the second boat in tow, across the lake to the priory. No sign of St Theodore's Rest showed through the fog, though from the distant island came the softly muted tones of a single bell, and by its sound the priest would find his way there.

The men who had escorted them this far now held back while the rowing boats pulled away, and each of them was watchful and alert for any danger that might, in that murky morning, be lurking unseen at their very elbow.

'I do not like it,' Osric said in a gruff voice, watching the slender hooded figure of the woman hug her bundle against her breast as the boat eased silently away into the fog.

'They will not be taken out there on the lake,' Thorald assured him. 'The deeper water is too hazardous for a skirmish, especially in this thick fog. If they were to be attacked it would have happened here on the marsh, or back there on more solid ground.'

'Not so,' Antony said quietly, shaking his tonsured head. 'If they are to be attacked it will be now, while their guards are absent.'

Thorald signed the cross. 'Then God protect them while their friends can not.'

'We must go back now,' Osric declared with urgency, using his pole to shift the boat through muddy water thickened to a dark gruel by weed. 'We must return to St Peter's without delay.'

From the rowing boat Michael watched the others leave, Osric the infirmarian urging his strange little vessel away from the edge of the lake and back across the marsh, the others following close behind. He saw them vanish into the fog, but the woman, huddled in her seat at the prow, did not turn her head to watch her guards depart. Michael felt the sweat grow cold on his skin and wondered if the woman grieved to leave the handsome blue-eyed priest behind. He did not know which stories were true, which were mere speculation and which malicious gossip. It was not for him to play the judge in these matters, only to do his best where it was needed and leave all else to his lordship, the Archbishop.

From behind him came the steady tolling of the priory bell, and as he pulled steadily toward the centre of the lake, the thick mist that always hung above the water rose and thickened to meet the fog now closing in around them. He could see the towed boat trailing sluggishly in their wake, laden with goods for the monks and sitting so low in the water that some of the sacks and bags already showed damp in places. Now other sounds, some close, some distant, reached his ears. He thought he heard a man's voice bark an order, the sound of an oar lifted clumsily from the water, the steady rhythm of a moving vessel. He lifted his own oars free of the water and set them in a resting position inside the boat.

'Ho, there!' he called softly, and again, with his hands cupped around his mouth, 'Ho, there!'

Seeing the woman stiffen with alarm, he leaned well forward and bent his head in an attempt to see the face beneath her hood. 'Have no fear, Mistress Elvira,' he reassured her. 'These men are coming on the Archbishop's business. They will take you and the child to a safer place until the authorities are ready to question you. They are not here to harm you. Have no fear.'

A boat now loomed out of the mist, a large, deep-sided craft that carried as many as a dozen men. At first glance Michael saw that all were darkly cloaked and heavily armed, some with their faces hidden beneath hoods or helmets. At second glance he saw that all were soldiers, with not a single holy man among them. As the boat bore down on them he felt the first sickening twinge of doubt, and there was an anxious ring to his voice when he called out:

'What's this? My friends, put up your swords. The woman and child are delivered into your hands in the name of my lord Archbishop of York. Put up your swords. You have no need of force.'

'Put up your tongue, priest,' a harsh voice said. 'We have no need of your instruction.'

He saw the woman cross herself and heard a sob catch in her throat. His hands gripped the sides of the boat, but the strength had suddenly drained from his arms and fingers.

'Safe conduct,' he cried. 'I am Brother Michael from St John's at Beverley.'

'Aye,' came the answering yell, 'we know you by your purple face and gathered features.'

'Then you must know I am about Archbishop's business. I was promised safe conduct.'

'And you shall have it, all the way to the bottom of the lake,' the gruff voice bellowed, and the soldier's companions guffawed loudly at the jest.

Now Michael felt the icy fingers of fear clutch at his

innards. His small betrayal of Simeon's trust had been but a scrap to catch the bigger mackerel. He was the one betrayed, and as that boatload of soldiers nudged his own boat sideways, and as the swords came out, he realised that he was to pay for his folly with his life. For a moment he dangled on his own indecision, whether to sign himself with the sacred cross in preparation for death, to snatch up the oars and try to row to safety, or to draw his sword and die in the child's defence. Then it was too late for one course or the other. He felt the first blow strike across his shoulder, a dull thump of a blow that seemed more like a punch than a cut from a sword, and so the sudden spurt of blood amazed him. As he fell forward he saw the woman cut down and the child attacked and it was then he saw the situation for what it was. As the woman fell her hood slipped back to reveal the face of one of Elvira's companion nuns, and the bundle that fell from her arms was not a living child but a bundled, swaddled shape with a painted face.

'Oh God, forgive me,' he tried to say, choking on the words.

Father Simeon had known, after all. He had read the betrayal in Michael's face and known what the young priest was too naive and inexperienced to see, that the boy and his nurse had been placed in mortal danger. And so Father Simeon had sent him to his death for that betrayal, and now, as a sword-blade sliced his forearm open to the bone, Michael knew there was more he could do than simply forfeit his life for his folly.

A strange fatigue had overtaken him. He felt no pain, only the dull blows falling here and there across his head and body. A sticky, warm liquid filled his mouth and threatened to gag him with its cloying sweetness. In laborious half-motion he managed to roll his body across the fallen effigy of the child, an effigy now saturated with the life-blood of the nun who had held it fast until her life gave out. His only concern now was that the killers should not see how they had been duped. This thing he could do for Simeon before he died: he could keep these butchers from knowing young Peter still lived.

'In the name of God!'

The words erupted from his mouth and echoed into the fog, loud enough, despite his wounds, to carry as far as St Theodore's Rest and beyond. At the same time he rolled sideways, clutching the bundle to his chest. He felt cold water rush into the boat, felt the nun's mutilated body slide overboard, and in another moment he too was sinking face-downwards into the lake. Calmly and without haste he folded his arms across his chest to trap the bundle there, and with a long sigh deliberately emptied his lungs of precious air. Then he sucked water into all the airless spaces to ensure that his body sank like a stone to the weed-tangled floor of the lake.

Osric and Antony parted company with Thorald at his ruined church on Holme Church Lane. They dismissed the jobber-lad with the donkeys, and made their way in haste to the old scriptorium. Simeon greeted them there without a word, though his face was tense and his eyes wide with unspoken questions.

'We saw nothing and heard nothing,' Osric said, 'but the place was ripe for ambush. The marsh mist added to the fog until a man was blinded by the very air he breathed.'

'Did they cross the lake?' Simeon asked.

'We did not wait to see,' Antony cut in. 'We feared for their safety, but we feared more for yours.' He strode into the room, to the rim of the well where Elvira sat with a cloak around her shoulders and the child held in her lap. She looked at him with grave dark eyes and thanked him with a smile for his concern. The child, when he touched its tiny head, looked back at him with its quiet stare and, in the way of all infants barely into the clamorous world of men, seemed wise in the knowledge of all that occurred around him.

'And now we leave for the convent,' Osric said. 'Is all prepared?'

'It is,' Simeon confirmed. 'They are to be kept in the Abbess's old apartments where the treasury once was housed. It has but a single door and its grounds are protected by a high wall. None but her most trusted women will have access to the place, save for the two Benedictine gardeners Antony has employed to guard them at all times. Who will think to search for them there, where those who seek to profit from the town's misfortune have also made their nests?'

They were to travel the short distance to the Keldgate Bar on foot. Elvira and her companion, Sister Catherine, were dressed in the plain, dark robes of monks, their faces and hair concealed, and the child was to be carried by Simeon in such a way that it resembled a bundle of clothing. A little group of monks and priests was unlikely to attract undue attention. In that still heavy fog, and with no goods or donkey to be stolen, it was hoped that they would travel to St Anne's without incident.

It was a vain hope, for men are ever at the mercy of the fates, and even as they left the safety of the scriptorium, the factors bent on destroying their plans were already in play.

Osric and Antony went out ahead of the others, their hands on their sword hilts and their senses alert. Behind them came the younger men, Mark and Richard, and after them the women, dressed as monks. Then came Simeon with his godson tucked beneath his arm and the fingers of his right hand resting lightly on the dagger at his girdle. They moved out slowly, testing the ground as they went, and within a few strides of the scriptorium door were halted by the clamour of a sudden skirmish down by the infirmary. They heard the cries of men and the clash of steel on steel, and they knew that the infirmary building had once again come under attack.

In one swift movement Simeon grabbed Elvira by the shoulder and placed her behind him, back inside the room. He handed the child to her, pulled the other woman to safety, drew out his dagger and blocked the open doorway with his body. They heard the cry of '*Looters! Looters!*' and the sound of many footsteps running in their direction. A moment later Osric and the others were engaged in a clumsy, half-blind battle in the fog as they tried to prevent the intruders reaching the scriptorium.

Simeon turned back briefly. 'Drop the bar in place and keep it there until I tell you otherwise,' he shouted, then pulled the door shut behind him and went to assist his friends in the noisy fray.

The bar was heavy, too great a weight for the elderly nun to lift unaided. When she called out for assistance Elvira returned the baby to his cradle and hurried to lend her own strength to the task of lifting and slotting the great beam into its metal brackets. They had barely shifted it partway from its housing when the door burst open and a man rushed in. He was a young man dressed in a leather skullcap and a mud-spattered cloak. His breath was laboured, as if he had come a good distance on foot, pressed hard by urgent matters.

'Father Simeon, are you there? I have ill news of . . .'

The man's voice halted in mid-sentence. He gaped long and hard at Elvira, his thoughts clearly written upon his rough peasant features. Then his gaze was drawn to the cradle where the baby lay. Elvira caught the intent in that glance and with a startled cry rushed to defend her charge. At the same time Sister Catherine let the heavy door beam clatter to the floor and made a brave rush to hamper the intruder. She flung herself upon him, clutching at the folds of cloth around his neck, screaming for God's and Simeon's help to save their innocent lives from bloody murder.

'Unhand me, woman! Get away from me!'

A short-sword left its scabbard between the nun's frail body and the soldier's muscular chest. It twisted sharply, sank into her flesh, jerked inward and upward in a savage arc that opened her body from groin to breastbone and turned her screams to gurgles in her throat. Her hands came down to clutch the blade. She fell to her knees, her face a mask of pain and disbelief, and the sword as it withdrew sliced through her fingers. Above her head, her killer turned his glaring gaze on Elvira, who hugged the child against her breast, her hood thrown back, her eyes great orbs of terror in her ashen face.

'Witch!' the man hissed. 'I saw you die out there on the

314

lake, you and the priest's bastard.'

Elvira shook her head, and as the man stepped forward she stepped back, trying to keep the high-rimmed well between them, all the time praying silently that someone had heard the Sister's screams and even now was rushing back to defend her and the boy.

He lunged with the sword. Elvira leaped lightly back and to one side. He lunged again, taunting her with the blade. Its point made contact with the sleeve of her robe, gashing the cloth and drawing blood from her arm so that she gasped and tried to set her shoulder between her attacker and the child.

'You'll die for this,' she said, knowing that she must hold the man at bay for as long as possible.

'Don't threaten me, witch,' he sneered. 'I fear no spells that you might cast.'

'I am no witch. The woman on the lake was a substitute, her child just a bundle of rags and bones. It was simple trickery, not witchcraft, that kept me alive. Why must you kill me? Why must you harm this child? What harm have we done that you should want us dead?'

The man leered at her, licking his lips and moving the blade of his sword in small, menacing circles in the air between them.

'I have my orders, witch.'

'Orders from whom? Who fears the truth so much that they would murder innocents rather than have it spoken?'

'*Elvira!*'

The sudden bellow from the door was enough to strike the stoutest heart with terror. The soldier wheeled, saw Simeon's greater bulk framed in the doorway, hesitated momentarily, then turned and lunged with his sword towards Elvira. She was not nimble enough to avoid the blow. Although she sprang sideways, turning the child away, the blade passed over her shoulder and breast to pierce the soft inner flesh of her left forearm, and as it withdrew it cut a red and bloody path across the baby's neck.

Simeon roared again as he leapt into the room. As the

soldier turned from his lunge he met the enraged priest head-on and with his sword half-raised, too late to prepare himself for his own defence. The priest's blade entered his body below his armpit, slicing through flesh and ribs with equal ease to find the vital organs lying underneath. The soldier's eyes bulged and the noisy rasp of air rushing out from his ruptured lungs was the only sound he made as he went down.

Now Osric and Antony burst through the door with Mark and Richard close on their heels. As the door slammed closed behind them they took in the scene at a glance. They saw the soldier fall to Simeon's sword, and the butchered nun now lying with her knees drawn up and her eyes turned glassy in death. And they saw the horror on Elvira's face as her bloody fingers closed the wound on the tiny baby's neck to keep the injured mite from bleeding to death.

'Dear God, the child!'

Simeon dropped to the ground beside Elvira. She leaned against him, her whole body trembling, and all that she could utter was: 'He's hurt . . . he's hurt . . .'

'How bad?' Simeon demanded, white-faced. 'How bad is it?'

'He's bleeding. I think the vein is cut.'

'Dear God!'

'Let me see. Let me see.' The wiry infirmarian loomed over the child, his expert fingers feeling for the wound. 'Let go, Elvira. I must inspect the wound.'

She shook her head. 'No, I cannot. He is bleeding. If I release the edges of the wound . . .'

'Elvira,' Osric said sharply, 'if you do not release him, how can I possibly do what I am trained to do?'

'But if the vein is cut . . .?'

'If it is breached then I must deal with it, and quickly, before he bleeds to death. Now let him go, Elvira.'

She would have resisted yet again, but Simeon placed his palm against her cheek and gently turned her face until her eyes met his, and the look that passed between them had no need of words.

316

'Do it slowly,' Osric urged. 'Careful, now, that's good, just a fraction more. Now, turn his head a little to one side. Antony, bring me the ivory stitching-pin, and some thread, I need a length of thread . . .'

'Take this,' Antony said, pulling the coarse stitching from his tunic so that the sleeve gaped open at the shoulder.

'That will suffice,' Osric nodded grimly, licked one end of the thread to smooth its fibres and passed it through the eye of the stitching-pin. 'We must move quickly now. Simeon, reach me that candle and hold it steady where I need most light. Elvira, turn the little one's face aside . . . tip his head so that his throat is exposed. That's it, now hold him still while I stitch the wound.'

The infirmarian worked with all the speed and accuracy of a man who had saved many lives on the battlefield. Two stitches were all it took the close the wound and after that, while Antony cleaned off the blood, Osric removed his heavy leather girdle, spread it out on the ground and selected certain items from its many slotted pockets. First he sprinkled the wound with a fine powder made from ground yarrow and poppy seeds, then smeared it with an ointment of Indian aloe to encourage the cut to skin over and heal rapidly. Then he placed a pad of linen against the baby's neck and bound it loosely with a strip of cloth to hold the dressing in place. By this time young Peter was wailing a protest as loudly as his lungs would allow. He needed to be quietened before his screams undid the surgeon's handiwork and set the wound to bleeding freely again.

'Put him to the breast, Elvira.'

Osric's instruction was for her sake as well as for the boy's. He had noted the chalky pallor of her face and the clammy chill of her hands. She was trembling violently and had sustained a deep sword wound on her inner forearm that must be cleaned and bound without delay. Before he attended to that he wanted her calmed and with a specific purpose to distract her.

'Please, Elvira,' Simeon whispered, and she shuddered at the sound of his voice. Then she slowly bared her breast and brought the baby to it, and all who watched gave thanks to God that the little boy was able to suckle despite his injury. Now Elvira meekly surrendered her forearm and allowed the infirmarian to apply a short row of his crude stitches to her flesh. As the wound was cleaned, closed and dressed, she neither flinched nor registered complaint. It was as if the incident had left her senses numbed, as if she had felt so much already that even physical pain was denied her now.

When the wound was dressed the infirmarian helped the others remove the bodies from the scriptorium. The soldier's carcass they carried to a spot outside the gates where the bodies of several looters already lay. The woman's they wrapped in cloth and set upon a handcart for the monks to take to St Anne's, where she would receive the full Christian burial to which she was entitled. Only after the bodies were cleared away did Osric draw Simeon aside to ask what had happened while they were dealing with the looters.

'It was a one in a thousand chance that the soldier arrived here at the precise moment he did,' Simeon explained. 'He had come to report that Michael, Elvira and the boy had been drowned while attempting to cross St Theodore's lake.'

'Then the boat was attacked, as we feared it would be?'

'It was indeed, and he, it seems, was one of the attackers. He must have come by way of the orchard gate and reached here just as we rushed out to deal with the intruders. Before Elvira and Sister Catherine could bar the door behind us, the soldier was inside the scriptorium. He recognised her at once, saw that Peter still lived, and decided to complete the evil work himself. And, Dear God in Heaven, he very nearly succeeded.'

'And he came alone?'

'That much we can say for certain,' Simeon confirmed.

'Then nobody beyond these walls can be aware that the woman still lives?'

'Nor that young Peter has survived.' Simeon gripped his friend's shoulders with both hands and searched his face for reassurance. 'Osric, he *will* survive?'

The infirmarian nodded. 'With care, and if the wound does not become infected.'

'And Elvira?'

'Her wound is serious. Her arm was all but pierced through by the sword, and what troubles me is that she is uncaring of it. The shock of this has robbed her of all feelings. She needs rest now, with plenty of good medicine, peace and quiet. The sooner we get her to St Anne's the better I will like it. If she falls ill, if she is unable to suckle the child ...' He left the rest of it unsaid, knowing that Simeon needed no reminders of the slender threads upon which the boy's life hung.

'We must leave at once then,' Simeon said at last. 'Elvira will travel on the cart with the body of Sister Catherine, and we can have her and the boy lodged under lock and key within the hour. Let Richard go on ahead to make sure that the side gate, the chapel door and the passageway are open. There must be no more delays to put their lives at risk. I want them safe, Osric. I want them *safe*.'

It was as he predicted. They made the journey through the fog-shrouded streets without further mishap, though they went fully armed and well prepared to deal with any happenstance. Elvira rode on the cart with Peter cradled in the crook of her arm and Simeon walking close beside her. At one point he found her hand beneath the folds of dark robing concealing her from view. He pressed her palm against his own, enveloping her small hand into his own. It was a protective, comforting gesture, and for a while Elvira watched his handsome profile through her half-closed eyes. She had been given a thick, sweet wine to drink before they left the old scriptorium, and she knew that something in the wine would make her sleepy and help to dull the pain she soon might begin to feel in her arm. Lulled by the rhythmic movements of the cart and comforted by the hand that held her own, she drifted upon the groggy edges of sleep, content to rest there until Simeon told her otherwise.

After a while she became aware of the change from cobblestones to smooth stone slabs beneath the wheels of the cart. The street sounds faded into the distance, to be replaced by the softer sounds of running water and choral voices raised in praise. She felt herself lifted and knew that she was in his arms, felt him walk with her across muddy, uneven ground, felt him stoop to pass through a small gateway set into a high stone wall, then through another door into a chilly passageway. She was vaguely aware of the opening and closing of many doors, the soft hum of women's voices, the sound of music coming from a distance, the scent of tallow candles, the brush of soft linen against her skin. And through the fog of sleep she feared that he would leave her and she struggled to tell him that, priest or no priest, celibate or not, she had come to love him with all her heart and soul. She did not know if she had merely dreamed or said the words aloud until her hand was pressed against his lips and his deep voice drifted gently into her mind.

'I know, Elvira,' she heard him say. 'I know you do.'

They made good time back to the infirmary and as far as they were able to ascertain, no word had spread of their brief visit to St Anne's. It was Richard's own idea to make it known that he and Mark and the monk Antony had taken the body of a nun back to St Anne's for burial. He let it be known that she had been killed by looters, and in return for his story he heard the whispered rumour that a priest, a woman and a child had drowned in the flooded lake while attempting to reach St Theodore's Rest.

Simeon was brooding by the fire when news was brought to them that the Archbishop of York had at last arrived in Beverley. The great man and his retinue had gone directly to the house in the Cornmarket, and already Sir Hugh de Burton and Sir Robert de Clare were petitioning him for interview. It was Father Alban who brought the news to the scriptorium, and while he was drawn aside to take refreshment, Osric and Antony held back to speak to Simeon.

'Nothing remains to displease the Archbishop, and yet the boy and the woman are safe, that much you can be sure of,' Antony reminded him.

'And we will be your constant guards until the Archbishop

hears your story and sees your miracle for himself,' Osric added. 'Once you have his confidence, once he is assured that you are neither fraud nor charlatan, then he will be sympathetic to your cause.'

'And when that happens,' Antony said hopefully, 'the truth about Peter can be revealed, his future properly determined and his purpose here in Beverley brought under his lordship's permanent protection.'

Simeon shook his head. 'How I wish I could believe that,' he said. 'But no, he is not safe and nor is she. I fear that none of us will ever be safe unless ...' He snapped his fingers to attract Alban's attention, waving to beckon the older priest to join their group. 'Alban, I want the truth in a single word. Will you give it, on the assurance that your answer never passes beyond these walls?'

The priest swallowed nervously, looked around at the faces of these men he had come to trust, then raised himself up to his full height and nodded his head.

'I will be truthful,' he declared.

Simeon looked closely into his face, the better to read any untruth or false colouring he might attempt to impart with his reply. 'The truth as you know it, friend Alban. Can I expect fair judgment when I meet my lord Archbishop?'

There was a silence into which no man dared speak, and all that showed on Alban's face was pity and regret. His answer to the question was firm and unfaltering, a simple 'No.'

'So be it,' Simeon said, then turned to stare into the fire with troubled eyes and said again: 'So be it.'

CHAPTER TWENTY-EIGHT

There was a small stone cell beneath the Canon's house in Moorgate, a deep, dark hole with a tiny window set at ceiling height and overgrown on its outside by garden weeds. In the summer months its walls ran with water, in winter they were lined with a layer of ice, and for much of the year its earth floor was a bed of unsavoury mud. It was rumoured that several prisoners had died there since the house was first occupied, and that their bodies had simply been dug into the ground and left to rot. There was even a legend that once a priest named Edwin, put there to contemplate some minor sin of pride, had been forgotten in his Provost's absence and starved to death before he was remembered. Some said that he was found in an attitude of prayer, kneeling in the mud with his head bowed and his hands clasped in his lap, devout and trusting to the last. Others whispered that he died in torment, his fingers all but destroyed by his desperate attempts to escape, his mouth and tongue horribly lacerated when thirst drove him to suck the moisture from the walls.

Now, a decade later, the cell known as Edwin's Hole held a different type of prisoner. This one was a common man, stocky and muscular, a carter by trade and a Beverley man by birth. He lay slumped in the muddy corner where he had been thrown, scarce able to move or even breathe without pain because his ribs were broken. Four men had dragged him from his home two days ago and brought him before the priest who had disturbed him at the holy shrine. He had been ready enough to admit his sacrilege, for his conscience had pricked him since the deed was done, and Harold the carter was not a man to look his accuser in the eye and boldly deny his guilt. He freely confessed to attempting to rob the holy shrine of St John, and to his amazement found himself further accused of beating Father Cyrus to the ground and making away with a dozen priceless jewels. Those charges were false and the indignant carter hotly denied them, only to find himself further charged with the heinous crime of murder. He had struck down a canon, so they said, the venerated, much-loved Bernard, and despite his protestations none would believe that the felon who robbed the shrine had not also struck the fatal blow.

The priest who came to hear his confession reminded the carter that neither the Good Lord nor his chosen servants are tolerant of liars who choose to meet their maker unconfessed.

'Repent or be damned,' he declared, and the carter, stubborn to the end, had adamantly refused to confess to crimes he had not committed. The guards had brutalised him then, and after that the priest came again in search of a full confession, only to find the carter steadfast in his original claims.

'Five precious stones I loosened,' he persisted through bloodied lips. 'If a dozen were lost then someone else has taken them. And I left the five where they fell when I ran off. I took no profit from what I did and I swear before God I never struck the priest. I hurt no one, not the holy Father nor the holy Canon.'

'Liar!' the priest insisted. 'In the name of God, confess your sins and be redeemed. A man hangs just as heavily for a sheep as for a lamb, and while it is too late to save yourself in this world, you still may preserve your soul in the next. Confess and be absolved. Repent of your sins.'

'God knows my sins,' was all the carter said.

And so the matter had rested until the guards came back and attempted once again to beat him into submission. The priest who had identified him as the tomb's desecrator was with them, and when the beating was over he demanded to know if the carter still dared deny that he had struck down Canon Bernard. He did deny it, and Cyrus de Figham, the priest on whose false word he stood condemned, had merely smiled and shrugged as if the fact were of no consequence.

Now Harold lay in the clammy mud of his prison cell, his knees drawn up to ease the deep bruising around his groin and belly, his arms bent across his body to hug his shattered ribs. He had vomited and now he coughed; every movement jarred his ribs and set his belly aflame, recalling the heavy blows from clubs and fists and feet, so that even in his solitude the violence continued. He prayed for mercy, although he knew such a privilege was never extended to robbers of holy tombs, and for death, which would be upon him soon enough if Roger de Pont l'Evèque was to be his judge. And he prayed, too, for his immortal soul, for when priests themselves were bare-faced liars who bore false witness against innocent men, how was a simple carter to know what God expected of him?'

The Archbishop of York's special investigation of the strange events at Beverley began in the early morning of 23 December, the eve of St Victoria's feast day. It was to be held in the Provost's upper hall, where broken windows had been replaced by either wooden shutters or thick wall hangings to help keep out the season's chill. Fresh rushes had been strewn across the floor and liberally sprinkled with dried lavender and rosemary, and censers hanging from the rafters emitted delicate coils of aromatic smoke to perfume the air. Six metal braziers, all glowing with crimson coals, were set around the room at intervals, and guarding them were acolytes and clerks of the lower orders, watching for stray sparks or fallen particles of cinder that might ignite the rushes.

The canons' chairs and priests' benches had been set in a

wide half-circle at the farthest end of the hall, the most important among them raised high on a dais and draped all about to keep the draughts at bay. The Provost's chair took second place to the Archbishop's private throne, which travelled everywhere with its illustrious owner in readiness for just such an occasion. When an archbishop sits down in his full church capacity, he must do so in a fashion worthy of his lofty station. It was a huge, wide chair of heavy oak, ornately carved with the faces and emblems of important saints, inlaid with gems and strips of polished brass, and with the winged angel representing St Matthew the Evangelist suspended like a canopy overhead. Before it stood a sable-covered foot-stool bearing, in finely worked gold and silver, the distinctive insignia of York.

On the morning of the inquiry, some time before the Archbishop had left his own house in the Cornmarket to make his way across town to the Provost's Hall, Jacob de Wold arrived at St Peter's unexpectedly. He wore a plain winter cloak over his office clothes and came without ceremony, accompanied only by his clerks and two priests for his protection. Not until he stepped into the scriptorium and threw back his hood was any man there aware of his identity. Young Richard was sent at a run for Father Simeon, who was working on the damaged roof of the little church. From the doorway of the scriptorium, the Provost's representative watched the agile young priest swing himself down from the roof and cross the wide enclosure at a firm and steady march. He broke his stride at the little bridge where a wooden crucifix was hung, made the sign of the cross and bowed his head in a brief prayer for Father Willard, then he continued on his way, hurrying to meet his important visitor.

'No trace of lameness,' Jacob de Wold observed, and met the quick glance of Osric, who stood beside him.

'No trace of lameness,' Osric confirmed.

'And there is much talk of miracles performed in his name.'

Osric shrugged. 'Talk is cheap, especially among the poor and the superstitious.'

'Talk is dangerous,' Jacob countered, 'especially amongst the powerful.'

'God's blessing, Father,' Simeon said as he reached the doorway. He was surprised when the older man gripped him by the hand, peered deeply into his eyes for a conspicuous length of time and then said gravely:

'Am I to believe the child is dead?'

'You are. All Beverley must be persuaded of it.'

Jacob nodded. 'Amen to that. God cherish him. There are many who will argue that this is the better way.'

'There are?' He held the gaze of this Provost's deputy, and an understanding of sorts seemed to pass between them. 'Why are you here, friend Jacob? Does my lord Archbishop wish it known that he may, if he so chooses, use the Provost of Beverley to carry messages to his rebellious priests?'

'I am not here at the Archbishop's bidding.'

'Ah, no message, then?'

'Only this, his reminder of the law: we must not reverence any man as saint, no matter how many miracles are done by him, without the sanction of the curia.'

Simeon's response was just as gravely spoken. 'And for my part I have declined to endorse what any man has said of me beyond the simple truth that I am healed of my impediment.'

'And yet they persist in speaking in detail of miracles and amazing deeds performed in the name of holy Simeon of Beverley. Their stories have reached the Archbishop's ears and brought your character into disrepute.'

Despite the serious implications so obvious in the words of the older man, Simeon was forced to smile at what he heard. 'The world has turned its upside under and its belly up,' he softly remarked, 'when a man who is said to raise the dead, heal the sick and perform good deeds is brought into ill repute for his goodly efforts.'

'Ambition and jealousy go hand in hand,' Jacob reminded him. 'Many are asking why a humble priest should be touched by a miracle while more powerful, more deserving men stand by unblessed.'

'Would these men question God's own judgment concerning where He bestows His blessings?'

'They would not dare, and they would be the first to condemn you to the fires of Hell for even suggesting such a thing of men in holy orders. It is your integrity they question, Simeon, not the grace of God. They will call you liar and brand your claims as falsehoods.'

'And yet my foot is healed,' the priest said softly.

'It is, my friend, and you may yet have cause to regret the healing.'

'Never. This is a gift from God, a miraculous healing, and I will challenge any man, right up to the Pope himself, who dares say otherwise.'

'Indeed, my friend. I do not doubt you will.'

Nodding thoughtfully, Jacob moved ahead of the others as they entered the scriptorium and gathered together in a close group by the fire.

'The Archbishop will soon be arriving at the Provost's Hall,' de Wold told them all, his eyes bright and keen below his shiny bald head. 'The streets have been lined since dawn with those seeking a blessing from the great man himself, and Hall Garth is packed with pilgrims, sight-seers and would-be witnesses clamouring for their lord's attention. The temporary walkways set across Hall Garth are straining beneath the weight of all those people. Already there have been reports of whole sections collapsing and many unfortunates drowning in the mud below.'

'When is the Archbishop expected to arrive?'

'Immediately after Terce and before mid-morning, and his humour will not be good, I fear. My clerks inform me that Hugh de Burton and Roger de Clare have petitioned him separately, each speaking against the other in aggrieved tones. They have furnished him with long lists of complaints and accusations, and each is seeking recompense for injury received at the other's hands. They will dog poor Geoffrey's heels all the way to the grave in their determination to grab the Provost's seat the instant it becomes vacant. They chatter and complain like quarrelsome fish-wives. Ah yes, there has been much to annoy and irritate this overlord of Beverley before his inquisition has even begun.'

Simeon lifted and dropped his shoulders on a sigh. 'I will not receive fair judgment from this Archbishop,' he said without bitterness.

Jacob nodded. 'You have a fair measure of the situation, and those who admire you the most are doing the least of all to advance or defend your cause. While they sing your praises too loudly to be ignored, your enemies accuse you of contriving this whole affair to your personal glorification. The Archbishop is intolerant of those who would be saints in their own lifetime, and he is impatient of Beverley and her powers. If you were a true man of York, if these events had taken place under his immediate jurisdiction, he might have been more sympathetic to your cause. As it is you come from nowhere, just a gifted but simple scribe, a priest without prior fame, and because of you he is put to much inconvenience.'

Simeon eyed him steadily, his gaze unreadable. 'Does he still speak of exile, then? The four knights who murdered St Thomas Becket were pardoned of his murder for no less a penance. What crime did I commit that can compare to theirs?'

'You are guilty of no crime, as such,' Jacob protested.

'And yet this Archbishop will condemn me to seven empty years in that wilderness we call the Holy Land?'

Jacob shook his head. 'He is not so keen on that solution now. I have reminded him of your long and arduous work in translating the Minster's charters and records into both French and Anglo-Saxon. So many of our old documents might have been lost or wantonly destroyed were it not for your constant diligence. Indeed, had you not brought our precious archives here to your scriptorium for copying, everything would have been lost in the flooding beneath the Minster.'

'But I did so without permission,' Simeon reminded him. 'I took it upon myself to claim what nobody else seemed to care about. We are not thanked for labours of love, Jacob. We are merely called upstarts and viewed with suspicion.'

'Nevertheless, your task is an important one for York as well as for Beverley and we, Cuthbert and Alban, Thorald and Antony included, have made it our business to speak out most forcefully on your behalf. Now that his own best scribe is dead of a lung disease, Roger de Pont could do worse that look to Beverley for that man's replacement.'

'I am grateful, Jacob,' Simeon smiled.

'Give your gratitude to the good Lord for allowing you such skills as will keep you here instead of sending you on a seven-year pilgrimage along with half the rogues and wandering vagabonds of Christendom. I doubt you would survive it.'

Osric laughed harshly at that. 'Simeon has strength and courage enough to make the journey if he has to. Let the Archbishop do the worst he can, and still he will not break this priest.'

'I doubt he would at that,' Jacob replied, 'and I do not challenge Simeon's fortitude. Like most of his friends I too have reason to fear that he would not travel half a mile before his enemies struck him down from behind, or fell upon him in the night while he was sleeping at the roadside.'

Their talk lapsed into thoughtful silence then and Richard, perched on a low, hard stool beside the fire, leaned over to pile fresh peat upon the grate. The others watched the sparks leap up a little way, then Jacob de Wold continued in his deep, calm voice. 'You are instructed not to appear at the inquiry, or even to show yourself beyond the boundary walls of St Peter's, until you are called upon to do so by the Archbishop himself. Word has gone out these last two days that the mystery child is dead along with the nurse who was to be a witness, albeit a dubious one, to your good character. I am to confirm the rumours as fact and report my findings personally to Roger. After that no word of adultery or fornication will be heard against you.'

'But the truth remains, young Peter was brought here ...'

'Hush! You must be silent on that score from now on, Simeon. We are all of us agreed that the child is dead. All else is sheer speculation and deserves no credence. This Peter of yours does not exist.'

'But he was seen by many, and Elvira's own husband will swear...'

'Elvira's husband has left for parts unknown, and as for the nurse herself ...' Jacob smiled and spread his hands. 'Her body lies somewhere at the bottom of St Theodore's lake, and how many credible witnesses can swear to actually seeing her here, beneath your roof? If your enemies should accuse you of keeping a mistress at the church's expense you will deny it, and rightly so, and there the matter rests.'

'And that is to be the sum of it?'

'No,' Jacob said, pointing to Simeon's healed right ankle. 'That, my son, that miracle of yours, is to be the sum of it.'

'This?'

'Aye that.' Jacob de Wold stood up, keen not to overstay the time of Terce lest the Archbishop arrive at Hall Garth with no Provost's representative to greet him. 'Think long and hard on it, Simeon of Beverley. The murderer of Canon Bernard has been found and will be brought to justice. The high altar was reconsecrated during a midnight Mass to which the public was not given access. A hundred and one statements are to be heard and recorded, crimes of petty heresy and blasphemy dealt with, healers chastened and preachers punished. By the time you are brought before your judges, Simeon my friend, your own pretensions to sainthood, however luridly your enemies' tongues describe them, will be all that remain in dispute.'

Simeon walked his visitor to the door and shook him warmly by the hand.

'My thanks to you, friend,' he said.

'God guide and protect you, Simeon.'

Jacob de Wold left St Peter's as he had come, anonymous in his dark cloak and hood. He and his small group, his clerks and protective priests, walked briskly from the main gate to the Minster Yard, keeping the great church on their left as they headed for Moorgate, intending to turn left into Keldgate to reach the only remaining bridge across the Hall Garth moat. They met a commotion near the prebendary house where Wulfric de Morthlund had his residence in place of his absent canon. A crowd had gathered about the house, a boisterous assemblage of excited men and women who were persuaded to stand aside to allow Jacob through only after his true identity had been established. He reached the core of the crowd and found a man hanging from the shattered stump of a tree. Someone had run about the town with news that the killer of Canon Bernard was to be moved to the Provost's Hall for interrogation, and that he would be escorted there by a single unarmed guard. Predictably, the townspeople had rushed to the house in droves, determined to take the matter of his guilt or innocence into their own hands. As the prisoner was dragged half-conscious from the house they fell upon him like a pack of wild dogs and had him hanged before any voice could protest on his behalf.

Before having the man cut down and offering a prayer for his immortal soul, Jacob instructed one of his priests to hasten back to St Peter's and inform the priests there of the carter's fate, and to bid them be more vigilant on Simeon's behalf. Then he went solemn-faced to the Provost's Hall, his thoughts more troubled and unsettled than before.

'The man was left unprotected,' he admonished Wulfric de Morthlund some time later, as they walked together towards their places in the crowded Provost's Hall. 'He was your prisoner, your responsibility.'

'Quite so,' Wulfric agreed. 'And the guard who allowed this terrible thing to happen will be appropriately punished for his lack of care.'

'Is that all?'

'All?' Wulfric echoed. 'What more would you ask of me?'

'I would ask you to consider,' Jacob growled through his tightly clenched teeth, aware that others, standing close by, should not be privy to their conversation, 'that the carter might well have been innocent of murder.'

'Then let us content ourselves with the knowledge that he was hanged for the desecration of St John's tomb, and for attacking a priest, two crimes we know he certainly did commit.'

Jacob de Wold stopped walking and turned to face de

Morthlund. 'Harold the carter was to be tried here, today, for murder,' he said quietly. 'The mob took him and hanged him by the neck for Canon Bernard's death, and for all we know he might have been innocent of that charge.'

'My dear lord Provost,' Wulfric declared with a short, stiff bow and a twinkle in his eye, conspicuously allowing Jacob the honour of a title to which he had no claim. 'The man was seen in the most suspicious circumstances by honest men whose word would never be disputed. He robbed our sacred shrine, attacked one priest and almost ran another down in his haste to escape just punishment. And as if all this were not sufficient to hang him, we have his own confession to the murder.'

'His confession? But I was led to believe . . .'

'The man confessed,' Wulfric interrupted with an amiable smile. 'You may take my solemn word on it, my dear lord Provost. And should it prove necessary for me to do so, I will swear on oath, before my lord Archbishop of York, that long before the mob could hang him for his crimes the carter confessed to killing Canon Bernard.'

With another bow de Morthlund turned away, a crimson-robed giant of a man in jewelled boots, his massive shoulders further broadened by the soft bulk of his fur-lined cloak.

Because he was an honest man Father Jacob crossed himself and asked forgiveness for his uncharitable thoughts. Then he scowled and muttered under his breath: 'May he who bears false witness in this life receive just punishment for his sins in the next.'

As he took his place on the dais he caught the eye of Cuthbert, Alban and Thorald in their turn. Like him they were concerned for Simeon's safety, and that concern would not be eased by news of this timely and convenient execution. When the common populace was whipped into a vengeful mob and manipulated by clever men, it would as readily hang a priest as a carter.

CHAPTER TWENTY-NINE

It was almost time for Vespers when the message came at last that Simeon was to make his way to the Provost's Hall to be examined by the Archbishop and his canons. By now there was little doubt that a priest of St Peter's had become the target of supernatural forces during the storm that brought to ruin half of Beverley. The question on most men's lips was this: had he been touched by God or deceived by the Devil?

'You could be judged an honest man,' Canon Cuthbert warned him in the gravest tones, 'and in the same breath condemned. Your fate no longer depends on whether the events of that night can be proved or disproved, for you only have to walk into the room to show that you are healed of your lameness. But they will ask, your enemies and your friends alike, if you are an innocent priest or the Devil's tool.'

'And I might well be exiled for years on either outcome,' Simeon observed. 'I might be condemned to a decade of pilgrimage to cleanse my soul of the Devil's favour, or else dispatched to Rome and then the Holy Land to give thanks for a miracle. On either decision I am lost. What must I do?'

'Protect the boy,' Cuthbert said.

'At any cost?'

'Only you can decide that.'

The sun was down and once again a heavy fog had crept in from the coast. Damp and chill, it clung to the roofs of buildings and stopped up alleyways, gathered in quiet lanes and lay in patches on the ground. By its cover Simeon had gone by flat-boat, taking the flooded pasture route to the convent of St Anne's, and for a short time had held his godson in his arms in the privacy of the Abbess's private chambers. Peter thrived despite his near-fatal injury, thanks to the quickness of the infirmarian's actions, and to Elvira's nursing. The puckered wound was vivid on his neck, the delicate baby-skin still drawn up and held by Osric's crude stitching, the two ends of the thread still hanging down, uncut.

'I have prayed by the hour,' he told the boy, 'and still no answer comes. The one who brought you here is gone now. He simply handed your guardianship to me and left your future in my hands. So be it, child. With neither guidance nor instruction I can do no more nor less than my heart dictates. If I am wrong then I will beg forgiveness, but for now I know only that you must live, and to that end I would sell my soul, if such a price were asked of me.'

The child looked back at him with its veiled gaze, its expression so still and solemn that he suspected, just for one uncanny moment, that every word he whispered had been clearly understood. He signed the cross on Peter's head, breast and shoulders, then pressed his lips to the child's small forehead and felt the sudden heat of tears stinging his eyes. That ache behind his breastbone was a reminder of his commitment to a cause he did not really comprehend.

'Is this what love is?' he asked, his eyes still closed, and when he opened them again Elvira was there, standing just inside the open doorway. Her own cheeks were damp with tears and the pallor of the sickbed was still on her skin. She nodded her head as if in reply to his question, and he saw in her big dark eyes that for her, too, love was an ache, a crushing, painful thing.

He handed the child into her waiting arms, touched his

thumb to his lips and signed another, smaller cross on the baby's forehead. Then he made the same sign on Elvira's head, between her eyes, and on a sudden impulse stooped to touch the spot with his lips. He felt a sudden tremor pass between them and was not sure where it began or ended, only that it was a thing they conjured and shared one with the other. A moment later he had the heavy door of the room closed fast between them, and with bright tears still glistening in his eyes he lifted his hood and strode to his waiting boat. He did not know when, or even if, he would dare return to St Anne's to see the woman and the child again.

And now it was evening, the Vespers bell was ringing and Simeon was on his way to give account of himself before the Archbishop and those other dignitaries of the church, and still that dull ache of parting hung in his breast like a heavy stone. It made him want to throw back his head and howl a protest to the heavens. Instead he kept his face grim-set and marched directly to the Provost's Hall, where he was shown into an anteroom and asked to await his lordship's signal to approach the dais. It was in that small, oak-panelled room that he finally gathered together the full strength of his own convictions. By the light of a single torch his shadow loomed dark and elongated against the wall, reminding him of the shadowed shape that had stepped out of an unnatural storm to change his whole life and everything in it. He recalled what his mentor, Father Cuthbert, had taught him as a child, that what can be resolved is soon forgotten, while the unexplained, the mysterious, is always remembered. That lesson of so many years ago showed him now the course he had to take.

'Dear God, this will not be easy,' he said aloud, and he heard the answer somewhere deep inside himself: 'Do what you must, for Peter's sake.'

Beyond the door of the anteroom some two hundred members of the church had gathered to take part in the inquiry. Many had cut off their beards and whiskers and shaved their crowns in haste to please the Archbishop, for if he had his way all men in holy orders would be compelled to do as much to show their obedience to the church. Like so many of the superior clergy of his day, he saw the simple tonsure as a token of the heavenly kingdom and a symbol of the wearer's desire to achieve perfection. More than this, it told him at a glance which priest was submissive and which held back, believing himself his own man still.

Within the last hour, Roger's anger had been tested to its limits by the mildest of men, and the clash had left him simmering with impotent rage. Stephen Goldsmith, church scholar and master craftsman, still steadfastly refused to turn his lands in Eastgate over to his lord Archbishop. He owned that acreage known as St Peter's Enclosure, and much would be gained by York if he would give it up. St Peter's Church had housed the Bishop of Beverley's remains before his sainthood earned him a loftier resting-place. It carried too much importance in the town. It should be closed and left in ruins, and all its upstart followers dispersed. But Master Stephen Goldsmith would sooner donate his lands to common monks, if he but dare, than sell them at an honest profit to his lord Archbishop of York.

There was a sharp intake of breath followed by a sudden hush in the Provost's Hall as Simeon of Beverley entered by its main door and began to walk slowly down the length of that great room to its farthest end where all the chairs were set. He looked impressive in his rich brown cloak and well-thonged boots, his head lifted up and his gaze held fast upon his far objective, the ring of hair around his shorn crown glowing like a band of gold in the torchlight. Every startled eye was on him as he made his way forward, dragging one leg behind him like a cripple.

Those on the dais watched him come, some half-raised up from their seats, others glowering suspiciously, still others with satisfied smiles upon their faces. When the hobbling priest reached the dais he lowered his gaze respectfully before the stern, unyielding man who had officiated at his ordination. The Archbishop's senior clerk and advisor, Egwin of Durham, rose elegantly to his feet and cleared his throat in a series of conspicuous coughs. Too short and slight to present an imposing figure, he had the satisfaction of knowing that his good, strong voice would fill the room when he began to read aloud the list of charges and complaints lodged against this calm-faced priest. There was no sound save for the occasional rustle of heavy robes across the rushes, but even before the clerk began to speak, the Archbishop waved him down with impatient gestures and turned in his seat to address Simeon directly.

'You are limping, Simeon of Beverley,' he observed.

Simeon bowed again and drew his dragging foot close to his body, lowering one wide shoulder in the process, so that he stood the way a cripple might. 'My foot was crushed in an accident while I was but a child, my lord,' he replied.

'So I was led to believe, and yet of late I have heard a different story.'

'My lord?'

His lordship's face now brightened with special interest. It had occurred to him that he might close this tiresome inquiry here and now. By managing this, the very crux of the Beverley matter, with the utmost care, he might pack up his household once again and start out at first light for his comfortable castle and lovely young mistress in Lincolnshire. A full day's travel, dawn to dusk, and he could be home in time for the lavish Christmas celebrations. With an elegant gesture of his fingers he instructed his clerks to write as he surveyed the priest with furrowed brows.

'Simeon of Beverley, have you received a miraculous healing of your crippled foot?'

Simeon lifted and lowered his uneven shoulders in a clumsy shrug. 'My lord, I am as you see me here before you.'

The Archbishop looked about him with a smile that was almost gleeful, noting the ripple of astonishment that passed through the gathering. He raised his voice to ensure that his words were heard in every corner of the room as he confronted the priest.

'Men are saying that you were given the blessed gift of healing by a divine messenger who came to you with a tempest running at his heels.'

Simeon spread his hands, his face a mask of innocence, and smiled a patient, almost sorrowing smile. 'They speak in error, sir, for I know of no such messenger,' he replied, and he recalled that Peter, Christ's disciple, made a similar claim to keep himself from notoriety by association.

Now the Archbishop leaned forward in his great carved throne and peered at Simeon through narrowed eyes. He could not have hoped for a more convenient outcome to his inquiry. At the moment of truth this wise young priest had chosen to take the line of least resistance, his arrogance subdued, and rightly so, in the presence of a higher power.

'And the matter of the child?'

'My lord?'

'Come man, do not play me for a fool by pleading ignorance of rumour. The whole town whispers of a mysterious child drowned with its mother in St Theodore's mere. They say it was your godson, or your bastard.'

Simeon met his gaze and knew that he had judged the man and the situation wisely. Roger de Pont l'Evèque of York would accept the olive branch that had been offered, and content himself with any verdict that did not demand the notice of his monarch or his pope.

The priest spread his hands. 'My lord, I am a simple scribe, a priest of St Peter's serving God and the Church in studious obscurity. Whatever fanciful stories men tell of me, I can but deny all knowledge of such a child, living or dead.'

'You have no bastard son?'

'My lord, you yourself witnessed my vow of chastity at my ordination. As God Himself is now my judge, that vow has not been broken.'

'Then you keep no mistress?'

'Indeed I do not, for I am celibate.'

'And you have no personal involvement with this child they speak of?'

'None, my lord.' In his imagination he heard the crowing of a cock protest the denial. 'I know of no miracle, no special powers, no mysterious messenger, no child.'

His answer sent a ripple of speculative talk around the hall.

The Archbishop raised both hands for silence.

'Do you have any comments of your own to add to this?'

'None, my lord.'

'So here is where the matter rests, with your denial?'

'For my part, yes,' Simeon replied, shifting his weight with clumsy movements so that this stern inquisitor might be reminded of his lameness.

The Archbishop leaned back in his seat until his face was in the deep shadow beneath the angel's wings carved into the canopy. Only his eyes showed bright and glinting as he massaged his chin thoughtfully and studied Simeon's face for any trace of defiance. When he found none he was well satisfied, for the issue would now remain contained within his jurisdiction, and he would be home for Christmas after all.

'Very well, you may return to your scriptorium,' he said at last, 'and there await the instructions of my clerk. I have a mind to employ your special skills for the benefit of my seat at York, on a project that will keep you and your copyists dutifully occupied for many years to come. Go now. Enjoy your obscurity while you may, for a peaceful existence is a blessing in itself.'

'By your leave, my lord.'

At the Archbishop's curt nod Simeon turned to leave. He knew that every eye in the room was once again upon him as he began the long walk back to the door. He looked at no man's face directly, but he was aware of Cyrus de Figham and Wulfric de Morthlund, of Canon Cuthbert, Daniel Hawk, Alban, Thorald and Jacob de Wold. He was aware of those who sighed in relief or smiled their satisfaction, and of those who nodded their admiration of his expediency, and of those who wept without shame to see their hopes of a miracle so readily and easily dashed aside. He knew that circumstances had made him, for a time at least, many things to many men. Now he had turned his disrupted life back upon itself, and as if the last two weeks had been erased, had made himself back to what he had been before, the lame scribe of St Peter's, nothing more. Walking now with his old ungainly gait, he limped along the gauntlet of gaping priests, dragging a seemingly useless, stiff-jointed foot behind him.

At the door were grouped a score of men who had not been summoned to offer statements or answer charges during the archbishop's inquiry. Antony the monk and Osric the infirmarian were among them. Grim-faced, they stood aside to allow Father Simeon to hobble by, and as he drew level only they could have heard the words he muttered out of the tightened corner of his mouth.

'Now he is safe,' he told them, and the cost of that blatant public denial was evident in his voice and in the awful greyness of his features. '*Now* the boy is safe.'

Word spread like fire from the Provost's Hall to the streets of Beverley, and with the inconsistency that marks men's nature, the priest so lately respected as a saint in the making swiftly became the object of society's scorn. They shifted with ease to attribute his so-called miracles to St John of Beverley, and those who were healed in Simeon's name now mocked the priest and blessed the saint in his stead. And because the target of their scorn was out of reach the over-zealous Vincent was selected, according to mob rule, as scapegoat, for he had healed the sick and preached new hope in Simeon's name, and he had lied. With the news of Simeon's denial and humiliation, those who had esteemed him felt themselves betrayed, while those who feared him snatched a chance to do him ill by whispering their encouragement to the mob.

It was a woman, Hannah the salter's wife, who found the body of Brother Vincent after the crowd had turned its wrath on him. He had been stoned to death by the Minster wall, and such was the frenzy of the attack that but for his robes he might not have been recognisable. Still clutched in his fingers, bloodstained and covered in mud, was the strip of embroidered border torn from Simeon's tunic. The woman pulled it free and clasped it tightly to her bosom and, keeping it well concealed beneath the dark folds of her clothing, took it home to hide like treasure trove. She was convinced that when the turmoil was over and men returned to their senses, that holy relic, once the focus of so much reverence, would prove priceless.

Immediately after the inquiry the gates of St Peter's enclosure were locked and guarded, and the heavy beam was once more dropped into its metal brackets on either side of the scriptorium door. Whether the lame priest Simeon was grieving for a mistress and a son drowned in St Theodore's Lake, or whether he simply chose, as cowards will, to avoid the consequences of his actions, was a matter of brief speculation in the town. Whatever his motives, he held himself from public view and if he kept the services of his Office as he should, he kept them in strictest privacy, with none but God to witness his devotions.

The year closed and the new year opened on a solemn note, and from the start it seemed that the disaster which had come to Beverley would have its repercussions played out on a far wider and more public stage. The storm had dropped like a rock into calm waters. It worked its damage where it fell and thrust its ripples outwards, touching the calmer waters at a distance.

No sooner had his eminence the Archbishop of York returned to his castle in Lincoln than news came back that he had fallen seriously ill. He blamed the marshes and the damp air of Beverley, and swore that if ever he had the misfortune to return there it would be with a lighted torch on hand to burn the whole town to the ground. He recuperated sufficiently to travel with his entourage back to Henry's court in February, but much of his vigour and zest for life was lost. He suffered cramps and deep pains in his joins. His bowels locked, his belly swelled, and from time to time he was visited by a fever of such fierce intensity that, had he been lower placed in this world, it might have seemed that he was tasting the Purgatory awaiting him in the next. And as his temper and his health declined he began to fear, as others did, that the blessed St John of Beverley had a hand in his continued torment. However his behaviour at the Beverley inquiry might be judged by those who were, before all else, his servants, he feared he had perhaps been a little over hasty, too lenient or too harsh, overly biased or too indifferent for the saint's approval.

He wrote as much in a private letter to Pope Alexander, the third pontiff of that name; a man who knew Roger de Pont l'Evêque for the clever profiteer he had become. Alexander received those rambling sickbed declarations with a cynic's caution. By spring the Pontiff too was mortally ill and beyond all caring for Beverley or York. He breathed his last uneasy breath as a scorching August closed without a breeze for its respite. He died with his disputes with the King of England still unreconciled, for Henry Plantagenet would answer to none of flesh and blood while Alexander, equally inflexible, assumed for himself supreme authority over all the kings of Christendom. When Henry installed his bastard son, young Geoffrey Plantagenet, as Bishop-elect at Lincoln, Alexander insisted that the lad, though never noted for his piety, should take up holy orders. Geoffrey's refusal was unequivocal. He was a soldier, not a priest. He would accept the prestige, the power and the income from his office, but he was a bishop now and a monarch's son, and no petty pope with delusions of royal grandeur would compel him to bow to the yoke of holy orders.

Thus the unseemly squabble between pope and crown dragged on for many months until Alexander, frustrated and indignant, threatened the disobedient Geoffrey with excommunication, a drastic course that would have wreaked havoc upon Henry Plantagenet's plans for his bastard son. And so to stay his hand the king made Geoffrey his royal chancellor, as Thomas Becket had been while he enjoyed his monarch's favour, and in a magnanimous gesture of concession he agreed to reconsider his choice for the Lincoln bishopric. By these sly means the Pope's wrath was impeded and King Henry had his way, for while he hotly contended every other candidate presented for the office, young Geoffrey held fast as Bishop-elect and the crown reaped a welcome harvest from the revenues of the vacant see of Lincoln.

By the end of the same year Roger de Pont l'Evêque was also dead. He had been forced to relinquish his place at court and return to his castle at Lincoln while the good weather held; from there had travelled by cart to his palace at Cawood, close to York. When it became clear to those who nursed him that this time the failing embers of his health had sunk too low to be rekindled, he was carried in haste the eleven miles north to his noble seat at York. He died there on 21 November and was buried in the choir he had rebuilt a decade earlier in the great Cathedral of St Peter's. He was interred by Hugh de Poiset, his life-long friend and respected Bishop of Durham. The entire parish mourned the passing of this great man of the Church, and most were content to bury his known faults with him, for among his friends and enemies were men of great influence, and who could guess which way either one would wear his coat now that the Archbishop was dead?

When the saintly Archbishop William died in 1154, three powerful men, Archbishop Theobold, Dean Robert and Archdeacon Osbert, all contrived to procure the election of Roger, then Provost of Beverley, as his successor. He was duly consecrated at Westminster Abbey in the presence of no less than eight bishops before travelling to Rome to receive the hallowed Pall from the hands of the Pope. He had been present at Henry's coronation, and later had dared to crown that monarch's son, the arrogant Young Henry. It was Roger de Pont l'Evêque who sat at the Pope's right hand ahead of Thomas Becket during the historic Council of Tours in 1163. It was Roger who, at the king's instigation, caused the clergy of his diocese at York to swear under oath not to support the Pope on the matter of Becket, after cunningly warning Henry that peace was impossible so long as Thomas Becket lived. He quarrelled at length with Richard of Canterbury and as the Scottish papal legate he tested his considerable powers against William the Lion, King of Scotland until, in a characteristic rage, he excommunicated that king for insubordination. His life had been anything but uneventful. Though none would call him a saint, as was his predecessor, history would certainly remember Roger de Pont l'Evêque, Archbishop of York, manipulator of kings and user of popes.

The third significant death that year was that of Beverley's Provost, the long-suffering Geoffrey. He died peacefully in his sleep after taking a light supper, and because his seat had been openly coveted for so long by ambitious men, there were whispers that a deadly poison had been mixed with his food or slipped into his wine. He was buried first inside the Minster he had served, in one of the crowded spaces beneath the damaged choir, but within the month his remains were secretly taken up and removed to Holderness. It was there that he kept a modest manor house set in a park containing deer, a place of beauty and tranquillity connected with the Humber by several waterways. Ironically, his seat at Beverley was claimed by neither Robert de Clare nor Hugh de Burton's bastard son, for York now had the King of England as its overlord, and that one had plans of his own for Beverley's future.

'Such, alas, is the fickleness of monarchs,' Cyrus de Figham declared, spreading his hands and turning his dark eyes heaven-ward, as if his own plans too had been frustrated by this turn of events.

'And such, alas, is the will of God,' his friend Wulfric de Morthlund added. 'While priests and knights conspire, His will be done.'

Both priests had grown richer, stronger and wiser on other men's ambitions, and conscience played no active part in the outcome of the game. If those knights whose interests they professed to serve received only disappointment in return for their generosity, they could extract scant compensation for it, for who could hold even dishonest priests to account for either the fickleness of kings or the Will of God?

At the convent of St Anne a refuge was quickly established for the care of all those children left orphaned or abandoned in the aftermath of the storm. By September two dozen women had given birth in the bare little hospital building erected in haste within the walls of the convent. Within another month these infants too had been abandoned, left in the care of nuns while their mothers crept away to pick up the shattered pieces of their lives.

There was a certain sister at the convent, a pretty young woman who veiled her huge dark eyes with lowered lids and kept her long black hair concealed beneath a modest wimple. She was known as Sister Cecily, a distant cousin of the Lady Abbess, and she had a child, an infant boy, who bore an ugly puckered scar on the left side of his throat.

This same Sister Cecily met with the blue-eyed priest on the thirteenth day of December, in the year of Our Lord 1181, a full year after the horror came down on Beverley. It was the feast of St Lucy, or Lucy light, the longest day and shortest night. They met in a small, wood-panelled anteroom just off the Abbess's private library, and stood with a chasm of empty space between them and the Abbess herself discreetly looking on. He watched her eyes and she watched his, and finally he mouthed her name, her given name, as if he dare not speak it with his voice.

'Elvira.'

She smiled and her eyes took fire. Then she whispered, no louder than a sigh. 'Simeon.'

It was the same. A whole year had passed and nothing had changed between them. Despite his vows he ached to take her in his arms and hold her close the way he had held her all those months ago in the darkened roof-space of the infirmary. He offered his hand and she placed her fingers lightly in his palm, and he felt again that sudden charge, that flash of something bright and forbidden between them.

The Abbess shifted in her seat and turned a page of the ornate Psalter resting in her lap. Her eyes were lowered now to the sacred words, her lips moving to shape each one as her eyes lighted upon it.

He spoke her name again and she spoke his, and after a whole long year of planning what they would say to each other when next they met, neither he nor she could find more words than that.

On the instructions of the Abbess, the boy Peter was brought in to meet the priest who would one day be his tutor.

He waddled into the room on sturdy but uncertain legs, took a fold of Elvira's skirts in his small fist and surveyed Father Simeon with a solemn expression. His eyes were large and very blue, his hair pale blond and straight, his head well-shaped. On his neck the deep scar was evidence of the would-be assassin's blade that had so nearly claimed his life when he was little more than a week old.

Simeon dropped into a crouch and watched the boy closely. Despite the passing of so many months he would have known him anywhere, for his heart ached with a familiar pain at the sight of him.

'God bless and keep you, Peter,' he breathed.

His one-year-old godson was a strong-limbed, well proportioned child, as handsome as any boy he had come across. His face was open and intelligent, his eyes alert, and when Simeon extended his arms a small smile flickered at the corners of the boy's mouth and he propelled himself forward into the big embrace.

Simeon hugged him as tightly as he dare, pressing the strong young body against his chest, feeling the soft hair brush a silken touch against his cheek and chin. Missing Peter had been a deep hurt inside him for a year, a constant pain that rarely gave him anything but a temporary ease. Holding him now, feeling those baby arms around his neck and knowing that in a moment he must leave him for perhaps as long again, the pain became an open wound that made him want to weep.

CHAPTER THIRTY

It was another cold December day. Somewhere a bell was tolling, though the next church office of the day was still an hour away. The bell's tone had a softly muted quality, as if the cold mist that hung close to the ground had wrapped itself like a blanket around the metal, and so produced a dull, lethargic sound. Figures were moving all around the Minster, though at this glum and darkening end of the day their numbers had been halved, as many were driven home to firesides or into the churches for shelter for the night. The ruin of St Martin's was a ragged heap of stones against the sky. Canon Bernard had lain a whole year in his grave, and as yet not a single fallen stone had been lifted up except to be carried away to some other place. The ancient baptism font had been salvaged from the rubble and placed inside the Minster for safekeeping. All else of value had been pillaged: the roof timbers and wooden doors, the coloured window glasses, the altar plate and cloths. Even the old graves in the crypt below the tiny choir had suffered plunder, for those high officers of the church who were buried there had worn fine robes and jewellery and carried valuable relics to their interment. And every day the man who was now the Canon of St Martin's viewed that heap of rubble with a bitter disappointment in his heart. While it lay thus abandoned, his own advancement hung in limbo, lacking the stone-and-mortar evidence of his status.

Looking beyond the ruin of St Martin's to the busy area around the Hall Garth moat, Cyrus de Figham recognised the priest by his heavy, dark-brown cloak and his distinctive limp. His black eyes narrowed into peevish slits as he surveyed him. He did not trust this Simeon of Beverley. A year ago he had seen him walk on two good legs, had witnessed his dance of joy at the miraculous healing of his lameness, had watched him sink to his knees in the street and weep like a child at the impact of such a blessing. And just as surely Cyrus had seen expediency, and fear of the far-reaching power of York, return that healed priest to his crippled state.

'You are a wise man, Simeon of Beverley,' he growled. 'Wise and clever, for you have learned that Archbishops can be pliable and peasants have careless memories. But Cyrus de Figham has your measure, priest. He has your measure.'

From the steps of Canon Wulfric's house in Moorgate, Cyrus observed the two who met Simeon at the Hall Garth drawbridge. Simeon had come by rowing boat from the other end of Keldgate, perhaps from the convent where a priest was needed for the special masses, and when he arrived the two were there to meet him. Heavy rain had swelled the moat around the Provost's Garth, had flooded the town ditch and stretched a great muddy lake over the southlands of the Minster.

Simeon's boat drew close to the outer housings of the drawbridge, and the waiting men stooped low to help steady him as he stepped on to the waiting raft. They were Osric, the old campaigner turned infirmarian, and the monk Antony, who went about in rags and dined like a beggar so that his precious *poor* might benefit from his frugality. Such sacrifice was offensive to de Figham, who knew that a man's ambitions were not always displayed in the cut of his cloak or the richness of his table. Some gained their ends through poverty and humility just as ruthlessly as others sought advancement by more obvious means. All men were driven by greed, and although its shape and size, its weight and its colours varied, the essence of it never altered.

Cyrus watched the three friends pole their way, all standing brace-legged on the little raft, from the town ditch to the higher ground close by the Minster Yard. The lame priest was the first to set his feet upon dry land, and from there he limped and lurched his way in the direction of St Peter's. Not for a moment did he allow his steps to veer towards normality. He was a cripple, that much was obvious to any with eyes to see, but Cyrus de Figham knew better than to place his trust in outward show alone. Because he trusted no one, he questioned everything, especially the obvious.

The fishmonger's daughter, Maud, had that day given birth to a son, a lusty, black-haired whelp with the Norman stamp on him. Cyrus had liked her better when she was swollen-bellied, for while the child grew inside her there was a measure of resistance that caused her no little discomfort and served to heighten his sexual pleasure. The midwife was in attendance and the girl had been prepared for her lying-in when Cyrus arrived for his appointment at the fish-monger's house. Gervaise protested, though feebly, that his daughter should be left alone now that the birth was imminent, while the midwife, probably following his instructions, dared to insist that the priest be turned away unsatisfied. She stood her ground, as stubborn and mindless as the animals she tended for her living, when Cyrus reminded her of his priestly standing. But he knew his rights and would not abdicate them. He and the fishmonger had a firm agreement, settled and paid for in advance, and no old woman with blackened teeth and cow dung under her nails would tell him otherwise.

The child was born before he left the house, for he and Gervaise had pressing business to discuss that would not wait for another time. The birth was fast and noisy, and in spite of her shrieks the girl dispatched her squalling burden with all the ease with which a plump pea is ejected from its pod. The midwife did her duty and hurried away, eager to be gone from the house before some poison touched the mother's wounds or filled her breasts with soured milk or turned the living child into a corpse in its cot. A midwife's lot was not always worth the fee she could demand, and while the ill-tempered priest still lingered, glowering over his wine, she dare not question the child's chances of survival and claim a coin for speaking the baptism rite.

Cyrus in his turn refused to perform the rite for a whelp that seemed as robust as a suckling pig. He did, however, step closer to the bed to scowl at the figure lying exhausted on the filthy mattress. Maud's face was beaded with perspiration and blanched as grey as paste beneath its surface flush. She had lost a great deal of blood and mucus during the birth, none of which the midwife had bothered to clean away. It soaked into the straw and sacking beneath her body while she just lay there with her eyes half-closed, showing no interest in her screaming offspring.

'If she should die while you are in my debt . . .'

'There is another girl,' the fishmonger hastened to assure him. 'A sister, Adelaide, just two years younger.'

He jerked his head and at his growled command a child in ragged clothes stepped from the shadows of the sloping roof. She was thin and under-developed, a skinny, flat-chested girl with sores around her eyes and matted hair of no particular colour. She could not match even the lowly value of the elder girl, but both men knew she would suffice if need demanded, and would shoulder her sister's duties if she must.

Now Cyrus stepped across the threshold and into the warm interior of Wulfric's de Morthlund's house, shrugging off his heavy cloak in the hallway. A smell of fish had followed him from the hovel in Fishmonger's Row. It clung to his clothes and stained his skin, and he was angered that a priest of his high standing could be brought this low in the name of honest need. As the door closed at his back he caught a last glimpse of Simeon in the distance by St Peter's wall, and he wondered if that priest was a genuine celibate, as they claimed, or if he too crept back to his bed from time to time with the tell-tale scent of fornication tainting his priestly robes.

In the scriptorium, damp cloaks were hung on the chimney wall and cups of warm, spiced wine were raised against the cold. A huge fire blazed in the grate, throwing its reflections into corners where shadows danced and twitched at the intrusion. The same flames were reflected in Simeon's eyes, flashing gold and yellow and amber in the blue so that his gaze was bright in the fire's echo. Young Richard joined them at the fireside, as eager as Osric and Antony for news of the boy. No word was passed between them on the subject until the door was barred and the stools drawn close around the hearth, then Simeon said:

'He is a fine boy, strong and healthy. He walks well enough, though he wants for practice, and he will be tall, I think.' He put out a hand to measure a certain distance from the floor. 'This high, and but a year old yet.'

The others nodded, well satisfied by the brief report.

'Does he bear a scar?' Osric asked, recalling how roughly he had stitched the wound in that tiny neck.

'He does, and it will mark him out as clearly as any brand, should his enemies ever hear of it.'

'His enemies will never know that he still lives,' Osric growled, determined that it would always be so.

'How did he take to you?' Thorald asked.

'Bravely,' Simeon smiled, 'He held my gaze and accepted my embrace as if he were of my own kin. Indeed, if I did not know better I might claim he knew me on the instant, as I would surely know him anywhere.'

'Is he intelligent?'

'Undoubtedly.'

'And well nurtured?'

Simeon nodded. 'Nurtured and loved as well as any child should be.'

The others nodded, satisfied, and fell into a lengthy and thoughtful silence. It was Osric who asked, shaping his words with care: 'And how is the woman? How is Elvira?'

Simeon looked at him directly and smiled with troubled eyes.

'The same,' he said. Just as he was intended to catch the

351

deeper meaning within the question, so he knew that Osric recognised the significance of his simply phrased response. 'Elvira is the same.'

Within the scriptorium extra benches had been set directly below the high windows, where the light was at its best. On each bench lay the copyist's pens and parchment, a small lump of pumice for keeping the parchment clean, a goat's tooth to polish it, a ruler, a rubber and a lidded well of ink. In a locked chest in one corner was a small store of paper, rare and very expensive, and the special ink, with wormwood added to keep the mice from nibbling at the precious sheets. In another sturdier chest were kept the Minster's charters and histories, and many of the ancient documents supposedly lost but found again amongst the debris of the Minster's flooded cellars.

Simeon considered his work as master scribe a true vocation. He was compiling a scrupulously detailed history of the town of Beverley and its Minster Church, and where past scribes had set the records down in French and Latin according to the custom, Simeon had them faithfully reproduced in Anglo-Saxon, the true language of the English. By now he had no less than seven carefully selected translators under his supervision, all dedicated clerks who used their talents to the glory of God and the preservation of their Minster's history. In return for their excellent work he allowed them regular periods of rest, fresh air and exercise so that none became too weary to cross-check a fact, verify a difficult word or question a doubtful phrase. And yet he was no easy taskmaster for all his care, for he was a perfectionist who kept his workforce under the closest scrutiny. No scribe of his would be guilty of copying down another man's mistakes, or of keeping a statement as undisputable fact simply because some past historian claimed it to be so.

One whole year after the horror came to Beverley, much of the town and its trade had been returned to normal. Dwellings and shops had been rebuilt, damaged businesses repaired, lost stock replaced and shattered lives restored. The great east window of the Minster had been replaced with plain glass at the expense of local tradesmen, and it was hoped that King Henry himself might be persuaded to finance the making and installing of a special window that would rival any other in the whole of England. Four men were lost when the crypt was finally cleared of mud and rubble and the damaged walls shored up. Their bodies, and those of the eighteen priests who perished in the storm of 1180, were brought out one by one and given full Christian burial, as was their due. Each priest had been mummified by the mud and slime in which he drowned, every corpse so well preserved that it was instantly recognisable and correctly named before it was blessed and laid to its final rest.

'So many good men accounted for,' Simeon observed, and Osric merely nodded grimly, knowing his friend was asking; 'Why not Willard?'

As the years passed the drains and waterways were cleared of debris and their smaller conduits unblocked, but the body of the terrified priest who sacrificed himself to the full fury of the storm was never found. There were times when Simeon suspected that his sense of loss was close to self-indulgence. Poor Willard's death would remain forever in Simeon's memory, for a man did not easily forget a scene of so much ugliness and so little dignity.

The times were not easy, and that disharmony between the powerful Minster of Beverley and the great Cathedral at York was not restricted to the Archbishop's see. As each year made way for the next, too little altered, for Henry demanded York for his bastard son and, keeping the see vacant, claimed its revenues for the crown. His fiery temper, that very Norman trait, did not improve with age. He had been kicked on the thigh by a skittish horse a decade since, and still that old injury caused him so much pain from time to time that he rolled on his couch in agony and cursed every horse that ever bore a man upon its back. After ten long years he had granted the scheming Eleanor of Aquitaine her freedom from house arrest at Winchester and Salisbury. It was an optimistic move, for she had ambitious sons and powerful friends to use against her lord. As for him, they said his heart had turned to stone when his favourite son, the twice-crowned Young Henry, died of the dysentery on foreign soil.

'Still, he has his precious bastard, Geoffrey, for his comfort.'

So said the ones who were closest to the king, who knew the colour of his heart as well as they knew the nature of his children. And if there was any sense or justice in the world, Richard and John would follow Young Henry's example and leave the future of England to the only one fit to wear its crown. Bastard or no, only Geoffrey had the makings of a king, with none of Aquitaine's malignancy.

While the country was uneasy and the town itself once more a hive of bustling activity, within St Peter's enclosure there was peace of a kind. The priests there lived quiet, industrious lives that moved no man to envy or suspicion. They tended the altar of their little church, kept faithfully to the religious offices, prepared their books, instructed the town's orphans in the word of God and attended the Minster services when required. And if one priest, the lame scribe, Simeon, was touched with scandal out of some shadowy incident in his past, few people now recalled the details of it, and fewer still were inclined to trouble themselves with the petty misdemeanours of a man in holy orders.

The little blond-haired, blue-eyed boy from St Anne's grew swiftly and settled contentedly into his lessons a full year earlier than anyone expected. He was a studious child, solemn and thorough in his determination to please his master. And as he grew a certain mystery grew with him, for he seemed to learn far more than he was taught, and he came and went like a swift and silent shadow; secretive, almost furtive in his movements. By the age of six he knew all the Offices by heart and sang them with a sweet, clear voice that was a joy to any ear. From the priests he learned his Latin, from the lawyers and clerks his French, and from the pilgrims and foreign traders the rudiments of many other tongues. He hungered for knowledge of the world beyond his own, its ways, its people and its strange beliefs.

'He is a rare companion,' a traveller once told Simeon after spending the better part of an afternoon sitting on the river bank, talking to the boy. 'He listens well. He perceives with his mind what his eyes may never see, and he feels in his heart what many men spend a lifetime struggling to understand.'

'He is an uncommon lad,' Simeon agreed. And so he was, for Peter rarely smiled and seldom spoke unless to ask a question. He shunned the company of other children and attached himself instead to any learned or well-travelled man who would have him. So persistent a thirst for knowledge troubled Simeon, for the boy behaved as if he knew his time on Earth was short, that his days were somehow numbered.

As the boy grew, old Canon Cuthbert liked nothing better than to spend time in his company, shedding the seventy years that divided them as a man might shed his boots or his cloak before an agreeable fireside. Sometimes he forgot himself and spoke at length on matters so lofty as to be beyond a small boy's comprehension. And yet young Peter hung upon his every word, wide-eyed and attentive, feeding a need that was insatiable. Their meetings were restricted to those times when Peter was brought to the Minster to attend the services or to the scriptorium of St Peter's for his formal schooling, though Father Cuthbert would have sworn otherwise. There were times when he could be heard in earnest conversation while he tended the high altar and the golden shrine of Beverley's Saint, and the younger priests who overheard would smile and shake their heads indulgently. They were too fond of the old man to correct him in his harmless dotage. If he needed to create an imaginary companion with whom to share his solitary conversations, all those who knew and loved him felt that he had earned the right to do so.

It was on a fine, hot day in mid September when the eight-year-old orphan, Peter, vanished from the little walled garden behind the Abbess's quarters at St Anne's. The Sister of Mercy known as Cecily was working with a group of women in the vegetable field, and had left her son alone with his

355

studies during the hours between the end of Terce and the start of the midday meal. Her morning's work completed in good time, she returned from the field a full hour earlier than expected. The bell had not yet chimed the noon hour to mark the office of Sext when she crossed the small paved courtyard around which the Abbess's rooms were set, and entered the long shaded porch leading to the garden. She used her own key to open the small arched door, and when she stepped into the sun-dappled space beyond, her heart lurched in her breast, for the space was empty. His books were neatly stacked on the stone seat where he had been sitting when she last saw him. His precious Bible, a rarity carried back from Italy by Brother Antony, when he had travelled there to meet the Pope, was wrapped in an altar cloth and left in a safe, dry niche in the garden wall. Nothing was out of place or in disarray, nothing disturbed, and yet the child was gone.

His foster-mother searched behind every bush and shrub and peered into the leafy branches of those trees that overhung the garden wall from the Abbess's garden beyond. She did so thoroughly but with little hope of finding him.

'Peter? Peter?'

She called his name softly, almost in a whisper, knowing he would not answer. The boy was gone as surely as if he had vanished into thin air. The garden was walled on three sides, too high and smooth for anyone to climb, and beyond the wall was a sheer drop to the steeply sloping banks of the Keldgate Lake. Even if Peter's whereabouts and identity had become known, no human intruder could have scaled that wall from the outside and made away with him. Not a window nor a gateway opened into the garden save for the small porch door through which she had come, and which she had locked carefully behind her. Only two other keys existed, one held by Simeon and one by the Abbess herself. This modest home of hers was as secure now as it had been in those days when it housed the convent's treasures, and yet the boy, locked in for his own safety, had vanished.

In the very centre of the garden stood an abandoned well

that had, before a decent stream was cut through the grounds, provided fresh drinking water for the whole of the convent. On the night of the great storm the well had overflowed, its contents forced upwards by the pressure of the floodwaters below. Spurting like a geyser, it had caused a muddy deluge in the garden and flooded the cellars below the Abbess's hall; it had taken many long weeks to clear the mess away. But now the great storm was misted by history and the old well stood benignly in the grass, its water lying two poles deep, a distance to equal the combined heights of sixteen men. She could hear it flowing down there in the distance, carried towards the town by a swiftly moving stream. Like most wells that had fallen into disuse, this one was covered by an iron grid designed to keep out birds and small animals, leaves and other garden debris that might choke the shaft and contaminate the water. Now Sister Cecily, once called Elvira, stared down into the black hole of the well and sighed deeply before making her way to the stone seat that was set against the farthest wall. There she sat with her hands clasped in her lap and her head slightly bowed, waiting. And while she waited she thought of the clammy darkness underground, and of all the men swept away to their deaths or poisoned by rat-bites while working on the waterways.

'May the good Lord protect and preserve him,' she said aloud.

Those years spent in the convent of St Anne's had kept her safe and given her the education she lacked, but it had not taught her to pray with any sense of genuine conviction. For Elvira there was little meaning in it, no comfort, no sense of being overheard by some greater power willing to turn itself to her assistance. She found it far easier to believe in the harsh realities of life, in joy and pain, in sorrow, love and hope. She believed in the priest who held her heart and in the solemn little boy who shared her life, and after these she needed little else.

He came as the bell began to chime for Sext. His small, pale hand appeared between the strips of metal forming the well's heavy grid, slipped a rusted catch aside and lifted one section back to reveal an opening wide enough for a small boy to climb through. Then came his fair head and narrow shoulders, and soon the rest of him slithered free and dropped lightly to the ground by the well's outer wall. He closed the opening and slid the catch back into its metal housing, and all was left as it was before: except that this time he had been discovered.

Simeon heard the Minster bell begin to chime the noon-time office of Sext. In its strong echo came the softer, sweeter voice of the little bell of St Peter's, replaced three years ago when the damaged tower of the church was at last rebuilt. The priest was standing at his own tall bench beneath an open window, taking full advantage of the good light streaming into the scriptorium. The base of his thumb was aching now and the insides of his fingers had become deeply ridged and stained with ink. Stooping low over his work, he narrowed his eyes and turned the paper this way and that, into and out of the sunlight, the better to judge the quality of his efforts. He was well satisfied with his penmanship, knowing that God in His wisdom demanded, and was offered, only the very best his master scribe could offer. Simeon had been blessed with a keen eye, much patience and a steady hand with which to execute his God-given skills. This gift, this blessing, had been offered to him in its entirety, requiring him to return it to its heavenly source in no lesser measure.

At noon on that fine September day Father Simeon was alone in the quiet of his scriptorium. His class of twelve orphans from St Anne's would not arrive for another hour, brought to him by a group of clerks and a priest who kept a dagger at his belt and a wary eye on one particular pupil. He saw in his mind's eye the boy, tall for his years and slender, fair and aristocratic in his bearing, and yet as wiry and elusive as a thief's apprentice. He smiled at the thought and felt his love for Peter shift like a physical thing in his solar plexus. He was a crippled scribe, a priest without distinction. He had once been touched with a miracle and had been allowed to trade that blessing for his loved ones' safety. For that he was content, and in his prayers he asked for nothing more than the endurance of the bargain.

The transcribers under Simeon's supervision had already left the scriptorium for the church across the enclosure, and from there they would cross to the refectory for their midday meal. Theirs was a placid, orderly existence. They worked and prayed, sang out their praises to the glory of God, slept a short night divided up by periods of prayer, worked and prayed and sang again. And as it was for them, so it had been for Father Simeon of Beverley these eight long years: eight years, and then he turned from his bench to find a hooded figure at his elbow.

CHAPTER THIRTY-ONE

'*You! Dear God in Heaven! You!*'

His scalp prickled. He felt the icy fingers of apprehension move like talons along his spine. For the briefest instant he stared into the pool of darkness in the folds of the hood where the shadows were deepest. He saw only blackness, and yet he had no doubt that he was looking directly into the stranger's eyes. And then the door of the scriptorium was flung open and two men burst in, and the figure vanished.

'We saw it!' a familiar voice cried out. 'We saw the one in the hood!'

'I know,' Simeon answered softly, and the strength of his body seemed to drain away from him, leaving him cold and empty and afraid.

Osric gripped the priest by the arm, his face grimly set and his eyes narrowed. His other hand was on the hilt of the short-sword at his belt, as if he would stand and fight even unearthly forces. There was hostility in his voice when he demanded in a caustic whisper: 'What does this mean, Simeon? What horrors will he bring upon us this time? In God's good name, what more does he want from us?'

Simeon shook his head, but even as he tried to deny the

most obvious explanation, the words he dreaded most were dragged from his lips.

'The boy ... he has come for the boy.'

'No!' Osric growled. 'Dear God in His mercy forbid that it be so!'

'What, after eight years?' Richard protested. He had been pacing to and fro in agitation, crossing and recrossing the spot where the hooded figure had stood only moments ago. 'It comes to claim him *now*, to take him back after eight long years?'

'What else? What else?'

'To warn us?' Osric suggested. 'To set us on our guard against our enemies?'

'Could that be so?'

'Why doubt it? Why think the worst?'

Simeon stared back at Osric with a look of anguish in his eyes. 'Because, my friend, we will be helpless to prevent it, if its purpose is to take the boy from us.'

'Why should it be so?' Osric demanded. 'Eight years ago that ... that apparition called the boy *the keeper at the shrine.* He is Peter of Beverley ... of *Beverley!* His place is here. By the Gods, Simeon, have we protected him with our very lives and loved him so for all these years, only to have him taken from us now?'

Simeon met and held the angry stare of his oldest friend. There were wings of grey in Osric's hair now, fresh lines marking his face and a certain stiffness settling in his joints, but he was as strong and as quick as ever he was, a soldier still, with a soldier's temperament. He was devoted to the solemn little boy who took so eagerly from any man what skills or lessons that man had to offer, and offered a special friendship in return. Like all those who had willingly become the boy's guardians and tutors, Osric the infirmarian loved him deeply and would not give him up without a fight.

'God grant it does not come to that,' said Simeon. 'What did you see, my friend? And you, Richard? Was there a word, a gesture that might tell us why it came?'

Both men thought hard before shaking their heads. They

had seen what Simeon had seen, the figure standing silently before them, and they could do no more than guess at what it meant. Richard lifted the cross that hung from his neck on a silken braid, touched it to his lips and began to pray. He moved to that corner of the room where a flickering candle marked the tiny altar dedicated to St Peter. There he signed the cross and sank to his knees in earnest prayer, his voice a deep murmur as he begged the Lord's protection on behalf of the town of Beverley. He had been fully ordained for five years now, and for him the priesthood was a true vocation. His journey towards it had not been an easy one, and somewhere along the way he had become convinced that the power of prayer alone, if it be truly from the heart, could alter the very course of a person's existence. There were times when Simeon envied him the uncompromising spirit of his faith. With such conviction in his soul a man might feel himself to be immortal.

While Richard prayed and Osric scowled, Simeon recalled the disaster that had marked the figure's first appearance in Beverley. It pained him still to think of all the many dead and injured, the hundreds made homeless, the waste and destruction of that dreadful night.

'I have not given that one a thought for many years,' he confessed. 'Indeed, I might even have convinced myself that he did not exist save for some trickery of light and shade or some subtle treachery of the senses.'

'There's wisdom enough in that,' Osric nodded. 'We cannot face each new day hampered by yesterday's terrors.'

Simeon had moved through the open doorway to stand in the fresh, warm air with his eyes half-closed against the glare. He was looking out beyond the orchard to the distant boundary wall where the backlands stretched for many miles, divided by lakes and man-made waterways, by the river Hull and its equal partner, the navigable Beverley Beck. There were campfires and makeshift dwellings dotted here and there across the marshes now. Animals grazed out there and children played, for one winter's floods had subsided and another's not yet begun, and the land was made firm again by the kinder seasons in between. At that time of the year, though the annual fairs had been and gone, the town still teemed with every kind of merchant and journeyman, with pilgrims and travelling tradesmen come to take fullest advantage of the profitable weeks remaining before the weather worsened. The harvest had been good that year, the produce plentiful, and for months the keepers of Beverley's five town gates had been reaping a rich harvest in coin and kind from the boats and carts and pack-horses streaming through. Another tempest like the last, coming today into this bustling place, would claim a hundred times as many victims as before.

'Dear God, deliver us,' Richard prayed, his voice now full and loud inside the scriptorium.

'Amen to that,' Osric growled between his teeth.

At Simeon's back the Minster loomed like a splendid sentinel over all, the plain glass of its great east window twinkling in the light, the pale blond surface of its stones given a soft blush of gold by the rays of the sun. The sky above was as blue and tranquil as it had been since dawn. There was no evil omen to be imagined there. No cloud had darkened or was put to flight, no storm was gathering its power and its fury up. No tempest dogged the hooded figure's heels this time.

'Dear God, deliver us,' Richard repeated, and Simeon whispered a soft, relieved response: 'Amen.'

It was Antony who ushered the pupils into St Peter's enclosure via the narrow iron gate leading from the bridge in Eastgate. They came in single file to the scriptorium, a line of diminutive, grey-clad figures in cut-down robes with over-sized hoods and loose leather sandals that slapped their feet as they walked. Simeon scanned each small face as it passed: his godson's was not among them.

'Where is the boy?' he demanded of Antony, and anxiety was in his eyes.

'She keeps him close by her,' Antony said. 'She is afraid for him, but she has come herself to . . .'

He needed to say no more than that. Simeon caught a

movement at the gate and looked up to see Elvira there, her slight, grey-clad figure flanked by two men. He strode towards her, stopped short, uncertain, and while they each put out their hands to greet the other, their fingers fell inches short of making contact. Her unexpected arrival was a bitter-sweet thing, bringing him joy and pain in equal measure. He no longer questioned his love for Elvira, nor did he ask that God forgive him for it. His sacred vow concerned the flesh, and he would strive to keep that vow in the face of this temptation. And he would love her as he must and make no apology for it, for his was a loving God who would not chide even a priest for losing his heart to a woman such as this.

'You should not have come, Elvira,' he told her, but even as he spoke the words, his eyes declared that he was glad to see her.

'I need to speak to you,' she said.

'I know. I would have come to St Anne's when the day's lessons were ended. You need not have come. The streets are full of dangers.'

She smiled and allowed him to steer her in the direction of the little cloister where he often sat or paced or stood looking out across the flat-lands and marshes lying between Beverley and the coast.

'I am well protected,' she reminded him. 'And besides, the streets are teaming with traders and entertainers, and crowds are already gathering around St Mary's chapel for a glimpse of the prisoners who will be taken to York today for trial. I passed unnoticed in my Sister's hood and cape, and I do not doubt that I will do as well on the homeward journey.'

Simeon felt the short hairs prickle at the nape of his neck. She tempted providence with her lack of concern for her own safety. He closed his eyes briefly and offered up the words: *God keep her safe from harm.*

In the cloister they sat on a slab of stone set where the sun's light fell slanting through the leafy branches of a tree. It made dappled patterns of gold across her skin, and when she threw back her hood it lit and lifted the hidden colours in her hair. Two priests passed by them, their hands clasped and their heads lowered in prayer, their voices two murmurs in perfect unison.

'You priests,' Elvira said when they were gone. 'Do you really believe God wants all this mindless devotion, all this *sacrifice*?'

'He surely deserves our praise for His goodness,' Simeon reminded her. 'And as for sacrifice, in that we simply follow His example. After all, he sacrificed His son for us.'

She turned her head to give him a sideways look. 'Indeed, and if we in turn give up our son for Him, what will remain of His wonderful scheme of things?'

Simeon chuckled at her question. There was no blasphemy intended in it. She merely spoke as she was able to interpret, with a simple, uncomplicated reasoning. God's grace did not fall short of those who dared to question other men's views of Him. One day she would find her way to God, albeit by a tangled path, and the love of God would not falter while she did.

'You must speak to the boy,' she told him, suddenly grave. 'I fear for his safety. He is as agile as a cat and comes and goes with the guile of street-child. I swear there is no lock he cannot open, no barrier he cannot breach.'

'Ah,' Simeon said, and nodded thoughtfully.

'Ah? Is that all you can say to his escapades?'

'I was thinking of the saint for whom he is named,' Simeon explained. 'For his faith he was given the power of binding and loosening. No lock could hold that one, either.'

'Oh? And did he prefer to spend his time underground with the water rats? Did he sneak from his studies to crawl in the sewers, climbing in and out of disused wells the moment his mother's back was turned?'

Simeon noted the anger and concern in her face. 'Peter does these things?'

'Whenever my back is turned. He says he has found a way to the high altar in the Minster Church, and there he keeps every sacred office with the Canons, and they not even knowing he is among them.'

'Ah,' Simeon said again. 'That explains his detailed

knowledge of things that should not concern him. It also confirms that Father Cuthbert is not so deeply into his dotage that he imagines a small boy where there is none. Does Peter admit to spending time with Cuthbert?'

'Yes, he admits it. He also admits to spying on sanctuary men and eavesdropping on private conversations between the Canons and their priests. He might even listen to what is said in the confessional, for all I know, and what would it matter to us if he did? Our first concern must be for his safety, and since he refuses to do my bidding, you must forbid him to climb down that dilapidated well ever again, Simeon. You must find a way to keep him out before he comes to some terrible harm down there.'

'I will speak to him,' Simeon agreed. 'But I will not promise you the result you hope for, Elvira. We must not forget that he has a purpose here, and this latest adventure might well be a part of it. He must be free to do as he feels he must.'

'Simeon, he is only eight years old,' she protested.

'And not like other boys of his age. He knows his mind, Elvira.'

She nodded and lowered her head to watch the fingers moving restlessly in her lap. She had wanted him to take the fear away, to make things right, but in her heart she had known she asked too much of him.

'I thought I saw the man today,' she said at last. 'The hooded man who drove his horse to its death to bring young Peter here. Of course, I might have been mistaken ...'

He heard the hope in her voice and knew that he dashed it with his reply.

'No mistake, Elvira. He was here. We saw him too.'

'I see.' She cleared her throat and with an obvious effort collected up the full measure of her composure before asking: 'Has he come for Peter?'

'I do not know.'

Elvira nodded. She looked into his eyes and saw what she did not wish to see, that he was just as anxious and unsure as she.

'Can he be stopped?'

He shook his head. 'No more than could the tempest that pursued him here.'

'I see,' she said again, then rose to her feet and prepared to leave the cloister. 'I must go back. There might be something I can do . . .'

He touched her arm very lightly and his voice was hoarse. 'My dear, there is nothing you can do.'

'I will not give him up,' she cried. 'He is my son. I will not give him up.'

'Elvira, Elvira. Peter is no more your son than he is mine, and neither you nor I can alter his destiny. He is not ours to keep. We knew that from the start. He was never ours to keep.'

Her eyes flashed and she tossed her head, freeing her long dark hair to the slanting sunlight.

'I will not give him up,' she cried again, then lifted her skirts and hurried away from him.

'Elvira, wait.'

Simeon went after her, caught her by the arm and with his free hand turned her face until her eyes met his. He saw the pain there, gathering with the tears to spill out in glistening drops upon her cheeks. Seeing her weep was more than he could bear.

'Elvira . . . Elvira . . .'

And suddenly she was in his arms, her body pressing hungrily against his own, her arms about his neck, her tears hot on his cheek. She murmured his name over and over as his strong arms held her fast, and when his mouth at last found hers, they both gasped with the intensity of the contact.

'God knows I love you . . . God knows I love you.' He spoke the words in whispered snatches against her mouth, unable to draw back from the heady sweetness in her kiss.

'My love, my dearest love.' She cupped his big face in her hands and kissed his mouth with a hunger that left him breathless. She felt the strength and hardness of his response, the searching tenderness of his lips and fingers, and then she heard, as he did, the haunting notes of the sacred *Te Deum* soaring like an anthem on the summer air. The bell of St Peter's began to toll, sweet and slow, as the pure, high voice of the cantor led the choir in its devotions.

'Oh God!' Simeon clasped her tightly in his arms. His heart still raced, his senses were ablaze, but he felt himself snatched back to reality with a brutal abruptness. Elvira still clung to him, her own heart racing and her breath unsteady. He held her as tightly as before, but they were still now, letting their passions ebb, keenly aware that this time, at least, his God and his church had stepped between them to keep his vows intact.

Several minutes passed while they stood in that possessive, almost despairing embrace. It was Simeon who moved to end it. He pressed his lips to her brow, then kissed her closed eyes in turn before setting her at arm's length. There was no need for words between them: their love had already found a way to express itself in all its depth and potency. He kissed her hands and she kissed his, and then they walked, still silent, from the little cloister and across the courtyard to where Father Richard and her other escort waited.

'Take Sister Cecily back to the convent,' he told them in a tight, unhappy voice. 'And see that she comes to no harm.' And to her he whispered, aching to touch her one last time before she walked away: 'God bless and keep you, Lady.'

There were four prisoners on the cart that trundled from the Provost's gaol in Hall Garth, around the Minster and along the uneven cobbles of Eastgate. Three men and a woman were bound by their wrists to the heavy poles of the cart, easy targets for the jeering crowds who spat and hurled rotting fruit and vegetables at them as they passed. The four were ragged and bloodstained, all worthless vagabonds who had banded together in a vain plot to rob the sacred tomb of St John of Beverley. The mysterious ringing of the church bells had brought several priests scuttling from their beds in the dead of night, and so the robbers had been easily apprehended. And having been caught in the act by priests whose testimony could not be disputed, they were declared guilty the moment they were arrested. They would receive short shrift at York, for the robbing of holy tombs could not be easily forgiven, and who would dare fix a worldly price upon such a sacrilege?

Elvira's escorts drew her aside as the cart moved out of Eastgate and into the market area where the crowds were thickest. It was on its way to St Mary's for the customary blessing, and from there to the great York Road and the long, bone-shaking journey to the capital. As the roar went up and the rotten apples and cabbages began to fly, Elvira found herself caught by a sudden surge of movement and propelled sideways by the press of excited people all around her. She cried out as something heavy struck her hooded head, and as she stumbled felt the bite of a man's sharp grip upon her arm. Though far from gentle, her rescuer had both the physical strength and the presence of mind to force her back until she was safely pinned against the wall of a shuttered shop, and then place his own body between her and the jeering, stone-throwing crowd. The danger was past in a moment, but when she made to free herself her rescuer held her fast and laughed aloud at her struggles. She had experienced sudden pain, fright and relief coming one after the other, but now she felt another thing entirely, and this disturbed her far more than what had gone before. She was trapped and vulnerable, held at the mercy of this muscular man who could, if he so chose, conceal her in his cloak and carry her away with him. She cast around for assistance, caught a glimpse of Father Richard anxiously searching the crowds and realised that she could not be seen with this stranger's broad body barring her from view.

'My thanks for your timely assistance, good sir,' she said as calmly as she was able. 'Now be so kind as to release me into the care of my companions.'

'Soon enough, little Sister of Mercy,' a cultured voice informed her. 'But first I have a mind to see the face beneath the hood.'

Too late she reached up to keep her hood in place. He

snatched it from her head, then grasped her by the shoulders and stared into her face with the look of a greedy man who had uncovered a priceless treasure. Her heart sank. She knew this man. She knew him by sight as Cyrus de Figham, priest and canon of St Martin's that was, a man as dark as Simeon was fair and reputed to be his opposite in every aspect of his character and temperament. He was every bit as handsome as the younger sisters at the convent claimed, and in his sly black eyes Elvira saw the truth of other stories, too. This man was a debaucher who hungered after forbidden fruits and did not allow his lusts to stop short at convent gates or children's bedrooms. He was looking at her now with lechery in his gaze. He licked his lips and leered, and Elvira felt her flesh crawl.

At that very moment someone called her name, her old name, from somewhere in the crowd.

'Elvira? Elvira? By the saints, can it be ... *Elvira?*'

The sound of that familiar voice struck fear into her heart and galvanised her into desperate action. She began to struggle wildly against de Figham's hold on her, knowing she must avoid recognition at all costs.

'Elvira! It *is* you!'

'*Sister Cecily!*'

The young priest who had been her escort reached for her as she broke free of de Figham's grip, and with one yank he pulled her back into the press of bodies and began to shoulder a pathway through to one of the narrow alleyways that led off the Butcher Row. She heard the other voice cry after her as she ran:

'Elvira, wait, Elvira!'

As he made to follow the fleeing Elvira, Erik the ditcher felt a heavy hand come down upon his shoulder. The man who had grabbed him was a priest, the black-eyed canon, Cyrus de Figham, and though he disliked the man, Erik was relieved not to have been apprehended by a bailiff. He was older now and hardened in his ways, still strongly built and good-looking in his way, only now his left ear had been cropped to his skull and there were two fingers missing from his right hand. A knight had caught him poaching on his lands beyond the Westwood. For the lamb he was required to forfeit two fingers, and for the beaver an ear, and but for the knight's good humour he would have lost his life.

'Why do you seek to trouble the Sister?' Cyrus de Figham demanded, his grip so tight that the younger man winced despite the thickness of muscle padding his shoulder. 'Speak up, you unsavoury dog, or so help me God I'll have your other ear.'

'She's my wife,' Erik blurted. 'She was stolen from me eight years ago and I was told that she was drowned. But that was her. I'd know her anywhere. That was my wife, Elvira.'

'Rubbish!' de Figham growled, and cuffed the ditcher smartly across the side of the head with his free hand. 'The priest who took her called her Cecily. She is one of the Little Sisters of Mercy from St Anne's convent. How dare you even imagine that such a woman could once have been your wife?'

'But father, I saw her with my own eyes. I saw her face, her hair . . .'

'And I say you are mistaken, thief.'

'As God is my judge, sir . . .'

Cyrus reached into his girdle for a coin, held it between his finger and his thumb and saw the ditcher's eyes ignite with greed and his tongue flick out to moisten his lips.

'I say you are mistaken, thief.'

'. . . Er . . . well, perhaps . . . the light is not good here . . . the crowds are thick . . .'

'You do not know the lady,' Cyrus growled.

'That's right,' the ditcher nodded eagerly, eyeing the coin. 'I was mistaken.' He went to snatch the coin away but Cyrus held it fast.

'Listen well, cur. You do not know her, and if you dare say otherwise, this dagger at my belt will take that other ear and all your remaining fingers, one by one.'

'Yes, sir . . . I mean, no, Father. I was wrong. I swear it. I was in error, a foolish mistake . . .' This time he managed to snatch the coin and flee with it into the crowd, and by the

371

time he had sunk but a quarter of its value in good ale, he would indeed be convinced that he had glimpsed a stranger and mistaken her for his long-lost wife, Elvira.

Cyrus de Figham stared into the distance where the yelling townspeople were following after the cart as it lurched and swayed towards St Mary's chapel. There was profit to be had from this if the ditcher's eyes were to be trusted, and he did not doubt the man's eyesight for a moment. If that young woman in the Sister's habit truly was his wife, then there were those who would be willing to pay, in coin or favour, for knowledge of her whereabouts.

'Elvira the ditcher's wife,' he said aloud, smiling a secret and malevolent smile. 'Or are you Sister Cecily, Little Sister of Mercy from St Anne, beyond the Keldgate bar? It matters not who you are, Lady, for all women are whores with a man between their legs. But I will have you. As God is my witness, I will have my fill of you before I hand you back to that stinking ditcher.'

As Cyrus turned, still smiling, and began to elbow his way through the people still gathered in the marketplace, he was unaware that other eyes had also witnessed that telling scene. This one had marked the woman's beauty and the priest's lascivious gaze as he held her in his arms. He too had seen the bribe and heard the ditcher's protests. And more than this, he had recognised the two priests who had been the woman's escorts, particularly the tall young man who had dragged her off into the crowd the instant she was spotted by the ditcher. That one had been Father Richard of St Peter's: Simeon's man.

Daniel Hawk was neither as handsome nor as arrogant as he used to be. Each one of his twenty-eight years was clearly etched in deep lines on his chiselled features, and revealed in the sparseness of his prematurely thinning hair. That a proud man such as he should begin to lose so splendid a head of hair so early was a happenstance well marked by many. At fifteen Daniel Hawk was tonsured for the Church, but after that his vanity, and his master's pleasure, kept the blade away. He discarded the tonsure and took to wearing his hair in the Norman fashion, long and thick, even binding it into the nape of neck with a pretty brooch or a strip of embroidered cloth. Yes, he was proud, and for that sin God took the object of his pride away from him.

There was a hint of bitterness now around his mouth, a certain watchfulness in his once-pretty eyes. He had become distrusting and suspicious of others, for after the soft days of his youth he had learned to live with uncertainty and to grab his opportunities where he could. No longer his master's pampered favourite, Daniel Hawk now had to fight for his survival. His weapons were flattery and servility, and the fresh young boys he procured from time to time to satisfy Wulfric de Morthlund's carnal requirements. He lived within the fat man's favour still, for only a fool would dare to fall outside it; only now his was a precarious existence, and he was forced to serve at the very table where once he had dined like a prince.

Now Daniel saw a way to please his master that he could not afford to overlook or allow to go to waste for sentiment's sake. If that woman masquerading as a nun was indeed the ditcher's wife then many influential men, including Wulfric de Morthlund himself, had been played for fools and kept that way for eight long years. And if she still lived then it was possible that the child lived also. And what would de Morthlund make of that, when a humble priest of no particular ambition had every reason to congratulate himself at his expense?

Daniel knew that his master was an unforgiving man, and just for once he was inclined to bless him for that fault. He needed a gift to put before the fat man, and although he bore no grudge against Father Simeon, when every little favour counts so highly, a man must be prepared to trade whatever, or whoever, comes to hand.

CHAPTER THIRTY-TWO

It was mid-afternoon when Simeon arrived at St Anne's, and by then he had been fully informed of all that had happened in the marketplace. His first concern was for Elvira's welfare. The wound on her head had proved to be no more than a tender lump that caused her small discomfort, but the threat to her future safety might prove incalculable. Richard had whisked her away just as the ditcher identified her, but in doing so he had spoken her new name out loud, and any man with half his wits could make the connection now between the two. And by some perverse twist of fortune her rescuer proved to be no lesser man than Cyrus de Figham, who surely would not rest until the mystery was solved to his satisfaction.

On his arrival Simeon went directly to the Abbess's quarters and spent some time in private with her in the little anteroom next to her first floor office. Mother Constance was over sixty now and her thoughts were seldom allowed to linger too long in the realms of the mundane and the ordinary. She had begun her life at St Anne's without vocation, being driven instead by a fierce determination to succeed and an even fiercer will to rule over others. And she had not fallen short of either one, for her convent had become a powerful force within the chapter at Beverley. She had increased its numbers, its lands and its dues, swelled its private coffers and greatly enhanced its status. And in the process she had achieved another life-long ambition: to see her name, the name of Mother Constance, Abbess of St Anne's of Beverley, counted amongst the great names of the Church.

Despite her gentle manner and her constant references to the will of the Almighty, this abbess could be as ruthless as a common market trader in the interests of her convent and the many men and women dependent on it. She had bartered long and hard before agreeing to offer sanctuary to Elvira and the boy, and it was upon this quest for profit that Simeon now depended. The Reverend Mother would not be keen to have a modest but steady source of revenue withdrawn from her convent. To protect it she might condone a certain subterfuge, or at least agree to close her eyes to it.

The boy was waiting in Elvira's garden. He rose to his feet respectfully as Simeon entered, and for a while they surveyed each other, the priest and the boy, with solemn and thoughtful gazes. Simeon's hand came up to touch the golden emblem hanging from a cord around his neck. For eight years he had worn that shield each day beneath his clothes. It bore the symbol of St Peter and the name of the horse that had burst its heart to bring this child to Beverley: Cephas, The Rock, *Peter.*

'Dear God,' he prayed silently, 'help me to understand Your purpose here.' And aloud he said: 'Peter, you have begun to disregard your mother's authority.'

'Only when necessary,' the boy replied.

Simeon smiled at that. 'And is it necessary for you to crawl into the bowels of the earth in order to eavesdrop on the private conversations of priests and canons?'

'Yes, Father, sometimes it is.'

'There is a definite purpose in it, then?'

'Yes, Father.'

The boy's reply was simple and direct. Simeon nodded and indicated the wide stone rim of the well where they might sit together in comfort.

'Perhaps the time has come for us to discuss certain matters, man to man and honestly,' he suggested.

The boy looked back at him gravely for a while, then slowly nodded and said: 'Yes, Father, I think the time has come.'

When the Reverend Mother entered the visitors' room the Canon of St Martin's had already been waiting there for the better part of an hour. Two casks of brandy and one of salt had arrived ahead of him as a token of his regard for the elderly abbess; they both knew it was a bribe, and that he would receive fair measure in return. He halted in his restless pacing long enough to greet his hostess with the civility she deserved, waited until she was comfortably seated in a corner chair, then marked the length of the room again with his long stride. The room was in shadow, for it was hung with heavy drapes and the Abbess had ordered that its candles should remain unlit. Because of the depth of shadow there, it was not until her guest reached the far window, where softly tinted panels of glass gathered sunlight, that she could be sure he was still as handsome as she remembered him. She was not to be disappointed. Cyrus de Figham was indeed the most striking of men, tall and broad and with an arrogant bearing, with rich copper shades in his dark hair and a quick-silver glint in his eye. She sensed his impatience to get on with the business in hand, and his resentment of her presence there was obvious even before he halted his pacing again to ask:

'Madam, is it absolutely necessary for one of your Sisters of Mercy to be so closely chaperoned in the company of a *priest*?'

She smiled at that. Like so many men in his position, he would have her believe him gelded by the priesthood. She could count upon the fingers of one hand the number of secular priests she had come across in half a century capable of practising even a small degree of self-denial. Priests were but men, base animals from the waist downwards, and a shaved crown could not make them otherwise.

'It is my wish that it be so,' she answered mildly, and saw his

376

black eyes glitter in response. This one she liked. He was not lacking in fire or spirit like some of the other priests who came before her begging favours or support. Like the very attractive Simeon who was her favourite, this one also had hidden strengths and exciting undercurrents she could admire. It had been her lot in life to master a great many men and even break a few, but her instincts warned her now that here was one who would bend to another's will for just so long as it suited him and not a moment longer. He was indeed a match for Simeon. Mother Constance chuckled discreetly to herself. Two strong men in one day for her to deal with, two interesting episodes within as many hours. Life still had its small amusements, after all.

The Little Sister of Mercy joined them there at last. She slipped in quietly, closing the door without a sound behind her, a small, dainty creature who stood in the shadows with her hands clasped to her bosom and her head lowered.

'You have a visitor, Sister Cecily,' the Abbess said. 'Our brother in Christ, Father Cyrus of St Martin's, wishes to speak to you.'

'Yes, Reverend Mother.' The modest reply was accompanied by a small curtsy.

Cyrus de Figham had ceased his pacing now and was standing with his arms folded across his chest, staring at the young woman's lowered head. He licked his lips, drew in his breath and released it in a lengthy sigh. He would have preferred to see her in full light, for he had a tantalising after-image of raven hair framing an oval face, and huge brown eyes as dark and fiery deep as were his own. He would also have preferred to meet her privately, but since the old woman insisted on being present, he would have to behave with maddening restraint. He would choose his words with extra care in order to make his proposition clear to the girl without risk of antagonising the Abbess. He had come to St Anne's in search of a God-fearing woman to help run his priestly household at Figham. It was a common enough request of any convent, only he would have this priest's whore know that he claimed her in total ownership in the bargain, so long as he could keep the abbess safely blinkered. The very last thing he wanted was to draw out that old feline's claws and have her slam her convent doors against him.

There was a grid set discreetly into the wall, high up but near to the spot where the nervous young Sister of Mercy was standing. Its cover had been slid back a little way, and on its other side an unseen observer watched and listened. If the Reverend Mother was aware of it she made no sign. If Cyrus de Figham had even suspected the presence of such a witness, he would have bridled his desire and left without uttering a word.

'You may speak freely,' the Abbess prompted.

Cyrus bit back the cryptic remark he was tempted to offer in response, stepped closer to the sister and smiled to keep the impatient edge from his voice.

'Do you remember me, Sister Cecily?'

'I do indeed, sir,' she replied. 'But for you I might have been trampled by the crowd.'

'A small thing,' he declared with a flourish. 'I only wonder why we have not met before. How long have you been here at St Anne's?'

'A long time, sir. When I first brought my son here I was . . .'

'A son?' he cut in. 'You admit to having a son?'

'Yes, sir. He's a good boy. He thrives here.'

'You were married then?'

'I was indeed, sir.'

Cyrus allowed a satisfied grin to spread across his face. Surely he had her now. She could not hope to avoid detection while she kept the priest's bastard by her. He knew her secret, and he who uncovers another's guilts is always the richer for the knowledge. And more than that, he knew of no better way to exercise superiority over another man than by keeping his son beyond his reach in servitude.

'I believe you have not yet taken your holy vows, Sister Cecily?'

She shook her head.

'Well now, I have a mind to offer you a place in my household. I am in need of a woman there and you seem suitable, and that boy of yours will be just as safe beneath my roof as he has been in the Reverend Mother's care. I will, of course, offer generous compensation to the convent for the loss of your services.'

'But I'd rather stay here . . .'

'What?' he demanded coldly. He had hoped she would not dare express a preference. 'What's that you say?'

'You are kind, sir, but our home is here, where we are happy and . . .'

He allowed his voice a cutting edge. 'You surprise me, Sister Cecily. By the grace of Almighty God your humble fortunes are to be altered. Would you deny God's will? Would you reject this gift He offers you?'

'But sir, my little boy is happy here . . .'

'The future of your little boy, *Sister Cecily*, is my chief concern,' he said angrily, grinding the words through his teeth. 'For his sake I advise you to reconsider. You and your son are in need of my protection . . .' He lowered his voice and hissed into her face, '*Elvira*.'

She flinched. 'Sir?'

'Ah yes, I am aware of your true identity, Sister. Erik the ditcher recognised you instantly as his long-lost wife.' He stepped in closer, confident now that he would have his way. He had managed to set his back between his quarry and the Abbess, and he used the cover to cup one hand possessively around the Sister's left breast. He fondled the soft flesh with his fingers, kneading and pinching without a trace of gentleness. Whispering now, he added persuasively: 'Do not think to escape me, *Elvira*. Do not dare to make an enemy of Cyrus de Figham. I will have you, priest's whore. Either I will have you or the ditcher will, and I'll put your bastard son where neither you nor Simeon will ever find him.'

'What's that you say?' The Reverend Mother had fingered her beads for a measured interval but now she shifted in her seat, cupping one hand around her ear and waving the other in the visitor's direction. 'Stand back, Father Cyrus. Stand

379

back, if you please. I can no longer hear a word you are saying.'

He turned and bowed but stood his ground. 'I am merely offering the Sister God's blessing and my encouragement, lady Abbess,' he said, and to the girl he hissed: 'I'll have you, ditcher's slut and priest's whore. I'll have you.' Under the pretext of signing the cross he seized her breast so tightly that she whimpered. Only then did he move away from her, swaggering towards the window where he turned to lift his hand in a flourishing gesture of dismissal.

'You may return to your duties, Sister Cecily,' the Abbess declared. 'And you, Father Cyrus, may take a glass or two of wine before you leave us.'

He bowed low in acceptance of the Reverend Mother's hospitality, then called out to the girl in an amiable tone of voice as she was about to hurry from the room. 'I will return quite soon, Sister Cecily, and I ask you to pray for guidance and think very carefully on my offer in the meantime.'

Once outside the room, the distressed young woman rushed upstairs to the Reverend Mother's private library and flung herself, sobbing, into Elvira's arms.

'I know, I know,' Elvira soothed. 'God bless you, Alice, for taking my place in there.'

'He'll come again ... He says he'll come again ...'

'And when he does, you will meet him in full daylight, and then he will know that he and his witness have made a grave mistake.'

'He is a priest,' the girl said, clutching her bruised and painful breast. 'He is a man of God, and yet he was hateful, lascivious and hateful.'

'Hush, I know what he is,' Elvira said again. 'I saw and heard everything through the grid.'

Alice lifted her tear-stained face. She had dark eyes and short brown hair, and she was small and slender enough to be taken, in shadow, for her friend. Her deepest fear was in her eyes as she clasped Elvira's hands in her own and asked:

'Oh Elvira. What will I do if he decides to take me in your place?'

'I do not think it likely,' Elvira said. 'You are a pretty young woman, Alice, but believe me, it was more than simple lust that brought him here to our quiet convent. And should lust become the one and only consideration in his plans, I am convinced he will choose to service it elsewhere. Our Abbess has a temper not to be courted lightly. She is dangerous force when her nest is threatened.'

'Even so, I fear the worst,' the girl confessed.

Elvira smiled and tried to reassure her. 'Have faith, and if you cannot trust to God then trust to Simeon. We are in your debt, dear Alice, and Simeon will keep you safe from the lecher, that much you can depend upon.'

From there Elvira went to the little garden, bolted the door behind her and sat by the well with her Psalter unopened in her lap. She could hear a bell tolling somewhere in the distance, and the voices of fishermen carried on the still air from the lake beyond the garden wall. In her mind she tried to conjure a memory of that other time, when she had been a ditcher's wife with a dead child and an empty belly and only the milk in her breasts to give her value. The memory of it failed to touch her. It seemed to her that someone else had been Elvira then, and that she, the new Elvira, had come into existence in the instant when the priest dropped from the rafters of St Peter's infirmary, in the instant she first looked into his eyes.

Close by where she was sitting now, the iron cover of the well had been disturbed, as if a strong man had taken a lever and prised the bars aside for easier access. She had seen the situation at a glance. Instead of chastising him for the risks he took, the priest had followed the boy on some foolish and surely perilous adventure underground. And while they shared their masculine activities, all that she loved, all that was life to her, was down in those tunnels with them.

They carried two torches, and in the bright flames their shadows loomed and lurched, now moving ahead, now travelling alongside, now creeping behind like phantoms at their heels. The boy led the way, sure-footed on stones worn

381

smooth and treacherous by years of flowing water. Here and there a flow cascaded from above, fed by the overflow from an open stream somewhere far above them. They were in a tunnel no wider than the fullest span of Simeon's outstretched arms, and so low in height that for much of the journey he was unable to stand erect. He walked with his knees bent and his back stooped over, twisting his head at an angle in order to see his way more clearly.

Grey water flowed calf-deep beneath their feet, supposedly clean enough to feed the wells along its course, yet dark with all manner of impurities and sharp with the acrid scent of human waste. From time to time they found the slender chimney of a well cut into the tunnel's roof, and here Simeon paused to stretch himself upright, flexing the stiffness from his muscles. Some of these older wells had been left to fall into disrepair, but as many more were still in daily use despite the poor quality of the stream that fed them. Standing inside their dark openings Simeon heard the murmur of distant voices, the sudden barking of a dog, the cry of an infant. They passed a grid barring a small opening into the yard of an inn at Lairgate End, and another set close to the Bedern in Minster Moorgate, and by the same bent route they came at last to the very foundation stones that had once supported the ancient parish church of St Martin's.

Here Simeon stood with his torch held high above his head, his memories of that night a heart-stopping blend of awe and horror. He could see the stone pillars reaching down like the roots of some mighty tree, and caught between them many years of silt and mud and gravel. He recognised the debris of the storm, the old choir stalls, the sections of the flooring cracked apart like the fragile shells of hens' eggs. And amongst it all could be seen the pathetic bones of men and women sucked down as the church that had been their only shelter caved in around them. He crossed himself and prayed for the souls of those who remained in that dark place.

Then he suddenly heard the sound of voices singing.

'By all the saints!'

Quickening his steps, he followed the stream around

another bend, and the sweet sound of the plainsong reached his ears more clearly. He saw that the boy had climbed through a ragged gap where a fall of rock had broken away a part of the tunnel wall some way above the level of the water course. He could see light from the smaller torch flickering on the other side, and the boy's slim shadow, stretched to giant proportions, looming against the wall. Simeon climbed upon a pile of fallen stones and stepped through the opening to find himself in a cavernous space so strange and unexpected that for a moment it took his breath away.

The boy had lit some torches from his own and set them, spluttering and spitting in the damp air, back in their metal brackets on the wall. By their light Simeon saw a shimmering lake of near-black water, and rising from it several rows of squat stone columns supporting a vast roof of rounded arches. In many places the pale, smooth stones were still covered over with plaster, and on the plaster were colourful paintings depicting such inspirational scenes as might remind small mortals of God's greatness. Here was the Fall of Eve, and over there the Expulsion From The Garden, and the Labours of the Months, and looking down from shadowed curves some martyred saint with uncomplaining eyes. Here was a wonder the like of which Simeon had never dreamed of: a subterranean church that seemed to float on an ebony lake while a choir of disembodied voices sang an anthem to the Grace and Love of God. He crossed himself and whispered: 'God be praised!'

'Do you know this place, Father?' Peter asked, and his soft voice echoed among the arches.

Simeon nodded. 'I had not guessed that any part of it still existed, but yes, I know this place. We are in the main section of the original monastery founded by our Blessed St John, then known as Bishop John. He lived and died here almost five centuries ago. Legend tells us that his original tomb still lies somewhere down here beneath the Minster's foundations, covered by many centuries of silt and mud.'

'And so it does. I know the spot exactly,' Peter whispered. 'My hands have touched the very stones.'

'Then you are blessed indeed,' Simeon said, awed by the very idea of laying his own hands there.

'Is it true, Father, that the original marshlands known as the "Beaver Lake" were drained by the ancient Saxons when they built the monastery church here for Bishop John?'

Simeon nodded. 'History tells us it is so. The passing of time and the variable nature of men's tongues have conspired to alter our name to Beverley, but we were "Beaver Lake" then.'

The boy stared thoughtfully at the water, where shimmering glimpses of coloured tiles and ages-old mosaics and long-drowned marbles tantalised the eye.

'And the 'Beaver Lake' will one day claim it back,' he said. 'Let another five centuries pass and all of this ...' he stared about him, then looked at Simeon with a strange sadness in his eyes, '... this blessed monastery will be gone, buried without trace, and no man will know for sure that it ever really existed.'

'They will know,' Simeon assured him, taking him by the shoulders and speaking directly into those deeply troubled blue eyes. 'They will know because we will tell them, Peter. We are the scholars whose task it is to keep such things alive for all time. We are the very voice of history. We are the ...'

He halted with a sudden shudder and it was left to Peter to say out loud the words he could not bring himself to speak.

'... the keepers at the shrine?'

Simeon pulled the boy into his arms and hugged him tightly. There was a certain strength in that small body, a particular wisdom in his innocence. And there was that other, more painful thing that Elvira too had noticed. It was an almost *unearthly* quality that seemed to say his time with them was limited.

The priest and his godson climbed into a little boat that had been moored against the paving stones where they had stood. Propelled by a single pole that reached to the solid ground beneath the water, they steered a slow and silent course across the shimmering lake, drifting beneath the

384

arches, drawn by the singing of the choir. Here and there they saw a fancy boss or a capital carved with the head of a saint. They passed a little flight of steps that rose from the water only to vanish into a mound of toppled stones, and a handsome arch with an oak door leading nowhere. They were underneath the Minster church itself, in the flooded lower chapel or crypt. On one side was that part of the crypt that had collapsed with eighteen priests inside. Its fall had pushed a landslide of rubble into the lake, and where it rested a number of columns were so badly undermined that even a modest movement of the water at their base might keel them over.

Peter steered the boat to the left, into the deeper shadows where another fall of rock had shattered massive stones and twisted iron gratings into grotesque shapes. There he pinned the boat against the stones and scrambled out, and in a moment he had vanished into an opening too narrow to admit a fully grown man. When Simeon passed the torch in after him, he was shown a cavern of perhaps half the dimensions of his own scriptorium, a dank, dark place where heavy stones were piled as makeshift shelves, and on these lay a profusion of church ornaments: chests and caskets, bowls, vases, candlesticks and lamps. Here were items of copper, gold, silver and brass, panels of stained and painted glass still held in their original leads, altar plate of finest design and quality.

'These are from St Martin's crypt,' Peter explained. 'And these from the cellars beneath the Provost's Hall, and these from our Minster's lower chapel and reliquary.'

'You gathered them here? But why?'

'To keep them from the reach of common plunderers, and from being carried into the Beck by flood water.'

'Do I see caskets?' Simeon asked, pushing his head into the hole and squinting in the torchlight. 'By the saints, boy! Are there holy relics hidden here?'

Peter handed his torch through the opening and climbed through after it. He wore no shoes and his hooded grey tunic was left unbelted. Around his neck was hung an oval amber bead that did not quite hide the puckered scar at his throat. He was slender and agile, with delicate hands and narrow, waif-like shoulders. And in the pale oval of his face his eyes were a deep and startling blue, their lashes the same blond as his hair, his pupils wide and black in the half-light. He looked at Simeon with his steady gaze and said at last:

'Father, these precious relics would have changed hands at a profit a dozen times by now, had I not gathered them up and brought them here. I sat with a man at the church door, a pilgrim from the Lowlands, who boasted that he carried the finger of St Emerita of Rome in a pouch under his shirt. Another had the toe of St Isidor, another a lidded jar containing the blood of St Britwald of Canterbury. You must be aware, Father, that many thieves consider the theft of a holy relic more profitable than that of a whole purse full of gold, and Antony says that even the Heathens now have learned to trade in the business of Christian Saints.'

An idea came to Simeon then. 'It was you,' he said. 'You were the mysterious bellringer that night. You warned the Canons that thieves were attempting to plunder the shrine and altar.'

Peter smiled sheepishly. 'Would you have done less in my place, Father?'

'I doubt it, boy,' he replied, ruffling the fair head. 'So this is your purpose, then, to watch for thieves and gather what precious items you can into this secret hoard?'

'Not my purpose, father. These treasures belong to St John of Beverley. I merely keep them safe for him.'

Simeon shuddered at the boy's choice of words. '*Keeper at the shrine,*' the hooded figure had named him, and knowing nothing of these words here was young Peter, just eight years old and already bending his back to that very task.

'I caught sight of a casket in the torchlight,' he said, still scowling at his thoughts. 'A heavy gold casket set with precious stones. A perfect copy, it seemed to me, of St John's own resting place.'

Peter shook his head. 'A visual replica, yes, but lacking either value or substance. It is designed to fool the eye, but a pilgrim's touch would crush it to so much painted dust. Stephen the goldsmith made it for St John.'

'So that the pilgrims might be misled?'

'Sometimes, when need demands it.'

'But can such deception ever be justified?'

Peter shrugged his thin shoulders. 'In these uncertain times, if the Saint is to be protected, can it be otherwise?'

'My boy, you have assumed a tremendous responsibility.'

'Yes, Father, I know that.'

They pushed off again in the little boat, and as they changed direction at one of the larger pillars, Peter indicated the mouth of a tunnel opening, just visible in the wall on the far side of the lake and to their right.

'That way lies the old well in your scriptorium. The tunnel is dry and the tread-bars in the well are still strong enough to bear a man's weight. Remember that, Father. And the lake at its deepest only reaches to my shoulder. Remember that, too.'

Simeon nodded. He chose not to question the hint of warning in his godson's words.

To the muted sound of a score of strong male voices, they drifted beneath the arches under the choir. Here the stone roof was cracked in a jagged line, and the weight from above, where the choir had suffered the greatest damage in the storm of eight years ago, had crushed the spines of the arches supporting it.

Beyond that place was the spot where the High Altar stood. A single great column of early Norman design marked its position, rising from floor to ceiling to sustain the heavy, solid marble altar from below. By some mischance the whole column had shifted sideways off its base so that it now stood the whole length of a man's arm lower than it should, and its massive base-stone stood beside it, a pale, round shape barely visible beneath the water. Squinting upwards into the darkness, Simeon could just make out the shadowed space by which the column's capital fell short now of its purpose.

'The altar,' he said, stretching up to spread the torchlight higher. 'The altar is unsupported from below. That means the tomb of St John is vulnerable.'

'St John will endure,' Peter said, as if all knowledge of such things was his to tap at will. 'He will endure. Listen, Father. Listen to the singing.'

The broken shaft of a well stood by them now, set like a neglected chimney-stack between the lake and a flatter section of the roof. Simeon knew of this well and the mysterious properties of the stream from which it fed. Bishop John had blessed its waters for all time, and after five long centuries the stream ran swift or slow, shallow or deep, according to the moment: but always fresh, always pure, as St John decreed. The well had its small, square opening near the high altar, close to the ancient sanctuary stone. Near its top a metal bracket was set, and from it hung the customary rope and bucket, now rarely used to draw water up. It was by this rope that Peter came and went, his whole weight suspended from that single bracket, his young life hanging on the good will of the saint he served.

Now that same shaft which offered Peter secret access to the Minster Church had become a sensitive amplifier to enhance the wonderful singing of the choir. For a while they listened, their hearts delighted by the rare quality of pure notes and subtle echoes, the priest with his arm around his godson's shoulders, their faces uplifted and flickering with reflected firelight. When the music ebbed at last the boy looked up at Simeon with a coppery shimmer of light and shadow in his eyes.

'Will you help me, Father?'

'Peter, it seems like sacrilege ...'

'But it must be done, and before the feast of St Matthew in three day's time. After that ...' The boy's voice faltered briefly. 'Father?'

'Yes, my son?'

'Will you help me? Will you help me do what I must do?'

Simeon glanced down at the upturned face and realised at that moment that he had never denied his godson anything, nor would he do so now, no matter how strange or disturbing the request. He signed the cross and remembered how, after an absence of eight long years, the mysterious hooded figure had suddenly appeared beside him in the scriptorium.

'Yes, Peter,' he said at last. 'I will do whatever I can to help you.'

As he spoke the words he felt the weight of something cold and shapeless settle on him. It was a touch of foreboding, and it left him chilled.

He stayed to fulfil his promise long after the choral priests had filed from the church leaving a single candle burning at the High Altar. Moving like shadows in the uncertain light, Simeon and Peter took the treasures of Beverley into their keeping. Here were the bones and dust of Bishop John, the prayer-beads of The Evangelist, the dagger of King Athalston. Here too were four iron nails that had fastened St Peter upside down to his cross, three brass pins from the crucifix in Rome, and a little bundle of bones and hair belonging to St John the Evangelist.

It was an awesome hoard for any man to handle, and priest and boy were silent in their homage.

'So be it,' Simeon said at last.

'Amen,' the boy replied.

As Simeon drew Peter away from his secret underground hole, that sense of foreboding hung about him still, for it was not for the whim of men to disturb the sleep of saints.

CHAPTER THIRTY-THREE

Daniel Hawk had been kept waiting in the corridor for almost an hour. Twice he had protested to Wulfric de Morthlund's clerk that the matter was of some urgency, but the bent old man had shuffled away with a perfunctory nod of his head and still the visitor had not been sent for. Nor had Daniel been offered the refreshment he had come there hoping to receive, and even now, with an empty belly and many hours to wait before supper in the refectory, he was too proud to ask a servant for the common courtesy that should have been his due. He knew that Wulfric de Morthlund was in his chamber with a young boy from the grammar school. He knew it well enough, for he himself had procured the boy for his master's pleasure. It made him shudder to recall the youngster's reluctance to appear before the man who was the subject of so many whispered rumours in the school-room. It was a dirty business, this search for ever fresher flesh to satisfy de Morthlund's appetites, but it appealed to the fat man's sense of irony to have his one-time favourite supply the sop that kept his temper sweet.

In the dimly lit corridor Daniel occupied a short bench set into a recess, sitting well back so that his body was mostly concealed in shadow. The smell of roasting meat invaded his nostrils, reminding him of his hunger, but at that moment he was more concerned with selling his information while it still had value. That snake-eyed Cyrus de Figham had seen and heard exactly what Daniel had witnessed. He too must suspect that the nun was Simeon's mistress and the ditcher's wife. He too must have set a price on what he knew. The edge was Daniel's, or so he believed, because the woman was desirable and Cyrus de Figham, like his fellow Canon, Wulfric, thought first with his loins and only after with his intellect. And added to that was the sin of pride that would prompt the boastful priest to lay his own claim on whatever belonged to Simeon. Thinking of Simeon of Beverley brought him a small but sharp twinge of regret, but it was quickly salved. His own warning, eight years ago, had saved the life of the woman and her son. Eight years of life and freedom he had granted them in three words timely spoken: *you are betrayed.*

'And so you are again, Simeon,' he said aloud, sucking the tantalising scent of roasting beef and mutton into his nostrils.

When Daniel was at last led upstairs by the shuffling and openly disdainful manservant, he saw that the heavy curtain covering the alcove to de Morthlund's door was swinging from its timber pole. He guessed that the previous visitor had just left by the crooked staircase leading to the yard. Neither the boys from the town nor the students from the grammar school were allowed to come and go by the main entrance. They came by the back stair on the pretext of taking confession or receiving some priestly chastisement, and they left the same way with their lips firmly sealed and their fortunes altered for good or ill.

Inside the sumptuous private chamber Daniel found a low trestle table laid with an altar cloth and set with dishes of warm bread, roasted mutton, whole roasted rabbits, little fancy tarts and plump fruit fritters, wine by the jug and bowls of fruit and nuts. In the centre was a huge meat pie stuffed with pounded beef, shallots, dried currants and figs, and the steam that rose from the funnel in its pastry crust was enough to send a hungry man's stomach into aching spasms.

With a grin that showed a few discoloured teeth, Wulfric de Morthlund turned with a flourish to greet his guest.

'Ah, Daniel, my Little Hawk. Come in, come in.' He beamed and spread his arms out wide as if he might welcome Daniel with a rare embrace. Then he stopped dramatically and, as the smile fell from his face, shook his head with a disapprovingly frown. 'By the gods, you're as thin as a runt, my boy. You look no better than a beggar. You need more flesh to cover those angular features of yours.'

Daniel glanced at the laden table and licked his lips. He wanted to say that regular meals and a little more care from his master was all he needed. Instead he shrugged apologetically. He felt the flush rise to his cheeks and neck when he saw the fat man staring at his head with a look of distaste.

'You had a good head of hair when you were young,' he said maliciously, and saw the pink flush deepen to a fiery red. 'You should make an effort to repair the damage.'

'My lord, when a man's hair . . .'

Wulfric waved his protest aside. 'I have it on the very best authority that a thick, well-salted blood pudding, made from young hogs and with a good measure of horsehair added, is an excellent remedy for baldness if eaten every day for a month at breakfast.'

Daniel bowed submissively. He would more willingly have lost a hand than surrender up his precious hair, and this man who was his lord and master was well aware of it. That he could be reduced to playing a passive role in his own humiliation was a vital aspect now in any pleasure Wulfric de Morthlund still found in their relationship.

Through gritted teeth he managed to say: 'Indeed, my lord, but there are as many more who believe that simple lemon balm rubbed into the scalp many times during the course of a day will eventually halt the loss.'

'Or ox piss,' Wulfric suggested. 'Ox piss is a certain cure.'

Daniel recoiled from the suggestion even as he nodded his agreement. 'I am sure you are right, my lord.'

'Then try it, for Heaven's sake. Or would you rather reach

your thirtieth year with a head as smooth and ridiculous as an egg?'

'My lord, it seems that every house in the country has its tried and tested remedy and yet, if any one of them was proved but half a cure, no man would need to suffer baldness even in his dotage.'

'I personally know of a man who restored his fallen hair by regular applications of fresh cow dung,' Wulfric cut in, his fat face coldly serious but his eyes glinting with cruel amusement. 'What say you to that, young Daniel? It stank to high heaven, but it cured the loss. He swears by it.'

Daniel swallowed. 'I'm sure he does, my lord,' he muttered miserably.

'You would do well to follow his example.'

'Indeed, my lord.' Daniel nodded and forced himself to smile in the hope of appeasing his master. He touched self-consciously at the area of sparse and thinning hair around the front of his head. That morning he had counted all the seemingly healthy hairs remaining on his pillow when he left his bed. He knew that another year at this same rate would see his skull completely naked.

Wulfric looked at the younger man as he might study a cow or a pig in the marketplace, and when he spoke again a touch of irritation was in his voice. 'That hood and tunic you are wearing are grubby and threadbare.'

'Forgive me, sir. They are all I own.'

'You look like a vagrant, and those shoes are hardly worthy of a *monk*.'

'Then I must apologise for them,' Daniel said, 'for I have no others to replace them.'

Wulfric began to voice another criticism, then threw up his hands in exasperation and snapped: 'By the gods, Daniel Hawk, there was a time when I tolerated you better.'

'Yes,' Daniel muttered, feeling his throat constrict with unexpected emotion. 'I believe there was such a time, my lord Wulfric.'

For a moment the fat man glared at him angrily, hugely impressive in his embroidered tunic and yellow cowl, scented with oil of musk and rose and lavender. He seemed undecided whether to have his guest thrown out into the street or else take him in his arms and warmly embrace him. At last he stepped forward to slap Daniel heartily on the back and lead him to a seat at the table.

'Come, lad, we'll eat together and swallow a glass or two of good wine, and to hell with blood-puddings and cow dung. What do you say?'

'My lord, I would be honoured.'

'Ah, honoured you might well be, my Little Hawk, but are you *hungry*?'

Daniel nodded and felt his stomach growl. 'I think I will do justice to your table,' he said, and to prove his enthusiasm drew his dagger and sank it into the very centre of the meat pie.

Wulfric de Morthlund watched his young guest lose himself in the urgent business of eating as much as his belly would hold at one sitting. The Hawk was ravenous, and the splendid dagger that had been a gift from his master many years ago now flashed its fine blade and jewelled handle incongruously against its owner's shabby clothes and scrawny features. These days he was reduced to taking his meals in the refectory, and only then if Wulfric considered his duties as a some-time clerk had earned him that privilege. What remained between them now was a series of cat-and-mouse games of malice and meek obedience, of dominance and servitude. Wulfric abused him because he had the power and the God-given right to do so, and he then despised his victim for his weakness, just as all men must despise the loyal cur that cringes at their feet.

Watching Daniel grab at his food without regard for the genteel manners he once held in such high esteem, de Morthlund felt a rare sense of compassion for the young man who had shared his life, and his bed, for thirteen years. He deserved a better end to it than this, and Wulfric de Morthlund, more than most men, could afford to be magnanimous. The boy should have a chest of new clothes, a decent winter cloak and sturdy boots, and perhaps the exclusive use of a small room on the ground floor. It was not to the Canon's credit that his clerk be seen begging shelter at the house of Antony the monk, or sleeping in the Minster with the paupers and the pilgrims. Not since the boy was fifteen had he lacked a master's generous protection. He had been handsome then, with pretty eyes and a good head of hair and a certain natural arrogance that suited him far more than the grovelling servility he had recently adopted. What touched Wulfric in spite of himself was the knowledge that neither fear nor greed nor even the vain hope of a better future kept that young man clinging to his master's favours. What kept him there was a loyalty that would not be bought with cash or kind, with gifts or promises. What kept him there was love.

The fat man was smiling benignly when Daniel Hawk sat back in his chair at last, dipped a corner of his lap-cloth in the water bowl and wiped it over his mouth and chin to clean away the grease. He was swift to return Wulfric's smile, and the grin on his face revealed good teeth and a sudden brightness that chased every shadow from his narrow features. Replete with a dinner of excellent quality, he sipped his wine at a leisurely pace and savoured the rare pleasures of the moment. He reached out and took an ivory toothpick from a silver dish, applied it to his teeth, then raised his replenished goblet in a toast to his host.

'My compliments, Canon Wulfric,' he declared. 'A wonderful table, sir. I have not dined with such delight for many months.'

'I see you are more your old self again, Little Hawk,' de Morthlund grinned. 'And if you dine half so well at supper tonight and at breakfast tomorrow morning, we'll soon put some decent flesh back on those bones of yours.'

Daniel sat forward in his seat and tongued moisture to his lips.

'Am I to stay the night with you, my lord?'

'If that is your desire,' Wulfric said, still grinning.

'Oh yes, it is, it is.'

'Then so be it, Little Hawk, so be it.'

'Thank you, my lord. Thank you.'

Now Daniel could afford to smile in genuine satisfaction. For the moment at least he was back in favour. There was supper to be had and breakfast promised, and there would be a whole night in between. The time was right, the moment had come to offer Wulfric the special sweetener. He must appear to be confident without betraying any trace of arrogance. He must not seem to have assumed the upper hand, for the fat man was rightly jealous of his position of power.

'There was a woman some years ago,' he said carefully. 'A ditcher's wife who left her husband for love of a priest.'

Wulfric's smile did not falter, but his eyes had narrowed. 'It is to your credit that you choose to speak of it in such simple terms,' he said. 'There was no mystery, no strangeness in it. That priest was a simple adulterer who sought to manipulate hysteria and foolish superstition to his own advantage.'

'And was made to pay most dearly for his error.'

'Nonsense. He received neither more nor less than he deserved.'

'He lost his mistress and his son,' Daniel reminded him. 'Surely a heavy loss for any man to bear?'

Wulfric smiled easily and spread his hands. 'Should a man continue to reap the rich harvest of his iniquity?'

'The woman and her child were drowned.'

'An unfortunate accident – timely but unfortunate.'

Daniel shook his head, watching the other's eyes. 'The woman lives.'

'What?'

'The woman, Elvira the ditcher's wife, mistress of Simeon de Beverley. She lives.'

Wulfric's expression did not change except to grow a little stiffer and more mask-like. His eyes, by contrast, were as bright and alert as those of a hungry bird of prey with something tasty brought within its reach.

'That is not possible.'

'I saw her with my own eyes,' Daniel told him. 'Erik the ditcher saw her too, and called to her by name, but she ran off like a startled rabbit at the sound of his voice. When he would have given chase Cyrus de Figham held her back and ...'

'Hold up! Draw breath!' Wulfric declared, raising his palms as if to ward off blows. 'You say de Figham also knows of this?'

'He knows as much as I, but I suspect he intends to bed the woman before he accuses her. He would not dare keep such a secret to himself.' He paused with a scowl and, because he had learned the value of creating a common foe, added with a sly innocence: 'At first it seemed to me ... but no, I must have been mistaken. The crowds, the swiftness of events ... indeed, I was mistaken.'

'About what, Daniel?'

'It was nothing. A mere impression, my lord, no more than that.'

'Then tell me, Daniel. I will hear it.'

'Well, my lord, it seemed to me that Father Cyrus and the woman ... that they had not met there in the street by chance. He had his arms about her and he was smiling as if she pleased him greatly. They seemed ...'

'Familiar?' Wulfric offered.

Daniel nodded reluctantly. 'It was but my impression of the scene. I normally trust my instincts, but in this case I must surely be mistaken. Father Cyrus knows your feelings on the matter. If he had prior knowledge of this, he would be here now, helping you to net these conspirators.'

'And is he here?' the fat man asked mildly. 'Did he rush to my house, as you have done, to alert me to the fact that I have been duped for eight years.'

'Which shows he is not aware you were duped,' Daniel offered.

'By your own admission he saw what you saw. He identified the priest's whore.'

'Well, yes, that is so, my lord, but to play you false, to be a part of this long plot against you ... surely he would not *dare*?'

'Oh yes, he would, if the profit outweighed the risks,'

Wulfric answered dryly. Then he grinned again and beckoned Daniel to move closer. 'Come, dear heart, refill your cup with wine and sit beside me here on my couch. I must hear your story, every minute detail of it, from its beginning. If I have been duped these eight years I will know of it, and may Heaven help any who dares take Wulfric de Morthlund for a dunderhead.'

Simeon and his trusted friends had gathered together in the small, dark chapel that was tucked into one of the quiet eastern corners of the Minster. Here an elegant sweep of rib vaulting carried their voices upwards, while a wide stone screen, elaborately carved, guarded the chapel door. Beside the screen stood Brother Justin with his Psalter open and his deep, full-throated voice raised up in prayer. At first glance he appeared to slouch against the carved stone figures of saints set in a row at his back, but a closer look revealed the twisting and thickening of the spine that was slowly turning that strong young man into a cripple. Nobody knew why his bones should curve thus, or why the joints of his wrists and fingers caused him so much pain. It was God's will, no man knew more than this, and brother Justin, just twenty-four years old, humbly accepted what was to be his lot.

The voice of the crippled priest sang out the Psalms before the chapel door. It would not pause unless some danger threatened, and the sound of those deep, melodious devotions ensured that the low hum of voices from within would not be overheard.

'Seven men have claimed sanctuary at St John's altar during the last week,' Father Cuthbert said, watching Simeon's troubled face and wondering how that little boy from St Anne's had come to copy, and to claim, every expression of Simeon's for his own. There had been times, though he would not admit to them, when he doubted Simeon's own denial that Peter was in fact his natural son. They shared a bond that was little short of uncanny, and their silences were often so lengthy and conspiratorial that one might believe them capable of communicating together without the need for word or outward sign. And more than that, the old Canon had taken Simeon in when he was only ten years old and now, in this equally solemn, equally studious blue-eyed child, he found those years brought back to him afresh.

'Seven men,' he repeated. 'All of them devout in their demeanour and diligent in their devotions.'

'All of them?' Simeon asked.

Cuthbert nodded, smiling. 'Not a fault have they to share between them.'

'Are they known to each other?'

'Not that I am aware. Two are brothers, young gentlemen who keep close to each other, but the rest claim to be fugitives from some personal injustice, coming from such diverse places as Chichester, Bath, Chepstow and Berwick-upon-Tweed. They are claiming sanctuary here for thirty days, which is their right, and after that our canons will speak in their defence.'

'One is a deaf-mute with a halting stride,' Father Thorald explained. 'He spends long hours crouching before the sacred shrine, no doubt praying silently for a miracle cure of all that ails him.'

'No doubt,' Simeon mused, his thoughts already running on ahead. He did not trust this unlikely clutch of sanctuary men, this small, impeccably mannered group who made such show of being strangers that none would guess they shared a common cause. Petitions had been dispatched to their respective accusers, but if Simeon's information was correct, those papers reached no further than the town boundary, for the men who were hired to ride with them had secretly taken bribes, and their letter-pouches were handed over in exchange for personal gain.

The familiar voice beyond the chapel screen dipped down to a softer hum, as if the singer had lost his place and both words and music momentarily evaded him. It was the signal that others were approaching, and Simeon looked to the door of the chapel as Antony and Osric strode in together. Both had been sent to question the sanctuary men, to lead their little group in prayer and glean what they could in the course of the brief encounter.

Simeon studied both men in their turn, Osric with his rugged face and wary soldier's eyes, and the Flemish monk, Antony, recently returned from a lengthy pilgrimage that had scorched his skin to the colour of an Arab's.

'Well?' he asked.

'They are not strangers to each other,' Osric said without hesitation. 'They pretend to be, emphatically so, and they claim to have travelled from different towns, but you may take my word and Antony's on it; they are not strangers.'

Antony nodded his agreement. 'My instincts run level with your own, Simeon. I too suspect they have a sinister purpose here.'

'Except perhaps for the deaf-mute,' Osric added. 'He keeps to himself and seems concerned with nothing but his prayers and his modest share of the sanctuary alms.'

'Then he is undoubtedly the cleverest of them all,' Simeon told him with a smile that lacked amusement. 'Few others could hope to deceive a man of your good sense.'

'What?'

'Simeon? What are you saying?' Antony asked, rising from his seat with a perplexed expression not unlike the ones the others wore. 'Do you doubt that he is as he claims to be?'

'He is no deaf-mute my friend. Nor is he any more lame than I am. It would seem he too has learned the art of walking with a crooked gait.'

Antony was looking at him with a scowl. 'How have you discovered all this, friend Simeon? Since when have you concerned yourself with the company of sanctuary men?'

'Not I. I do not know these men.'

'Then who?'

Reluctant, Simeon shook his head and said: 'I have a reliable informant.'

'Informant?'

'Someone who can be trusted. His word is good. We must not disregard it.'

'The boy,' Father Cuthbert suddenly announced. 'For some time now I have had a niggling idea that the young rascal was up to something. It is Peter who is Simeon's informant.'

'Can this be so, Simeon?' Osric demanded. 'Is Peter your accomplice in this?' And when Simeon nodded in reply the grim-faced infirmarian rolled his eyes and said: 'By the gods, you are his godfather, his guardian. How can you even *think* to use him for such a dangerous undertaking? If these men are no more than common scoundrels and they discover that he has been your spy, carrying tales against them . . .'

'Enough of this!' Simeon flared. 'What in God's name do you take me for, Osric? Do you really believe I would send Peter into the very laps of thieves and desecrators?'

'Desecrators . . .?' The rest of Antony's question was left hanging in the air, for brother Justin had once again drifted from his steady course in the chanting of the Psalms. In the silence a company of sandalled feet and swishing robes passed by the door of the chapel. During the lull, Simeon took what appeared to be gems from a deep pouch at his belt, handed them out amongst his friends and waited for the intrusion to pass them by. When the singing resumed in earnest it was Father Richard, holding his arm before him, who stepped into the light and broke the silence.

'I know this gem,' he said, aghast. 'I know it by its distinctive shape and blood-red colouring. It is one of the larger gems from the shrine.'

'And here's a chrysoprase,' Thorald said, turning a polished, golden-green stone in his fingers.

'And this is one of the milky opals,' Antony exclaimed. 'By the saints! The shrine has been plundered!'

Simeon shook his head. 'The shrine is exactly as you saw it last.'

Osric was scowling as he turned a violet-toned stone the size of a dove's egg over and over in his fingers. 'Simeon, how have you come by these?'

'Peter brought them to me. You will find gems just as pure and genuine as these embedded in the shrine.' He glanced at Osric and smiled. 'I think our brother Osric is not so easily mystified, eh, Osric?'

The grizzled infirmarian placed the bright amethyst on the stone seat where he had been sitting, took up a candlestick and brought it down with a crash. The gem was crushed to powder beneath its heavy base, leaving its brilliant surface twinkling in tiny granules on the stone.

'Imitation,' he growled. 'And only a master craftsman, a tiler or a glazier of the greatest expertise, could produce so fine a finish upon such base matter.'

When he would have crushed another, Simeon stayed his hand, collected the remaining jewels and returned them to the pouch hung from his belt. He watched as Father Cuthbert rose from his chair with a great deal of effort, and only when his mentor had gained his feet did he offer an arm for his assistance. Cuthbert was a proud man who needed to feel that some things, at least, were still within his limited capabilities. He shuffled forward on Simeon's arm, only now responding to the young priest's earlier assurance that the shrine remained as they had seen it last.

'Are we to believe then, that worthless baubles such as these are decorating the holy shrine of St John of Beverley?' he demanded.

Simeon nodded gravely. 'We think these sanctuary men are well-practised violators of holy shrines,' he told them. 'They take whatever they can lay their hands on, anything from precious relics to simple altar cloths and plate. They carry fake gems of every size and shape, and where they can they exchange them for genuine treasures.'

'Dear God, we offer them sanctuary and they use it to plunder our altar at their leisure,' Antony breathed.

'If they have robbed St John,' Thorald declared. 'I personally will take no less than seven hands to repay the outrage.'

'Not on St John's account,' Simeon told him. 'Many of those gems were lost before these men ever came to Beverley. Do you not recall that a man was hanged for stealing from the shrine on the night of the great storm eight years ago?'

'Aye, conveniently hanged, as we all know,' Osric said. 'He died still swearing that he had left his hoard behind, yet it was not found and returned to the church until several months later.' He paused to massage his chin with a calloused hand. 'And as I recall, the finding of that little hoard helped make that rogue de Figham a Canon, albeit Canon of a pile of rubble.'

'Those gems were no more real than these,' Simeon told him, lifting up the leather pouch by its twisted thong. 'But whether our Provost and my lord Archbishop were aware of it at the time I cannot say. I suppose it is feasible that Cyrus de Figham had the first copies made and brought to the Minster as a gift, and that the Provost either accepted them for the sake of appearances, or because he too was duped into believing they were real.'

'Duped by Cyrus de Figham,' Richard said. 'As cunning as a fox, that one. He pretends to return the stolen gems and instead replaces them with clever copies. And even now he could claim that he did so in good faith, to set the tomb to rights until the real gems were found. Ye gods, he might even have kept the true gems for himself.'

'Indeed, but that is merely speculation,' Simeon warned. 'And remember that our task is not to accuse Cyrus de Figham of duping the masters of our church eight years ago, even though we would all believe such a thing of him. The fact remains that only a half dozen genuine jewels were left in the shrine when the sanctuary men arrived a week ago.'

'Six? *Six?* But only a dozen, at most, were stolen during the storm, and there are *scores* more set into the casket.'

'Six!' Simeon repeated.

'Impossible,' Antony said emphatically. 'You must be mistaken, Simeon. Only that many remaining? I tell you it is impossible!'

'And I tell you it is a fact, my friends. If the thieves were left to carry out their plan, they would be the richer by six gems, no more than that.'

'But what of all the rest?'

'I suspect they were prised loose one by one over the years, replaced immediately by a duplicate, then sold on at a handsome profit and with little risk of the theft ever being discovered.'

Once again the voice outside the chapel door began to falter. A line or two of a psalm were repeated out of turn and softer than the rest, but after no more than a minute or so the voice rose up again as clearly and as confidently as before.

'So,' Father Cuthbert said at last. 'The boy discovers a plot to steal from St John, and that discovery leads us to discover that the shrine has been systematically plundered since the first gems were prised away eight years ago.'

'I fear there is more to it than that,' Simeon said gently. 'Gentlemen, these thieves have not come to Beverley for the sake of a handful of pretty baubles for which few men could offer anything like their true value. They are here to fulfil a far more sinister and damaging purpose. Oh yes, their aim is personal wealth, of that there can be no doubt, but the true value of their target cannot be estimated in coin alone. Believe me, my friends, not even Henry, King of all England, could hope to raise enough to purchase for himself what these men are here to steal from us.'

He felt Father Cuthbert grip his arm more tightly, and in that place each man had held his breath, dreading to hear the words spoken out loud.

'These men did not come here for St John's treasures but for his sacred relics. They are here to steal from us our greatest prize, *the saint himself.*'

CHAPTER THIRTY-FOUR

Simeon let his cloak hang loosely from his shoulders. Another night was closing in, creeping like a warm mist off the marshes. Tomorrow would be the eve of St Matthew's Feast, the twenty-first day of September, in the year of Our Lord, 1188. Nearly a decade had passed since that storm of almost Satanic proportions had battered the town of Beverley. In that time courageous efforts had been made to repair the damage: whole streets of houses and shops had been rebuilt, corn mills and warehouses repaired, ditches retrenched.

In the Minster church all seemed to have been returned to its former glory, though much timber had been used in place of the more expensive stone. Carved oak stood well beside columns of chiselled sandstone or marble, and even the shattered arches had been repaired, in places, by curves of sturdy timber. Large areas of plaster now rested on beds of smoothly finished wood, and on these the beautiful wall-paintings had been lovingly restored. With the help of donations from local squires and merchants, the ornate stone seats of the choir had been replaced and its flooring repaired. Sir Hugh de Burton had personally designed the choir's new canopy, a splendid affair carved in oak by master craftsmen and topped by a dozen slender, spear-like pinnacles that reached up and were lost in the shadows hanging below the roof. Even the shrine and its protective screen of intricately woven metal was once again a thing of splendour, lovingly restored by that expert in his craft, Stephen the goldsmith. Once again the interior of Beverley Minster could snatch a man's breath away with its powerful beauty. Only its great east window still kept the memory of that terrible night. Its faceted sections of plain glass caught the shifting tones of the sky, echoed the movements of the clouds and reflected the silver glints of moonlight as if in a pool whose surface was oddly fractured. It was without doubt a splendid feature of the church, and yet it fell far short of what it once had been.

Simeon stood at the edge of the little orchard, looking up at the Minster's moonlit profile looming beyond the enclosure wall. He missed the colours, the blood-red and the deep, luminous blue, the brilliant golds and greens, the delicate pastels. And he knew he was not alone in mourning the loss of that sacred work of art.

He had returned to St Peter's enclosure via the boundary wall that skirted the wetlands. There was a deep ditch beyond the wall, and a tangle of growth on either side that could trap a man like a fly in a spider's web. But Simeon knew just where to climb and how to place his feet, how far to jump from the top, and at what angle, in order to clear every obstruction and land with safety on the inner side. Even in darkness or in the deceptive shades of twilight he was sure-footed enough to scale that ancient and forbidding wall without mishap.

Tonight he had passed the secret grave in the north-east corner where two high walls met, and in the bright moonlight he had remembered another time, too many years ago, when he had crouched to bury a tiny bundle there. The spot was overgrown now and neglected, and the grave where Elvira's son lay buried had long since succumbed to Nature's prolific handiwork. He had remained there long enough to whisper a solemn prayer for the child's eternal soul, and left with a heavy heart because, try as he might, he could not recall its name. With neither name nor grave to its credit,

406

with none to remember, to mourn its loss or plead its case in Heaven, how would God ever know that small soul as His own?

He was still troubled by his thoughts as he strode towards the infirmary where Osric had promised to keep a simple supper for him. His trip tonight had been virtually uneventful. He had followed a ragged, strenuous course beyond the boundary ditch, tracing an east-handed, roughly circular route around the town and back to St Peter's via the Beck and the wetlands. His path took him by the settlement at Groval, along the edge of the woodland close to Molescroft, across the lower West Wood where the land was uneven and treacherous, beyond the lake at St Anne's, through open pasture to Long Lane and the Figham meadow, then across the Beck to the wastes around St Nicholas's Church. One third of the distance he had done at a run, testing the strength of his muscles and the full extent of his stamina, and he knew that any young sportsman in the area would be hard-pressed to pass him on the way. He had long since determined never to waste the blessing that had come upon him during the terrible storm of eight years ago, though circumstances dictated that he should not wear his miracle for all to see and all to wonder at. In daylight he did not dare to walk or run like other healthy men, for to the world he must appear the same, a lame scribe dragging a useless foot behind him. But at dead of night, outside the boundaries of Beverley, lost in the darkness beyond the street fires and the eyes of men, he could be for a while as God had made him, whole again. Of all the many-worded prayers of thanks he had offered up for his healing, this surely was the most meaningful of all: that he should choose to run himself weary on his two good feet, blessing God with every stride.

When Cyrus de Figham left the convent of St Anne's early that evening, he was in a rage that taxed his well-practised powers of self-control to their very extremities. It compressed his mouth into a bitter line and blanched his skin to an ashen grey. The lengthy walk from the convent to his house at Out Ings, overlooking Figham meadow, failed to reduce the simmering heat of his fury. To add further irritation to his already soured temper, two separate incidents along the way had left their mark on him. The first was a common scuffle just outside the Keldgate Bar, where a group of vagrants was gathered around a campfire, cooking a meagre supper in a pot over the flames. The biggest and strongest among them, a man with rotten teeth and nostrils that were clipped to mark him as a thief, stepped into Cyrus's path as he approached. He was a swaggering braggart with massive fists, thick legs and a heavy dagger fastened at his belt. The campfire's glow was insufficient to light the traveller's face in any detail, or else he might have better judged the measure of his victim.

'There be a toll for passing into Beaver Lake,' he drawled, using the ancient countryman's name for the town.

'And since when do citizens afoot surrender coin for entry here?' Cyrus demanded.

'Since I decided it be so,' the man replied with a bellow of drunken laughter, and there were answering guffaws from around the nearby campfire.

Cyrus lowered his voice to a savage hiss. 'Step aside, you cur, or you will eat the filth of the town ditch for your supper.'

The man roared his amusement and set his fists on his hips in a brazen gesture. A woman with her skirts hitched high above her knees came swaggering into view.

'Hear that, me lass?' the lout demanded. 'Hear what the fine gent says? Taste the town ditch indeed, and him no bigger than meself and wearing a pretty priest's frock under his cloak.'

'And a pretty purse at his belt, I'll wager,' the woman said, nudging the man with her muscular elbow.

'There be a toll for passing into Beaver Lake,' the man said again. 'And if the purse be empty I'll settle for that fine cloak you're wearing.'

He raised one unwashed hand to touch the sable hood and that was his undoing, for the touch of the vulgar poor was, as far as this priest was concerned, no less abhorrent than the

408

embrace of a leper. His hand came up in his own defence and his dagger was in it. The blade found soft flesh and slid inside without resistance. For a moment the man just stood and gaped in disbelief. Then he lowered his head in time to see the blade withdrawn and the warm blood rushing after it. He grunted and staggered backwards, lurched against a section of damaged fencing on the bank of the ditch and fell into the water with a splash. Cyrus marched on through the Bar, his boots sounding a hollow ring on the timber boards of the bridge and his shadow looming hugely against the paler underside of the Bar's tall arch. He left behind a scene of much confusion, with the woman shrieking at the top of her voice for help in fishing her injured husband from the filthy water before he was swept away.

The incident was of little consequence to Cyrus now. A man of his standing did not concern himself with the debris of the streets. But there had been a second occurrence, somewhat less eventful but potentially more significant than the first. It happened in the open regions between the impressive Eastern Bar on Flemingate and the sprawling Figham Meadow. He had crossed the stinking, narrow ditch that ran a parallel course with the Port Beck before forking away to join the main stream at Lund. There he had seen another man striding out in the darkness, a tall, broad-shouldered man in a gentleman's hood and tunic over tightly thonged braes and high leather boots. This other was on the far side of the Beck, marching across a patch of rough ground in the direction of St Nicholas's Church, and there was something about his size and bearing that was strikingly familiar.

'Simeon!' The name was pulled from him on a growl of malevolence. 'Simeon of St Peter's.'

Still holding on to the stile by which he had crossed the ditch, he lowered himself into a crouch and stared into the gloom. As he watched without showing himself, the other priest lifted his face to the silvery eastern window of the Minster, and by the moon's glow his features were distinctive. This one was indeed Simeon of Beverley, albeit in a borrowed hood, Simeon the lame priest, owner of the woman Cyrus coveted and could not have. He watched him sign the cross and turn away to move at a steady pace across open ground, running as only a man can run who savours every ounce of strength and vigour in his body.

'Damned trickster,' Cyrus spat through his teeth. 'No cripple ever moved with such grace and power. And when you beckoned, Simeon of St Peter's, no miserable little ditcher's wife ever spurned your advances and sent another woman in her place.'

He turned away then, nursing his jealousy as closely as he nursed his rage, and strode away, cloak billowing at his ankles, towards the shadowed mouth of Figham Lane, and from there to his well-restored house in Out Ings.

The house was in darkness save for the flickering glow of candlelight and firelight that escaped through narrow chinks in the draped windows of his chambers on the first floor. The door slid open as he approached it, for Brother John, his faithful steward and confessor, had watched for his return since dusk. The younger man saw at a glance the shape and colour of his master's mood, and he guessed that the Reverend Lady Constance had set too high a price on one particular Sister of Mercy.

'It did not go well, my lord?' he dared to ask.

'Not well at all. They take me for a fool.'

'A fool, my lord? But who would dare?'

'It is a conspiracy,' Cyrus declared. 'The priest and his whore conspire against me, and that Devil's instrument who keeps the convent reaps a handsome profit from their games.'

He flung himself into a high-backed chair beside the fire and sat with his elbow bent and his chin resting upon his fist, glaring at the flames.

John watched him as he poured out wine, noting the set of his dark profile and the way the firelight danced and glinted in his black eyes. He guessed that his master had been too long unchallenged, too long deprived of manly stimulation. Even the satisfaction of gaining St Martin's had left a sour taste on his tongue, for what prestige was there to be had from a pile of rubble? He was a Canon now, but his status was centred only around the altar in the Minster Church. The revenues that should have been his by right were siphoned off by other churches and other altars. And eight years on, the disputed bishopric of York determined that no funds were made available for the rebuilding of St Martin's. Thus thwarted in his main desires, Cyrus de Figham had become a powerful man without direction: a dangerous thing indeed, for power too long reined in was likely to turn inward upon itself in sheer frustration.

Without looking up from the fire, Cyrus reached out to accept the glass of wine John offered. He was aware that servants had entered the room, bringing with them platters of steaming food that filled the air with the scents of spit-roasted meats and hot, rich sauces. John stooped to place the bread and the honey-pot close to the fire to keep warm, and as he did so Cyrus turned his attention from the flames to look at him. He was a strong, plain-featured man; a native Northumbrian with a thick, muscular body and short legs, he made up in brute strength and bull-like stamina for what he lacked in height.

Brother John had proved himself well in Cyrus's service. He valued his position but did not play upon it to his own advantage beyond what was expected of a respectably ambitious man. He knew his own worth and his master's value, and so he was content to look to Cyrus de Figham's interests before his own. Like any wise man who sought a lifetime's security, he was keenly aware of who must lead and who, ever watchful of the pitfalls, must follow.

'You were right to suspect the priest of St Peter's,' Cyrus said petulantly. 'I saw him with my own eyes, wearing a borrowed hood and running like a stallion newly turned out from its stable. He prospers, John. That lame priest prospers while I flounder in the vacuum created by the empty see of York.'

'Simeon is a poor man,' John said carefully.

'Aye, and content to be so. He has all he desires. He serves the altar of St Peter's. He is the master of his little church, a respected historian and a scribe of some renown.'

'He is but a small fish in a small pond,' John reminded him. 'And as a scribe and a scholar he must work long hours. Surely you would not envy him his daily toil, my lord?'

'It is his self-content I envy.'

'Small fish must learn to be content with little.'

'But he has all he desires,' Cyrus complained. 'Dear God in heaven, how many men achieve that much in a lifetime?'

John made no attempt to answer his master's question. Instead he poured more wine and drew the table closer to the hearth. He had been busy these last two days on his master's behalf, busy and successful, but the gains had not come cheaply and he had learned better than to spill his achievements out like so much worthless chicken feed. Better to wait until the perfect moment to ensure that this offering was well received. He piled several of the more succulent pieces of skewered meat on to a separate platter, dribbled the oily sauce over all and handed the platter to Cyrus. Despite the blackness of his mood, temptation in the aromatic steam reminded him that supper was late and he was extremely hungry.

His thoughts were fixed on his latest visit to St Anne's convent. This time he had sent a barrel of salt and a length of fine silk cloth ahead of him, along with a half-dozen beaver pelts and a lady's girdle decorated with coloured beads and exquisite embroidery. His gifts were gratefully accepted, and when he arrived there for his appointment with the Abbess, he found good wine laid out for him and a bowl of fruit and nuts for his refreshment. The deal was settled when the girl was brought to him. She was to become a part of his private household, and in return the Abbess took his gifts and his promises and willingly put her signature to the deal.

'She was not the ditcher's wife,' he growled, surveying John from under puckered brows. 'Oh yes, she was the one I spoke to on my previous visit, I have no doubt of that, but not the ditcher's wife, not the woman I held right here in my

412

hands two days ago in the marketplace. They tricked me, John. They attempted to fob me off with a substitute, a pretty enough young thing, but not the ditcher's wife, not Simeon's woman.'

'Will you not be content with her, since she is already bought and paid for?' John asked.

Cyrus shrugged. 'If I must. She will certainly do to warm my sheets and calm my frustrations and, as you do well to remind me, John, she is amply paid for, and therefore mine by right.'

'And yet you did not bring her back with you?'

'No, I did not,' Cyrus growled. 'I left the convent in a rage, thanks to that witch, that wrinkled old ...' He shook his head, lost for words to express his indignation. It bruised his pride as well as his temper to be so cleverly taken in by a woman almost twice his age. 'You know, I have a mind to demand the return of my gifts in full and have the girl snatched in secret, when it suits me.'

John smiled at that. 'And who would protest at that? If one of her prettier young Sisters goes missing off the streets, the Abbess would hardly dare accuse the respected Canon of St Martin's of the crime.'

'I suppose she was desirable enough in her own way,' Cyrus recalled, then placed his fingertips to his forehead and closed his eyes with a groan. 'But the other one, the one in the marketplace, now she was a beauty of a different mettle. She had spirit, and eyes like polished ebony, and that mouth of hers, so soft and full ...'

'And she was Father Simeon's whore,' John said, to illustrate how well he understood the situation.

'Aye, Simeon's whore,' Cyrus nodded. 'But perhaps I am mistaken in assuming that he keeps her at the convent. It is possible that the Abbess merely sought to capitalise on my search for a dark-eyed woman amongst her sisters. She cannot know how fixed I am in my intent. Ye Gods, I would willingly surrender the better half of my possessions if I could steal but half of Simeon's smug contentment away from him.'

413

'He must have done you a terrible wrong, my lord Cyrus,' John observed, knowing full well it was not so, that the venom spat by an envious man befouls the innocent before it finds the guilty.

'Do you doubt it?' Cyrus snapped. 'For eight years he has duped us all into thinking his whore and his bastard were drowned trying to reach St Theodore's Rest. He pretends to be a cripple, a scholarly scribe much dedicated to his work and flawless in the pattern of his devotions, and all the time he laughs behind our backs. He mocks us all with his content. While his smug self-satisfaction pricks my peace of mind and sticks in my craw like bile, you can be sure he wrongs me.'

Now John was almost ready to speak his piece. He poured warm honey over a baked fruit pudding and watched his master eat it with his fingers. John had been forced to buy the information now in his possession, and by the act of offering payment he had placed a value on something previously thought to be worthless. The woman who took his coin would hardly count herself content with it while she might as easily sell the same commodity elsewhere. If one man is prepared to buy, another can be persuaded to match his price. The woman knew John as Cyrus de Figham's man, and she would reason that what could be sold to one canon might just as easily be sold again to another. Even now she might be babbling her story into the ear of Wulfric de Morthlund's creeping catamite, who slept like a dog on the steps of his master's house in the hope of intercepting just such an opportunity to ingratiate himself once more.

John smiled. At that moment he was untroubled by the prospect, for Daniel Hawk had fallen from grace and was without privilege of any kind. He would therefore be forced to nurse his information in respectful silence until de Morthlund rose from his bed in the hour before Sext tomorrow, and even then his plea for audience might be rejected. If the fat man had an interest in the ditcher's wife or the priest's son, it would not be exercised until noon at the very earliest. Cyrus, on the other hand, would make it his

414

business to be at the convent at dawn.

John held back for a few more minutes, watching Cyrus clean his fingers meticulously on a dampened napkin. Then he cleared his throat and said:

'You have made no mistake, my lord. The woman you seek is indeed living in seclusion behind the convent walls.'

'What?' Cyrus's quicksilver eyes narrowed to slits.

'The woman is kept there,' John repeated. 'As lately as this very evening, even while you were conducting your business with the Abbess in one part of the convent, the woman Elvira was attending to her motherly duties in another.'

'Right there?' Cyrus asked. 'Right there under my very nose?'

John nodded. 'It seems she was taken there by Simeon and his friends in the wake of the storm eight years ago. She had a gaping sword wound on her forearm and a suckling infant at her breast.'

'An infant?' Cyrus echoed.

'A newly-born. A boy. He too had a sword wound, here ...' John marked the spot on his own neck with his finger. '... And both mother and child were closely nursed for several days until it was known that both would survive their injuries. During that time the lame priest was in attendance, but after that he kept away and the nurse saw little of him, though she always suspected that he came and went by way of a secret passage or a doorway cut directly into Elvira's private section of the convent.'

Cyrus sat upright in his chair, impressed. 'Am I to understand that you have stooped to spying on my behalf, friend John?'

'My lord Cyrus, I consider it my privilege to help you whenever I may.'

'And at your own expense, no doubt?'

John spread his hands. 'Well, my lord ...'

'I will see to it that you are repaid two-fold at least,' Cyrus assured him. As always at such moments he was sharply reminded of a time when he might have lost this man's respect and loyalty for the sake of a decent cloak. He nodded and said again: 'I will see to it.'

'Thank you, my lord.'

'Now tell me, John, where may I find this ditcher's wife, this priest's whore?'

'She is kept at the convent, just as you suspected, but in a safe chamber close to the lakeside wall. She is well protected by the Reverend Mother and her women.'

'But you know of a way to reach her? A secret passageway? A concealed door?'

John shook his head. 'Nobody knows how Simeon comes and goes.'

'Then how in God's name am I to get to her?' Cyrus demanded, throwing up his arms in exasperation. 'I can hardly take it upon myself to storm St Anne's with an army of fighting men. Nor will I resort to scaling high walls and risking life and limb merely to dip my snout in Simeon's private trough.'

Now John allowed himself the luxury of a wide, self-confident smile. 'Such risks are quite unnecessary, my lord.'

'Then how...?'

'She will come to you willingly enough when you demand it of her.'

'What?' Now Cyrus too was smiling. He turned his head to watch John from the corners of his eyes. 'You know of a way to make her come to me?'

'Indeed I do, my lord Cyrus.'

'If that is so then you will be amply rewarded for your efforts, friend John.'

'And you will claim for your personal use that which Simeon values most of all.'

'How is it to be done? What risks will be involved?'

'It will be easy, my lord,' John smiled. He accepted the glass of wine his master offered and watched the malicious glints come and go in those deep black eyes. 'As easy as snatching an eight-year-old boy from his bed.'

Cyrus de Figham flung himself back in his seat, uncaring of the wine that spilled from his glass, threw back his handsome head and roared with laughter. To a determined man an eight-year-old boy was no more tedious a burden than a squealing piglet in a sack brought home from market for the supper-table. He would grab the whelp as bait to lure the woman to him: it was as clear and uncomplicated a plan as that. And he would do it with an easy conscience and a proper show of indignation to still any protests the conniving Abbess Constance might choose to offer. He would simply march into that convent while the Sisters were at their dawn devotions and take what now belonged to him by right.

While Cyrus de Figham and his faithful clerk raised another glass of wine to their joint venture, the prebendary house in Minster Moorgate was buzzing with activity. The informant from St Anne's would soon return there with the Canon's party after describing in detail the place where the boy and his mother were hidden. She would be rewarded in coin and protected from reprisals, for this Canon was set to benefit handsomely from her endeavours, and for his reputation's sake he must be seen to be generous with his thanks.

'I have him,' de Morthlund growled as Daniel helped him hang and pin a crimson, silk-lined cloak around his shoulders. 'I have that devious priest and all those others who have helped him in this outrageous eight-year subterfuge. And what part has Jacob de Wold played in all this, squatting as he does as Beverley's counterfeit Provost in an empty seat? Well, what part? What part has he in it?'

'He must certainly have known of it, my lord.'

'Aye, known of it and had a hand in it. Ye gods, I'd give my teeth to know what princely sum he hung upon his silence all these years.'

'And princely it must have been,' Daniel nodded. 'He wields so much power, albeit with a genial hand, that wherever he leads the rest are sure to follow like mindless sheep.'

'Like mindless sheep they are indeed, my dear Daniel,' he agreed. 'And if I have my way they will follow their leader all the way to the slaughterer's blade.'

Daniel smiled. He was more than satisfied with this turn of

events, for now his fortunes were once again reversed, his position in his master's affections fully restored. By sheer tenacity and diligence he had managed to set his master on a course that would take him all the way to the Provost's seat, scattering powerful men and women like ninepins as he went. Then he would waste no time in bringing the full weight of his imperious personality to bear upon the dignitaries at York, for the Chapter there must see to it that these crimes against the fabric of the church were brought to book. And then the interests of Geoffrey Plantagenet himself must be discreetly served, for despite the bleatings of the Pope, it was only a matter of time before Henry brought his bastard to the Archbishop's throne at York.

Wulfric flung back his cloak and stood with his hands on his hips and his legs apart, assuming a royal pose that drew a long sigh of approval from the younger man. By the time they reached the convent every soul there would be sleeping, lost in those precious hours of uninterrupted sleep before the sacred Office of Matins began at 2 am. And in the flurry that would surely follow his arrest of the adulteress and her whelp, he would insist that Cyrus de Figham be amongst the first to explain his guilty knowledge of their existence. Let him deny it if he dare, for there were two witnesses who would swear to seeing him embrace the woman, Elvira, in full and open view in the marketplace.

'I'll have this business settled to my satisfaction,' he declared as he swept from the room with his cloak in full sail around him. 'And in the process I will crush this upstart Simeon like a common beetle beneath my shoe.'

And so he would, if his secret plans came to fruition. He needed a scapegoat for another matter, and when Simeon stood accused of wrongs that could not be denied, it would be an easy task to have him burdened with a much more heinous crime. The people of this town were fiercely jealous of their saint, their prosperity depending upon the thousands of pilgrims who flocked each season to his shrine in search of cures or miracles or blessings. Without St John the people of Beverley would fall beneath York's shadow, and obscurity and famine would surely follow. They would take swift revenge upon the priest who employed a handful of sanctuary men to plunder the holy shrine and steal the precious relics from their resting place.

CHAPTER THIRTY-FIVE

'Simeon!'
The voice was an urgent whisper in his ear. It yanked him from his sleep with a start. He reached for his short-sword, had his fingers clasped around its hilt even before he was fully conscious. He knew the door was safely barred and all the windows fastened, and yet someone had called his name, of that he had no doubt. He rolled sideways from his mattress, his eyes wide open in the darkness, and dropped lightly, with a cat-like grace, from the higher rafters to the floor. On a ledge close to his ladder a single candle spluttered, its flame reflected in the dish of water in which it stood for safety's sake. Around and above it danced a hundred flickering shadows created wherever the meagre light touched upon the greater darkness, and beyond those shadows a blackness hung like a heavy mantle everywhere.

Simeon crouched, his sword at the ready. The dirt floor was cold beneath his bare feet, the night air chilly on his naked chest and shoulders.

'Who's there' he demanded, seeing nothing.

'*It is I, Brother Simeon.*'

He felt the fine hairs stiffen at the nape of his neck. His scalp grew tight across his skull and goose-flesh invaded the skin along his forearms. That other one, that harbinger of grim events, had come again. Simeon's thoughts flew first to the boy, then to Elvira.

'I am needed,' he exclaimed, coming to his feet.

'*Not yet.*' The voice came from the darkest section of the room. It was deep and familiar and had a soothing, reassuring quality. '*The time is not yet.*'

Simeon stood beneath the timbers where his bed was set and peered into the darkness beyond the candle's glow, seeing nothing but shadows.

'Not yet?' he asked. 'Why then are you here if not to warn me of some danger coming?'

'*There will be danger soon enough.*'

'Why are you here? Why now?'

'*To offer a blessing, Brother.*'

Simeon licked his lips and nodded grimly. 'I fear I will be in need of it before all this is over.'

'*You will, and more.*'

Simeon nodded again. He was not afraid of what might be to come. He only feared that he might fail, and by this failure lose, or leave without protection, those whom he loved the most. He crossed himself from lips to breast and from shoulder to shoulder, then sank to one knee and clasped his hands before him. Head bowed, eyes closed, he whispered a few words of the *Jesus Prayer* and prepared himself to receive the other's blessing.

'*In nomine Patris, et Filii, et Spiritus Sancti.*'

'In the name of the Father, Son and Holy Ghost,' Simeon repeated.

'*Dominus vobiscum.*'

'*Et cum Spirituo.*'

The blessing was short, the words a mere whisper just beyond the clear range of his hearing. He felt what might have been the touch of a hand upon his head, and then his senses told him that the figure, silent and invisible, was already drawing away.

'Wait! When is it to be?' he called out after it.

'*Soon.*'

'St Matthew's Feast? Before? After?'

'*Soon, my Brother. Very soon.*'

The candle spluttered sideways as if a door somewhere had opened to let a chill wind in. It almost died, but righted itself at last to burn as evenly and as bravely as before. From beyond the enclosure walls there came an ominous rumble, the sound of distant thunder. Simeon feared that history was about to repeat itself, and that this was the onset of a second tempest, but when he flung the door open and stepped outside he saw that the sky was clear and glittering with stars as bright as gems. The breeze was warm and dry, heavy with the sweet fragrances of late summer fields and gardens. It brushed his cheek as lightly as a caress, reminding him of the gentle Elvira, whose touch was no more than swan's down on his skin. That very evening she had placed her small palm over his heart and looked so deeply into his eyes that he fancied he might drown in the tender depth of her gaze.

'I will not be parted from you, Simeon,' she had whispered, and he had said, uncaring at that moment of God's will: 'Nor I from you, Elvira.'

Now Simeon closed the door of the scriptorium and dropped the metal bar in place across it. He turned to peer into the heavy shadows at the far end of the room, beyond the well and the ladder leading up to his bed in the roof-space.

'When will it be?' he asked softly. 'In the name of God, help me to be prepared for what is to come. Tell me *when!*'

Even as he asked the question, he knew no answer would come to him from the shadows. The hooded figure had served its mysterious purpose and had vanished into the night.

The great Minster Church of St John of Beverley was in darkness when Wulfric de Morthlund and his party began their journey to St Anne's. A flat boat was waiting at the landing by the Hall Garth bridge, and the man in charge of it muttered an anxious prayer when he saw the mountainous proportions of the man he had been hired to carry. The watercourses were running shallow at this time of year, their currents slow and sluggish. Without assistance, any boatman would be hard-pressed to pole that bulk and all its hangers-on the two miles from the Hall Garth landing to the convent.

From a slender window cut into the stone a man was watching. He was a young man dressed in a travelling cloak and with a broad-sword hanging at his hip. His rugged profile and his thatch of fiery hair stamped him as a stranger to these parts, and his accent proved as much. This foreigner had come down from Berwick-upon-the-Tweed. He was a Scot, or close enough to being a Scot to prompt most decent Englishmen to shy from his company. They were a treacherous bunch, these border men, and best avoided. This one had come to Beverley in the dead of night as a desperate fugitive, and at the high altar, by the episcopal seat of Bishop John, had claimed the ancient privilege of sanctuary. As was the custom, he took the required oath of obedience to the Archbishop and his minions, admitted his misdemeanours, rendered his fee and vowed to be of good and honest behaviour. In return he was given his full entitlement of board, lodging and protection for thirty days and thirty nights, and the Canons were bound to do all they could to reconcile him with his pursuers.

The young man scratched at the coarse red hairs making up the beard concealing the lower half of his face. There were no pursuers galloping at his heels, no angry accusers to be pacified. He was here to join his six companions in a quest for wealth beyond the dreams of ordinary men. They expected to carry away sacred vessels, chalices, urns and vases by the sackful, boxes of coin and altar gifts left at the shrine by hopeful pilgrims. And this man with the fiery hair and beard had a special part to play in these events, for he was to take but a single item from the tomb: the golden casket bearing the precious relics of St John.

He heard a door open and close below him and a voice called out.

'Come down, Fitzburn. We must be about our business.'

'There's time enough, Ulric.'

'Not so. Some of the men will soon be too drunk to know what they're about. Come down, then, and let's get on with what we were hired to do and be gone from here before these pious Canons take us for the thieves we really are.'

This jovial voice came up from the pool of darkness where the stair wound down to the foot of the tower. A tiny altar candle burned down there to mark the spot where an elderly priest was murdered many years before. Some said his killer, a robber of sacred tombs, was hanged by a vengeful mob before he could be brought to justice. Others whispered that a holy priest had done the deed and craftily laid his guilt upon an innocent man.

'Come down, Fitzburn,' the voice called again.

'All right, give me a moment.'

The young man peered through the window slit to see the flat-boat moving off with several men helping the boatman by bending their backs to extra poles. At the front of the boat a torch burned in a metal sconce, at the rear a stool was set for those unable to stand erect throughout the journey. Now Wulfric de Morthlund was perched upon the stool, a huge crimson mound that kept the boat well down in the murky water. To help balance his considerable weight the other passengers all were gathered close to the lighted torch, hindering those who struggled to pole the boat along the shallow watercourse.

Inside the stone tower the man using the name Fitzburn leaned close to the newel stone as he swung himself lightly down to the foot of the winding staircase. He bent his head low as he stepped through the narrow pointed door that opened into the retrochoir behind the high altar. The others were already gathered there, crouched in the flickering half-light by the shrine. The brothers from Chichester had found and plundered the chamber where the altar wine was stored. They had already drunk beyond their fill of it before passing what remained to their companions. One man among them was drinking from a huge chalice of finely worked gold, a cup bearing elaborately carved handles and so heavily encrusted with gems that it could only be lifted in a two-handed grip.

424

A certain Bishop had already put first claim upon that particular item, for St John himself and the martyr Thomas Becket could be counted amongst the great men who were reputed to have drunk from it.

Although once open to the touch of every pilgrim who made an offering, the golden shrine of St John and the precious dagger of King Athelstan were now encased within a cage of fine metal mesh, a precaution taken by the Canons after several of the altar casket's valuable gems were stolen. Fitzburn knew well enough that the remaining jewels, less visible now and supposedly better protected, were nothing more than fakes produced by a clever local craftsman, beautifully reproduced but virtually worthless. The casket itself held little real interest for him, despite the considerable weight of gold and silver reputed to have gone into the construction. His sights were set on far richer spoils than this.

Fitzburn glanced all about him, then signalled for another man to join him in a last inspection of the church's interior. This one was Kagar Jen, an ugly brute of a man who called himself a Lowlander but would not own to any particular country of origin. He was a mercenary of sorts who sold his services wherever and to whomever they might fetch him profit or fresh adventure. He played the part of a deaf-mute to perfection, and no genuine cripple could hope to match the pitiful lameness he could assume at will. He used a stout crutch tucked into his right armpit, leaning on it in such a way that his upper torso seemed horribly deformed. The two men moved around the church together, a staggering, silent cripple and his striking red-haired keeper.

The church was empty save for a few poor stragglers who had managed to hide themselves in the shadows when the last priests came to clear them out. An old man lay in a corner with his legs drawn up and his mouth wide open, struggling for every breath. Another was slumped awkwardly against a wall, and the ugly rigour gripping his limbs was proof that he had been dead for several hours. Some poor wretch issued a prolonged, choking cough while another

425

cried out for mercy and relief. A priest was lying prostrate by the altar of St James, too engrossed in his devotions to even note who it was who passed him by in the darkness.

Fitzburn and Kagar Jen returned to the area of the shrine and signalled to their companions that the time had come to carry out their task. Kagar Jen removed his crutch from the folds of his wide cloak, turned it top-to-toe to reveal its massive iron hammer-head and sturdy shaft. Two blows were all it took to smash the screen and open one side of the tomb. Another two destroyed the tombs of those ancient abbots, Brithun and Winwald, and another broke the seal on the box that held the prayer-beads of John the Evangelist. Then he marched down the short flight of steps to the tiny oak door of the treasure house, and with a few blows had the thing unbarred.

Fitzburn used the blade of his dagger to prise the joints of the mesh apart at the spot where other hands had previously gained entry. He reached within, only to cry out in disbelief as his fingers closed around not the genuine, solid casket of St John but a cleverly painted shell, a fragile thing of little substance that collapsed and splintered in his hands to reveal the empty, worthless space inside.

'*Dear God in His high Heaven!*'

The sudden commotion around the High Altar brought the lone priest hurrying from the lesser altar of St James. He came running with his skirts hitched up and his mouth agape, and when he saw that the shrine was violated he flung up his hands and let out a cry of horror. The sound stopped short at the cold steel blade that sliced into his throat. A man in a leather skullcap stood before him. He saw a leering grin, heard a drunken stream of profanities and felt a jab of pressure on his windpipe and a sticky warmth spill over his clothes. He was still alive, though barely so, when he heard the cry go up: '*The tomb is empty!*'

Kagar Jen lumbered back to join his companions at the tomb. He was wielding his monstrous hammer like a weapon and his face was a mask of thunderous rage.

'No treasure house there,' he growled in his deep, thickly

accented voice. 'Down there is nothing. Beyond the door nothing but rubble and waste like a big black mountain. No treasure. Nothing.'

'And nothing here,' the most drunken of the Chichester Brothers drawled, kicking out at the damaged altar. He cleared his throat with an ugly sound and spat out the result. 'Not a thing of any value. No gold or silver, no relics, no jewels. And where is the dagger, the priceless jewelled dagger of King Athelstan? They have tricked us, robbed us of our prize. God damn these priests and their deceit.'

While the others rampaged through the church in search of sacred treasures, Fitzburn held back, sword at the ready, prepared to defend his own prize if he must. By now the Bishop's chalice was concealed in a sack and fixed to the girdle beneath his cloak. He would not go empty-handed from this place. A priest lay dead, the shrine and altar were defiled, the holy wine dispersed amongst the desecrators. The scales were burdened against them. A priest had died and seven sanctuary men would hang for it. The holy relics were gone, and who but the same unholy seven should answer for the theft?

'We were as good as hanged before the first blow was struck.' He ground the words between his teeth, seeing this intrigue now for what it was. 'And while we swing for this empty tomb, who claims the spoils at our expense? Who claims the spoils?'

'The Devil who brought us here.' His answer was voiced by Kagar Jen, who rested his hammer now against his shoulder and stood with his legs apart and his features grim. He was a simmering, smouldering volcano ready to erupt. 'We go.'

Fitzburn stared back at him, then nodded sharply and confirmed the words: 'We go.'

As they turned to leave, Fitzburn stumbled heavily into a small shape that must have been hovering silently at his heels. He staggered and grabbed out with both hands to steady himself, and found himself holding a frail-looking little boy in a pale grey hood, a boy whose eyes were so large and blue that in the light from the altar candle they were almost luminous.

'Ye gods, lad, I all but crushed you underfoot.'

He set the boy firmly on his feet and released him, and in an instant he was gone, darting away like a startled animal to vanish into the shadows beyond the shrine. In the brief skirmish between colliding with the boy and regaining his balance, Fitzburn had not been aware of the light touch of fingers beneath his clothes or the slash of a sharp blade at his girdle. Only now did he find the weight and bulk of the Bishop's chalice conspicuous by its absence.

'The cup!' he roared. 'That thieving son of a sow has cut my sack and lifted the Bishop's cup!'

He made as if to give chase but the big Lowlander held him back by grabbing his shoulder in a vice-like grip.

'No time,' he growled. 'We go now.'

'But that chalice is priceless . . .'

'Then we take more to compensate. Come, we go now to make good this night's treachery.'

Fitzburn reluctantly agreed, knowing the young thief might even now be well beyond his reach. Church rats knew every hole and niche that would hide them from their pursuers. He had as much hope of reclaiming the chalice as he had of finding one scuttling rat among a thousand others.

'Damn!' He spat the oath as he strode away. 'His face was pretty as a painted angel's and his hands as expert as a hardened thief's. By the gods, I swear I'll clip that rodent's nostrils to the bone if he ever crosses my path again.'

They left by the small exit in the western wall beyond the greater transept, and before the door swung closed behind them another man had joined them.

'Let the others stay for the hanging if they will,' Ulric growled. 'I reckon we three have a score to settle elsewhere.'

Fitzburn and his two companions hurried across the churchyard to St Martin's and quickly concealed themselves amongst the ruined stones and ragged arches. Moments later they emerged on the far side as three innocent men about their private business, walking upright together at a steady and purposeful pace. They reached the large prebendary house in Minster Moorgate, where the Canon of St Andrew's lived in princely fashion, playing the so-called notables of Beverley and York like so many painted pieces on a chessboard. The door was opened by the elderly steward, who would have turned the late-callers away, had he been given half a chance to do so. Instead, the huge iron head of Kagar's hammer touched him almost lovingly in the centre of his forehead, and he sank to the floor with a sigh, his skull crushed.

Other members of Wulfric de Morthlund's household rushed to see what had gone amiss in their master's absence. One glance at the intruders and the murdered steward sent them rushing out through the rear door to the safety of the yard. Only one of their number, a young man with a clear view of the world in which he lived, had the presence of mind to grab what he could that was of value as he fled the house.

The sanctuary men ransacked every room in turn. They took what they could carry away and demolished what remained. They broke open elaborately decorated chests to slash the rich garments stored there, destroyed fine cupboards simply to lay waste the personal riches kept inside. The sanctuary men stuffed their pockets and pouches, even packed their hoods and the loose tops of their boots with valuables. And while they pillaged whatever came to hand, the giant Lowlander strode from room to room with his great hammer, reducing to ruin the splendid things he found there. As the three prepared to leave the house, their clothes bulging and their backs stooped by the sheer weight of plunder they carried, the lower edge of Kagar's cloak snagged against the corner of a chest. He yanked it free, dislodging the chest and the candlestick upon it. Two lighted candles fell to the floor and spluttered out. A third rolled free and came to rest near the curtained alcove where a small bench was set. In the draught of night air from the open door its flame flared up, died down and flared again, a small tongue searching for something dry, like dusty tapestries and door hangings, to feed upon.

In the Minster church the four remaining sanctuary men vented their fury upon the holy screen and sacred altars, tombs, windows, anything that sheer brute force could damage or destroy. They were met by priests, most of whom had rushed from their beds or their night-prayers unarmed, and once again the blood of innocent men was shed on consecrated ground. And when the sanctuary men had done their worst they lurched drunkenly away to nearby Minster Moorgate, intent on settling their private scores with Wulfric de Morthlund. They left the church doors wide open in their wake, and soon the human creatures of the night were slinking inside in ever increasing numbers. They came at first like cautious shadows, wary and fearful, and what they saw dismayed them. The highest authority in their lives had been reduced to rubble before the rage of ordinary men, and those whose duty it was to maintain God's Holy Order had fallen before the sword and bled as freely as worthless beggars. The Devil waits patiently at every shoulder, and when the yoke slackens or falls away he takes his chance: within minutes of stepping across that hallowed threshold, those God-fearing men and women of Beverley were rampaging through their Minster church in an orgy of wanton destruction.

It was the darkest, deepest hour of the night and Simeon was crouched on the stone floor of the scriptorium with his back against the wall and his chin lolling on his chest. He was wearing boots now and his hooded cloak hung loosely around his shoulders. His dreams were filled with startling images. A phantom steed more than twice the size of any living beast reared up, snorting and white-eyed, out of a broiling, copper-coloured sky. It bore a hooded rider on its back, and in the rider's arm was clutched a bundle, and in that bundle lay the destiny of Simeon, lame scribe of Beverley.

'How soon?' he muttered, twitching in his sleep. 'Help me.

430

Tell me how soon.' And then, as if the new thought had just been brought to him in the dream, he called out softly: 'And how? How will it come to us this time? How?'

And suddenly Simeon was wide awake, his eyes smarting and his throat and nostrils scorched. He sprang to his feet, hearing the warning bells and the distant cries of panic, and he knew he had the answer to his question: *Fire!*

CHAPTER THIRTY-SIX

Daniel Hawk turned his head sharply, straining to identify certain sounds beyond the grunts of labouring men and the lapping of water around the flat-boat. His nostrils flared at the scent of woodsmoke on the still night air. All along the watercourse were clusters of makeshift shelters where thieves and beggars banded together to share a miserable existence. Their flickering campfires were strung out along the bank, each with a company of dark, anonymous shapes huddled around it. Few men would dare to pass this way at night without an escort, even if a boatman could be found who was brave enough, or foolish enough, to carry such a vulnerable cargo. That very month a boat had vanished while making the return trip from the convent landing. It was supposed that this outward journey had been marked by thieves who lay in hiding and, seeing him later return alone, determined to unburden him of his fee. Nor was the boatman spared, for only a wealthy man can toss his purse to a robber and hope to buy his safety with the contents.

Despite the weight of his cloak and the almost oppressive warmth of the night, Daniel felt a cold shiver run down his spine. These waterways could be dangerous, even life-threatening places. Wulfric de Morthlund snapped his fingers in the air and the sound pulled Daniel from his thoughts with a start. He stepped to the rear of the boat where the stool was set.

'What ails you, Little Hawk?'

'This place. It makes my flesh creep.'

De Morthlund smiled up at his grim profile. 'Have courage, dear heart. We will soon be there.'

'Courage?' Daniel echoed with a sharp glance at his master. 'It is not want of courage that unsettles me.'

'Patience then, dear heart,' Wulfric soothed. 'Have a little more patience.'

'I do not like this. We should have gone by road.' Daniel sniffed the air. 'Do you smell something burning?'

'Of course I smell something burning. This is September.'

'Listen! Do you hear it? A bell is ringing the alarm.'

De Morthlund shifted his great weight on the stool. 'Some farmer's field alight, perhaps. The land everywhere is as dry as tinder.'

'Not a field-fire. There is woodsmoke on the air, and closer to home, I think.'

Wulfric grinned and shrugged his bulky shoulders. 'As you see, despite the laws concerning *couvre-feu*, or curfew, as these illiterates call it, there must be a hundred campfires burning in the town tonight.'

'Thatch!' Daniel declared. 'A smell of burning thatch. Do you not recognise it?'

'Daniel, Daniel, do not distress yourself over a dropped torch or a scorched thatch in some filthy hovel,' de Morthlund admonished patiently. 'These peasants are always burning their pathetic shelters to the ground. Such matters can be of little consequence to us.'

'Unless it takes hold,' Daniel muttered under his breath, and he fancied he could detect the merest whisper of a breeze across his cheek. 'Unless it spreads.'

The landing was in darkness when the boat arrived. A metal brazier half the height of a man stood on a tripod near the door, its coals cooled to black save for the bright glow at the fire's heart. Here and there the crimson flared to gold and tiny sparks flew up, stirred to fresh life by a breeze that only moments ago had been barely discernible.

It required the combined efforts of four strong men to hoist the Canon of St Andrew's from the lurching flat-boat to the smooth steps of the landing. The boat sat low in shallow water, creating a wide discrepancy between its deck and the landing stones. Each man climbed up with difficulty, turned and helped someone else ashore, and those who crouched to hoist the Canon up were hard-pressed to complete their precarious task.

When settled on dry land, Wulfric de Morthlund called: 'Boatman, you will wait here until I have settled my business with the Abbess. And you there! Use your stick to rouse the doorman. Would you have me standing here all night?'

There was a flurry of activity as the sound of urgent banging echoed in the stillness. Presently the doorman came running with his drawers half on and his cap askew. He came down breathless and red-faced, while the woman paid to share his bed sent a shower of coarse complaints down after him. He opened the trap in the door and thrust his face inside, recognised de Morthlund's bulk and hastened to unfasten the bolts.

'My lord, you are not expected,' he blustered. 'We are not prepared, but if you will be so kind as to wait inside, I will rouse my lady Abbess and . . .'

He ducked away nervously, fearing a blow as de Morthlund's hand made a gesture of dismissal.

'You will do nothing of the sort and no, I do not care to wait *anywhere* on some woman's pleasure, whether that woman be Lady Abbess or Queen of all England. Take me to the walled garden behind your mistress's private rooms, the garden where the woman and the boy are kept.'

'My lord?'

'Don't play the imbecile with me,' de Morthlund growled.

'But my lord, I swear . . .'

The fat man grasped him by the ear and twisted sharply. 'The garden,' he growled, and began to propel the unfortunate man in ungainly fashion along the sheltered walkway that skirted the main inner courtyard.

They passed the school rooms and the dormitories, where the daughters of lords, knights and gentlemen lived as boarders during the course of their education. Several young laywomen, some Sisters of Mercy among them, had been startled from their beds or from their prayers by the clamour at the main door. They peered through shutters or partly opened doors as the visitors swept forcefully through the courtyard. The party made an impressive sight, de Morthlund marching on ahead with his great cloak billowing and the doorman, wriggling like a captured eel, teetering by his ear from one outstretched hand. And behind the huge priest strode seven men, among them the handsome Daniel Hawk resplendent in a fine new cloak.

Among these watchers was Alice, Elvira's dearest friend. Her heart was racing and her eyes were as round and as bright as nut-brown beads. While the others stood agape, she pulled a plain dark shawl about her shoulders and lifted one section of it to cover her head. Then, moving like a quick shadow, she slipped out by one door and in again by another, scrambled up an unlit stair and ran on bare feet along the timber floor beneath the roof supports. A second staircase took her down to where the Abbess now had her private rooms and there, disregarding one of the stricter rules of the convent, she pulled frantically and unceasingly at the cord that rang the inner bell.

After a while the door was flung open by a red-faced Sister Margaret, the senior auditor. She was wearing a gown of crumpled white linen, a shapeless thing that covered her from chin to wrist to ankle. On her head was a close-fitting sleeping cap, also of linen, that covered her ears and forced her face into a tight, unflattering oval. She was far from pleased by the interruption.

'What is it, girl?' the woman demanded. 'I trust, for your sake, that you have good cause to disturb your superiors before the hour of Matins?'

'The Abbess ... please, I must speak to the Mother Abbess at once,' she gasped, still breathless after her dash from the dormitories.

'Calm yourself, and do try to keep your voice lowered,' the auditor snapped. 'The Abbess is sleeping soundly and must not be disturbed. Come back at the Matins hour.'

Just then a small, slight, white-clad figure appeared at Sister Margaret's elbow, her face a pink mask in her linen skull-cap. Her presence prompted the anxious girl to release a rapid tumble of words.

'Another Canon has come in search of Elvira,' she blurted. 'This time it is Wulfric de Morthlund, the Canon of St Andrew's, and he comes with seven others to aid his cause.'

'Why was I not informed of this? Why have I not been sent for?'

'He would not allow it, Mother Abbess. He would not be detained at the gatehouse and even refused to send a messenger on ahead. He has the doorman by the ear and is marching to Elvira's lodgings at this very moment.'

'What? Surely he would not dare to play the master here, within my very walls!' The little Abbess had paled with indignation.

'He dares,' Alice said.

For a woman of her advancing years the Abbess then moved with surprising swiftness. Within minutes she had slipped a grey robe over her white cotton shift and pulled a woollen over-robe across her shoulders. She stepped on the lid of a chest to reach the shelf set high upon the wall behind it, and from the layers of dust there she removed a key. She stared at it for a moment and was about to drop it into the pocket at her girdle when a second thought came to override the first. Only Simeon knew this key existed. If this pompous canon was so bent on gaining access to Elvira's secret place, let him break down the door, if he had the courage, and take to himself the consequences.

'Sister Margaret, go find the gardener's boy,' she ordered, setting the big key back upon its shelf. 'Have him take the best horse and ride at speed to St Peter's with news of this intrusion . . . and be sure he does not mention Elvira or the boy by name. Tell him to speak to no one but Father Simeon or his chief infirmarian, Osric. Go quickly, this matter is of the utmost urgency. Alice, you will come with me.'

Ignoring the stouter boots she favoured now that her blood ran thinner in her old veins, Lady Constance slid her feet into a pair of open sandals and hurried out with Alice running obediently at her heels. Long before they reached the smaller courtyard leading off the cloisters, they heard the thunderous pounding at the porch door and the bellowing voice of Wulfric de Morthlund demanding entry. The door would hold, even against his mighty forearm. Elvira's chamber was once the convent's treasure house, so its access door was cut from a narrow piece of solid oak, well fortified with metal, and its lock was stout enough to withstand any onslaught. When they reached the porch leading to the garden door they found it crowded with men, each jostling with his neighbour in the confined space, all bent on passing through that oaken door.

The Lady Constance, Abbess of St Anne's, slowed her steps at the open end of the porch, slid her hands into the wide folds of her sleeves and gathered her anger into manageable proportions.

'*My lord Canon!*' She offered him the full title of his assumed office. Her voice was high and cracked with age, but there was a certain authority in it that would not be ignored. The banging stopped and men stood back respectfully. In the hush that followed her small but piercing voice demanded: 'By what right, sir, do you intrude upon the peace and privacy of St Anne's?'

Wulfric de Morthlund came slowly to the entrance of the porch, his shoulders stooped in the confined space. He glowered at the little Abbess and, framed by the narrow, pointed opening to the porch, he seemed enormous. He pushed two men aside and stepped forward with his hands on his hips until he loomed like a giant over the tiny woman who challenged his presence there. If it surprised or angered him that she was not intimidated by his size and bearing, he gave no indication of the fact.

'I believe you are harbouring a fugitive on your premises, madam.'

'I most certainly am not.' Her answer was swift and emphatic.

'I say it is so,' he insisted.

'And I say it is *not* so,' she countered.

'Do you call me a liar, lady?'

'I do not. I simply advise you, my lord de Morthlund, that you are misinformed.'

'Misinformed?'

'Indeed, as was my lord de Figham when he was here.'

'What? Has Cyrus de Figham already been here?'

'He has, my lord. He came to see this very young woman, Alice. He sought to employ her in his own home, though he was bent on calling her by another name. He seemed convinced that she was other than who she claims to be.' She eyed him pointedly and added: 'He too was obliged to leave here empty-handed.'

Wulfric snapped his fingers and Daniel stepped forward to whisper in his ear. In the brief exchange the fat man's gaze moved from the Abbess to Alice and back again.

'Cecily,' he said at last. 'Where is the black-haired woman known as Sister Cecily?'

'Sister Cecily?' the Abbess echoed, feigning ignorance of the name.

'Yes, madam, the same Sister Cecily you have wilfully harboured here, in scandalous defiance of your church superiors, for the last *eight years*.'

'My lord, I say again, you are mistaken.'

He smiled at that. His hand came out, pink and fat, palm uppermost. 'Then the matter must be settled here and now, to the full satisfaction of these many witnesses who seek only to protect the interests of the church. I will have the key to the garden door, Lady Constance, if you will be so kind.'

Her steady gaze did not falter. It would take far more than a show of brute strength and a shower of petty threats to frighten her. Men judged her weak and of little consequence, a mere woman, pious and heavily burdened by her years. They judged her on their own terms and rarely saw, until too late, the ingenious strength beneath the frail exterior. In her lifetime this lady had manipulated men of every rank and calibre, from brutish soldier to ambitious Abbot, from bullying knight to pompous Archbishop. She was not about to see herself defeated by a small-minded canon with the girth of a calving cow and the sexual tastes of a sewer rat. Her smile became benign, almost apologetic.

'Alas, my lord, no key remains to fit that particular lock. The garden has not been used for longer than a decade. By now it must have fallen into a state of disrepair. It was small and unproductive, with a poisoned well and a terrible stink from the lake beyond the wall. There is no key. We have no need of one.'

'The garden has a living-place,' de Morthlund said.

'Hardly that, my lord. It is barely more than a gardener's shelter, and since we no longer employ a gardener for that old place . . .' She spread her hands and smiled again.

'You describe the perfect place in which to conceal a fugitive,' de Morthlund told her.

'I assure you, sir, there are no fugitives here.'

'Then let me see as much with my own eyes. The key, madam.'

'I have no key.'

'Then I will have my men break down the door.'

'So be it, but have a care, my lord. The Chapter of York shall have a full report of this night's events.'

'Indeed they will, my lady. I will personally see to it.'

'And how will you justify this ill-mannered intrusion, my lord, when the garden is found to be empty?'

De Morthlund glowered. 'Then let me suggest we make a compromise,' he said. 'Send for your ironsmith. Have him open this door so that it may be proved, *to the satisfaction of the council at York*, that you harbour neither fugitive whore nor priest's bastard on your premises.'

The Abbess knew he had her. To deny so reasonable a request was to give these gathered witnesses good reason to speak and speculate against her. She had done her best for Elvira and the boy. For eight long years she had kept them safe, albeit at a handsome profit for her beloved convent. She

439

had kept back the key and she had sent urgent word to Simeon at St Peter's. None could ask more of her than that. She would not hang her reputation upon the uncertain hook of Simeon's cause, not now, while she stared this beast of a man in the face and saw that he recognised her story for the lie it was. She glanced around at all the men and women who had crept close enough to see and hear everything that was taking place. She must not lose face or credibility before these people. Better to give Elvira up than to have this monster break down the door and brand their Abbess a deceitful profiteer. She pointed to a kitchen-man with swollen, red-rimmed eyes, and even as she spoke, her mind was moulding these new events to her own advantage.

'You there!' she said sharply. 'Go quickly to William the ironsmith and bring him to me here.' And to Wulfric de Morthlund she said, loudly enough for everyone to hear: 'Be kind enough to rest here in the porch until the ironsmith comes, my lord. And I will wait beside you if I may. If there are fugitives hidden in my convent then I will know of it, and I will know which members of my house have betrayed my trust and authority to keep them here.'

With a bellow of laughter de Morthlund bent his head in a mocking bow and indicated the two stone benches set along the walls of the porch. He waited until the Abbess was seated, then lowered his great bulk on to the bench opposite hers. With his fists placed on his hips he settled down to await the ironsmith, and while he did so he watched the calm, still face of the Reverend Mother. He did not trust her story for a moment, for it seemed to him that her integrity, like her tongue, was too slippery by half. It would be interesting to see how loudly she proclaimed her innocence when the priest's whore and his son were found hiding behind her very skirts. She would be ready enough to strike a bargain then for the preservation of her position.

Behind de Morthlund's shoulder there was a deep niche cut into the thickness of the wall, holding a small marble figure of the Blessed Virgin. The hole at the Virgin's back was covered by a piece of stiff leather pinned to the side wall of the room beyond, and through that secret aperture Elvira learned that she had been betrayed.

'Mother, we must go now, before the ironsmith comes and we are discovered.'

Peter was standing near the door, his precious Bible and Psalter wrapped and knotted into an altar cloth. Already the room had been stripped of their few possessions, the bed tipped on its end as if no longer in use, the firestone turned so that no tell-tale scorch-marks betrayed the presence of recent fires. Twigs and leaves and withered flowers, long-dead weeds and fine topsoil were strewn so haphazardly across the floor that the wind might have blown such garden debris in through the open doorway. To any eye, even the most critical, it was obvious that the gardener's shelter had stood abandoned for many years.

'Come, Mother,' the boy whispered again, and slipped his small hand into hers to give her courage.

With her free hand Elvira smoothed her foster-son's hair as she smiled down into his solemn, upturned face. Eight years ago, when he was a helpless new-born, his life and safety had been placed in her care. Now they had come full circle with their roles reversed. Now she must have the same unquestioning trust in him.

'I am ready, Peter,' she said at last and, hand in hand, they walked together into the darkened garden.

The ironsmith came at last with his cloak askew and his woollen hose unlaced. His apprentice, half-dressed and shoeless, scuttled behind in a clumsy crouch, stooped by the weight of a huge leather bag filled with the assorted irons of his master's trade.

Rush lights were brought to illuminate the porch and blazing torches were set in iron sconces around the court-yard. Many of the curious onlookers had crept back to their beds to snatch a last hour of rest before the night-time offices began at midnight. As many more were still crowded around that corner of the courtyard where the porch was set, eager to see the outcome of the intrusion. Inside the porch the ironsmith worked on his knees before the door, with his skinny apprentice crouched, shivering, beside him.

Daniel Hawk had stayed close to his master for a long time while the ironsmith toiled to free the lock, but the smell of fat from the rush lights soon became oppressive in that confined space. After a while he chose to pace the cloisters instead, striding the half-sheltered walkway on restless feet. The scent of woodsmoke was heavy on the air. It troubled him. These over-crowded towns, with their lean-to timber hovels, were potential death-traps. There was an official *couvre-feu*, or cover-fire, from 9 o'clock at this time of the year, and by now every iron at every hearth should have been in place to seal off the flames and cool the coals. Campfires, candles and cooking fires alike should be properly extinguished, so that decent men and women might go to their beds at a Christian hour and plotters and schemers find cold comfort in their gatherings. A lord might rest easy once the fires were out and the populace safely off the streets for the night, but in certain areas the law was impossible to enforce. The more unsavoury elements of the population no longer even troubled to offer bribes to the curfew stewards. They simply laughed at the town laws, kept their fires alight at will and challenged any man to tell them otherwise.

A whisper went up that the door was breached. Daniel grasped a lighted torch from its sconce, pushed his way through the gathered crowd and went ahead to light his master's way. They quickly discovered that the area beyond the door was deserted. The only entrance to the hut stood open upon an empty, cold interior. There was no priest's whore here, no sign of the woman or her child.

'Bring more torches,' de Morthlund ordered. 'Search every inch of this place. Search the roof-space and the garde-robe, if there is one.'

'My lord, the place is deserted.'

'Then look elsewhere,' de Morthlund spat. 'But find her. By the gods, I will not leave here empty-handed.' He turned to the Abbess where she stood with her hands in her sleeves and a small smile on her face. 'You have not defeated me yet, madam. You are keeping the woman here and I will find her.'

The Abbess bowed her head and smiled serenely, then grasped Sister Alice by the arm and glided silently away.

'Madam, it is a miracle,' Alice whispered. 'Elvira is delivered from her enemies by the hand of God.'

'Hush, child, her name must not be spoken here,' the Abbess hissed under her breath. She heard one of the searchers confirm that the barred metal cover of the old well was still in place and firmly locked from the outside. She smiled afresh at that, for when the door was first thrown open she had glimpsed a small, pale hand slipping through the bars to refasten the bolt from the outside. It was not the hand of God that delivered Elvira from her enemies; it was the hand of a small boy who bore a striking resemblance to the priest who claimed to be no more than his guardian.

'Have you searched everywhere?' Wulfric de Morthlund demanded. 'The roof timbers? The corner holes? The bushes?'

'We have, my lord, and found nothing.'

'Is there no secret door, no hidden passage?'

'Alas, no, my lord.'

De Morthlund turned a furious glare upon Daniel, and then he hissed, with venom in his voice: 'You told me she was here.'

'And so she must be,' Daniel insisted.

'Then find her, Daniel Hawk, or so help me God you'll bear the consequences of this indignity. *Find her!*'

He stormed from the garden to watch the search from the courtyard, seated upon a stone bench beneath the criss-crossed timbers of the half-roof. He could see the sky in places where the thatch was in need of repair, and all around him he could see the other buildings with their darkened windows. There was a white-clad figure at the window of an upper room, a small, frail shape with the glow of flickering candlelight behind it.

'Damn you,' he growled, convinced that the Abbess was enjoying every moment of this futile search. She had dared to trick him, to play him for a simpleton, and while she kept him dangling upon the fumblings of an incompetent ironsmith, Elvira and her son had been spirited from the premises. That two-faced old woman had played him false and he, Wulfric de Morthlund, had allowed himself to become the laughing-stock of this hen-house.

He was still seated thus when the messengers came to inform him that his house was looted by sanctuary men, his servants murdered or fled with their pockets filled, his treasures pilfered.

He rose to his feet, his face reddening and his eyes bulging. The messengers, startled, took several rapid paces in reverse.

'There's worse, my lord,' one dared to blurt from a safer distance.

'Worse? *Worse?*' de Morthlund bellowed.

'It burns, my lord.'

'*What?*'

'My lord . . . it burns.'

'My house?' *My house?*' The fat man struck his own chest with his fist and roared again: '*My house?*'

'Torched, my lord. Put to the torch by the sanctuary men. And the fire is spreading. Already it runs along Moorgate gathering everything in its path. A stiff breeze is carrying blazing thatch hither and thither in every direction. The lean-to dwellings in Hyegate and the carrier's yard are well ablaze. It is everywhere, my lord. The fire is everywhere.'

'No, I will not suffer this,' de Morthlund blustered. 'I will not . . .'

It was Daniel Hawk, rushing back across the courtyard with a lighted torch held high above his head, who dared give voice to the awful truth. The unthinkable was happening. Beverley was alight. The town was burning.

'I knew it,' he declared. 'My instincts warned me of it. Dear God, oh Dear God in Heaven . . . *the town is on fire!*'

A roar like that of an enraged beast suddenly filled the courtyard. Wulfric De Morthlund stood with his fists clenched and his head thrown back, and the sound that issued from his open mouth struck fear into the hearts of those who heard it. It was a wild and murderous roar that set his rolls of fat to quivering, and when it came to an end he stood wild-eyed and purple-faced, and once again the men stood back from him. When at last he made a move it was to snatch the torch from Daniel's hand and wave it above his head with another roar, aiming his rage at the upper window where the Lady Abbess still stood.

'Keeper of whores!' he screamed at the top of his voice. 'Devil's hand-maiden! Deceiver! My house ... my property is lost! While you have kept me here by your trickery...'

'My lord ...'

'Keeper of whores,' de Morthlund shrieked again.

Then he laughed as if insane and swung the lighted torch in a wide arc that sent men and hot sparks flying away in all directions. When the torch left his hand it soared like a comet into the air then fell, bouncing and rolling and shedding hungry flames, over the dry thatch of the cloister roof.

'If Beverley is to burn,' he screamed, 'this cursed Abbess shall have her share of it.'

CHAPTER THIRTY-SEVEN

The fire rampaged like a mad beast through the town, devouring and destroying as it went. No sooner was a thatch consumed than the breeze caught up its blazing remnants and tossed them into the air. Like fiery predators these parcels of flame swooped down in search of easy pickings amongst the drier roofs. They took hold wherever they settled, and one by one the roofs of Beverley fell like so much corn before a plague of deadly locusts.

There was a carter's yard in Dedde Lane beyond the market cross and the small enclosure of St Mary's church. It was little more than a huddle of lean-to buildings hunched around a cobbled area where carts and barrels and building materials were stored. Every item of the carter's trade was there, and all of it combustible. His horse was tethered to a centre post, its cart piled high with bales of rushes intended for the floors of the Provost's Hall. The animal stamped and snorted in its traces, tossing its head as its flaring nostrils picked up the scent of fire on the breeze.

Beyond the carter's fence a dozen fires raged. Men and women used poles with hooks lashed to one end to drag the burning thatch away in the hope of saving their homes. They worked with more desperation than expertise. In many cases their efforts merely served to bring the roofs crashing down into the houses, and then the contents became fresh fodder for the hungry flames. Others worked with such haste and lack of care that they were guilty of depositing bundles of fire willy-nilly in the streets. And in the general panic that scourge of all misfortune, the looter, slipped unhindered in and out of open doorways, snatching what he could.

In the carter's yard the big horse whinnied and side-stepped on the cobbles, pawed the air with its forelegs and whinnied again. The urgent ringing of warning bells competed with a growing clamour of voices as more fires took hold, and the nervous horse detected the scent of hysteria on the air. Above the fence the sky was very dark, with an orange glow hanging low over the town. A spray of sparks went up ahead of the breeze, and with them flew loose bits of straw and burning cloth. Some part of this debris dropped into the yard, where much of it cooled on the smooth stone cobbles and only the smallest particles drifted by chance into the loaded cart. There it smouldered, unseen and unsuspected, until a little tongue of flame began to lick out at the dry rushes in which it had become embedded.

The street outside the carter's yard was packed with people when the first blows from the horse's hooves struck at the inside of the gates, straining them outwards against their wooden bars. Then the bars splintered and the gates burst open, and the terrified beast launched itself into the street, dragging the now blazing cart behind it. Men, women and children scattered before this new danger, screaming in panic as the beast bore down on them with its fiery cargo scattering bundles of blazing rushes everywhere. Snorting and rolling its eyes, the horse charged through the market area in a blind panic, attempting to out-run the crackling, spitting fire that raced at its heels. Seeing that half the town might be set alight by the burning rushes, several brave men jumped into the horse's path, waving their arms or their hoods in its face. To avoid the yelling men in its path, the horse veered to left and right, driven by yells and flapping garments, down first one alleyway and then another, until it reached the crowded Butcher Row. From there it was dragged along the frontage of a row of timber-built shops, shedding a large part of its load in the process.

At the far end of Butcher Row, where the street forked off in two directions around the Fishmarket, one of the curfew bailiffs had his house. He had gathered his family and his valuables together when he heard the clamour of the fire bells. He would not risk his life and theirs to defend four timber walls and a roof from either fire or looters. Instead he made ready to make a dash for the little port at the head of the beck, and from there to safety until the fires were out. When he opened the door of his house he saw the frenzied horse and its blazing cart careering along Butcher Row, leaving a trail of havoc in its wake. The horrified bailiff judged the situation at a glance. There was no time to usher a pregnant wife and five young children away before the danger was upon them, and nothing would turn that demented beast when it reached the fork at the end of the narrow street. It would meet the sudden obstruction of the bailiff's house and rear up in mindless panic, dumping its deadly cargo everywhere. The bailiff acted instinctively in defence of his helpless family. He drew his sword and rushed to meet the horse head-on. He leaped sideways at the last instant, lashed out as it pounded by him, cutting its front legs from under it. The labouring beast went down with a scream of agony, dragging the cart over and on to its side a safe distance from the house. The traces snapped and the main section of the cart turned over several times, sliding and bounding across the junction, scattering its fiery load. The bailiff threw up his arms and screamed, knowing he was doomed. An instant later he was engulfed in a shower of flames. He rose up from the midst of it, screeching and beating vainly at the flames devouring his clothes and flesh. Blinded and choked and mad with pain, he moved once again by purest instinct, stumbling for home. His family were huddled together in the farthest corner of the room when the door of the house burst open and the ball of fire that was their lord and master staggered inside.

The big stone and timber house now known as Antony's hospital stood in Keldgate close to the ruin of St Martin's church. Long Lane and the landing at Hall Garth were on its right, with the Provost's Hall in its splendid grounds beyond the moat and its massive timber drawbridge. St John's passage and the lower end of Moorgate were on its left, with a portion of Hyegate visible from its upper windows. It faced the Minster, now that the parish church was reduced to rubble. Once the prebendary house attached to St Martin's, it stood unwanted now that Cyrus de Figham was Canon there, for he had his greater house in moated grounds at Figham, and nothing would induce him to give it up. His generous and timely gift of the Keldgate house to Antony for the benefit of the town's poor people had helped earn him a canon's seat at Beverley. De Figham had been a hero then. The great tempest had changed his fortunes and altered his reputation for the better, and he had been swift to capitalise on his new status. Only that empty Archbishop's seat at York had thwarted his ambitions, for it prevented the rebuilding of the parish church and robbed St Martin's Canon of its revenues.

Now Antony was preparing to evacuate his house and move every person in it to a place of safety. De Morthlund's house in Moorgate was still ablaze, with tongues of flame licking the air and showers of sparks lifting this way and that on the breeze. Already the fierce flames had spread along Hyegate, quickly becoming a raging inferno that devoured every scrap of wood and thatch in its path like a ravenous beast. The night was filled with screams of pain and fear, with the howls of dying animals and the cries of helpless people cornered by the flames. The fire, too, had its voices. It crackled and spat as it ate its way through the town. It sucked air noisily to itself and with an ominous *whoosh* of sound breathed fresher, stronger flames into the night.

Gervaise the fishmonger cowered in the Minster doorway, holding his sullen, black-eyed grandson by the coarse woollen fabric of his hood. All his children and his house were lost, his livestock burned alive before he could turn them

449

loose, his livelihood gone and everything he owned gone with it.

Inside the hospital, Antony the monk surveyed the chaos from an upper window.

'It's winning,' he declared without emotion. 'The beast is winning.'

Between the hospital and de Morthlund's house lay St John's Passage, with its timber-built grammar school buildings and its little row of thatched-roofed houses leaning drunkenly against each other. The breeze was strong and lacked any true direction, so that the path of the fire was impossible to predict. An airborne scrap of burning thatch, a hot spark carried on a capricious breeze, and Keldgate too would be ablaze.

The deaf-mute who worked in the kitchen across the yard was tugging at Antony's robes and gesticulating wildly with both hands. He led the monk to the little wooden ladder leading to the roof timbers, and into the farthest corner overlooking the rear of the house. Through a gap in the eaves Antony could see the watercourse running parallel to Keldgate. Its waters seemed molten, reflecting as they did the eerie, orange glow now hanging over the town.

Close by the end of Lairgate the orange-tinted watercourse swept out and back in a great loop, then made its way almost directly to the wide lake beside the convent of St Anne's. It was then that Antony understood what had so excited the kitchen boy. Dense smoke was rising from inside the convent walls, and from the smoke huge flames licked up. The convent was on fire.

The monk raced down two flights of stairs and at the bottom collided with Father Simeon. The big blond priest was helping to lift the sick and the crippled on to carts that would take them to the port where boats and rafts were waiting. His shirt was open and the golden bridle-piece hung flat against the muscles of his chest. His face was streaked with soot and his eyes were bright, and just for a moment Antony was struck by that detached, almost other-worldly calmness that marked this Simeon out from his fellow priests.

'The convent, Simeon. The convent is ablaze.'

Even as he spoke the warning, Osric the infirmarian came running from the Minster Yard with a young man at his heels.

'Wulfric de Morthlund is at St Anne's,' he gasped. 'He's there to arrest a woman and her child. This lad was sent to warn us, but he was attacked and his horse and boots taken from him by robbers. Much time has been lost. The woman and the boy are in danger.'

'The fire has reached the convent,' Antony told him. 'I saw it from the roof.'

'Then we must go at once,' Osric declared.

'No, wait.' Standing between them, Simeon lifted his face and turned his head as if to catch some distant, half-heard sound. He shuddered then and closed his eyes, and when he opened them again he shook his head. 'We are needed here.'

'What?' Osric clasped Simeon's arm in his steely grip, and the studded leather band encircling his forearm was hard against the other's flesh. 'Would you put her life and the boy's at risk?'

'Peter will bring her out,' Simeon told him softly. 'You and I must go in search of Father Cuthbert.'

'But there is no way,' Osric protested. 'Wulfric de Morthlund has them cornered, and now the fire has reached them. There is no way, Simeon.'

The blond priest shook his head again and looked more deeply into the infirmarian's eyes.

'Trust him, my friend. Peter knows a way. He will bring Elvira out.'

'But how? In the name of God how will he . . .?'

'Trust him,' Simeon said again. He turned to Antony and said: 'This lad will stay to help you with the carts. Take great care, Antony. The town is running alive with looters and they will offer violence if you challenge them.'

'God guard and protect you,' Antony said, and gripped him briefly by the shoulder before returning to the task of clearing the hospital. He did not turn his head again to watch

Simeon and his infirmarian hurry away. He was a man whose Christian faith was veined with simple superstitions and in the midst of danger and uncertainty he chose not to witness the leaving of a friend.

As the two men ran from the hospital they saw that the nucleus of the fire had already leaped across the open space from one side of Moorgate to the other. A group of priests were dragging away burning sections of the grammar school roof, but even as they worked at it a thread of flame was racing along the eaves where bits of thatch and birds' nests made perfect kindling.

The Minster was packed from wall to wall with families who had gone there to escape the fires and looters. The sanctuary men had done their worst, for neither a plate nor a candlestick remained, and barely a figure or pane of glass was undamaged. Some men had lit a small campfire near the high altar and were huddled around it, talking together in lowered voices. Simeon pushed his way through the crowd, stamped out the fire and lifted one of the men by the hair until their faces were very close together.

'The whole town is alight and you make fires here,' he growled, and there was real fury in his voice at such a mindless absence of care. 'Well, I have seen your face and I will remember it, and if our church goes up in flames you will be held responsible.'

'But there are others with campfires . . .'

'And I will hold *you* responsible for them.'

'What? But Father, there must be a thousand people here . . .'

'Then you and your friends here will need to be extra diligent,' Simeon warned. 'Together you will guard this Minster from fire, and if you fail you will pay for that failure with your lives. Do you understand me?'

'Yes, yes,' the man cried, unable to nod his head while Simeon's fingers threatened to tear his scalp from his skull. When the priest at last released him he fell sprawling amongst his friends, knowing that he had become a marked man. There had been real menace in those hard blue eyes.

That priest had a dangerous coldness in him that few would dare to challenge openly. The man glanced up at the lofty roofing of the church and recalled that heavy masonry brought down in the storm eight years ago had been replaced by timber. Struggling to his feet, he rubbed his scalp, and lashed out with kicks at the legs and rumps of his companions.

'On your feet,' he yelled, infuriated by his loss of face. 'The Holy Father has given us work to do. We must see that every fire and candle and every torch is put out. We must protect the Minster Church. Come on! Get up, you idle dogs! We have a job to do.'

As Simeon had anticipated, they found Father Cuthbert in the turret stair where his old friend, Father Bernard, had been cruelly murdered eight years earlier. He kept an altar candle burning there, set on a tiny shrine near the lower steps where the one-time Canon of St Martin's church had been struck down while at his prayers. There was a scent of woodsmoke in that dark and narrow place, and a chill that was best avoided by a man well past his physical prime. Father Cuthbert was sitting beside the candle, his head hung forward and his eyes tightly closed. The small flame jumped in the draught as the door was opened, and Simeon winced to see it set so close to the old man's robes.

'Father Cuthbert?' Simeon's voice was as low and soft as a whisper as he squatted beside the sleeping priest and touched him very lightly on the shoulder. He would not wake him harshly from his sleep, for old men's dreams are precious things and must be relinquished gently.

'Ah, Simeon, my boy,' the old Canon smiled. 'And our dear Brother Osric too, I see. Is it time to go to St Peter's already?'

'You sound as if you were expecting us,' Osric smiled.

'And so I was. He told me you would come.'

'He?'

'That boy of yours,' the old man said to Simeon, leaning heavily on his arm as they stepped through the narrow door. 'I went to the high altar to see if I could help repair the

453

damage to the shrine ... such wicked sacrilege. While I was praying there, young Peter appeared beside me, took me by the hand and led me here. His intervention was a timely one. I believe two of our younger, stronger priests were injured when the crowd came rushing in. I owe my safety, perhaps even my life, to that boy of yours.'

'Praise be to God,' Osric exclaimed. 'If Peter was there then he too is safe. Wulfric de Morthlund does not have him.'

Simeon smiled and winked an eye at his old friend Osric.

'I told you he knew of a way,' he said, helping Father Cuthbert to his feet. 'And Elvira is safe, he will have seen to that. Hurry now, we must get Father Cuthbert to St Peter's.'

In Eastgate a large band of men, some priests and foreign sailors among them, were tearing down the lean-to hovels erected along the banks of the ditch outside St Peter's walls. They worked with hooks and long staffs, with scythes and sticks and with their bare hands to clear away the poor dwellings before the fire could reach them. Similar groups had been dispatched to other parts of the town, for Father Thorald, who was the instigator of the scheme, would tear his beloved Beverley down rather than see it fed to the flames. He worked alongside the strongest of his men, wielding his axe with the energy of those half his age.

Father Cuthbert stopped to sign the cross and speak a simple prayer. He was looking toward the smaller market area at the end of Eastgate. Already the fire had spread this far. Flames and billowing clouds of smoke were belching out from the blackened, charred remains of homes and warehouses. The screams of trapped animals matched the cries of hurt and frightened human beings, and the dry, hot scent of the inferno carried with it the stench of burning flesh.

'How bad is it?' the old priest asked.

'Already it rages beyond our control,' Simeon admitted. 'It burns from Moorgate and the grammar school to the convent outside the bar, from the sheds behind St Mary's to the mouth of Eastgate here. And even now I fear the worst is yet to come.'

454

'Dear God, how many innocents will we lose this time?'

'Too many,' Simeon told him softly.

They brought Father Cuthbert into St Peter's by the main gate. Several priests were on duty there, bringing the sick and old, the women and small children inside the enclosure while keeping the able-bodied men outside. Already that part of Eastgate lying between St Peter's wall, the east end of the Minster and the Bar at the mouth of Flemingate was jammed with people, many struggling with bundles or sacks containing all the worldly goods that they could carry. Many more led tethered goats or cows, or carried lambs and piglets slung across their shoulders. There was little sign of panic here despite the numbers. Between the Minster and St Peter's church, with the port and the Great Beck at their backs and the entire length of Eastgate lying between them and the burning town, they felt themselves secure. Only those gathered closest to St John's, those nearer to Hyegate and Minster Moorgate, could see and hear the blaze and feel the heat of the inferno on their faces.

Simeon and Osric protected Father Cuthbert with their own bodies as they elbowed and heaved a pathway through the tightly-packed crowds. When the going became more difficult and the old man began to show signs of distress, Simeon lifted him into his arms and wrapped his cloak around him so that his frail body was perfectly insulated from all harm. Even after they reached the safety of St Peter's, he held his beloved Canon close against him, barking out instructions over that fragile head.

'Send the women into every part of the grounds to watch out for random fires started by flying sparks. Let any man, woman or child seeking food and shelter here first earn the privilege. I want every sign of smoke, however small, reported at once, and every spark doused before it can take a hold. Let them watch the orchard and the woods, the pasture and the meadow, and every building here, including the church.'

He paused to stare up at the thatch-and-timber roofs of the dormitory, refectory and infirmary, all of them set close

455

enough to the Eastgate wall to be ignited by a stray spark. Then he glanced at St Peter's church, where the sound of priests at their devotions drifted from every window.

'Get those priests out here and give them work to do,' he said to Osric. 'God knows our needs already, without their constant prayers.'

'I'll set them all to work with buckets to damp down the roofs with water from the ditch,' Osric shouted, already moving away to attend to the task. 'And after that is done they can help to keep the fire-watch.'

Not until Simeon reached the scriptorium did he open his cloak and set Father Cuthbert gently back on his feet.

'You are safe now, Father.'

'Thank you, my son. As ever, I am in your debt.'

Simeon smiled grimly at that and asked, not expecting any reply: 'Who keeps account?'

As Simeon stooped through the doorway Elvira rose from the stone rim of the well where she had been sitting, and his breath caught in his throat at sight of her. Her skirts were wet from knee to hem and the short hood covering her shoulders had been torn in several places. Her eyes shone with a feverish brightness in the torchlight, and she hugged her body with both arms as if she had been chilled to the bone. In a few short strides Simeon was by her side, sliding the warm cloak from his own shoulders to enfold her slender body in it. He smoothed her hair with his big hands and looked into her pale, small face as if he might read a thousand secrets there. He saw her dark eyes brim with tears that spilled over on to her cheeks, and seeing those tears he issued a soft, low moan and gathered her into his arms.

'Elvira, Elvira ...' He murmured her name against her hair, for the moment content to hold her close to him. She was small and light in his arms, as sweet and as dear to him now, after eight long years, as ever she had been. His voice was hoarse when he said: 'I thank God from my soul for your safety.'

'We must thank your godson for that, Simeon,' she whispered, clinging to him. 'Our enemies were at the very door. If Peter had not known a way...'

'Hush. It's over. You are safe now.'

'You always told me that one day I would need to trust him without question. I knew it, yet still I was afraid. I thought the fear would stop my heart in my breast. Oh Simeon, I was so frightened...'

'I know, my love, I know.'

For a moment longer he pressed her close in his arms, and when at last he held her away from him she was smiling a little through her tears. He did not doubt her courage for a moment, for she had more of that than any woman he had ever known.

He felt a light touch on his arm and turned his head to see Father Cuthbert watching him with a twinkle in his eye.

'Perhaps the pretty Elvira will be content to keep an old man company in your absence, Simeon?'

Elvira nodded and Simeon lifted her fingers to his lips. She knew then that he would leave her in order to help fight the fire, and she knew that she would suffer a thousand tortures in his absence. It seemed to her that the whole town had passed into a state of insanity. There were fires in every street and looters rifling through every abandoned home. She and Peter had picked their way beneath the town, passing by open well-shafts and half-covered drains, and every step had taken them from one unseen misfortune to another. Those dark, damp underground tunnels had echoed with the most fearful sounds; such screams and cries as had struck cold terror into her heart.

'Must you go?' she asked.

He nodded gravely.

'Go safely, then,' she whispered.

'If it is God's will.'

'If He is just, how can it be otherwise?'

He smiled at her reasoning and kissed her fingertips again.

'Where is the boy?'

'He too is stubborn,' she told him. 'He would not stay here with me, no matter how I pleaded.'

'I will find him,' Simeon promised. 'You must have faith, Elvira. All will be well.'

'If your God wills it,' she said, and there was sadness and a hint of bitterness in her voice, for she had ever been baffled by the vagaries of God's will.

Simeon took the lighter, shorter cloak his Canon offered, flung it around his shoulders and fastened the jewelled clasp across his chest. Her dark eyes watched him as he and Osric prepared to leave, but she made neither sign nor answer when he turned at the door and said again: 'All will be well, Elvira.'

At the convent of St Anne, men and women worked side by side to bring a dozen separate fires under control. The cloister half-roof, with its large area of dry thatch and timbers, had burned with the ferocity of a furnace. Then the breeze plucked off the blazing remnants of it and scattered them across the cluttered convent grounds.

The convent's chaplain, a sparse and timid man with failing eyesight, was rushing from one building to the next, clearing the occupants out. His name was Fabian and he was no longer young, but he was determined to snatch as many lives as he could from the jaws of the ravenous beast that was loosed among them. He found a score of young women, Sister Alice among them, cowering together in their dormitory, where heat and dense smoke from the burning roof had driven them into corners. Father Fabian herded them out of the grounds by the lakeside gate and set a handful of armed priests and men-servants to guard them. And after that he returned to the blazing convent, for those still trapped inside were in need of his help. He gave no thought to fighting a fire that hemmed them in from every side and already ran beyond any man's control. He thought only to get as many people out as was humanly possible while there was still time to save them.

Searching now for the Lady Abbess, the elderly chaplain dashed up a crooked stair that led to the high room above the dormitory. At the far end of the room a second stair would take him downwards to the Abbess's apartments, and from there he could reach the lakeside gate by way of the dry ditch running parallel to the wall. Now he took the steps two at a time until he reached the upper floor. When he pushed the door open he felt a sudden, sucking wind grab at his clothes so that the skirts of his cassock pulled tight around the backs of his legs, buckling his knees and dragging him into the room. And just as suddenly as the wind turned tail on itself, released his clothes and flung him backwards, blowing a scorching gust into his face. It was the door that saved him. It slammed with a tremendous crash between him and the fire, leaving him to lurch and stumble down the darkened stair to safety. He did not know how badly he was hurt until a young man looked into his face and screamed in horror.

'Wait! Don't go in there!'

The chaplain's cry came out too late to stop the young man fleeing towards the dormitory stair. In a blind panic he raced for the upper room, threw back the door and let a fireball out.

The chaplain ran toward the treasure-house porch where several men and women had taken refuge dangerously close to the half-timber structure. The Lady Abbess was among them, and she was trembling as she tried to offer comfort and hope to her frightened flock. He saw at a glance that one of her legs was broken below the knee. With a muttered apology for her discomfort, he stooped and lifted her almost effortlessly into his arms.

'Master Fabian, is it you? Dear God in Heaven, your face ... your poor face ...'

As he carried the Abbess to safety, those who had stayed to fight the fire with buckets of water and beating brooms abandoned their futile efforts and followed him. Oblivious to his weariness, uncaring of his injuries, Fabian led the way along the dry ditch to the little gate set into the high stone wall. He passed through the gate to the crowded area on the slopes above the lakeside, hugging his precious burden to his chest, leading a small army of coughing, sobbing survivors.

With loving care he set the Abbess to rest on a man's cloak on the ground, where caring, capable hands were waiting to tend her injured leg. When he tried to rise up again his heart gave out. He issued a small, strangled sound as his body pitched forward and rolled down the slope to the lake. And there it floated, still and unprotesting, with its fire-blackened face turned up and its arms outstretched.

CHAPTER THIRTY-EIGHT

In the Provost's Hall Jacob de Wold had supervised the storing away of the precious journals and records of the church. The Provost's rolls were there, the church accounts, personal letters from the Bishops, Archbishops and important Papal legates. Here were papers signed with royal signatures, documents bearing the great seals of Rome, Westminster and Canterbury. And here were many other irreplaceable things; rare books and maps, priceless treaties and icons that were the envy of many greater churches. Now all were safely concealed beneath the tiled floor in the lower chapel, where dirt pits had been dug for the purpose and lined with sheets of lead and ceramic material thicker than the width of a man's palm.

Despite the precautions, Jacob was uneasy. From the upper windows of the Provost's Hall he could see a large proportion of the stricken town and much of the wasteland lying to the south and south-west of it. At least two thirds of the more densely populated area was ablaze. The sky was filled with curling columns of smoke and fiery cascades of crimson and orange sparks. To his left he could see the bustling port at the head of the Beck, and by the light of many torches and braziers he saw frightened people scurrying from the town like rats deserting a sinking ship.

461

In theory the moated grounds and the Provost's Hall were safe from the spread of a common fire. At the first alarm bell Jacob had ordered the drawbridge raised and posted guards at every bridge to keep the masses out. If the fire spread to the Minster Church there was every chance that those now sheltering there would seek refuge in the moated Provost's grounds. They must, like the dangerous animals they were, be kept at bay. As servants of God, he and his priests and clerks had a certain obligation to the needy of the town, but their first and foremost duty was to the Church itself; to keep its property and its treasures safe.

When a clutter of lean-to dwellings went up in flames on a patch of ground off Keldgate, a frightened woman gathered her children together at the watercourse. She found a raft, a single length of wood that had been burned along one edge, and one by one she piled her brood on board. There was no room for her to travel with them, so she waded waist-deep into the filthy water and, keeping the raft ahead of her, pushed the little ones to safety through the flames. Her task was not an easy one, for the watercourse was choked in places with piles of charred debris and smouldering thatch. She stopped well short of the Hall Garth landing where a crowd was gathered, pulled her children up the bank and dragged her small bundle of possessions after them. After a lengthy search she found a weak spot in the timber barrier and managed to crawl through into the dark, safe grounds beyond. There were guards patrolling the woods and pastures and all the Provost's animals were herded together in a fenced enclosure, goats and cows, sheep and pigs alike, all bleating and bellowing at the scent of fire on the air.

The woman ushered her children deep into the thicker woodland in the dark shadow of the Provost's Hall. She found a spot closed in by trees and there she held the youngest to her breast and rocked it to and fro, hugging the others to her as best she could. She was wet and shivering with cold, and she was frightened. She had seen her husband and the eldest of their children burned to death. She had seen two women raped by looters, another beaten to death when she tried to protect her husband from attack, and she feared the people of Beverley even more than she feared the fires sweeping virtually unchecked through every street.

Now her teeth were chattering and her children whimpered and shivered in the cold night air. She had no blankets, no warm dry clothes, no food, no comfort of any kind to offer them, and in her distress she did what any other mother would have done: she lit a fire.

It was a small, insignificant fire, a modest source of heat and comfort made up of twigs and leaves and other debris lying inches deep on the woodland floor. It caught the spark from her flint almost greedily, for the woods were as dry as tinder and even in that sheltered spot the breeze was brisk enough to fan the flames. Soon the little fire began to spread. It became a reaching, grasping, urgent thing with its own will and a fierce, unsatiable hunger. It reached for the trees, licking at roots, darting into branches, slithering in a flaming stream of fire across the ground.

From his window Jacob de Wold saw first the stream of fire at ground level, moving beneath the trees. Then, with a sudden flash that flung it upwards, the fire took hold and huge flames burst high into the dark branches of the trees. In moments the woodland was a crackling inferno and the breeze was carrying tongues of flame and sparks in every direction. Jacob turned from the window, grey-faced and hollow-eyed, and looked to the many priests and clerks gathered on their knees in the Great Hall. Sick to his soul with apprehension, all he could manage were two small words: '*It's here!*'

Cyrus de Figham knew his house was safe. The fire could come two ways, neither of which would pose any real threat to his property. It could run along Flemingate, where it would meet the port and two lesser waterways, or it could pass around Hall Garth and out across the marshland and the Figham meadow. And either route would leave it to burn itself out before it reached his home. Already the families who worked his fields were gathered close to every wall, for de Figham would pay them well for keeping the looters out. He was sure they would cheat him if they could. At the very least they would conspire together to tell of looters when there were none, and so claim a purse of silver to share between them. It mattered little to a man of his means, for the cost of paying them out for a pack of lies was but a fraction of what the looters would take from him. As an extra precaution the household servants were also armed and on their guard behind locked doors and shuttered windows. Their job was to defend the house, should the need arise, against the very people employed to protect it. Cyrus de Figham trusted no one.

Several messengers had been to the house since the fires started, and Cyrus had rewarded them all in coin for their information. He took the news of the convent blaze with silent fury at his own procrastination. He should have taken the ditcher's wife and her son while he had the chance, regardless of any offence he might have caused the Lady Abbess. He had let that chance slip right through his fingers. He had allowed those sly, conniving nuns to dupe him, and the priest's whore might be anywhere by now.

He left the house in the company of Brother John and two strong men who would be well rewarded for taking good care of their master.

'My lord, do not go out there,' John had implored, as much for his own sake as for de Figham's. Such nights as this struck terror into him, and the last thing he wanted was to be out there on the streets, tempting fate, looters and cut-throats alike with his presence.

Cyrus ignored the pleading of his clerk and steward. He would not remain cooped up in his house like a coward while lesser men than he enjoyed the night. Fire fascinated him. The raw, uncertain power of it filled him with a special kind of excitement. Fire was an animal that could not be chased, cornered and slain like any common beast. It knew no fear, and neither hid nor ran from any living thing that dare pursue it. And it was evil, for it destroyed and devoured according to its appetites and the Devil take the consequences.

As he strode from the house, Cyrus could see the fire raging in the distance. Already it was unstoppable. It lit the whole town with an orange glow and set the sky alight so that the stars paled into insignificance behind such a show of dazzling sparks and dancing flame.

'We are taught that God made the Heavens and the Earth,' he grinned, his eyes bright and his face lit with exhilaration. 'But never doubt that the Devil himself made fire. No merciful God could create a thing so wild, so inherently *evil* as this murderous, rampaging thing. Just look at it, John. See how our foolish townspeople, even our priests, scuttle like frightened ants before it. *There* is your God, my friend. There is your *true* God.'

Under cover of his cloak Brother John crossed himself and mouthed a silent prayer. He feared to be caught in the slipstream of divine retribution if God Almighty took offence and struck de Figham down for his blasphemy.

They crossed the Figham Meadow near the sparse, low hedge that ran alongside the narrow ditch. The meadow and the marshland had been given an eerie quality by the twin glows of red-gold fire and silver moonlight. Here and there the walkers came across patches of scorched grass where smouldering thatch, carried on the stiffening breeze, had fallen to earth, flared for a while and then burned out for want of better fuel. Here too were animals who had fled the fire, and in the shadows groups of men and boys chased after them. There would be rich pickings everywhere while the fire still raged through Beverley.

'My God! The fire has crossed the moat!'

They had almost reached the Hall Garth enclosure and now they could see that the Provost's house and the woodland beyond were well ablaze. All those buildings repaired or rebuilt in timber instead of stone following the tempest of 1180, were providing fuel for the fire now. Huge flames were dancing from roof to roof. Fields of blackened trees stood shrouded in fire, a strange, biblical harvest growing in the Provost's grounds. Orange flames and black smoke belched from all the lower windows, and even as they

465

watched, long tongues of flame licked up the spiral staircase at the south end of the building.

'Look! Look there, in the Great Hall!'

The others followed where Cyrus de Figham pointed. They saw a figure at the arched window close to where the Provost's seat was set. They saw him struggling to open the stairwell door and Brother John yelled out a warning, knowing the wind and the roar of the fire would snatch the words away as they passed his lips.

'No! Go back! The fire is in the steps. Don't open the door!'

Oblivious to either the warning or the danger, the man at the window struggled with the door. At last it opened and he fell back, felled by a blast of hot air, and in that instant the fire was in the Great Hall. It leaped like an army of yellow imps for the dusty drapes and heavily embroidered wall-hangings, slithered across the panelled walls, cavorted in the rushes on the floor. It rolled and turned like a hungry serpent towards the wooden rafters where painted saints and bible tracts and snatches of Psalms were hung like so many banners to be devoured. The man who had admitted the fire now scrambled to his feet and began to run, but even as he fled in panic, the flames leaped every timber above his head to run him down. It carried him sideways in a ball of fire and flung him through a window in a shower of flame-tinted glass. When he hit the ground below he was still struggling, with fruitless movements of his limbs, to outrun his fate.

At first sight the Minster appeared to be ablaze, but then Cyrus and his companions saw that all the flames were on the outside of the windows, leaping in bright reflections on the glass. Every corner, every inch of space outside the great walls was claimed by a desperate soul seeking deliverance. A heaving mass of humanity surrounded the church on every side. They writhed about in witless panic, clambering one atop the other like cockroaches in a stinking nest.

'As if the walls of any church will save them now,' Cyrus scoffed quietly. Then he cupped his hands to his mouth and bellowed: 'Fools! The fires of Hell are loosed upon you! Run for your lives! Your God no longer has jurisdiction here!'

'Father Cyrus! My lord!'

In the flickering light John's face had turned deathly pale and now wore an expression of horror. He was deeply shocked by what he saw and heard. Cyrus de Figham's eyes had a devilish glint and his smile was cruel. To those who gaped at him, now, he seemed to derive an almost lustful excitement from the anguish and destruction all around him.

The two servants who were there for his protection stepped hastily back from him, glanced at each other briefly and then, without a word, turned on their heels and fled. Only John stood his ground, rooted to the spot by fear and indecision. He dare not run lest his master draw his sword and cut him down. Nor would he dare stop running if he escaped, for Cyrus was a vengeful man who would rather kill an enemy than forgive him. And yet he also feared to stand so close to that madness in his master's eyes.

'My lord . . .'

'Don't grovel,' Cyrus warned. 'Pull yourself together and follow me, for there's work to be done here.'

'Work? But my lord . . .'

'Don't argue, boy. Every priest and canon of any standing will be making for the Minster, and I will not be made conspicuous by my absence.' Cyrus growled the words as he strode towards that area where the crowds were at their most dense.

They met Wulfric de Morthlund in that area where Long Lane, skirting the Figham Meadow, joined the Minster Yard. The fat man was dazed and horribly dishevelled. His hands and face were bloody and his clothes were torn. He and his Little Hawk had fought their way through the pandemonium in the streets to reach their home in Moorgate, only to find a heap of charred and smouldering timbers sinking into a bed of white-hot flames. Hyegate was an impassable inferno from end to end. Nearby, in inner Keldgate, the house of Antony and its immediate neighbours were well ablaze. Across the way, the Hall Garth landing and the drawbridge

467

spanning both the watercourse and the moat were engulfed in flames, set alight by the burning debris carried downstream by the water. Beyond them almost the whole of the Provost's grounds had become an inferno. The fire had burned a horse-shoe course around the town, and at its open end lay the Minster, St Peter's enclosure and, beyond the two, the port area and the safer lands of Figham.

Wulfric de Morthlund looked neither right nor left as he ploughed his way through the crowds, carrying the limp body of Daniel Hawk in his huge embrace. They had been attacked by armed looters who pounced on them from an alleyway in Hyegate, and Daniel had been injured fighting bravely to protect his master. When Wulfric saw that they were sadly outnumbered, he threw down his purse, his rings and his jewelled girdle to distract the thieves, then drew his dagger and screamed at Daniel to flee and save himself. For once in his life the young man disobeyed a direct order, unable to think of his own safety while Wulfric was in danger. He stayed to help, and for his pains was savagely cut down. And now de Morthlund, exhausted and with his lungs burned raw by smoke, gently set down his burden and grabbed a hooded monk who worked nearby.

'Help him,' he croaked, his eyes streaming and his voice cracked. 'He saved my life when he could have saved his own. He's badly hurt. I think he's dying. Help him.'

He did not recognise the monk as Antony. In his distracted state he only knew that Daniel might not survive, and that if he lost his Little Hawk the world would be a sadder place for him.

'I cannot help him,' Antony said, after a brief examination of the young man's injuries. 'He needs the infirmarian's skills to close those wounds. Give him your cloak and stay with him here. I will send Brother Osric to you when I can find him.'

'He saved my life,' Wulfric repeated, as if unable to comprehend that any man would do as much for him. 'He saved my life.'

Standing nearby, Cyrus de Figham viewed the brief scene

with a snigger of contempt. How easily the mighty, the pompous and the vain could be brought this low. Along with all the favours he had received from his obese master over the years, that young man had taken more than his share of humiliation and abuse. Now the roles they had played for so long had been reversed, for in his senseless and bloodied state, Daniel Hawk had triumphed over the fat man. To win the game outright all he need do was die.

Within minutes the monk had proved himself as good as his word. He came running back with Osric hard on his heels, and the tough infirmarian had with him a bulky leather bag with all his medicines and instruments inside. By the time they were bending over the fallen man, Wulfric de Morthlund's fleshy face was glistening with tears, and no one could judge which tears were induced by heat and smoke and which by grief.

Cyrus de Figham scowled suddenly, his attention snatched from the obese canon and his catamite. He had seen another priest he knew, a handsome, strong-boned priest with a thick blond tonsure, a dusty, smoke-streaked face and eyes as blue as cornflowers.

'Simeon de Beverley,' he said out loud.

The blond priest had his hood pulled down and his cloak flung back over one shoulder. He wore high boots and walked on two good legs, his crippled ankle and his limp forgotten. He was searching the crowd anxiously. He touched and blessed and offered what comfort he could where it was begged of him, but all the time his blue eyes searched the teeming press of bodies for a more familiar face. A voice called out and his head jerked round to meet it, and his features lit with a sudden brightness.

'Father! Father! Here I am! Father!'

Simeon lurched forward, reaching out, and his voice was hoarse and thunderous in reply: '*Peter!*'

The two met in a fierce embrace. With both hands Simeon lifted the boy from the ground and clutched him against his chest, enfolding the slender body in his muscular arms. The boy was laughing through his tears. He was a small boy with pale blond hair and wide blue eyes set in a delicately boned face, and he hugged the priest now as any son might hug the father he loved.

'God damn you, priest,' Cyrus de Figham breathed. 'God damn you for your healed foot and your bastard son.'

He watched them through narrow, hate-filled eyes. Gervaise the fishmonger had a black-eyed grandson that was sired on his daughter Maud before she died in her sixteenth year. That boy was almost eight years old now. He was tall and strong and sharply intelligent, as cunning and as crafty as most boys twice his age. He was a fine lad by any man's standards, and Cyrus de Figham despised him with a passion. He would no more countenance the idea of owning that whelp as his own than he would have considered taking the fishmonger's unsavoury daughter as his wife. And because he bore the grandson of Gervaise such burning ill-will, he was all the more resentful of this priest's continued pleasure in his son. Cyrus had come so close to putting an end to it, and but for this cursed fire he might have succeeded. It cut across the sensitive grain of his vanity to be counted amongst the many who had been taken in by this so-called *innocent*. He would forfeit his soul to be the one to expose this man of virtue as a felonious priest who stole a poor man's wife and sired a bastard on her, then kept her on church property as his whore for eight long years. This priest's vows were a mockery, an insult to the church, and Cyrus burned to see him come to grief for his deception.

He stood back, closing his cloak around him and melting into the crowd, as Simeon was joined by two other men in fine priestly robes. One wore his hood too close to be recognised, but the other had his hood thrown back, and there was no mistaking Father Gilbert, that sharp-minded priest of higher orders who claimed a dubious, distant kinship with the late Roger de Pont l'Evèque of York. This man was a co-conspirator of Simeon's, for he had been among those who witnessed young Peter's baptism, those traitors to the church who had kept their guilty silence now for almost a decade. One side of Father Gilbert's face was badly blistered. Half his tonsure had been burned away and part of his ear with it. Even from a distance it could be seen that the skin across the backs of his hands was as charred and discoloured as was his ragged cloak. Father Gilbert paused to place his hand on the blond head of the boy. It was a tender, loving gesture, and for that moment his fire-ravaged face was softened. Then he turned to Simeon and his expression once again was grave.

Standing off to one side of this, Cyrus saw Gilbert pointing back to where the Provost's ground still blazed with flames that licked at the sky as they were carried upward by the breeze. He heard a few words: 'Jacob ... four canons ... several priests ... a wall of fire ... fallen timbers ... trapped ... burned' and from them gleaned the nature of the message.

When Simeon hugged the boy again before setting him down and stooping low to speak to him, Cyrus felt his spirits lift in unexpected anticipation. Perhaps his lost chance had come again. The brief reunion was already interrupted, and the priest and the boy were about to be parted again by circumstances. Simeon pointed to the Minster Church as if instructing Peter to wait for him there, then indicated the Provost's Hall where he must go because his help was needed. And when Simeon released the boy, Cyrus would have him, and when he had him the woman would come at his call and Simeon de Beverley would learn who was master here.

'*Cyrus de Figham!*'

He started at the sound of his name. The voice was so deep, and had such an oddly penetrating quality, that it might have originated inside his own head. Touching the hilt of his short-sword, he whirled in time to see a tall, dark-robed figure turn from him and move swiftly away in the direction of the moat. He started after it, only to alter course after a few strides when the other disappeared into the crowd. That hooded, unusually tall individual was known to him. It was Simeon's man, the one who first brought the child to Beverley, who officiated at its baptism and after that was

471

never identified. The man had called his name and ducked away, clearly expecting him to follow, but Cyrus was not so easily taken in. He caught a glimpse of Simeon and the others shouldering their way through a press of people, then turned back to see the small boy in the grey robes slip from view. With an angry curse he went after him, and in a few moments he stopped and cursed again, knowing that the hooded man had distracted him just long enough to make certain that the boy escaped. He was still growling profanities when he came face to face with Brother John. The younger man was smiling nervously and looking to his master for approval as he held a wriggling, grey-robed figure by its skinny shoulders.

'Good man' Cyrus said. 'Good man.'

He hooked a finger under the boy's chin and lifted his face to examine his features more closely. Blue eyes looked bravely into his, eyes as clear and knowing as Simeon's own, with the same unflinching, almost judgmental gaze.

'Well now, what have we here?' Cyrus demanded. 'You're a handsome lad, and what a pair of eyes you have, young Peter.' He turned the boy's face a little to expose a puckered, crimson scar lying across his pale throat. 'Who is your father, boy?'

When Peter made no answer de Figham squeezed his chin more tightly and said, with menace in his voice: 'Speak up, boy! Name your father.'

Unable to move his head against de Figham's grip, Peter strained to turn his gaze toward the church. Several large pieces of burning thatch were dipping and turning like huge fire-birds on the breeze, heading for the vulnerable timbers of the Minster roof. The two men followed his gaze, and for a moment they were left off guard. With a squirm the boy was free of the hands that gripped him. He darted away, slithering between men's legs and women's skirts, a small, quick shape determined to have its freedom.

Cyrus and Brother John gave instant chase, thrusting a way through the crush of people gathered around the Minster doors. They saw the boy slip inside and duck to the left, and

472

when they followed after him it soon became clear that he had entered the tiny, narrow turret that housed the mason's stair.

'I have him,' Cyrus grinned. 'He has trapped himself. I have him.'

His gaze went upward to the little aperture leading out from the turret walls high above them. A narrow walkway was set along the inside of the Minster walls. It was used by the stonemasons who kept the decorated stones in good order, by the plumbers who set the leads and glasses into the upper windows, and by the roofers whose job it was to keep the weather out. The boy had a key to the perfect hiding place, but a man with cause enough could flush him out. Cyrus made a grab for John's hood, pulled him roughly toward him and hissed into his ear.

'There are three more turrets on this side of the church. When he steps on to the walkway, watch him well, and be waiting for him at the foot of whichever stair he uses for his escape. I want him, John. I want him.'

'I will do my best, my lord.'

Cyrus twisted the other's hood until its folds stretched tight across his throat. 'I want more than your best,' he demanded. 'If you lose him again you will live to regret your carelessness.'

'Yes, my lord.'

As John shouldered his way into the main body of the church, Cyrus craned his neck to see the high aperture slide open and the small figure of the boy step out on to the walkway.

'I'll have him,' he whispered, elbowing several women from their places of safety in order to open the turret door and step inside. 'I'll have the priest's bastard now.'

CHAPTER THIRTY-NINE

There was little that Simeon or anyone else could do to help those who were trapped in the inferno of the Provost's grounds. There was a house outside the grounds, across the moat with Keldgate on its lower side and its frontage in Long Lane. It was a stone building, long and low, with leads on its roof and a high brick wall as shelter on two sides. Once a dormitory for priests, it was now a makeshift hospital where the injured from the Hall Garth blaze were carried. Among them was Jacob de Wold, who had fought bravely to get his priests and canons to safety before the fire took hold. His hands and head were burned and his spine injured when a blast from the fire flung him backwards into a pile of fallen timbers. At great risk to his own life, a younger priest had hoisted the semi-conscious man across his shoulders and raced with him down several flights of steps, across the smouldering herb gardens and over the high wooden fence beside the moat. That prompt, courageous rescue undoubtedly saved Jacob's life, but the rough and ready handling might well have inflicted irreparable damage on his already injured spine.

Simeon and Osric did what they could for Jacob. They dressed his burns with betony and hog's grease and smeared his body with an ointment made from boiled knitbone root with sugar and licorice, coltsfoot, mallow and poppy seeds added. Then he was tightly bound from shoulder to ankle to a length of stout timber and given a few drops of tincture of poppy to ease his pain.

'Will he survive?' Simeon asked when the work was done.

Just then a wild-looking priest burst in, his scorched robes hitched into his girdle and his feet and legs singed.

'The Hall Garth defence poles are burning. Unless this rogue breeze drops, the flames could easily reach the church.'

'Will any of us survive?' Osric answered Simeon with a question of his own.

'If God wills it,' Simeon said.

'Aye, and if the wind drops.'

They used hooked poles and wire loops to drag the fencing down, rolled every piece into the moat where eager hands were waiting to smother the flames with water or with spadefuls of earth. And while they were at this work a runner came to tell them that some children were trapped in the cellar of Antony's house, and the monk had gone back into the flames to save them. Two men stepped in to take their places at the fence as Simeon and Osric rushed to help their friend.

'Dear God, I thought he was safely at the port by now,' Simeon yelled as they ran.

'And so he was,' Osric shouted back. 'But could we hope for one moment that he would stay there while he might be needed more urgently elsewhere?'

They slowed their steps as they were confronted by the burned-out shell of Antony's house. It was a skeletal structure made up of charred beams and blackened stones, gaping windows and a ruined roof. Inside this ugly crust the fire still raged, sending great billows of smoke and heat into the air.

'Holy Mother of God!' Simeon crossed himself as he made the exclamation. 'How can anything be alive in there?'

As if to answer him a cry went up from a knot of people gathered as close as was humanly possible to one of the side doors. The onlookers fell back as a dark shape filled the doorway with a sheet of orange flame leaping at its back. In a sudden hush Antony of Flanders stumbled from the jaws of Hell to the land of the living, breathing men. And he carried two children with him, one on either arm, and both unhurt.

As the awed onlookers dropped back the priests ran forward to catch the monk in their arms and lower him gently to the ground. He surrendered his charges only under protest, and they were given over into the willing hands of priests who would not easily forget such heroism. For a while the exhausted monk could neither speak nor open his eyes, for the heat that had scorched his lungs and burned his brows and lashes right away. He could only point back at the house and with frantic gestures indicate that others were still trapped. Almost without a second thought, Simeon and the infirmarian were on their feet and running for the house. They stopped, aghast, to see another figure amid the flames. This one was very tall and wore a deep black cowl that fully concealed its face, and both its arms were raised to bar them entry. Flames danced across the dark folds of its robes and the fire hung like a deadly curtain all around it.

'Do you see it?' Osric gasped. 'Do you see the spectre?'

Simeon nodded, feeling the fierce heat on his face and chest. 'I see it.'

One sleeve of the black robe lifted then and a single finger emerged from behind the folds. The two priests followed where it pointed, saw the great Minster Church still safe but lit with the glare of reflected fires at every window. The distraction was brief but sufficient to save their lives, for as they turned back the entire side wall of the house had begun to bulge and heave as if the full force of the fire were thrusting against it from the other side.

'Ye Gods!'

The two priests turned and ran as they had never run before. Yelling an alarm, they raced for their lives, scattering the crowd of onlookers ahead of them. As Antony staggered to his feet they grabbed him, one on either side, and half-carried, half-dragged him away from the danger at their backs. The wall came down with a terrible roar and a crash

476

of fallen masonry, and the blast of air produced by the impact was so intense it knocked them off their feet. They fell in a tumble in the street, and not until the dust and smoke had cleared could any one of them be sure the others had survived.

Behind them the big house had been reduced to rubble. Thick dust and smoke blew up from it. Flames licked swiftly over the smoking rubble, searching for food, for wood or cloth, paper or flesh amongst the fallen stones. The figure that had barred them from the door was gone, but the after-image of it hung in Simeon's mind.

'He was trying to tell us something.' He coughed out the words with smoke from his aching lungs.

'Do you doubt it?' Osric spluttered. 'He told us the house was about to collapse. He kept us from being crushed beneath the wall.'

'There was more,' Simeon insisted. 'I'm certain there was more.'

As he spoke he squinted through streaming eyes into the swirling smoke and dust that surrounded them. He heard a voice call his name and responded instantly by helping a groaning Antony to his feet. He felt all over the tough little body for obvious injuries and, finding nothing more serious than superficial cuts and bruises and a few scorched patches, clasped the monk to him in a rough embrace.

'I thank God for your safety, Antony,' he said hoarsely.

'And I thank Him for yours, my dear friend,' Antony said. Still coughing, he reached out and grabbed the infirmarian by the loose folds of his cloak, pulling him close to share the moment. 'You too, you crusty old soldier,' he grinned. 'We three have much to be thankful for.'

'Our lives and safety many times over, and even now ...' Simeon stopped abruptly and narrowed his eyes against the dust-cloud. 'Look! Look over there. Do you see something?'

'Only this wetness in my eyes,' Osric told him.

Simeon rubbed his own face with his hood, dashing the tears away. 'There was more. I know he came to tell us more.'

'Dear God, has the fire spread to St John's?'

'I don't believe so,' Simeon said. 'But I must go there at once. I am needed.'

'What is it, Simeon? What is it?'

Simeon was already moving away, the others close behind, when he said very calmly: 'It's Peter.'

They saw him as they cleared the area where the Hall Garth landing and the drawbridge were still smouldering. The smoke thinned out here, fanned away by the now westerly breeze. Peter had slipped through a wooden flap and was running along the narrow outer ridge of the roof over the South Transept. He moved like a swift and agile little animal, leaning inwards against the steeply sloping roof to help maintain his balance as he ran. With every step his feet were placed so close to the rounded edging stones that it seemed he might slip and plunge to his death at any moment. He carried what looked like a man's cloak folded over one arm, and he was clearly intending to reach that spot where fragments of burning thatch were taking a hold on the roof. In another moment he was there, and with a flourish threw down the cloak so that it covered the flames to starve them of the air they needed. Then he used his hands and feet to beat them out, until the fire was smothered. His dangerous task accomplished, he then swung the cloak over the edge of the roof and shook it vigorously to drop the now harmless scraps of thatch on the heads of those people jammed against the walls below.

'Peter.'

Simeon spoke the name softly, almost in a whisper, and yet the boy turned his head at that very moment and seemed to look right into his eyes. The exchange was brief but so intense that Simeon felt himself transported back eight years to that night when the Minster and much of Beverley lay ruined in the wake of the tempest. He had fallen to his knees in the rubble, exhausted and injured, hugging a new-born child to his breast and vowing with all his heart for every man to hear: 'I will not give him up.'

'Peter,' he whispered again, and everything in him reached out to push that small figure back from the edge of the roof, as if by love alone he might keep him safe.

'By all the Saints!' Antony exclaimed. 'The boy has put the fire out. *He's put it out!*'

'Get down now, boy,' Osric said in a quiet voice, willing the youngster down from that high place.

As if obedient to their wishes, Peter turned his gaze from Simeon's and began to retrace his steps with less urgency. He halted suddenly as he neared the aperture that had allowed him access to the roof. The heavy door of the trap was swinging upwards, and as Peter backed away, the figure of a man appeared and made a grab for him. On nimble feet the boy turned and ran, but even as he reached the other end of the roof and struggled to open a second trapdoor there, his pursuer was already half way along the ledge.

'Cyrus de Figham!' Simeon exclaimed, and as the hated name passed his lips, he was throwing back his cloak and racing for the church with his two friends at his heels.

Peter dropped through the trapdoor and released the heavy cover so that it slammed shut only inches above his head. He stepped to his right on to the slender stone ledge that ran the whole length of the inner wall on that side of the church, and there he paused to allow his senses to adjust to the darker shadows and the change of perspective. He was high in the curves and contours of the great church, above the lofty arches where so much of the delicate ribbing of stone, brought down or damaged in the tempest, had been re-placed by wooden substitutes. Far below him the floor of the south transept was a dark mass of humanity shifting this way and that in undulating waves.

Peter flung the darker cloak about his shoulders to cover the softer, more visible grey of his hooded robes. He slipped off his sandals, the better to keep his balance on the narrow ledge of stone. Then he ran as far as the corner angle and along the shorter ledge that topped the big south door and its soaring arched windows. Another angle brought him back along the opposite wall of the transept. He stopped quite still when he saw the square of dim light as the trapdoor opened,

479

and then the shadow of that black-eyed priest dropped lightly down to follow after him. Peter lifted the cloak to cover his fair hair, for only the width of the transept divided them at this point, and de Figham's eyes would soon become accustomed to the gloom. As the priest set out to follow the course of the ledge, the boy moved off in the opposite direction, his bare feet silent on the stones.

At the corner where the transept met the main body of the church, he stopped to peer down before climbing into the stairs of the centre tower. The old font from the ruin of St Martin's now stood close by the entrance to the choir. All around it the Minster church was packed to every corner with frightened people, so many in number that none could sit or even crouch, and all those standing were forced to jostle each other for every scrap of space.

In the gloom below him at the tower's base, Peter saw the pale face of a man turned up. He recognised the features as those of the cruel exorcist, Brother John, who was Cyrus de Figham's personal clerk and steward. The man had been watching for him, and now he intended to cut him off at the first turret staircase he attempted to descend. The tower had been his obvious choice, but that escape was, for the moment at least, closed to him. The next stair was at the far end of the choir, and after that the turret where Father Bernard had been murdered. And beyond that place was the last way down from that side of the church, the turret in the furthest corner near the great east window.

Peter glanced back to see Cyrus de Figham edging his way toward him in the gloom, then down to see the exorcist looking up. His only chance to escape this trap was to make a dash for the next turret and hope that he could double back without being seen. If the exorcist was convinced that he would come that way, he would concentrate his efforts on ploughing a way through the crowd to cut him off, and perhaps not see, until too late, that Peter had changed direction. And if the boy could then slip back to the tower exit before de Figham reached it, he could be down the stair and outside the church before they even knew that he was gone.

He judged his moment and made sure the exorcist saw him make a dash along the ledge. He was rewarded by the sound of a small commotion from below as John lashed out in his efforts to get ahead of him. Peter turned and ran back the way he had come. He had almost reached the corner by the tower when Cyrus de Figham loomed around the angle of the wall and reached for him.

'Come here, boy.' His voice was low and silky. 'I have no wish to cause you harm. Do not make matters more difficult than they need to be.'

Peter shook his head and backed away. The priest came after him, coaxing and beckoning, his face in shadow but his eyes aglint. When he reached the halfway mark along the ledge, Peter turned and made a dash for the turret stair, only to find himself confronted by a man on all fours who was carefully inching his way along the ledge toward him. The man was a vagrant and a thief. He wore a leather skullcap to conceal his mutilated ears, a filthy short-cloak over a ragged tunic, and he stank of the gutters and alleyways in which he lived. His eyes rolled now and he groaned out loud when he glanced down to see the slender pinnacles of the choir stalls reaching up like ornate javelins from below. The sheer drop over the rim of the ledge clearly sickened him, yet still he came on, inch by steady inch, crawling toward a certain profit.

'Here lad,' he lisped around a mouthful of rotten teeth. 'Come here to me. You're worth a shilling in reward, my lad. I'll not be cheated of it by the likes of him.' He jerked his head to indicate the priest now closing in at Peter's back, then fixed a leering grin upon the boy. 'Come, lad. Come here to me.'

Peter froze, knowing he was trapped.

'Pay no attention to that animal,' de Figham instructed. 'He'll sell you for a shilling to any man who'll take you on as whore or slave. I believe your father will pay much more than that.'

'My father?'

'Come lad, you know as well as I that Simeon de Beverley

481

is your natural father. He loves you too well for it to be otherwise.'

Standing with his back against the wall, Peter glanced at the man still picking his hands-and-knees way along the ledge on his right, and at the tall priest now standing only a few strides away on his left. He had glimpsed another man down there in the church, cleaving an uncompromising pathway through the crowds with his big hands and his broad shoulders. Behind him came two others, equally resolute in their purpose. As the first man reached the tower door he turned up his face and locked glances with the boy, telling him that help was close at hand. All Simeon needed now was time, but Peter, caught like a bone between two dogs, had little of that.

'My godfather will have you punished for this,' he said calmly, hoping to hold both men at bay until Simeon could reach the walkway. 'You have no right to lay hands on me.'

Cyrus grinned. 'Might is right when the Devil is loose,' he scoffed.

'The Devil, sir?'

'Aye lad. The Devil and all his fiery, murderous imps. They have first claim on Beverley now.'

'Not here,' Peter corrected boldly, holding the priest's attention. 'Never here. Never in this holy church of God.'

The door to the tower had opened at de Figham's back and Simeon, treading as silently as a hunter stalking prey, stepped from the stairwell. Peter moved back a little way, drawing de Figham after him, and offered a change of tactic.

'Father Cyrus, if I agree to come with you ...' The breath caught in his throat as a rough hand closed around his lower leg. He had miscalculated. He had stepped too far. With a gasp he lurched forward and back, clutching at the smooth stones behind him for support. Cyrus reached out to grab him from the front, catching him by the hood as his leg was yanked roughly backwards, pulling his foot from under him. He cried out as the man in the skull-cap lurched to his feet, grunting and grabbing at everything in his reach, as much to claim his shilling profit as to keep his precarious balance on

482

the narrow ledge. There was a struggle, a brief, frantic confusion of arms and legs, and then the man began to topple backwards. His bare toes alone made contact with the stone. His heels hung over the edge, drawing his body down. His left arm paddled vainly at the air in search of something to hold on to. His right hand clutched at Peter's hood as if the weight of that small body would keep him upright. And then Cyrus de Figham, holding the boy as tightly as he could and aware that they were all about to plunge over the edge, reached out with his free hand to pluck that other's fingers loose from Peter's hood.

With a scream the man fell backwards with his arms flailing. The scream was short-lived, for his body met one of the sharp-pointed pinnacles of the choir stalls and he became impaled there. For a moment he writhed, his head and limbs still straining upwards to the shadowed ledge. Then he took hold of the pinnacle protruding from his body, and with a defeated sigh fell back and hung spread-eagled above the crowd.

High on the ledge, Cyrus de Figham braced his back against the wall and set his feet more firmly on the smooth stones of the walkway. He was holding Peter out beyond the ledge so that the slightest mischance would send him to his death. He turned his head to look at Simeon, and there was a cruel glint in his quicksilver eyes.

'Another step and you've lost him, priest,' he smiled.

Simeon held back. He had stopped dead in his tracks when the vagrant fell, too grateful that the boy was safe to care that a man had died. Now he saw that Peter's feet barely skimmed the ledge. He was hanging by his cowl, his body as still and as limp as a child's toy, his gaze on Simeon, trusting the priest to save him.

'Do not harm him,' Simeon said, his voice betraying nothing of the anxiety that caused his heart to pound in his chest. 'Bring him back from the edge. If you dare harm him, Cyrus de Figham ...'

The black eyes glittered, lit with the same sense of power and exhilaration that fired their owner's blood.

'Well, priest? What then? What if I harm this whelp of yours?'

From a distance of only a few strides Simeon met the black stare with his own and answered with a frosty calmness in his voice: 'Then I will kill you.'

At that de Figham laughed out loud, and as he did so the folds of Peter's clothes became disturbed so that the priest was obliged to adjust his grip or let him fall. The darker cloak hung free of his shoulders now, but instead of letting it fall Peter hugged it close to him as if to gather extra courage from it. His eyes once again sought Simeon's, and in the brief exchange each read the other's intentions.

'Well, well, we see your true colours exposed at last,' de Figham bellowed, his laughter subsiding to a throaty chuckle. Then his eyes narrowed and he growled: 'I have a mind to make this matter public, to bring it before the council at York for a higher authority to judge.'

'You will do as you wish ...'

'Step back, priest. Come no closer if you truly value his safety. Here are my terms. I intend to take full charge of the whelp until his future can be decided by our superiors. You will deliver the whore, Elvira the ditcher's wife, to me also. Do you agree?'

'I do not,' Simeon whispered, holding his rage in check. 'I will not place them in your hands.'

'Then the boy will ... *fall.*'

'And you will join him,' Simeon warned.

Cyrus grinned. 'Would you do it, Simeon of Beverley? Would you really kill to avenge the loss of him?'

The answer was a simple 'Yes'.

'*Fraud!*' de Figham hissed. 'You sanctimonious fraud! My God, when it comes down to it, you are no better than the rest of us, for all your fine words and your saintly vows. You are a man like any other man, and I see murder in your eyes, priest. As God is my judge I ...'

He got no further than that. Still hanging by his hood, Peter saw his opportunity and grasped it bravely. He flung the dark cloak into his captor's face and, mimicking the movements of a hooked fish, twisted his body towards Simeon. At the same time Simeon grasped a section of carved stone in one hand and made a grab for his godson with the other. For a moment it was as if a single movement joined them all in a quick, decisive dance. De Figham felt something soft and black flap into his face and, with a startled shout, instinctively reached up with both hands to protect himself. And as the boy twisted free, Simeon's muscular arm went around his body and snatched him back to safety. Then, as the boy's feet touched the walkway, Cyrus's cry took on a different sound. He flung the cloak aside, reached for a hand-hold and, finding none, fell sideways over the edge. Simeon made a spectacular lunge that sent him crashing to the ledge on his belly, the air slammed from his lungs by the impact. Now he was pinned to the narrow ledge with his left arm over the side, and the weight that hung from it threatened to drag him over. His fingers had locked themselves around de Figham's wrist, and only the strength in them could prevent that black-eyed priest from falling to his death.

Cyrus de Figham hung helplessly in space, his right arm almost ripped from its socket, his fingers stiffened by the crushing force of the grip on his wrist. He saw his own feet dangling in the air, a score of upturned faces in the gloom, and the body of the vagrant, grotesquely skewered, hanging. And looking up he saw the beads of perspiration and the terrible strain on Simeon's handsome features.

'Well, priest, you have me,' he gasped.

Simeon clenched his teeth and growled a protest from the depth of his big chest. The ledge was too narrow to offer leverage and de Figham's weight was pulling him over the edge. Already his grip was weakening. He could feel the powerful pulse that was de Figham's life-force beating its own tattoo against his palm, and he knew he held this priest's life in his hands.

'I cannot hold you.' He forced the words between his teeth, straining with every muscle in his body to pull the other upwards. 'I cannot hold you.'

'Don't murder me, priest,' de Figham rasped. 'The Devil take you and yours if you murder me.'

'Father...'

'Keep back, boy,' Simeon groaned. 'Keep back! God's teeth, I cannot hold him!'

He felt de Figham's wrist begin to slip as his own grip weakened, saw the carved and twisted pinnacles of the choir stalls reaching up like deadly spears in search of flesh. And even as Cyrus de Figham's life began to slip away through Simeon's fingers, another hand, scarred and steely strong, reached down to grab the doomed priest by the shoulder.

'Thank God,' Simeon muttered.

He rolled back from the edge as Osric took the main weight of the burden from him, and together they clawed and heaved, accompanied by a stream of grunts and moans, to haul de Figham to safety. Then Osric pulled him, limp and exhausted, along the ledge to the turret. Having come so close to death, it took some time for him to regain his composure, but when he did he was the same man, unchanged by the experience.

'Expect no thanks from me,' he spat, flinging off the infirmarian's hands now that the firmer, safer ground was beneath his feet.

'You may keep your thanks,' Osric snarled in reply. 'I would have been well content to see you dead, de Figham, but not by any fault of Simeon's. He is the one to whom you owe your life.'

Now other hands were helping Simeon gain a safer purchase on the ledge. For a while the monk from Flanders held him safe in his strong embrace, then quietly insisted that Simeon remain crouched on the ledge until the stress and cramps began to ease from his muscles. Only after his arm and shoulders had been well massaged and the circulation restored almost to normal was he allowed to make his cautious way to the small door in the tower wall. He looked back along the ledge to the farther turret in time to catch de Figham's parting glance. There was neither gratitude nor truce in it, only that cold black stare filled with a quiet hatred.

486

'Father?'

The sound of Peter's voice was as healing to his senses as balm to an open wound. Simeon turned to lift him into his arms, and at that moment Cyrus de Figham narrowed his eyes and mouthed the vow:

'I'll have you, priest. One day I'll have you.'

Osric was the last to step off the treacherously narrow ledge. He gripped Simeon's arm affectionately, then allowed his hand to rest briefly on the small fair head that nestled into Simeon's neck.

'We saw what was happening from below,' he said softly. 'You were a fool to risk your life for his. You should have left him to his fate.'

'You can say that?' Simeon asked, hugging the boy.

'I can, and you can be sure I will remind you of it. You should have let de Figham fall.'

'What? But Osric, I could not have held him any longer without your timely assistance. *Yours* was the hand that pulled him back when mine had weakened. *You* were the one who saved him.'

'Not so, my friend,' Osric said coldly, wagging his finger in Simeon's face and setting his own face grimly. 'Never say I saved de Figham. I did what I did for the sake of your soul, not his. I saved *you!*'

They were still confronting each other thus when the noise from the crush of refugees packed into the church below took on a more sinister quality. Panic flashed through the crowd like a lightning bolt with hysteria on its heels, and with it every sheltering person began to screech and fight to the death as they made a crushing stampede for the doors.

The roof high above the northern transept was suddenly ripped asunder with a terrible sound. Sections of burning wood and balls of molten lead rained down upon those below. Tendrils of searching flames shot out to reach the chancel and the chapter house. That which they dreaded most was happening. Despite their efforts and their prayers, the fire was in the church.

487

CHAPTER FORTY

When they reached the foot of the tower steps they found the door was barred. Some blockage on the outside jammed it shut, and although they applied their combined strengths to it, their efforts came to nothing.

'The choir turret,' Osric shouted, and led the others back up the spiral stairs and across the very ledge where Simeon and the boy had almost lost their lives. Simeon kept Peter's face turned into his neck as he moved with careful, shuffling steps along the walkway. Down below, the panic-stricken people had turned upon each other like a pack of savage animals in their desperation to escape. Above the chaos hung the impaled man, his body horribly arched, his sightless eyes wide open. And above them all the roof of the great church was ablaze, and already the upper windows were beginning to crack and shatter in the intense heat.

That turret, too, was locked from the outside.

'This is Cyrus de Figham's doing,' Osric growled.

'How could he do that after we saved his life?'

Osric scowled at Simeon. 'You cannot change the nature of the beast. You know he could do it and feel no twinge of either guilt or regret.'

They returned to the ledge and stepped around an angle

that took them to the turret stair where Father Bernard died.

'Wait there,' Osric said, and hurried down the steps to check the door.

Standing high in the church, Simeon and the monk exchanged worried glances. They were much closer to the fire now. The smoke was in their nostrils and their eyes. It funnelled across the roof, rolling and turning in response to every draught, and behind it the flames were following, gaining an ever stronger hold. At every window the saddle-bars of lead had begun to warp and twist and fling their glasses out like deadly bow-bolts. And the heat in that high place was already unbearable.

'May God forgive those fools who mended His stricken church with wood instead of stone eight years ago,' Antony muttered. 'They lacked the courage to stand against the penny-pinchers of York, and so they made a kindling-box of our blessed St John's, and now the fire will take it all.'

'Come down! The door is open!'

At Osric's triumphant shout they all went down into the narrow shaft that housed the stair, descending in a blind spiral through the smoky darkness. Every window was an open slit that revealed a portion of the stricken town, and the air that filled the turret scorched the lungs of those inside.

They burst from the turret into the mayhem of the church, where screaming, clawing people formed dense crowds at every door, jamming the exits so that few escaped and many were trapped. Scores of bodies lay where they had fallen, trampled and crushed by a thousand stampeding feet. The central area around the high altar and the shrine was deserted except by those beyond hope of fighting their way to the doors.

Osric stared about him. 'We're trapped,' he yelled above the clamour. 'Every exit is blocked by the crush. Those crowds are hundreds deep at every door.' He pointed upwards, shook his head and added: 'We'll not get out of here before that roof comes down.'

'To the shrine,' Simeon shouted back, grabbing Antony

by the shoulder and pushing him on ahead. 'Get to the shrine.'

He held Peter more closely as burning debris rained down on them from the blazing roof. Some fell on Antony's head and shoulders and Osric, raging against the heat, plucked away bits of flaming wood and molten saddle-leads with his bare hands.

They found the shrine and the altar wrecked beyond recognition, for what the sanctuary men had begun the common looters had completed.

'The shrine!' Osric exclaimed, a look of horror on his face. 'My God, the shrine!'

'The shrine is safe. Only the shell is destroyed. The shrine is safe.'

'And the holy relics?' Antony asked, grabbing Simeon by the arm. 'What of the holy relics?'

'Safe. All are safe.'

'Thank God for that!'

'There's no way out of this,' Osric yelled. He was standing in a half-crouch with his sword and dagger raised, as if the soldier he had been could hold back the flames and the smoke with sharpened steel. 'This fire has us trapped.'

Now Simeon set Peter on his feet and smoothed the fine blond hair from his pale forehead.

'Son?'

'Yes, Father?'

'We must go down into your secret place.'

'Yes, Father, there is no other way.'

He looked into the huge blue eyes. The boy was tired. He had endured far more already than his tender years deserved. Now Simeon must ask even more of him.

'Will you help us, Peter?'

'Yes, Father,' the boy nodded.

Simeon smiled grimly, then turned to the others and asked: 'Who wears the stoutest cloak?'

'I do,' Antony said.

'Then use your dagger to make stout strips of it, enough to shape into a rope that will bear a man's weight. Our only way out is through the tunnels.'

'Tunnels? What tunnels?' Osric demanded.

'The remains of the old monastery lie below us,' Simeon told him. 'Ancient tunnels, ditches and watercourses run in all directions underneath the town. Come, lift the lid from the Minster well. Its upper side is heavily tiled to blend with the floor of the shrine, and that will keep the fire out.'

'I had forgotten this well existed,' Osric said, bending his back to the task of shifting the small, square lid aside.

'It was Peter who rediscovered it. We will tie our makeshift rope to what remains of the altar's base and lower ourselves down to the old abbey floor below.'

'But there is water down there,' Osric told him, peering down.

'Only the ancient freshwater stream that still runs into the well. Beside it on both sides is solid ground. You will feel where the wall ends as you slither down. Swing yourself under it and you will be on safe ground.'

'Will there be light?'

'Not much, and we dare not risk taking torches down. We must go in darkness. Peter will show us the way.'

By now the fire was raging almost directly above them. Some timbers fell from the roof of the north choir aisle, and through the wall of fire they could see that the chapter house had become a huge stone stove packed tight with blazing boards and rafters.

Osric was the first to lower himself through the small, square aperture and into the deep, dark shaft of the altar well.

'There is a rope here,' he called out. 'It is hanging from a metal bracket set into the wall.'

'Don't touch that,' Simeon warned. 'It will not bear a grown man's weight and it must be left where it hangs. Peter needs it.'

Osric went down quickly, feeling his way with his knees until he reached the gap in the shaft. He swung himself under it and at last his feet touched firm ground in the pitch-darkness of the ancient abbey that lay beneath the Minster.

491

At his signal Antony quickly followed, and when the make-shift rope swung loose, Simeon prepared to make the drop. The flames were all around them now, the smoke so thick that he could barely see. He was loath to leave while Peter stayed behind, but they both knew the makeshift rope must be released and the tiled cover eased back across the well's opening. There was too much at stake to leave anything to chance, too many precious things down there to risk any future discovery of those passageways. And Simeon feared that while the Minster burned, any one of those hidden tunnels might suck the fire up. In his mind he saw Elvira at the well in the scriptorium, and some Devil's breath sending a gush of flame into her face. He shoved the thought aside.

'Come quickly after me, boy,' he said, dropping down, and minutes later yelled back up the shaft: 'Peter, come down!'

He would remember those moments as the longest, most painful moments of his life. Because they were standing now beside the shaft, they could not see the rectangle of light high above them, nor could they judge, amongst all the sounds down there, what noises might be coming from above. They could not even know for sure that Peter was capable of replacing the heavy cover whilst hanging in the black hole of the well-shaft.

'How will he close the cover?' Antony asked, giving voice to all their fears.

'He knows how,' Simeon said. 'He has moved that weight many times before.'

'Aye, that may be so, but not while his skin was scorched and his lungs filled up with smoke.'

'He will do it,' Simeon told him.

They waited in silence, three anxious men standing together in that eerie place, and when he sought their faces in the darkness, Simeon guessed that they too were praying.

'He will come down soon,' he said aloud, praying it would be so. 'He will come.'

At last in the blackness there came a whisper: '*Father!*'

'Oh, God be praised!' He groped for the boy and held him in a brief, hard embrace.

'We must hurry, now,' Peter said. 'The smoke grows thicker all the time. The air in the tunnels will soon be too bad to breath. Join hands and follow close to each other. The way is dry and free of obstacles, but it is very narrow in parts and there is no light. The roof is also low in places, so be wary of it.'

They moved off in single file with Peter leading. As their eyes became accustomed to the gloom, they glimpsed the ancient monastery arches and saw long shafts of light flung down into a glittering ebony lake. Where Simeon had so recently heard the ghostly singing of the choral priests, now all he could hear were the screams of dying people, the falling timbers and the crackle of fire from the great Minster high above them.

'How do you know these places, Peter?' Antony asked, but the boy was already stepping ahead into a darker, narrower place.

'I know them well,' was all he said.

They came up in St Peter's church, the men squeezing awkwardly through a shallow opening in an alcove behind the altar. For a while they remained there on their knees, offering thanks for their deliverance. Only then were they able to look each other in the faces and laugh out loud, to slap each other's backs, ruffle Peter's hair and hug him fiercely, one by one. And in their shared thanksgiving Simeon wondered if they, like himself, felt more like weeping.

Later they stood outside together, watching the Minster burn. The flames were now at every window and door, shooting upwards from the ravaged roof and licking out from every turret window. The number of unfortunates who had burned to death inside the church was impossible to calculate. The clamour at the doors had become so great that many had died right there, crushed to death, suffocated, their bodies creating a solid wall that kept the victims in and the would-be rescuers out. In the angle of the church the ancient, many-cornered Chapter House was burned to a

493

blackened shell that belched enormous billows of dark smoke into the sky. Priests, clerks and monks stood all about the grounds alongside white-faced women and men who were not ashamed to weep like children for their losses. Even the crowds outside the walls were silent now. They had watched almost the whole of their town razed to the ground in a single night, and now the Minster itself was to be taken. No greater tragedy could strike them down after this. If the worst was here, right before their eyes, what more was there to dread?

'We have lost our Saint,' a young priest sobbed, weeping and wringing his hands as he watched the spectacle. This one was Richard, loyal, stout-hearted Richard, whose fine brown beard, his pride and his joy, had been all but singed away by the fire he had bravely helped fight for so many hours.

'Oh ye of little faith,' Simeon admonished gently. 'The Saint is not lost, Richard, nor will he ever be lost or forgotten while those who love him still survive. Believe on it, my friend, with all your heart. St John of Beverley is not lost. So long as there is a Keeper at the Shrine, neither he nor his precious Beverley shall perish.'

Simeon was standing on the little hillock where a tree had been planted and a cross erected in memory of those who were lost in the Great Storm. Elvira stood beside him with her body leaning close to his. Peter, still trembling a little, stood between them, his fair head touching Simeon's chest close to the spot where the golden headpiece hung on its silken cord. Simeon's fur-lined cloak was around his shoulders, its soft folds also encompassing the woman and the boy.

'What will happen?' Elvira asked him in a whisper.

'Along with our Saint, we too will survive,' he told her. 'Every stick and stone of it we will rebuild, bigger and better and stronger than before. This 'Beaver Lake' is not finished yet, nor will our Minster be allowed to die. In a thousand years we will still be here. In a thousand years, Elvira. Believe it, for I *know* it to be so.'

She nodded her dark head and after a moment of contemplation asked: 'And what of us, Simeon?'

He turned to her then and she was reminded of the first time she had looked into his eyes. They were the same, as if the eight years between had dropped away. She saw two pools of startling blue, alight and dancing with fiery reflections of amber and gold, and once again she fancied she had looked to Heaven and found the sky on fire.

'Do you understand how it must be for us, Elvira?' he asked her softly. 'The risks? The many enemies seeking to do us harm? And most of all my solemn vow of celibacy?'

'I know,' she said. 'I know.' And he believed she did.

'*Simeon!*'

He would have known that uncanny voice among a thousand others. It seemed to reverberate inside his head, sending a shiver down his spine and leaving an echoing vibration in his breastbone. He caught sight of a tall, black, hooded figure detaching itself from the deeper shadows around the scriptorium door. It seemed that his heart turned over on itself, or faltered and missed a vital beat, as he looked at it. For a moment it stood quite motionless and by some sixth sense he knew that it was watching him. It signed the cross with a slow, deliberate movement of its right hand, then placed a finger to its lips as if to swear the priest to secrecy. When it lowered its hooded head in a brief bow, Simeon, knowing he had met that unseen gaze directly, nodded his own head in acknowledgement of their covenant. A mysterious bond had been forged between them all those years ago, and this was a mutual confirmation of it. This much achieved, the figure turned and walked away, and Simeon watched after it until he saw it step into the crowd of onlookers and move, unseen by any, toward the blazing Minster Church.

'Father?'

Young Peter turned his face up to Simeon's, a rare smile playing about his solemn features. He held out his hand, palm uppermost, and on it glistened several drops of moisture that caught the Minster's leaping flames and came alive like sparkling gems.

'Look, Father! God in His compassion weeps for us! He weeps for us!'

Simeon lifted his face and, feeling the same coolness on his cheeks murmured, right from his soul:

'*Heaven be praised!*'

Now all about him men were dropping to their knees. That cynical old soldier, Osric, and stubborn Antony the monk, the awesome Thorald with his thunderous temper, young Richard and the wise old Cuthbert with Henry in attendance: all falling down to give their personal thanks. And then the first notes of the *Te Deum* began, rising softly at first, but soon swelling up into a mighty hymn of praise that rose above the sound of crackling fires as other voices, near and far, joined in.

'We will endure,' Simeon whispered, lifting his wet face up. 'We will endure.'

And so they would, for it was over now. God in His mercy was sending in a new day, with all the hope and pardon each new day offers. The fires still burned throughout the town, the Minster Church would be destroyed, but the nightmare at last was over. God was compassionate indeed, for as the priests were singing in the dawn the heavens opened with a majestic roll of thunder and the rain began to fall.

POSTSCRIPT

Following the great fire of 1188, Beverley's Minster Church was rebuilt and rededicated to St John the Evangelist. It was again severely damaged by the collapse of the central tower in 1213.

St Martin's Church was never rebuilt. Its scant remains lie beneath the south-west corner of the present nave.

The old Norman font is now located near the present Minster's south door.

The relics of St John of Beverley were not recovered until nine years after the fire. His casket, including four iron nails, three brass pins, six beads, several scraps of bone and hair, '... and a dagger, much corroded', vanished again in the disaster of 1213 and were not located for a hundred years.

St John's episcopal seat, the sanctuary chair, still stands on the left of the High Altar.

As recently as 1960 the water in the disused well to the right of the High Altar was tested and found still to be pure and sweet.

The ever-mysterious tomb of the unknown priest, to whom this book is dedicated, rests on the east side of the North Transept.

In 1221 Stephen Goldsmith gifted those lands in Eastgate

described as St Peter's Enclosure to the Dominicans, or Friars Preachers.

Excavations undertaken in 1960–1983 at the side of the Old Friary enclosure in Eastgate revealed the foundations of a Mediaeval church, much of which lies in the trench of the present railway station. Also found was evidence of twenty-six burials, some grave slabs, tiles, masonry, cooking pots, jugs, spouted pitchers, fragments of painted window glass and pieces of leather shoe-soles, all dating from the eleventh and twelfth centuries. Many skeletal remains were also uncovered. Details of these excavations can be found in: *Excavations at the Dominican Priory, Beverley* by P. Armstrong & D.G. Tomlinson (Humberside Heritage Publication No. 13).

LEONORA

Domini Highsmith

**IN A MAN'S WORLD, SHE REFUSED TO SUBMIT
TO THE WILL OF MEN...**

Daughter of a philanderer, gambler and spendthrift,
Leonora is scorned by her mother's family, the aristocratic
Cavendishes. They see her as a poor relation while she is
consumed by a burning desire to be one of them. From
the moment she sets eyes on their family seat, the
magnificent Beresford Hall, she vows that one day it will
belong to her.

When her father gambles away her inheritance and steals
everything his family possesses, they are left to face
destitution in the harsh world of Regency England. Only
Leonora's betrothal to a man she loathes can save them,
but while she barters her future for his patronage, her
dreams of greatness refuse to be surrendered. She *must*
become Mistress of Beresford, for she is obsessed by the
power behind the Cavendish name, and by the
handsome, secretive gypsy Lukan de Ville, whose illicit
kisses have kindled another, more dangerous kind of fire
inside her.

However the odds are stacked against her now, by any
means and at any price, Leonora Shelley is determined to
have both ...

LUKAN

Domini Highsmith

**THE GENTLEMAN AND THE GYPSY.
THEY LONG FOR THE LOVE OF ONE WOMAN.
BUT WILL SHE DESTROY THEM BOTH?**

Her family destroyed by her father's gambling, Leonora
Shelley decides once and for all to claw her way into the
glittering lifestyle of her aristocratic Cavendish cousins at
Beresford Hall.

But Leonora is driven by twin obsessions: her lust for
power and her passion for the dangerous and enigmatic
Lukan de Ville. Half aristocrat, half gypsy, Lukan's fate is
shaped by the complex intrigues of the family he serves.
And now at the head of that family stands Lady Leonora,
wife of Lukan's dearest friend, and the object of his fiery
desire.

In a storm of passion and jealousy, tragedy and danger,
Lukan is the sequel to the bestselling *Leonora*.

| ☐ Leonora | Domini Highsmith | £4.99 |
| ☐ Lukan | Domini Highsmith | £5.99 |

Warner Books now offers an exciting range of quality titles by both established and new authors which can be ordered from the following address:

Little, Brown and Company (UK),
P.O. Box 11,
Falmouth,
Cornwall TR10 9EN.

Alternatively you may fax your order to the above address. Fax No. 0326 376423.

Payments can be made as follows: cheque, postal order (payable to Little, Brown and Company) or by credit cards, Visa/Access. Do not send cash or currency. UK customers and B.F.P.O. please allow £1.00 for postage and packing for the first book, plus 50p for the second book, plus 30p for each additional book up to a maximum charge of £3.00 (7 books plus).

Overseas customers including Ireland, please allow £2.00 for the first book plus £1.00 for the second book, plus 50p for each additional book.

NAME (Block Letters) ....

....

ADDRESS ....

....

....

☐ I enclose my remittance for _____

☐ I wish to pay by Access/Visa Card

Number ☐☐☐☐☐☐☐☐☐☐☐☐☐☐☐☐

Card Expiry Date ☐☐☐☐